NEF HOUSE PUBLISHING

Until the Next Sun
Dead Again: Book Two
Copyright © 2024 Bruce Jamison

ISBN: 978-1-965393-05-5

Until the Next Sun

Dead Again: Book Two

Bruce Jamison

To my wife: I cherish every day we spend together. Our lives have grown busier with every new chapter, and you meet every challenge with a grace that inspires me to be a better man, husband, and father. To my son: Watching you grow fills me with a happiness I never knew existed. You're going to be the world's best big brother!

PROLOGUE

I remember the final thoughts of Tekşan, the red mage. He intended to slaughter every undead skeleton in the mountain kingdom of Jallfoss. The human wizard would have carried out that aim if Beast had not put Henry's sword through his head. I took offense at his intent, as I am one of those skeletons he resolved to murder.

I do not recount these events in jest toward the man. As I read through his entries in this metal tome, I realize his talent for magic, even if I disagree with him on certain interpretations. His prowess in combat was nearly our downfall. Fortunately, he let his rage distract him, and his group of Ikritian Acolytes died in battle at our hands.

I want to say that I'm filling these empty pages with the intent of honoring the man, but the truth is I have no better place to document the happenings of this graveyard under the mountain—a difficult task, compounded by the fact that all details of the past elude my memory.

I have read through this spellbook several times over, and each time I do, I glimpse new insights into the mind of the red mage. From Tekşan's musings, my time with the dwarves of

Hjardharfell, and our discoveries in Lundarbrekka, my interpretation of our situation is taking form.

Henry was the first of us to awaken. I assume he obtained an Ikritian Drift Amulet by sheer luck and subsequently killed a human. By doing so, he accidentally discovered how to return consciousness to animated skeletons. For that, I am grateful.

Henry is a warrior. Not of the military sort, though he is a natural leader, and the three of us have chosen to follow him. His tactical prowess and situational awareness in the battles we have fought have kept us from dying a second time . . . barely. He's also the one who gave me the name *Buddy*. He rests now, but moments earlier, his Drift Amulet allowed him to connect with the Necromancer who destroyed this mountain nation.

"The Emperor of Ikrit. He used the boy's death to pry into my mind. Lord Stavros is the Necromancer, and he's coming to stop us from reaching the Empress." After Henry's unexpected account, our quest to resurrect the Empress, Lady Destria, took on a sense of urgency. The boy to whom he referred was one I initially deemed inconsequential. Henry impaled the young Acolyte with a javelin and left him for dead. How the boy managed to find his way back to the Necromancer leads me to believe he was more resourceful than I had originally credited him.

The memories and visions aren't coming to me as easily as they do to Henry. My mind is a cemetery on a moonless eve— foggy and decrepit. It's fitting, though, to match the bones that make up the entirety of my body.

The third member of our undead group is an elf who has elected to be called *Beast*. Her natural speed can only be matched by Henry's Vitus-fueled attacks. With her stealth and affinity for self-conjuration, she is a deadly warrior, though she is as quick to anger as she is with a blade.

Then, we have the self-proclaimed emperor. Ox, who believes himself to be the long-dead ruler of this mountain nation, is a brute of unbelievable Strength. How bones alone, without the aid of muscle and tendon, can generate such force remains another mystery of the Necromancer's resurrection spell. More incredible than his raw power is his ability to regenerate and his knowledge of healing magic. I must study him more to see if he can provide insight into regaining the flesh that no longer covers our bones.

Our company's fifth and final being has proven itself useful as of recent events, and thus I have decided not to kill it. Muji is a trogold, a cave beast that hides its cunning and mischief through feigned innocence. He gained many Tiers from killing Smyrna's Golem and is a proficient artificer—much more so than the gnomes of Hjardharfell. I feel he may have more to offer our troupe than I first imagined.

A short time has passed since we defeated the magic-eating construct and only slightly longer since we've been awake in this underground mausoleum. We've retrieved the Magma Blaster for the dwarves, which should allow them to restart their forges and take back their mountain from the monsters assaulting Hjardharfell. The other item obtained from the golem's hold is the set of Flow Bracers. The dwarf King, Thorodd, believes the Bracers may hold the key to resurrecting the empress's ghost and restoring this mountain's undead inhabitants. I am skeptical.

I do, however, look forward to another meeting with the only mildly impressive dwarf in existence, Thorodd's daughter and a decent illusionist: Torgga. Of all the dirty machinists that call themselves dwarves, she is the least offensive. Our auras were attracting cave animals and monsters, and we would have been killed again in the maze of caverns if Torgga hadn't intervened. Even though dwarves can't see the magical emissions, she believes that if something has a green aura, its soul attached to its body inside the mountain. That also applies to skeletons upon our resurrection. Red auras surround any being from outside the mountain, mainly the Acolytes. The red auras drive any undead creature mad, including the four of us. Animals have the natural ability to sense auras and can even hide their own. Why can the undead see red auras, and why do they elicit such a violent, uncontrollable response? The effect is rather inconvenient, but we've slowly learned to resist the call to malice, either through practiced mental resilience or the addition of Tiers granted by the Drift Amulets.

Luckily, Torgga stumbled upon us before our green auras attracted too many monsters from the Underdeep. After an introduction to the dwarven kingdom of Hjardharfell, she gave each of us an enchanted ring that masked our auras and other sensory excretions, leveling the battlefield between us and the monsters of this cave. The enchantment was only a minor advantage, but apparently enough to see our way to Smyrna's Golem and allow us to retrieve the dwarven devices.

After nearly losing our second lives defeating the stone guardian of the dwarven treasure store, we have taken a moment of respite in a quartz cavern. We can't rest for long, as the dwarves require the Magma Blaster, and the Empress's ghost stands waiting for the Flow Bracers. If Lord Stavros truly is the Necromancer, I fear our time is scarce.

CHAPTER 1

Buddy fanned the black squid ink with a skeletal hand until he was satisfied it had dried. He had the urge to softly blow on it but then chuckled to himself, imagining what a skeleton with neither lips nor lungs would look like trying to create a substantial current of air. He still had the impulses of a human body, but he didn't know if those were the whims of his anatomy or just old habits. The urges comforted him in knowing that he had been a human at one point, not an undead monster conjured from a place of evil. That satisfaction was slightly inhibited by a nagging desire for a strong cup of çuwabee tea that his fleshless body couldn't enjoy.

The blue mage closed the cover of the tome in his lap. It was a heavy book, and his companions had often asked him why he insisted on lugging it around the caverns of the dwarven Underdeep. That was until the knowledge it held had saved their lives on several occasions. One such experience was in the very cave in which they currently slept.

Buddy had used the tome's insight to defeat what Tekşan called an *amalgamator*. The amalgamator was a horrid monstrosity with a flowing body composed entirely of various bones, weapons, and armor. After its defeat, only a skull remained—a skull that now set attached to one of Ox's mismatched pauldrons. The remains of the amalgamator had given up trying to fight Ox and now slept beside the skeleton on his shoulder. Buddy assumed it was sleeping because it had ceased clacking its teeth together. As Ox dozed, he snored loudly with a rising and falling rib cage, even though he lacked the same lungs that prevented Buddy from blowing on the wet ink.

He wasn't sure of Ox's race, but the hulking brute claimed to be a descendant of cloud giants. Buddy discounted that claim because true giants were allegedly several stories tall, but that didn't take away from the brute's impressive size. Ox was nearly eight feet tall, with shoulders as broad as an actual ox and bones thick enough to be from one as well. Buddy thought he could have been an ogre or an oversized orc, but his structure was too humanoid, and his posture too upright. Buddy had tried to use his Drift Amulet's Assess Ability to divine Ox's race, but it only returned the word *"unknown."*

No armor they'd found had been big enough for Ox, so they'd had to piece together scale, plate, and chain from the armory in the arena in Ammerthall, the underground city from which they had first awakened. He almost looked like the body of an amalgamator made of bone, leather, metal, and of course, weapons. Ox wielded a massive war maul, four feet long and every bit of forty pounds. Initially enchanted with lightning, Buddy and Muji had since charged it with the mage's force spells, multiplying the weapon's deadly bludgeoning properties.

The small campfire in front of Buddy had begun to die down. They didn't need the fire for heat or cooking, but the group found it comforting nonetheless—old habits again. Since the flames had begun to wane, the light in the quartz-lined cavern took on a soft bluish green hue. Patches of lumimoss, a bioluminescent fungus, clung to the walls and ceilings of the lower caverns of Jallfoss. Here it was mostly blues and greens, but in the lower, warmer sections of what the dwarves called the Underdeep, the lumimoss turned to purples and reds. Ox had hypothesized that it was due to the temperature. Buddy couldn't refute such a notion and thus had ceded to Ox's superior knowledge of biology.

Across from Buddy, on the far side of the waning tongues of flames, Beast sat with her back against smashed remnants of a quartz boulder. She rested with one knee up, and the other leg stretched out. She had one of her two daggers unsheathed and was slowly twirling it in her hands. The light blue sheen of its razor-sharp edge hinted at the frost magic it contained. The weapon's cold caused the moisture in the air to condense and form a tiny puddle on the ground.

Beast wasn't paying attention to the dagger or the puddle. She cast a spiteful glare at Ox, annoyed at the volume of his snoring. They had only known each other for a few short days, but the skeletons had grown accustomed to each other's mannerisms. Even without muscle and skin on her face, Beast's delicate elven skull was as expressive as any living being would be capable of, especially when she was irritated.

A heavy, dark cloak concealed her leather chest armor along with a menagerie of weapons. She'd stowed daggers and knives of all sorts, a short bow and quiver of arrows, vials of poison, and any number of other deadly weapons.

Beast had taken a liking to the trogold long before he'd proven himself useful and had even given him the name *Muji*. Though the cave creature was obsessed with Buddy and anything magical, he would often cuddle with the elf and accept affection from her that the blue mage would never offer. The trogold was absent at that moment, but if he wasn't meddling with the Flow Bracers or the Magma Blaster, Buddy wasn't worried. According to the red mage's tome, trogolds loved to interact with magical items, a fact which Muji had repeatedly proven true.

Henry sat across from Ox, stirring in his sleep. Lord Stavros had reached deep into the warrior's mind, and the interaction left him frazzled. He slept now, but he tossed and turned, and Buddy was sure Henry was experiencing more of his visions. Fire, deserts, necromancers; Buddy would have been jealous of Henry's haphazard divinations, were it not for the ominous nature of the premonitions. Hopefully, these visions would eventually prove useful to their quest.

Buddy had only met a small number of mages in the few short weeks since he'd woken. Torgga was an advanced dwarven illusionist with whom he'd spent many hours discussing the intricacies of magic. His only interaction with Tekşan was through a brief combative exchange, though the red mage's metal tome had provided the foundation Buddy needed to forge his magical arsenal. The gnomish wizard he'd met, Gnaz, was a novice artificer at best, with talents behind even Muji's Abilities. Buddy assumed Gnaz's level of proficiency was a more accurate depiction of common magic users, but if they were truly the best Hjardharfell had to offer then Buddy could understand why the dwarven stronghold was on its heels against the deluge of cave monsters.

By all standards, Buddy was an exceptional mage, specialized in evocation. He was also fairly proficient with minor divination which allowed him to detect magic in objects and beings, a trait he denied he shared with the Trogold. However, the Drift Amulet provided much more thorough insight regarding assessment and associated lore of items and beings. It was dependent on the user's Perception, of which Buddy wasn't lacking, so he had no qualms utilizing the item's impressive Abilities.

He'd attached a Drift Amulet inside his own ribcage with a piece of leather taken from a fallen Acolyte, but he untied the strap to look at the item. It provided little information besides the half-filled **9** for his Tier, and halves of crimson and azure, indicating his Health and Vitus were full. As he observed the Amulet, a glyph resembling an eye carved into stone appeared over the item. It didn't block his vision, but one with a lesser Resolve could be distracted by something like that in their sight. He mentally selected the glyph and allowed it to display its information.

Identify

Item: Drift Amulet (Epic)

Description: Accessory (Enchanted). Ikritian magic item used to increase the Tiers of Acolytes. Created by the Ikritian Emperor, Lord Stavros, this item contains powerful Necromancy and Divinity Enchantments. This item's Abilities scale with use and Tier

Abilities:

> **Essence Siphon III (Necromancy). Transfer Soul Essence of defeated enemies to advance the user's Tier**
>
> **Assess III (Divinity). Display more advanced information about items and beings. Expanded details and hidden knowledge are now available**
>
> **Status III (Divinity). Display more advanced information about the user**

Henry's revelation that Lord Stavros was the Necromancer responsible for the undead curse made sense, considering the Drift Amulet's enchantments. The irony of a skeleton using

Necromancy hadn't escaped him, but he wasn't ready to fully examine the morality of his actions in the current context.

Finished with the Amulet, he turned his attention to Henry. The warrior claimed to have been physically affected by visions of a desert, but Buddy was unaware of reveries that could cause such an effect. He examined Henry, allowing the Drift Amulet to fully expand its descriptions.

Assess

Name: Henry
Race: Human Skeleton
Tier: 9
Health: 69/69
Vitus: 90/94
Attributes:
   Strength (STR): 22
   Mobility (MOB): 32
   Fortitude (FOR): 23
   Acumen (ACU): 17
   Perception (PER): 29
   Resolve (RES): 31
Resistances: Physical, Lightning, Poison (Immune)
Weakness: Fire

Buddy noted the rapid expansion of Henry's Status, even though it somewhat lagged behind the other three skeletons. Buddy found the progression curious, and even allowed himself to entertain the idea that Henry's visions were behind the hindrance.

Henry wore a complete set of studded leather armor he'd found in the chamber of the Gladiator Supreme, the winner of an annual contest in Jallfoss. It would have been loose on his bony frame, but since he'd donned it over top of an enchanted chainmail suit, it fit him well. He was an expert in almost any weapon, but the one with which he was most proficient, a double-edged xiphos, had been sacrificed to stunt the golem's deadly magic. Henry had used it to restrict the golem's life-stealing abilities, lodging it in the gears around its metal heart. The sword had been melted by the Muji-induced flame from the Magma Blaster, and the blade was destroyed down to the hilt. Luckily, Buddy had managed to retrieve its remains before leaving the crumbling chamber.

Buddy tucked the heavy metal tome into the leather hip pouch on his belt. Beast turned her glance to Buddy, and they exchanged slight nods. They had rested long enough, and it was time to start making their way back to the dwarven stronghold of Hjardharfell.

Buddy summoned a tiny amount of his force magic and sent a blast toward Henry. The bolt hit him on the shoulder, jostling him just enough to rouse the warrior from his sleep.

CHAPTER 2

Jacoby spat until his saliva ran dry, but the fetid taste wouldn't leave his mouth. The unsavory sensation of putrid flesh on his palate was almost enough to pull his attention from the ghastly occupants keeping him company in the small dwelling. He had yet to be grateful for the distraction.

The color had started to return to his pale skin, but his body still felt sluggish. His heart pounded heavily, forcing thick blood into his aching muscles. The nausea had somewhat abated after several rounds of vomiting, but whenever he thought of the hunk of rotting meat he'd found in his mouth, bile started to climb back up his throat. He hoped the sickness he experienced in his body was just a severe case of food poising, but that didn't explain the loss of his memory or the blood spattered on his clothes.

With a heavy sigh, Jacoby sat with his back against the red sandstone wall of the tiny abode. He had cleared enough of the debris to sit and collect his thoughts. He noticed the roof above him had caved in. It was old wood, but from the look of the splinters, it had fallen quite recently.

Broken rafters dangled from their inlays, leaving a gaping

hole in the center of the one-story home's roof and threatening to tumble down completely from the slightest disturbance. Light shone through the opening, coming from a globe in the sky, but the sky was stone—the same red sandstone that composed the building where he sat. He was in a cave and judging from the height of the ceiling, it was massive.

Jacoby wasn't ready to explore until he made sense of the dwelling around him. It looked like a single-family home, twenty feet wide and twice as deep, with a stone entrance at the front. The wooden door had long fallen off the rotted frame and lay smashed a few steps beyond the entrance. Other similar-looking buildings sat across a wide, sandy street.

The debris from the roof obscured the home's furnishings, but Jacoby thought he could make out a hearth, some form of plumbing, and some basic furniture that had decayed beyond use decades earlier.

He gripped the Amulet he'd found while repairing his broken bootstraps. The polished crystal, inlaid in silver with a robust steel chain, seemed strangely familiar to him, but his memory still wouldn't cooperate. The crystal was divided into two halves. One half was a dark blue, like looking into deep ocean water. The other half was completely clear, except for a small portion of the bottom that was blood red. It had a black flashing **1** on the surface that looked like it had been painted on with dust. Jacoby brushed the number with his thumb, but it didn't rub away. He turned the Amulet over and ran his fingers along the single word: *Jacoby*.

As he examined the jewel, a glyph hovered over it. He focused on the glyph and a wealth of information revealed itself to him. He saw red and blue bars in his vision that matched the configuration of the Amulet, indicating the two were linked.

Item: Drift Amulet (Epic)

Description: Accessory (Enchanted). Ikritian item crafted from a
rare flow crystal. This item's Abilities scale with use and Tier

Abilities:

> **Essence Siphon III. Transfer Soul Essence of defeated enemies**
> **to advance the user's Tier**
>
> **Assess I. Display basic information about items and beings**

Something about the information and its connection to the Amulet seemed intuitive, but his foggy memory wouldn't allow him to make the connection.

He'd found the Amulet neatly tucked away in his boot, so he'd chosen to believe the name on it belonged to him, but as he tried to remember anything about himself, his mind drew a blank. The harder he tried to focus, the cloudier his thoughts became. He gave up, and instead focused on the glyphs in his vision, allowing them to activate in the same way as he used Identify on the Amulet.

Item Ability Discovered: Status I (Drift Amulet). Display basic infor-
mation about the user

Status Effects:

> **Soul Anchor: +2 Health per hour**
>
> **Skeletal body: STR -20%, FOR -20%, Damage Resistance:**
> **Physical -1 (Bludgeoning -2), Environmental +1, Poison:**
> **Immune**

Name: Jacoby
Race: Undead Human
Tier: 1
Health: 8/30

Unknown: 20/20
Attributes:
    Strength: 12
    Mobility: 13
    Fortitude: 10
    Acumen: 10
    Perception: 12
    Resolve: 14

Jacoby rubbed his eyes and shook his head, trying to make the information from the Amulet stop saying that he was an undead human. He felt very much alive, but the glyphs and his absent memory weakened his confidence.

Before waking up in the rubble-filled home, his only recollections came from somewhere beyond him. Henry, Stavros, Koş . . . those weren't his thoughts. An old man had killed a boy. A skeleton wanted to find a ghost. It didn't make sense. Unable to find an answer, he clasped the chain around his neck and tucked it into his shirt, then dismissed the Amulet's display.

Even more confusing than the strange glyphs were the three beings that joined Jacoby in the stone dwelling. He didn't want to call them human. Two dead men and a skeleton stood in silence, like they were waiting for a signal to begin some activity. The fear of what that activity might be left Jacoby hoping we wouldn't be around to find out.

If they were moving at all, it was nearly imperceptible. Jacoby thought he saw them occasionally sway, like a grossoak tree in a faint breeze, but it could have been the dizziness playing with his eyes. He'd tried to talk to them, hoping to get some reaction—something that would explain what was going on—but they didn't answer. They were covered in blood and stripped of everything but their undergarments. They stared ahead at nothing with milky, dead eyes.

They were young, only a few years into manhood. One of the youths was short and stalky, and the other tall and skinny. Jacoby could tell by their lean muscles that they were soldiers, and they had been through some sort of training that had molded their bodies. However, they'd been dead for long enough that their skin had turned pale and begun to droop. Jacoby smelled carrion, but he couldn't tell if it came from his own mouth or their rotting bodies. He eyed one of them, mentally selecting the glyph that appeared over the dead soldier.

Name: Unknown

Race: Undead Human

Health: Full

Magic: None

Attributes:

    STR: 7

    MOB: 3

    FOR: 2

    ACU: 0

    PER: 8

    RES: 0

The race was the same as his own: undead human.

They must have died recently, within a week. Jacoby wondered if their skin, muscles, and organs would eventually melt away, leaving them looking like the third occupant. The skeleton was much shorter with no skin on its boney frame. Like the men, it gave him no reaction.

The final puzzle piece was the green aura emanating from

their bodies. The skeletons' aura hung close, flowing over its frame like gentle ocean waves, while the men's billowed around them, rising like a fire consuming a tree. Were the auras responsible for animating the dead, or were they just an indication? Jacoby had no idea.

With the waves of nausea slowly receding, Jacoby started to feel pangs of thirst and just a bit of hunger. He slowly scanned the room, and what he found gave him another reason to be uneasy about his situation.

Two sets of bulky platemail, two rusty swords, and two leather packs were strewn on the ground. One of the men was missing his boots, but Jacoby still had his, and Jacoby wore the same undergarments as the men. Between the three men, the two undead and Jacoby, an entire set of gear was missing. He felt like a single person had been there and looted the bodies since those men had died, but with one exception.

Two of the leather packs had dried jerky, bags of nuts and bread, and a hefty waterskin, which Jacoby gulped down with gratitude, thankful to wash away the aftertaste of rot that was still in his mouth. Strangely, a third set of water and rations lay scattered on the floor. Whoever had looted the dwelling didn't take the sustenance.

Had there been a fight? Jacoby felt he was on the same side as the dead men, but why had he been spared? There was a bloody hole in his shirt but not in his chest where the red-brown outline indicated—more mysteries.

Whatever had happened here, Jacoby felt it probably wasn't safe. He needed to protect himself. He donned the heavy, awkward armor, strapped the pack around his waist, filled it with the rations and water, and attached a sheath to the other side of his leather belt.

He picked up the better of the two blades. The sword felt

comfortable in his hand, and it seemed sturdy enough, though the edges were chipped and dull.

Assess

Item: Short Sword (Mundane)
Description: Weapon, chipped sword intentionally suboptimal for
fighting Jallfoss undead. Hardness 5, Structure 15/20

The blade would have to do until he found something better.

The sound of rattling bones outside startled him, and he almost dropped the sword. The noise was the first he'd heard from beyond the stone room since he'd woken. It was quickly followed by the thuds of running footsteps and the snap of cracking bones that rang through the air like tree branches splintering from a wood cutter's ax.

"First house on the left, that's what the boy said." A man's gruff voice echoed. "He claimed Jacoby, Skid, and Flash had already resurrected. Let's get eyes on them, though I'd prefer not to fight the Senior. Even undead, he's probably still tough as nails."

These men knew him. They were searching for him. The two dead men in the room with Jacoby must be Skid and Flash, but the words from outside disturbed him.

Undead? They expect me to be undead? Jacoby took an awkward step forward. His armor was cumbersome and didn't fit him well, but his body seemed to know how to move to keep it quiet. He walked through the stone entry and onto the broken wood that had once served as the dwelling's doorway.

Status Effect: Enraged (Severe)

Rage and anger replaced every other emotion in his addled brain. The red blaze surrounding the men filled his vision, burning away any coherent thought—only unbridled fury remained to commandeer his faculties. He had to extinguish the offensive radiance, and nothing would matter until he did so.

"Master Jacoby, you're alive! Thank Minoa's dusty star. Koş said you'd been—" The man didn't have a chance to finish. Jacoby's blade left its scabbard and removed the man's head from his shoulders. The dull blade wanted to stick, but Jacoby's slice hit with such precision and force that it deftly found its way through muscle and spine.

The other man fumbled with his blade, eyes wide with shock. Before he could draw it, two dead men and the skeleton charged from the doorway. The soldier made the fatal mistake of turning his attention to the charge, and Jacoby slipped his sword between the soldier's plates and into his chest.

The soldier winced at the attack, and the two dead men impacted him with enough force to send his helmet flying. The skeleton was just a few feet behind and joined the pile, all three ripping into flesh and tearing him to pieces.

Jacoby bounded toward the pile, ignoring the man's gurgling screams. He raised his sword the slice the man, but as the soldier died, the red aura contracted and disappeared like someone had closed the cover of a lantern. The rage drained from Jacoby just as quickly. With sanity and control returning to his mind, Jacoby looked down in horror. What had he done? The men were happy to see him, and he'd violently killed them in cold blood.

Then the thoughts flooded into his head, and Jacoby dropped to his knees. Sadness and terror. Broken trust. Both men knew him; knew him well and admired him. They felt the fear of being attacked and the sadness that Jacoby had slain them. Jacoby reached for his blade without looking but the chipped edge gouged into his hand, cutting deep and drawing blood. He pulled his hand back but didn't bother to look at the wound.

The undead men and the skeleton had also stopped their attack, standing and returning to their silent watch. The man's red tunic had been torn to shreds and was covered in blood. Jacoby could no longer make out the features of his face, but he saw platemail underneath, much higher quality than what he wore. The man had a sword still in its sheath but had dropped a black metal club. The club was octagonal in shape, thick at one end and tapering down to a metal ball at the base of the grip.

The intensity of the emotions faded, but Jacoby couldn't explain his actions. When the rage overtook him, he couldn't control those urges, though his sword seemed to know where to strike to snuff out the aura. What had driven him and the three undead to attack these men?

Jacoby looked at the headless soldier on the ground. The man wore the same tunic and armor as the other. Jacoby wasn't sure about the skeleton, but he was now confident the first two dead men were once his companions. That didn't explain why he was alive, and the other two were not. Glyphs flashed in his vision, but he ignored them.

The clink of armor and shuffle of sand, accompanied by the muffled voices of men, pulled him away from his thoughts. A dark tunnel, three times his height and twenty paces wide, curved into darkness. The sounds of the approaching soldiers grew louder.

He had so many questions, but he knew he wouldn't be able to control himself if he saw them. They would kill him, or worse, he would kill them. Even if these men were his fellow soldiers, he had to escape.

Jacoby turned and ran, stopping for a second to pick up the metal club on the ground and take the man's sword from its sheath. With blood still dripping from his hand, Jacoby dipped into an opening between two houses and sprinted down an alley, his heavy armor not making the slightest sound.

CHAPTER 3

Flames broiled around Henry, the white-hot inferno swirling in violent blasts. A wall of fire before him roared with such a force that it almost seemed solid as he clawed his way forward. The flesh on his hands melted away, revealing pale bone that quickly charred. The heat didn't subside, but the pain soon faded like a distant memory along with his melted nerves. He only had precious few seconds to reach her if it wasn't already too late.

"Henry!" the woman cried out to him. He knew the voice, but he couldn't picture her face. He heard the pain in her speech, but there was something more prevalent. Fear? Desperation? Sadness? Henry couldn't tell. He only knew he had to reach her.

The world around him spun, and the flames faded into darkness along with the woman's cries. Henry's hand instinctively reached for his sword, but he grasped only air, finding his sheath empty. His vision darted between Buddy and Beast as he realized he was still in the caves of the dwarven Underdeep.

The dream, if he could call it that, felt so real that he expected to see burnt flesh and charred bone when he examined his hands. Shaken by the experience, and with the woman's desperate cries ringing fresh in his ears, he dove into his status, hoping to distract his mind. He parsed through Attributes and Resistances, and focused on the major changes that had resulted from his second trip to the desert.

Haruspex

Status Effects:

> **Soul Anchor: +2 Health/Hour**
>
> **Skeletal body: STR -20%, FOR -20%, Physical Resistance -1 (Bludgeoning -1), Environmental +1**
>
> **Second Path of the Desert. STR - 3, MOB -3, Max Health -5, Fire Resistance -5, Lightning Resistance +5**

Thresholds:

> **MOB +10%. -10% Vitus requirement for all transmutation Abilities**
>
> **PER +10%. Transmutation Abilities Extend to Equipment. Divinity Abilities Expanded**
>
> **RES +10%. Mental Damage Resistance +1, +1 Vitus regeneration per hour**

The Desert Path status effect had dropped his Strength back down and once again he was without the **10%** bump to the Attribute, but he still had three others above **25**. The effects of the Mobility and Resolve thresholds were straight forward, but Perception? He'd used the PER threshold enhancement to transfer the Harden Ability to his shield. That made sense, as it was a transmutation Ability, but what about divination? Either the Tier of Haruspex or his heightened PER allowed him to see the school of magic associated with each of his Abilities, but Haruspex was his only divination skill.

Too exhausted to focus on the information before him, Henry waived his hand in front of his face and dismissed his display. The glyphs and numerals faded, and he noticed Buddy looking at him.

"Anything more this time?" Buddy asked softly. Henry had grown used to the way the skeletons communicated with each other. Their jaws didn't move to converse, voices emanating from inside their skulls and projecting out. It was creepy, but now familiar in the short time they'd traveled together.

"No. More of the same." Henry unconsciously reached for the hilt of his sword again. "The woman's voice is desperate, but I can't locate it through the flames. The heat melts the flesh from my bones as I search for her. She only says my name, then I wake and it all fades. The harder I try to concentrate on her voice the further it drifts from my head."

"Shame," Beast said, tracing a line of frost on her fingertip. "The Necromancer could have at least given you back your memory after you showed him our plans."

"Stavros . . ." Henry whispered the name like it was a curse. "The dwarves thought the Necromancer had retreated to the depths below, but he's installed himself as the leader of the Ikritians. We don't have much time."

"We'll deal with the Ikritian ruler when the time comes," Buddy said. "For now, Henry, how is your Status?"

"I'm mostly healed from the fight, but several of my Attributes took a hit after my desert vision." Henry waved his hands through his display. "I'm having trouble understanding some of the information, especially in the heat of battle. I'm sure Damage Resistance is important, but it takes me too long to interpret all the numbers. Take mine for instance . . ." Henry brought up his Status and read it to Buddy.

Damage Resistance:

Physical: 5

    Bludgeoning: -1

    Slashing: +1

Environmental: 4

    Poison: Immune

    Fire: -5

    Lightning: +5

Magical: 2

Mental: +4

"That information is very important," Buddy said, and Henry felt like he was about to get a lecture from the mage. "Positive numbers show you're more resistant to that specific type of damage, while negative values reveal a weakness. I'm surprised a tactician like yourself doesn't take advantage of such information."

Henry shrugged. "I try, but it's hard to focus on every single enemy."

"Then why don't you change it to something more useful?"

"You can do that?" Henry asked.

"Of course. Though your Acumen is low, you should be able to will your display to meet your needs. Small numbers are inconsequential. Try hiding any Resistance with a value lower than 5, then eliminate the numbers completely. When you get stronger, or face stronger enemies, simply allow it to adjust accordingly. You can also designate negative numbers as weaknesses."

Henry considered the mage's guidance and decided to give it a try. Surprisingly, his display molded to his intent with little effort, like the divination magic had been listening to Buddy the whole time.

Resistances: Physical, Lightning, Poison (Immune)
Weakness: Fire

"That's much better. Thank you, Buddy," Henry said, and scrolled through the rest of his display, seeing what else he could clean up.

Before he could ask the mage for more advice, a heap of bone and armor stirred across the campfire from Henry and Buddy. "Ugh, I should have you all flogged for disturbing my sleep." Ox's maw dropped into a yawn wide enough to fit a normal-sized skull. The massive skeleton stretched his arms and legs, spanning most of their campsite. One of his feet contacted a quartz boulder that weighed several hundred pounds. The rock skidded away like an oversized pillow on a king's bed. "Consider yourselves lucky you're my only choice of company."

As Ox roused himself, the amalgamator skull that had merged with his shoulder plate began to clack its jaw. It labored to bite Ox, but it couldn't reach him. It struggled to attack, despite Ox's skull being twice the size of the amalgamator's. "A pleasant morning to you as well, Gator. At least one of my minions has the wherewithal to great their emperor properly."

"Get rid of that thing, or I'll do it for you." Beast pointed the tip of her dagger at the skull.

Ox turned his head to stare at the smaller skull attached to his shoulder plate. It could rotate side to side and up and down only a bit, and it appeared to have rooted itself into Ox's armor. Ox tapped the possessed skull on its forehead, and it snapped its jaw, trying once again to bite him. "Gator is one of my most trusted minions. Besides, he taught us how to beat the fiery rock monster. If memory serves me correctly, I had to save *you* during that battle as well."

Beast crossed her arms over her chest and glared at Ox, but the towering skeleton seemed more concerned about interacting with Gator than acknowledging Beast's annoyance.

Ox had stopped the golem from crushing Beast, but she had dragged his mangled body from the crumbling ruins. They'd faced many challenges in the short time since they woke, but the four of them, five with Muji, were an effective team when it came to battle. Also, Henry couldn't argue with Ox's reasoning. They did use a similar tactic to fight Smyrna's Golem as they had with the amalgamator, though what saved them was Henry's lost sword and Muji's unexpected use of the dwarven Magma Blaster.

Henry surveyed their campsite. It was a vast circular room with a single exit—a short offshoot from the main tunnel that looked like an abandoned mining venture. Veins of purple and white rock snaked through black hexagonal quartz pillars that lined the walls.

Haruspex

Item: Purple Quartz (Mundane)

Description: Component. Can be used to craft various items. Hardness 3, Structure 4/5

Henry didn't know much about mining, but he suspected the dwarves deserted the room when it didn't yield more than the worthless rock. The alcove served as a decent campsite, but provided little cover and protection for the dangerous monsters of the Underdeep.

Once again, Henry reached for his sword but found only an empty sheath, reminding him of the lost weapon. He had a few javelins, a shield, and a small dagger, but he didn't like being without something for heavy combat.

Buddy noticed Henry examining his gear. He reached into his pack and pulled out the melted remains of Henry's xiphos. The sword once had the ability to drain Vitus from its victims and transfer it to the wielder. Henry had unknowingly used that sword to kill a Master Acolyte, and with the help of a well-placed Drift Amulet, he subsequently gained his undead life.

Buddy tossed Henry the hilt of his sword. "I had hoped to gather more from the room, but this is all I could manage before it crumbled around us." Henry gladly accepted the gift, examining what remained of the familiar blade.

Haruspex

Item: Akşam Xiphos (Epic)

Description: Weapon (Enchanted). Ikritian sword crafted with an extremely rare flow crystal (Legendary). Hardness 30, Structure 9/100

Lore: This magical weapon was created by the great sorcerer and Emperor of Ikrit, Lord Stavros. First used to defeat a cursed ettercap set loose in the Ikritian capital, this xiphos was gifted to Cirilo Galantis, the current Commander of the Acolyte Bastion

Ability: Drain V (Necromancy). Severe damage has rendered this item inert

Haruspex was the strange Ability from his desert vision that took over the Drift Amulet's Assess and Status functions. As the Ability had grown, he'd learned to gather more information about stronger items and beings. Similarly, Consume had overridden the Amulet's Siphon ability. Ox had also experienced the same change in his Abilities, albeit without the accompanying visions. The giant skeleton didn't seem to think anything was abnormal, but there was very little Ox cared about beyond booze, women, and fighting.

Henry thanked Buddy for recovering his weapon. Even though the blade had been destroyed, the flow crystal it contained was still the highest quality of any item they'd found so far—Legendary—even though its magic had been hindered by the damage from the golem and Blaster.

Without Henry's sword stifling its magic, the golem would have sucked the skeletons dry, and they'd be lifeless bone piles, unable to regenerate under the mountain's spell. Buddy and the dwarves believed that the regeneration spell was a curse from the Necromancer, and that the auras they saw were the Empress's counter to whatever Livadi and the Necromancer had tried to do. Henry felt there was more to the story than that, but he had was no way to tell without delivering the Flow Bracers to Destria's ghost.

"The Flow Bracers!" Henry exclaimed. He'd been too busy recovering to examine them before, but he opened his leather pack and pulled out the treasure. They were made from shiny metal, almost white, and inlaid with dozens of tiny, perfectly clear flow crystals, with one larger crystal on the back of each hand.

Haruspex

Item: Flow Bracers (Legendary)

Description: Dwarven Armor created to harness the power of the Source Crystal. Contains flow crystals (Transcendent). Hardness 50, Structure 123/150

Lore: Few civilizations can match the prowess of dwarven engineering. For thousands of years, the will to survive in the harsh underground world of Jallfoss, along with the ambition to dig deeper, have driven the innovations of Hjardharfell. Numerous engineers have made their mark over the millennia, but few so much as the dwarven Flowsmith, Smyrna Skibibidi. Many will

say that Smyrna was more gnome than dwarf. That claim is hard to refute, given his proficiency as an artificer. These Bracers are one of his final creations—a gift intended for Empress Destria.

So much for the sword being the most powerful magical item we've found. Henry had never heard of Transcendent quality, but it was likely higher than Legendary.

As the golem's lair collapsed around him, Henry was in such a rush that when he pulled off the Bracers, he also took the arms from the dwarven skeleton. Henry pulled the bones from the Bracers, and a piece of brown cloth fell to the ground. At first, he thought it was a tattered piece of clothing, but it was neatly folded.

Henry sat the Bracers on his lap, then picked up the cloth and carefully opened it. Scrawled in charcoal was a diamond shape with lines, swirls, and dwarven writing.

Buddy watched Henry examine the Bracers. The armor emitted such an enormous amount of power that it overwhelmed the mage's faculties, and he almost had to shield his eyes before turning off his Mystic Revelation Ability. When he dismissed the Ability, the drawing on the cloth caught his attention. He plucked it from Henry's hand and examined it closely.

"Look," he said, tracing the lines and mouthing dwarven words, "The writing on this sketch goes into great detail about the precision of a flow crystal's cut when connecting to . . . something. Unfortunately, it's smeared, and I can't read most of it. There are several references to Vitus. S*team,* as the dwarves call it."

"What does that mean?" Ox turned his attention away from Gator, and the skull clamped down on his finger. Two of its front teeth cracked on the giant digit, but it didn't seem to notice.

"When the golem held me in its grasp, I got a good look at the flow crystal in its chest. That crystal and this drawing are too similar to be a coincidence," Buddy mused, not looking up from the drawing.

Henry held up the melted remains of his sword and compared its flow crystal to the sketch, noticing that even though the metal was destroyed, the stone had remained mostly unscathed. "The drawing looks like the flow crystal in my xiphos. My sword's Drain ability and that of the golem were similar, but the golem drained Vitus, Health, *and* the capability to resurrect. My sword only stole Vitus. As far as I know, it has never drained life or stopped something from resurrecting."

"I think that dwarf whose hands you've stolen was Smyrna himself," Buddy replied. "Maybe he created the golem's heart per this schematic. The Ikritians made your sword. It's a rough copy . . . incomplete.

"You talk like it's something you could recreate?" Henry asked, but he also wondered why Buddy would want to do something like that.

"No. From what I understand, there are two parts to the process, and both are beyond me." Buddy neatly folded the cloth and tucked it inside the cover of his metal tome. "The first is the way the stone is refined. That's what I believe your stone lacked, though the dwarves may be able to recreate the cut. The second part is a spell. It's referenced on the cloth, but there's not enough information to get started. I am, however, sure of one thing. It's definitely a necromancy spell. If your theory about Stavros is correct, that would make sense."

"But why would Smyrna use necromancy?" Beast stopped twirling her dagger and took an interest in the conversation. "He was a dwarven engineer. How would he even be capable of that?"

Buddy shrugged and started to answer, but the pad of tiny footsteps and a muffled squeak interrupted their conversation. Muji the trogold hopped over and around the bones and rubble that littered the cavern's floor. The knee-high creature usually traveled on all four feet and only stood to observe something or interact with the skeletons. Now, he padded toward them on two feet, clutching something the size of his own head. His pointy ears with singed tufts from the Magma Blaster and his large, black, shiny eyes were the first things they could make out. He plodded toward them with his long bushy tail swinging wildly to help him keep his balance. Normally, Muji was grey and white, with wild matted hair that obscured his long limbs. He tended to get dirty while exploring, so his appearance changed from sooty grey to muddy brown, depending on where he had most recently ventured.

Buddy had read in the red mage's tome that trogolds were mildly intelligent, solitary creatures but quite curious. They had an affinity for magic and any items containing it, which sometimes led them to inadvertently activate item Abilities, much to the detriment of their own safety and those around them.

Muji matched that description perfectly. From the moment Buddy had saved the furry creature's life from a pack of hungry lizards, the trogold had been enamored with the mage. Buddy had tried to chase him away with lightning and frost bolts, but the trogold never stayed away for long.

Luckily for the group, Muji turned out to be a proficient artificer. He could channel Buddy's elemental spells and Ox's healing magic into flow crystals and weapons. He had even activated the dwarven Magma Blaster and destroyed Smyrna's soul-eating golem. In the process, the tiny trogold earned himself a healthy number of Tiers thanks to the Drift Amulet that Beast had tied around his neck. Unfortunately, they had yet to find out what those Tiers meant for the creature, besides an impressively expanded Status.

"Have you made him your thrall yet?" Beast asked.

"No, and I don't intend to," Buddy huffed. He had explained to the other skeletons that a thrall was a magical contract between a magic user and another being—the two would share power and magical affinity. Buddy had been insulted by the trogold's repeated requests for the connection, even after Muji's artificing and heroic acts. The mage would never admit it, but he was just as attracted to any magical item as the trogold was.

"It's a good practice to reward your minions for their good deeds," Ox said with a chuckle.

As the trogold traipsed near, they could see he carried a large rock and was covered in red dust. He stopped in front of Buddy and held up the rock. "Beak, beak," the trogold chirped, clutching the rock with long skinny fingers, lifting it as high as he could.

"I see," Buddy said, plucking the rock from Muji's grasp. Buddy waved his hand, and a swirl of water formed around the stone, washing it to reveal a clear flow crystal.

"Beak," Muji dropped down to all fours and shook the red dust from his fur.

Beast scratched Muji's head and cooed affectionately. "What did he bring you?"

"He's covered in rust. I believe he pulled this out of one of the inert golems that lay in piles in the surrounding tunnels. I hope he didn't accidentally activate one."

"If we beat that big one, even an army of little ones would be nothing," Ox said. He wasn't wrong. According to Thorodd, the famous dwarven engineer, Smyrna, had created the soul-stealing golem to defend against the Acolytes and the

Necromancer, but he'd accidentally activated it, and it killed him. It was much bigger and meaner than the other golems they'd found that were meant to be used for mining and moving heavy loads for the dwarves.

A tiny cave lizard scurried across a rock near the group. Muji's eyes locked on the lizard, pulling his attention away from Buddy. The lizard was a thousand times smaller than the ones that had tried to eat him, but the trogold never passed up the opportunity for retribution. Muji pounced, and the lizard scurried away in time to avoid being eaten.

Henry tapped on the huge flow crystal with a bony finger. "Can you do anything with it?"

Haruspex

Item: Golem Heart (Epic)

Description: Accessory. This flow crystal is enchanted to control and power dwarven golems

Lore: The mindless automatons carry out the instructions imbedded in their enchanted hearts. Be wary, for those enchantments may have degraded over a century of neglect

"Degraded. That's putting it lightly," Henry remarked.

Buddy slowly pushed Henry's hand away as one would that of a child before responding. "Maybe I can use it to store or amplify magic. Or maybe Torgga would be interested in it."

Ox took the opportunity to give Buddy a good ribbing. "I don't know much about seducing dwarves, Barney, but maybe they like rocks as much as other women love flowers. I wish you luck with that approach."

"I am not trying to seduce Torgga," Buddy snapped. "She's the only dwab with any magic potential, and I want to make sure she has every opportunity to excel. That is it."

Ox let out a sharp chuckle. "You must convince *yourself* that. Not us."

"Dwab?" Henry asked.

The questions forced Ox to erupt with laughter, and Henry imagined that if the huge skeleton had eyes, he would be wiping tears from them. "It's an affectionate term for beautiful dwarven ladies, Herbie."

"It is a general term for dwarven females!" Buddy rebuked, then tucked the golem heart into his pack. "Enough talk. We've dallied for too long already."

Henry went to heft his own bag over his shoulder, but a sound from Muji that wasn't one of his normal chirps froze him in place. The trogold had stopped chasing the lizard and now arched his back and bared his teeth. Tiny incisors glistened under the snub nose of the cave creature, and its fur stood on end, doubling the size of his body and tripling that of his twitching tail.

Henry followed the direction of Muji's attention to the opening of their cave. "Enough talk, indeed."

CHAPTER 4

"The mighty pine flexes in the wind. It weathers the storm." Bharat closed his eyes as he chanted the funeral prayer. "Its needles stay green through the harshest winter." His voice rasped with age and weakness, a mixture of low groans and high creaks, like a water wheel that had ground through its bearings.

"As does our faith," the circle of elves responded. Twenty elves in white and brown robes surrounded the High Sage, all on their knees with their heads pressed against the wooden floor of the worship hut.

"Spread your branches to the sun." Bharat held open palms in front of him. Three elves in full Sentinel gear knelt in the center of the circle. Between the three elves and the High Sage lay a fourth elf on a bed of fresh pine boughs, wearing only a thin white tunic and had his arms crossed over his chest. His eyes had closed the previous day for the last time. The dead elf's cloud-white hair was pulled back, highlighting the sharp features of his face and pointed ears.

"We are grateful for our protector's sacrifice," the elves chanted in unison. The hut was meant for a larger gathering, but their

numbers had dwindled in the years after the Turning. It was a vast building supported by giant pine logs and a thatched roof with walls made of thick layers of animal hides. The small ring of elves with the Sage at the center made the place of worship seem empty and vacant—nearly as void as the eyes of the skeletons that surrounded the elves and lined the walls along the building's interior.

The skeletons stood in frozen silence, adorned by a mixture of high-quality elven armor and the gear of fallen Acolytes. Most of the skeletons were undead Acolytes themselves, as they were generally hardier than the bones of the average Jallfoss human. There we no elven skeletons amongst those undead. While not outlawed, it was taboo to include the bones of an elf in one's Guard.

Fire from metal braziers outside the elven circle cast shadows on the skeletons, playing tricks with the light and dark that shone through their eyes and gaping smiles, giving a hint of life behind the deathly gazes.

Taljipura knelt before the Sage. A hint of light made her open her eyes, and she saw the head of a young elf from the corner of her vision. The boy peered under a fur flap of the hut between the legs of one of the peripheral skeletons.

"Jai," Taljipura cursed under her breath. She'd knelt for hours as the ancient elf drug out the ceremony. Her knees ached, and her patience had grown thin. Seeing the young elf peering in had sent her already short temper to boiling. The lowlife thought he was worthy of being near the funeral blessing. And to be looking at them between the legs of her own champion Guard? If it weren't for the sanctity of the ceremony, she would pull him into the tent to be lashed before the High Sage.

Though she directed her anger at the worthless, dark-haired

boy, Mayur was the one that had let her down. The dead elf before her had been the anchor of her troupe of Sentinels just a day earlier. Before the Turning, Sentinels were forest elves that protected the mountain valley of Amera from encroaching beasts. After the Turning, the High Sage had reformed the Sentinels as groups of blessed high elves that commanded Guards composed of undead skeletons.

Along with Surat and Lata, the two elves that now knelt beside her, Taljipura had led Mayur in her group of Sentinels into hundreds of battles against the *Sprigs*. Ghara's monsters only came a few at a time, but they were strong enough that only the Sentinels and their skeletons had a chance in a fight against them.

The previous day, they had gotten surrounded while venturing into Jallfoss, and a Sprig had landed a fatal blow on Mayur. The Sentinel's Guard of three skeletons instantly turned on them. Taljipura, Surat, and Lata barely escaped with their lives. They returned later that evening to recover Mayur's body back to the elven forest valley of Amera.

Those peasants had better be grateful. It took me forever to train Mayur, and it's going to be even harder to replace him, Taljipura thought as Jai caught her stare and dropped the flap.

The elves couldn't bury Mayur's body. In less than a day he'd return as one of the undead and attack them. The only thing they could do was dump him in one of the dwarven air vents and send his body to the bottom of the mountain. It was difficult to tell how much time the dead had left before returning, so Mayur's body had been tied with thick cords to prevent him from rising during the ceremony. Such was the danger of fighting Sprigs inside the mountain instead of out. When an elf died inside Jallfoss, they became the enemy.

"May the wrath of Ghara wash over her servant." The High

Sage lifted his frail arms to the ceiling as Taljipura brought her attention back to the ceremony. The crystal on Bharat's forehead glowed with a dark earthy brown. It was ornately carved and set in a circlet of light, silvery metal in the shape of pine branches. His white robes of pure marrowbella silk were lined in golden thread. Now that his arms were spread, one could make out the antlered head of a Spriggan on the back and front of his robes, meant to resemble the original form of the forest god herself.

"May our penance return peace to the forest." None of the elves moved as they prayed with their heads down.

"Rise, Sentinels of Ghara. Remember those lost and receive this blessing as you go forward to protect us." Bharat's robes hung loosely on his thin frame, making his shoulders look like tent poles. The wrinkles on his weathered face were deep enough to make Talji think of cracked dirt on a lakebed during a drought.

The circle of elves sat back on their heels. Talji's back popped as she rolled her shoulders, thankful to stand after hours of fighting off cramps all through her body.

The three Sentinels stood and opened their eyes. Heavy fur capes draped their shoulders and covered white leather armor. The armor looked like it would offer more protection from the cold than it would from an attacker, but it was as hard as it was light, boiled in pine sap and troll blood until it became more durable than steel. Boots and gloves made of leather and fur rounded out their ensemble.

Each elf had a short bow strapped to their backs, a quiver at their side, a light elven short sword, and a series of daggers sheathed in their belts. The armament of the three elves was of Superior quality and second only to the fine thread and craftmanship of the High Sage's robes. Each wore a circlet on their forehead, holding back white hair and revealing pointed ears. Similar to the Sage's, the brown flow crystals set in their circlets were only slightly larger than a pine seed and much less ornate. Finally, each wore an Ikritian Drift Amulet they'd salvaged from dead Acolytes tucked safely under their armor.

The ceremony had drug on for hours, but Bharat always made it a point to highlight the sacrifice of his Sentinels and emphasize their importance. The undead and the Sprigs had forced them out of their mountain castles, and it was everything Bharat could do to hold together the few hundred high elves and the several thousand forest elves. The blessing he bestowed before sending Sentinels forward was as much for show as it was for ritual. "You carry the hope of all the elves of Amera with you into battle. May your efforts redeem our weakness."

"Thank you, High Sage," Taljipura replied, then turned and quickly left the worship hut before Bharat could change his mind and extend the funeral ceremony yet again. The nine skeletons standing around the exterior moved in unison to follow the Sentinels out the fur flap of the wooden hut.

It was neither rumor nor hidden knowledge that the Sage favored Talji most of all his Sentinels. She had once been a member of his personal escort and had kept him rich and in power for the last century of turmoil. In return, he'd blessed her Guard with the finest elven armor and weaponry in the forest. It wasn't much compared to the high-elven weapons left behind in the castles of Jallfoss, but still enough that she could focus on battle while other, lesser Sentinels had to scavenge their own armaments from the hazards of the mountain, usually leading to their doom.

Taljipura formed her group of four elves from the most

elite families. There was little selection since only a few hundred high-borne had been outside the mountain castles when the Turning happened a hundred years earlier. Mayur had been a good elf and a strong warrior, one of the best with a partisan she'd ever seen, but his heart had been too soft to do some of the things being a Sentinel required. She wasn't surprised he'd died trying to protect her. Surat and Lata, on the other hand, were vicious and just greedy enough to keep them loyal.

Lata was the youngest of the troupe, only a few years past two hundred. Her hair was always neatly braided, and she was beyond proficient with a bow. She despised the forest elves and fought the Sprigs hoping to one day return to the castles and be removed from the forest forever.

Surat was much older, maybe approaching four hundred. He claimed to be the only high elf to have trained with the original Sentinels before the Turning. He was a proficient evoker, but it was doubtful if he had ever been good enough to train with the Sentinels of old.

Surat and Lata loved to extort the forest elves. There wasn't much gold to go around since the dwarves had stopped mining after the Turning, but they would force the poor elves to give them food and fur in return for *active protection* from the Sprigs, as they called it.

The three made their way outside the tent to find that a group of elves had gathered. About a hundred forest elves stood in the dirty snow around the prayer hut's opening. They all had the shabby furs of the poor farm dwellers and the long brown hair typical among forest elves. Each one had a pine bough in their hands, like the ones that lay under Mayur's dead body. It was a sign of respect among the forest elves, though the gesture irritated Talji more than she was willing to admit.

Bharat embraced their traditions, but Taljipura hated living in the forest, and she longed to return to life in the castles of Jallfoss.

"Hey, Talji. Looks like your fans are here," Surat quipped. Talji shot him a mean look that shut his mouth quicker than the back of her hand could have. Surat looked away, not wanting to draw any undue attention to himself. Talji allowed her coterie to refer to her informally when they were hunting, but a Sentinel should know better than to be so unprofessional in public. It also bothered her that Surat was being disrespectful to the forest elves' sign of respect, and it frustrated her further that she was annoyed by that.

The gathering of forest elves lowered their eyes as the three Sentinels and the nine, armed skeletons made their way past. As they trod through the dirt and snow, a young girl ran up to the skeletons. She wore light furs but didn't seem to mind the cold. A small woven cord held a flat circular rock to her head.

The girl stopped just in front of Lata's Guard and lifted her palm. "Hold!" the girl commanded. Fear gripped the forest elves, but none dared interfere. They all stood in shocked, uncomfortable silence.

Lata channeled her Guile through the circlet on her forehead and into the skeleton the young girl addressed. The skeleton stopped and turned toward the child. It opened its mouth and released a blood-curdling scream that sounded like the dying throughs of a mountain troll. The villagers cowered in fear, and the young girl shrieked and ran away crying.

"Children . . . they're all children," Surat chuckled with a derisive sneer.

Talji motioned toward one of the paths that led into the pine forest. "Speaking of children, we're making a slight detour. I need to chat with Jai."

—

Jai had been caught. He knew it was useless to run away and that Talji would eventually find him. He wasn't welcome anywhere near the worship tent, but he couldn't help himself. *Why do we have to worship something that only brings us suffering?* He thought as he ran, but he would never say that out loud for fear of five lashes to the backside.

Mayur was the only one in Talji's group who had ever been nice to him. The other three would smack and taunt him whenever he tried to get close, but never in Mayur's presence. The only other person besides Mayur and Jai's own parents that had shown they boy kindness was a lone Ikritian farmer who often traveled through Amera to collect plants and herbs.

Jai remembered one time when the other three Sentinels weren't around, Mayur had helped Jai learn to focus his Guile. "It has many names," Mayur said. "Dwarves call it *Steam*. Humans call it *Vitus*. If you sneak up on Acolytes and listen to them, they'll call it *Merq*. No matter what its name, it refers to your mental constitution when controlling magic. The more Guile you have, the more powerful and numerous your spells become."

"Why do you need spells if you can just use your circlet?" Jai asked, pointing to the yellow stone on Mayur's forehead.

Mayur smiled. "The circlets are Bharat's magic. They let us counter the Necromancer's spell and use his undead to fight Sprigs. Unfortunately, we all know those Sprigs are getting stronger, and our Guard can't always be relied on to protect us. They wouldn't hesitate to rip us apart if I were to remove this circlet." Mayur motioned to the three armored skeletons standing just outside the firelight.

It was late, and Mayur had allowed Jai to join him by his

fire outside the Sentinel's stone house. Most of the high-elven Sentinels preferred to live on the outskirts of the main settlements as they'd never taken to the rural lifestyle of the forest elves. The few remaining evokers among them had used their elemental magic to form buildings that resembled the castles they could no longer call home.

Mayur instructed Jai as the youth dumped a handful of moosel nuts that he'd gathered from the forest into the campfire. "The minds of the undead are hard to control. As experienced as I am, I can only hold three in my Guard. Any more and they'd break loose of their bonds."

"I don't understand," Jai said. "Why are skeletons hard to control? I heard that when you kill one, the Drift Amulets only transfer their hate. You don't even get memories. The minds are nearly blank."

"That's precisely why they're hard to control. With no memories and few thoughts to convolute their minds, the spell doesn't have much to work with."

"I heard that the Sprigs have thoughts when you kill them, at least according to the Drift Amulets," Jai wondered aloud. He knew that the Sentinels used the Ikritian Drift Amulets to power up through Soul Essence they took from the Sprigs. "Why can't you just control them instead and not worry about fighting."

Mayur laughed and stirred the moosel nuts around the burning coals. "It's not that simple. The *Hold Undead* spell in our circlets only works on the *undead*. Hence the name."

Jai sat quietly and considered Mayur's words. It made sense. Ghara once summoned creatures of the forest— everything from elk to bears to the bees that pollinated the mountain crops. Since the Turning, the forest god had only unleashed horrible monsters that corrupted the surrounding land.

Jai looked at Mayur's guard. He hated Bharat, but he was thankful the High Sage had found a way to use the Necromancer's undead to counter the corrupted god's minions. He just hadn't ever realized those minions were living creatures.

Those poor animals were being forced to attack, though not in the same way the Sentinels were using the mindless skeletons. Jai had spent countless hours watching from under the arena stands as the Sentinels practiced. It took years of intense training to master one's Guard, so the Sentinels went to a place called the *Theater* to hone the skills of their undead and, subsequently, their control over them.

The Theater was little more than a set of stone stands built into the side of a steep hill. A rocky field sat before the stone seating, with wooden stands on the opposite length. The short sides held a series of wood and metal cages that housed captured Sprigs.

The Sentinels would trap weak Sprigs and use them for training and entertainment to pass the time. Jai understood the utility of it but felt it was cruel how the Sentinels would surround the Sprigs with their Guard and tear them apart. Not that Jai had any sympathy for Ghara's monsters, but he wasn't fond of watching any creature suffer.

On the other hand, the Sentinels' Guard had always fascinated the younger forest elves. They would spend hours discussing aspects of each held skeleton, classifying their Attributes and Abilities, even though none of the forest elves possessed Drift Amulets. The strongest Guards, knowns as *champions*, were the toughest skeletons, and capable of tremendous feats.

Talji's champion was the deadliest Guard in all of Amera, even without its magical armor and sword. It was fast and incredibly robust. Some said she had captured a high-ranking

Acolyte and killed him herself. Jai didn't doubt the rumor based on Talji's ruthless nature.

Mayur reached into the fire and pulled out two moosel nuts, cracking the steaming morsels in his hand. Jai marveled at how strong Mayur had to be to reach into the fire and not even flinch.

"Remember, Jai. It's not the Guard that makes the Sentinel." Mayur sat one of the moosel nuts on the bench next to Jai to cool. "The Guard is only as strong as its Sentinel's aptitude to control it. The circlets gain their potency form the wearer, not the other way around."

From that day, Jai had not stopped training. Running, jumping, carrying logs, and hiding like the forest Sentinels of the past used to do. He would spend hours every day working with his sling and practicing his magic every night until he fell asleep from exhaustion.

As Jai sped from the worship hut, a tear streamed down his face. *I'm probably the only one crying for you, Mayur*, he thought, *I wonder if Talji, Lata, or Surat even care that you're dead.*

Jai despised Talji, along with every other high elf, with the minor exception of Mayur. Just because they were high-born with white hair didn't make them better than the forest elves.

Bharat gave the best living places to the high elves and treated forest elves like chuborgi boars, but the Sage spurned Jai most of all. Jai knew the reason for Bharat's hatred, but there was nothing he could do to change the past, so he pushed the thought from his head. Jai was only a baby during the Turning, and he and his parents shouldn't be held responsible for his sister's crimes. If Bharat wanted to blame Jai for his sister's involvement with the Turning, the old geezer could go straight to the afterlife, for all Jai cared.

No. He refused to be held back by his family's problems.

Instead, he would become the greatest Sentinel ever and save all the forest elves from Ghara's monsters. Then the high elves could return to their castles and leave them alone forever.

Jai sprinted past snow-covered huts as he made his way out of the village. The forest elves had lived in the high mountain valley of Amera for much longer than the humans and dwarves had inhabited Jallfoss. They were hardy people who embraced the cold pine forest the way their cousins from far away did their swamps and jungles. But since the Turning, times had gotten hard. The land now withheld the usual bountiful harvests and produced barely enough to sustain the elves. To make matters worse, the constant barrage of Sprigs made essential maintenance on housing very difficult. Many starving elves couldn't farm since the forest god's monsters interfered with any harvest. They could have abandoned Amera long ago, leaving the Acolytes to sort out the mountain, but they were stubborn and refused to give up. It didn't help that Bharat was their High Sage and worshiped Ghara with a furious zealotry, no matter how many evil Sprigs she sent their way.

Jai ducked between tiny wooden huts and vaulted over piles of firewood, knocking a few pieces to the ground. He heard a shout from the wood's owner, but he kept running, ignoring the protest. Even if he weren't in a hurry, he wouldn't have stopped to interact with the villager. Very few had been nice to him since Bharat had all but exiled his parents shortly after his birth. Jai understood that the other forest elves didn't want to risk Bharat removing the protection his Sentinels provided, but it had made growing up challenging for the youth.

Jai passed two human skeletons that stood at the edge of the village. Their bones were frail and sun-bleached. Each wore a mixture of metal plates meant to act as armor and held rudimentary wooden clubs. The poorly equipped sentries were the best skeletons this section of Amera could manage, and they were armed far less than Talji's Guard. The feeble undead watchmen would do little to defend against an attacking Sprig besides holding it back as the villagers fled.

Settling into a steady jog, he welcomed the exercise that distracted him from the tears welling in his eyes. He would honor Mayur the only way he knew how—training himself until he was strong enough to become a Sentinel.

CHAPTER 5

Muji let out a low grow that was far too deep for the normally playful trogold. It was both a threat to whatever was coming and an effective warning to the skeletons. They looked toward the only entrance to the quartz cave. Muji had growled at enemies before, but it was more of a challenge. This growl had fear in it.

Buddy unbuckled the strap that held the three bronze dwarven bucklers at his waist. They hovered and began to orbit the mage slowly. Beast nocked an arrow, and Ox tightened his grip on his hammer.

Henry picked up a cracked Acolyte kite shield he'd found in the amalgamator's remains and secured it to his wrist bone with leather straps. It was lower in quality than the lion shield he'd found in the Gladiator Supreme's chamber, but that armor had been lost in Lundarbrekka. Keeping his eyes on the entrance, he retrieved one of the javelins that he'd placed against a quartz boulder and held it ready.

Black smoke began to roll into the room, slowly at first and just a few inches deep, but it grew thicker and darker as it spread toward them, covering the piles of bones that once composed Gator's body. Several dark figures appeared in the stone entranceway, and a creaking sound echoed through the cavern like tree branches rubbing against each other in the wind. The smoke didn't appear to have come from a campfire. Instead, it was thick, stratified near the floor, and looked like it would be sticky to the touch.

An enemy approached, but the skeleton's had never fought anything preceded by something like the black fog that now inched toward them. Muji's growling intensified as the intruders drew closer.

Status Effect: Fear (Moderate): STR -10%, RES -30%, HAR -10%

Henry fought to steady trembling hands. Fear was the emotion, but whatever could make a skeleton feel fear had to be worse than a soul-stealing golem. He looked for a place to run, but the dark figures blocked the only exit. Henry noticed that the other three skeletons were experiencing the same Status Effect, as they hadn't moved or spoken.

Henry's focus went to steadying his nerves instead of discerning weaknesses in the coming enemies. It wasn't normal for him to be this distracted by emotion. It was almost like fighting the rage that came from the Acolytes' auras.

That was it. He realized where he'd felt it before. It was exactly like the rage that the red auras induced. It was artificial, like the emotion was coming from outside him, but that didn't make it any less forceful.

Then Henry realized that it wasn't smoke coming from the intruders. It was the collection of their auras. He'd never considered an aura could be any color other than green or red. If every aura reflected the individual's soul, what did that say about these intruders?

When Henry's aura wasn't hidden by the dwarven muffle spell, he'd been told it looked like a rigid beetle carapace, hard and crystalline. Beast's was hard to see. It snaked over her bones like a tiny vine. Buddy's swirled around him like a billowing thunderstorm. Ox's aura was the most massive of any he'd encountered. It spun around him and enveloped everything within thirty feet.

However, all of their auras were green, marking that their souls had melded with their bodies inside the cave. Red came from outside and caused rage. The approaching auras were black and causing fear, but Henry was getting better at overcoming aura effects. He forced his mind to calm by focusing on the task at hand.

Status Effect Subdued: Fear Dismissed
RES +1
HAR +1

"The smoke, it's an aura. The black is causing fear instead of rage. Fight it in the same way," he shouted to the others.

"That's why I allow you to lead, warrior minion." Ox shook his head and rolled his shoulders, happy to be pulled from the effect on his mind, though resisting that fear was easier said than done as the smoky aura began to billow and surround the figures entering the room. The black smoke slightly obscured them, but their features were unmistakable.

The intruders were skeletons, at least partially. Long, thin bones flowed together and bent where joints shouldn't have been. Thick muscles and tendons partially covered the bones, but they didn't connect in places that made sense. The muscles looked more like clothing or a tattered robe than the actual structure of the creatures.

Six of the monsters made their way into the room, and Henry couldn't tell if they stood on legs and moved mechanically or if they were gliding through the smoke. They had eyes in the bony sockets of their enlarged, globular skulls, but without facial skin the eyes seemed filled with an intense frenzy that didn't match their floating movements. A few strands of sinew connected their jaw bones to their skulls, forming sadistic smiles.

What stood out most was the monsters' hands. Their hands flowed into three dagger-like claws, almost as long as the rest of their arms.

The spikes that make up their hands grew longer. The creaking sound they first heard came from the boney claws rubbing against each other. Like the bow of a ghastly violin, the appendages let out a brutal song of agony.

Henry pushed the fear aside and tried to focus on tactics. "They must have followed us from below. Did the red mage write about these?"

"No," Buddy answered. The question jolted him out of his fear, and allowed him to prepare blue fireballs in his hands. "I don't believe he ever made it far enough to find out. I only recall a few references to the Necromancer's soldiers tearing men to shreds and sowing fear."

"Close enough. Whatever they are, they're not here to talk," Beast said, her daggers glowing bright blue with their frost magic.

The monsters spread into the room just like the smoke that preceded them. Instead of making a direct approach, they fanned out and Henry realized they were trying to surround them. They were intelligent, and that made them even more dangerous. "We can't let them flank us. They're smart, so be careful."

"Then I suggest we don't wait for them to encircle us before we take the initiative," Ox offered.

"Agreed," Henry responded, cocking back his arm and launching a javelin at the approaching monsters. Henry had faith in the accuracy and power of his throw, but as slow and deliberate as the creatures had approached, he didn't expect their agility. Henry's target dodged quickly, and he noticed that a normal creature with legs would have dipped before it sprang. Instead, there was no drop, only a quick strafe, and the creature easily evaded. "Damn," Henry cursed. He had to get closer if he wanted to land an attack.

"You're going to need this." Beast flicked one of her frost daggers toward him. It left a dim blue spiral of cold flakes in its path that slowly settled to the ground. Henry caught the blade by the handle and spun it into a reverse grip.

With the fear aura still urging him to flee, Henry didn't want to waste the brainpower it would take to devise and coordinate a strategy. Instead, he rushed the monsters. Ox must have been thinking the same thing because he charged alongside Henry.

Ox's heavy footsteps thudded beside him, and out of the corner of his eye he saw Ox reach down and scoop up a heavy fragment of a quartz boulder and launch it underhand at the intruders. That's when the cave erupted into chaos.

The monsters raised their clawed hands and pointed their long fingers at the approaching skeletons. The bone spikes that formed each finger shot forward, extending well over twenty feet. A lattice of bone filled the cave, crossing and weaving together to create a deadly forest that ripped through the stones in its path. The claws easily pierced Ox's thrown boulder, tearing it apart and sending the pieces crashing to the ground long before reaching its target.

The claws not aimed at the boulder were directed at the

charging skeletons. Henry saw the attacks coming at him with deadly precision and couldn't ignore the effect they had on the massive hunk of quartz. Despite the setback that accompanied his vision of the desert, he'd gained Strength and Mobility with his Tiers, just not enough to prevent his body from lagging behind the speed of his Perception. Though he saw every attack, his reaction time was still limited by the speed he could coax from his bones. Nevertheless, he managed to dodge all but two of the claws, which pierced his shield like it was made of paper.

Ox presented a much bigger target than Henry and wasn't so lucky in dodging the assault. Half a dozen claws, not hindered at all by his mixed armor, empaled the huge skeleton and halted him in place. The massive damage from the claws forced Ox to focus his Vitus on repairing his bones as they shattered under the barrage. He would have been torn to pieces if he hadn't been able to supply a constant stream of healing magic to himself.

The claws around Henry withdrew only slightly slower than they had extended, and he hacked at them with Beasts daggers. The blade glanced off the hard bone, not leaving so much as a scratch. Then, with their claws retracted and reset, the monsters pointed their deadly fingers at Henry again. Their wide eyes and cruel smiles seemed to target him with murderous intent, but Henry was ready this time.

He opened the channels in his mind to allow the Vitus to flow through his body, energizing and strengthening his bones. He crouched his legs and sprang forward, aiming with Beast's daggers at the center of the chest of the closest dreadful clawed monster. *Dread claw,* Henry thought, *that was an appropriate name for them.*

Blitz

Harden

Henry's magic launched him forward within feet of his

target, but the two dread claws on either side loosed their spears toward his path to intercept his charge. Henry saw they would hit him before he landed the attack, so he suspended his surge and allowed the deadly claws to cross harmlessly, just inches in front of him.

More claws followed close behind, aimed directly at Henry now that he'd stopped charging. Luckily, Beast and Buddy joined the battle. As the assault sped toward Henry, Buddy's bucklers plowed into the attack. The mage had surrounded the shields with his blue fire, and he must have reinforced them with force magic because the claws deflected off the spinning shields enough to miss Henry—an expert series of parries, by the warrior's standard. Henry dodged backwards, avoiding another bone spear, and tried to assess one of the monsters.

Haruspex

Type: Dread Claw

Health: 63/63

Vitus: 48/48

Attributes:

    STR: 18

    MOB: 28

    FOR: 15

    ACU: 12

    PER: 11

    RES: 8

Resistances: Physical, Mental (Immune)

Weakness: Magic

Lore: The Necromancer's minions guard the lowest depths of Jallfoss. Some claim these monsters can eat the souls of their victims

"They're weak to magic," Henry shouted, trying to maneuver for a strike with Beast's dagger.

A puff of green smoke behind one of the dread-claws signaled Beast's arrival to the fight. She'd used her teleportation magic, or self-conjuration, as Buddy liked to call it, to route them. As soon as she appeared, she let loose a piercing shriek. A few of the crystal pillars that littered the cave floor spiraled with cracks, and the two intruders nearest Beast retracted their claws and gripped their heads Before her shriek ended, two other dread claws shot their spears at her, forcing her to retreat.

She teleported clear of the barrage and reappeared behind one of the monsters still holding Ox. The monster was ready, retracting its claws and swiping at the elf before she could scream again. She tried several more times but couldn't get close enough to strike. The two dread claws that she'd hit with her shriek had a black substance that looked like blood dripping from their ear holes and eyes, but they had otherwise recovered and continued their attacks.

Blasts of Buddy's lightning and fire targeted the monsters. Unfortunately, their claws were just as effective at stopping magical attacks as they were against flying boulders, countering the information Henry had gleaned from Haruspex. Two dread claws continued to attack Ox, and he had to use all his focus to heal his body and stop them from rending him apart. Beast couldn't find an opening to land an attack, and it was everything Henry could do to dodge the relentless web of deadly spears. The skeletons were getting overwhelmed.

"I don't think they're tiring," Henry yelled between dodges. The monsters were more intelligent than any enemy they'd come across thus far, but what made them most dangerous was their tactical approach. Whenever one was moving or recovering, another was attacking to cover it. They were working together, and their sadistic smiles made it seem like they were enjoying playing with their prey, trying to surround their foes and keep the skeletons on their heals. His admiration of their tactics and the rush of battle helped to reduce the effect of the fear aura, but Henry still fought the urge to flee the battle.

"We need to even the odds," Buddy said, igniting blue flames around his hands. Instead of launching another fiery attack, he dropped to a knee and forced his palms to the ground. Dozens of lines of blue magic snaked along the black stone and flowed toward the melee. They reconnected into two swirls of magic, forming a spiraling blue pool. From each pool, a column of blue fire rose to nearly Henry's height. The columns formed into vaguely humanoid shapes with arms and legs that melded apart and together like tongues of flame in a blast furnace.

When the magical beings had fully emerged from the pool, white-hot blazes formed their eyes, and the two beings rushed toward the fray. The way they glided across the cave floor left Henry feeling wary of the magical attackers, but as Buddy advertised, they served their purpose of evening the odds of the battle.

The fire men harassed the dread claws with a barrage of blue fireballs half the size of Buddy's. The monsters countered, but their claws went right through the fiery bodies, not phasing them or even slowing their progress.

The fire men continued to launch their magical bolts and tried to chase down the dread claws, but the monsters evaded. The distraction worked enough to give Henry the breathing room he needed to charge.

He called on the power of his Vitus once again, visualizing bolts of white magical energy flowing into his legs and powering him in the absence of muscles.

Blitz

He sprang forward again, seeing an opening in a dread claw

that had gotten distracted by one of the blue fire men. What he didn't see this time, until it was too late, was a quartering attack from behind him. It was a glancing blow that disrupted his charge and sent him rolling across the ground.

Harden

The two creatures that evaded the blue fire men took the opportunity to attack Henry. He flooded Vitus into his bones to reinforce them against the assault. They held . . . barely. Henry tried to recover to his feet, but the monsters must have sensed the vulnerability like a pack of gnolls stalking injured prey, and they attacked.

He saw the wave of claws rolling toward him and knew what to do to avoid them, but his bones wouldn't respond with the speed he desperately needed. He cursed the frailty of his skeletal body as the monsters chipped away at him.

In the heartbeats between dodging the vicious spears, Henry took a quick mental account of his Vitus. He had enough to charge up for another Blitz, hoping to land a heavy blow, but they would most likely dodge it again. Then he would be in the same spot, and he didn't feel like the other skeletons would gain the advantage before his Vitus ran out. The dread claws were just too fast to land a heavy attack.

The idea hit him like a bolt of Buddy's lightning. He didn't need one heavy attack, but several small ones. And not necessarily attacks, but just movements. He charged his body with Vitus, and instead of expelling it all at once, he metered the flow into small amounts to specific joints. Another volley of claws approached and Henry directed his arms to counter. To his surprise, his shield and dagger responded as he'd asked, parrying the claws to the side with unexpected speed, leaving him completely unharmed.

Ability Discovered: Blitz III (Transmutation). Increased mastery of mind and body allows for a wider range of employment. Bolster attacks and defense with metered bursts of strength and speed. (STR +4, MOB +2, FOR +4, ACU +2, PER +2)

The claws he'd just dodged retracted quickly, and he followed them back to the monster, dipping and dodging strikes from two others. It was hard to coordinate the flow of Vitus to his movements, and he found himself overcorrecting. A claw glanced off his shoulder and spun him to the side, but he redirected his magic to counter his momentum and propelled himself forward. By the time he approached within striking distance of his target, he had started to get the hang of his upgraded Ability.

The dread claw raised its spear-like fingers and prepared for another attack. Now within a few feet of the monster, Henry could clearly see the bulging muscles inside its bone armor pulsing, almost as though they were feeding into its skeletal structure instead of powering its movements. The claws shot forward, creaking with an audible groan that sounded like the bone itself resisted the unnatural growth. Henry poured Vitus into his joints as the claws extended toward him, speeding up his movements just enough to allow him to escape the attack and nimbly dodge past. He sliced with Beast's dagger as he spun past the dread claw, slicing between the boney structure and deep into its dark muscles.

The frost magic left the spots where it cut frozen and immobile, and the creature's claws contracted like a balloon with the air let out of it. Henry pivoted and ducked under a sloppy attack as he maneuvered his body into position. He lifted his dagger and jammed it under the chin and into the creature's skull.

Henry locked eyes with the monster. Throbbing purple veins lined their white sclera, but as Henry drove the blade further up through its skull, he could see a black iris streaked with tiny flakes of metallic green surrounding a pure black pupil. Its eyes dilated and shook before breaking their lock with Henry's. Purple and black gore sprayed from every opening in the dread claws skull as Henry scrambled its brane with Beast's dagger. Its eyes rolled, no longer being controlled by the monster. As Henry pulled the dagger free, it toppled backward, dead before it hit the ground.

Henry's mind stopped as if all the thoughts in his head had disappeared. For a moment, no awareness existed within him save for a palpable quiet that seemed to press against his soul.

Then he heard a rush of wind, feint and distant at first but quickly gaining in intensity. The sound built until a flash of blue erupted in his vision, jolting him from his daze. It had only been an instant while he absorbed the nothing of the monster's mind, but the other two dread claws on his flanks had already moved to attack. The blue fire men blasted the assailants with enough fire to stay their assault on Henry, if only for the moment it took the warrior to regain his senses.

Henry dodged another volley of spears and charged the nearest dread claw as he screamed his findings to the other skeletons. "Brains!"

"What?" Beast shouted with an annoyed tone. She'd also managed to dodge her way past the claws and maim her target. It stumbled as purple globs oozed from the cuts in its muscles, but it hadn't dropped it yet.

"Their brains and muscles control their bodies. Hit them in the head." Henry yelled.

Ox took the opportunity to lunge at the two distracted dread claws that had been holding him in place with their relentless offense. He wrapped a hand around each skull and lifted them off the ground. They tried to fight back, filling the massive skeleton with bone spears and shredding his armor, but Ox's healing magic held firm and reconstituted his bones as fast as they were damaged.

He violently rattled them by their heads, their brains clattering and limbs snapping like a ship's flag under the force of a gale. Ox shook and squeezed until their organs liquified, spraying purple globs through the battlespace, then he dropped their limp corpses like a child discarding a broken toy.

Opposite the cave from Ox, Beast continued slicing through the muscles of her opponent, leaving it helpless and immobile. Now it was her turn to toy with her prey. She played with it like a cat, slicing deep at it struggled to evade. Its attacks now little more than sluggish movements. She tired quickly of the game and jammed her dagger between the joints at the nape of its neck. It crumbled to the ground in a heap of bone and shredded muscle.

Buddy's fire men had teamed up on one of the monsters and surrounded it. Their attacks had finally dealt enough damage to slow its movements. Scorch marks covered its bones, and clumps of muscle had been charred black. As the two columns of blue fire collided with the enemy, they enveloped it, searing any remaining flesh and cooking it alive. It died with a silent, wrenching scream.

One more. Henry zeroed in on the last dread-claw. The creature stood between him and the exit, but it didn't flee. Instead, it raised its claws for a final attack. Henry spread Vitus through his bones again, thrilled that his reflexes could finally keep up with his mind. A burst of magic propelled him toward his adversary. He planted his foot and pressed hard, thrusting for a killing blow.

Blitz

Henry's magic gave out with a loud *pop!*

With a jumbled mind from drained Vitus and no Strength to stop his momentum, he tripped and rolled along the black stone floor. Claws flew toward him. Henry hadn't any way to dodge nor the Vitus or time to harden his bones.

Bronze bucklers intercepted the spears inches from Henry's head. Then, a quartz boulder bigger than Henry was tall collided with the monster, smashing it and smearing gore along the floor until it shattered against the far wall.

Henry's new attack was more than adequate, but the drain on his magic was tremendous. Henry hadn't even realized he'd burned through his Vitus until it was gone. Ox and Buddy had saved him, and he was grateful there were more battles in the future for him to perfect his control over new Ability.

Beast pointed her dagger at Buddy and asked accusingly, "What were those things? And why did the black auras cause us fear?"

"Your expectation for me to know that is unrealistic." Buddy scoffed and pulled out his metal tome. He flipped through the pages until he came to the drawing of the dwarven Underdeep. "From the map, we haven't even touched the lower caverns of Skutarbrekka and Hraunfass, so I assume something followed us from the depths."

"Our enemies' potency continues to grow, but not as quickly as ours." Ox hefted his massive war hammer over his shoulder and stood triumphantly, scanning the carnage in the room. "I am impressed that my minions have gotten much stronger after our battle with the golem." A small plate of his armor fell to the ground with an echoing *tink*. All was quiet for a moment, then every piece of riddled mail below his chest crashed to the stone floor.

The remains of his pieced-together armor hung from his shoulders in shambles, completely shredded and useless, but he either didn't notice, or didn't care, as he continued to bask in the glory of victory.

With his Vitus slowly returning, Henry found himself more able to form words. He wondered why the dwarves hadn't mentioned black fear auras and dread creatures with bone spears for fingers. They also hadn't mentioned the soul-stealing power of Smyrna's Golem and piles of bone, armor, and weapons that came to life.

Henry hoped Buddy could explain some part of the mystery. "Did the red mage say anything about black auras? And where did you get blue fire men to fight for us?" he asked.

Buddy's three dwarven bucklers, still covered in blue flame, orbited the room in a random series of circles like they were searching for another target. With a wave of his hand, the flames dissipated, and their orbit drew closer to the mage until they were within a few feet. He grabbed the bucklers from the air one at a time and secured them to his hip with a leather tie on his belt. He took his time, leaving Henry's question hanging before he answered with an appreciable amount of annoyance. "The *blue fire men,* as you call them, are fire elementals. As my Acumen increases through training and Tiers from the Drift Amulets, I've learned to grant a certain amount of automation to my spells in the form of these allies. With more training and an expected increase in Tiers, they will grow in number and capability."

Henry didn't know why, but the fire men—no, fire elementals—had disturbed him almost as much as the dread claws. However, Buddy's understanding of his own skill development impressed Henry and further solidified his faith in the mage's capabilities.

Satisfied that all the enemies had been dispatched, Buddy pulled the metal tome from the leather pouch at his hip and began thumbing through the pages. "Tekşan did not refer to black auras. However, one passage briefly affords a second-hand account of monsters that cause fear Effects. That would make sense, as humans can't visually perceive auras."

"Ghakk." A grunt from Ox made everyone turn toward him. The dread claw's deadly spears could destroy a massive boulder, but the chips they had taken out of Ox's bones had already healed. Most of his armor had fallen to the ground or lay in shambles on his frame, but the shoulder plate with the amalgamator's skull was still firmly in place. Ox returned a confused glance, then looked at the smaller skull near his head.

"Did you say something?" he queried the amalgamator.

"Ghakk," Gator grunted, and for once, wasn't trying to bite at Ox.

"Weird," Beast muttered, tilting her head slightly and approaching Ox to get a closer look at the skull, "Maybe Gat . . . that thing was shaken by the black auras too."

Buddy turned back to his tome, seeming to have already lost interest in Gator's newly expanded vocabulary. "Weirder so is the fact that we gained Soul Essence toward the next Tier, but the memories and emotions were replaced by nothing . . . a very repressive nothing . . . but still a resounding emptiness."

Henry thought back to the battle and remembered the empty feeling. Where he usually expected to experience the last thoughts and emotions of a dying enemy, the minds of the dread claws felt more like the nothing world he was in before he had first awoken in the tiny stone hut in Ammerthall. But there was something else. "More than silence, there was intent. Almost as though they wanted our minds to be as still as theirs." Henry's theory sounded absurd, even as the words came out of his mouth.

"I felt the emptiness, too. That must be how blank Ox's head feels all the time." Beast climbed on Ox's back, sending more broken pieces of armor dropping from his body as she scaled the brute and tapped Gator with an arrow from her quiver.

"My head is filled with the death throughs of my enemies and the vision of a beautiful woman's bosom in my face," Ox replied.

Beast hopped down and gave him another annoyed look, but a low sizzling sound coming from the dread claw's bodies drew their attention. The dark muscles on their bodies and other soft tissues in their skulls had begun to dissolve into ash and flake away, wisping as though they were carried by an updraft, even though no wind flowed through the cave. As the muscle deteriorated, the heavy bones settled, no longer able to hold the skeletal structure.

Henry approached one of the corpses as the last bit of flesh ashed away. He nudged the bones with the toe of his boot, causing the pile to fall apart. Henry shook his head in disbelief; another skeleton was concealed inside the bones of the dread claw. "It's a human! There's a human skeleton inside the corpse."

"And this one as well," Beast offered, pushing the bones from a second dread claw heap.

Ox kicked aside the bones of a third. "This one's a dwarf."

Henry pushed the strange bones of the dread claw away from the human skeleton, noticing that it was mostly intact, but strangely, no green aura—or black aura for that matter—was forming around its structure. He expected at least a small green swirl to start within a few minutes of an enemy being defeated, but perhaps that was an Effect of being encapsulated by a dread claw. That assumption would back up the lore from his Haruspex that claimed dread claws could steal their victim's souls. "The dread claws are just shells formed around the skeletons like a suit of armor."

"*Dread claw*? Is that what we're calling them?" Beast asked with a hint of sarcasm.

"Well, that's what I've been calling them in my head," Henry replied. "But look at the skeletons inside them. No sign of an aura."

"*Dread claw* seems appropriate." Buddy raised his palm, and a dwarven skeleton lifted from the remains and hovered in the air before the mage. "Henry is right about the skeletons. I find it uncomfortably similar to the Effect of Smyrna's Golem." Buddy dismissed his spell and the floating skeleton crumpled to the ground.

All together, they found three human and three dwarven skeletons inside the shells. The skeletons were in surprisingly good shape, but there was nothing unusual about them.

Henry picked up one of the spear-like fingers that made up their clawed hands and examined it closely. It was long, maybe six feet, as it hadn't fully retracted when its owner had died. He jabbed its tip into the quartz floor. Black and purple stone chipped from the impact but didn't dull or even mar the point. It looked like bone, but it was harder than steel.

Haruspex

Item: Dread Claw Bone (Epic)
Description: Component. Can be used to craft various items.
    Hardness 30, Structure 100/100

The end that had been connected to the monster's hand

separated from a ball joint after the dread-claw's flesh dissolved. Henry searched through the rest of the remains, noticing that all the dread claw shells were epic-quality components, but he only found three other claws that suited his purpose. They were of varying lengths and diameters but almost perfectly symmetrical. His javelins had taken a beating and were virtually useless at this point. However, these claws were much more robust. He wrapped some leather around the center of the claw to form a grip and took another look at the item.

Haruspex

Item: Dread Claw Javelin (Epic)

Description: Weapon. Due to poor craftsmanship, the range and accuracy of this weapon is limited. Hardness 30, Structure 100/100

Henry was slightly offended at Haruspex's assessment of his crafting, though he felt that with a little more modification from a strong enough tool, he could turn them into effective weapons.

Now that the chaos of battle had quieted, Muji ventured back out of Buddy's pack. He poked cautiously at the bones, but when they didn't move, he started gnawing on them. He wrapped his clawed forearms around them and kicked with his back legs like he was disemboweling a lizard. His efforts caused more bones to topple, and a few cave insects skittered from their hiding places. Muji pounced on the scurrying bugs with a sharp, "Beak!"

Ox bent over and scratched Muji behind the ears with a finger nearly as long as one of the trogold's legs. "I agree, little one. We feast on the corpses of our fallen enemies." Then he said in a louder voice, "Your thrall is a true warrior, Benny. You have trained him well."

Buddy had been reading his tome and refused to look up, but Henry could see the mage was annoyed. He snapped closed the metal tome and placed it in his pouch opposite the dwarven bucklers. "The dwarves owe us answers in exchange for their Magma Blaster. Let us return and light their forges."

The skeletons gathered up their supplies and prepared to depart. Henry agreed they needed answers from the dwarves, but he was also eager to get underway before more dread claws tried to ambush them.

CHAPTER 6

The crackle of burning wood was the only sound interrupting the evening's silence. The flame's intensity grew as it consumed the dry kindling of the dead Acolyte's funeral pyre. Harvest season had barely begun, but the night had a biting chill despite the lack of wind. A vast, cloudless sky stretched above the plain, revealing brilliant constellations that old men used to tell the stories of long-dead heroes. Such a view could only be taken from the quite, rural farmland, far from the light pollution of Ikrit's capital. Two of the four moons had just started their evening journey across the sky. A third turned a deep orange as it sank below the horizon, following the sun, and the fourth had yet to rise for the evening.

There was no body burning on the pyre. It was ceremonial by nature, one last chance for the Bastion to pay their respects. Since the founding of the Acolytes one hundred and fifty years earlier, every fallen member had been buried in a graveyard a short walk beyond the Bastion's outer defenses. It served as a reminder to every Acolyte and recruit of the bravery of dead heroes and the danger they would face, both in war and in Jallfoss. Before this massacre, the Bastion— Command

Brigade, as it was formally called—had never been struck with such a significant loss, either in numbers or experience.

A few dozen Acolyte Instructors and nearly fifty recruits stood in quiet reverence. Commander Cirilo took a long swig of whiskey from his flask. "Fifteen," he said, mostly to himself. Sentient skeletons had murdered fifteen Acolytes in the training grounds of Jallfoss, if the boy's account could be believed. Four of those were seasoned warriors who had fought beside Cirilo and had even saved his life on numerous occasions. The other eleven were freshly-minted Junior Acolytes on their first time through the mountain. Only one of which had returned, and he now lay buried a few hundred yards away after having succumbed to grievous injuries.

All had been killed in Ammerthall, the ground-level city and the safest location, on a routine training mission. Cirilo took another heavy swig of whiskey as anger welled inside him. The Acolytes were his. He would never let a soldier enter who mountain who wasn't ready.

"Our response team should be exploring the mountain by now. I'll be on my way with four of my best Acolytes, before the pyre dies." Cirilo handed his flask to the man standing beside him.

Lord Stavros accepted the container and raised it to his lips, pulling a heavy drought from the metal ampule. He wore brown traveler's robes, simple in design but woven with pure marrowbella silk and enchanted with enough defensive magic to ward the Bastion's entire stronghold.

His silver hair was tied into a low knot at the nape of his neck, and his short grey beard with just a few hints of black was neatly trimmed. He took the flask with weathered hands that matched the wrinkles and liver spots on the Great Lord's face. Despite his age, the Emperor's deep hazel eyes gathered the light from the fire and shone with the intensity of a midday sun. "Your mission in the mountain is of the utmost importance. You may be the only one to save us from the Necromancer's darkness. However, your presence here is no less crucial. These recruits saw a young Acolyte, just a few months their senior, return on the verge of death. They heard his desperate story, and now your duty is to ensure they internalize the harsh lessons of the mountain."

The pyre's wood shifted and settled as it burned, releasing thousands of tiny sparks. The updraft from the heat lifted them in a swirling column, interspersing them on the backdrop of the starry sky before they winked from existence.

Cirilo and Stavros stood a dozen paces from the nearest Acolyte, but the Commander still lowered his voice to protect their conversation. "Jacoby and Sigurjon taught those harsh lessons as well. They'd been through that mountain hundreds of times. Allito and Tekşan were no strangers to battle either." He took his eyes off the pyre and looked directly at the Emperor. "What changed this time? The skeletons are mindless dullards. How could they have regained their sentience?"

Stavros took a second, longer swig of the whiskey from Cirilo's flask. The sweet liquid hit the tip of his tongue, giving him initial hints of vanilla and caramel. Then, as the draught rolled to the back of his mouth, the taste changed to that of toasted grains with a touch of salt and spice, bringing him back to his youth and the memories of the smoked salmon he loved from the Banda Sang Coast. He held the whiskey on his tongue, a second for every year that it had been aged. He didn't know how long the alcohol in Cirilo's flask had sat in charred barrels, but judging by how smooth it was, at least twelve. Finally, Stavros took a deep breath through his nose and slowly exhaled out his mouth. The bitter sting of fired ileata moss filled his nose from the evaporating vapors of the spirit, every bit as smokey as the funeral pyre before him.

Barley, water, and yeast were the only three ingredients. He knew more about the nature of magic than any man, dead or alive, but he still marveled at the artistry behind a skilled craftsman. A beautiful statue chiseled from a rough block of marble, a delicate stringed instrument extracted from the wood of a mighty grossoak, or in this case, an entire banquet of flavors and smells distilled from boiled grain and water, then left to set for years in a wooden barrel.

Stavros let the whiskey slide down his throat, enjoying the burn. Cirilo patiently waited for a response from the Emperor. The long pause didn't make him uneasy the way it would have Commander Alicos, and Stavros was grateful for a brief moment of enjoyment as he collected his thoughts. "Lord Livadi and Lady Destria banished the Necromancer back to the source crystal a hundred years ago." Stavros knew that wasn't an accurate account of the events that had unfolded in the mountain. Still, it was the version of the truth that had been told for a century. "She gave her life to hold back that evil. Her spirit was the only thing keeping the Necromancer at bay all those years. But, if the forces of darkness make it to her, all is lost. Evils far worse than skeletons will swarm from the mountain and overtake Ikrit.

"The sword that Jacoby carries was meant to dispel the Necromancer's curse, but somehow, I failed in its construction. Retrieve it if you can. It would be a terrible weapon for someone other than an Acolyte to wield."

Cirilo remembered the mission. Under the order of Lord Stavros, Cirilo sent Jacoby and a group of elite Acolytes to the highest mountain top to stop the resurrection spell. They suffered heavy losses on the expedition, and all he found was the ghost of the long-dead empress who couldn't be bothered to even acknowledge their presence. Cirilo and Jacoby never understood why using the sword on the Empress' ghost would stop the curse, but they trusted Stavros. Even though it was faulty, Cirilo knew of the weapon's power to harvest Vitus from adversaries, and he intended to bring it back.

Cirilo nodded, acknowledging the order. "I had been there to see her spirit a decade before Jacoby's campaign. She was peaceful, beautiful. My hand passed right through her, and nothing we did could elicit a response from the floating soul."

Heavy footsteps crunching dry grass approached them from behind, but neither turned to look. "Commander Cirilo," the man huffed, "the team is ready to leave upon your order."

"I'll be there shortly," Cirilo responded. The man turned and ran back, understanding that he'd been dismissed.

"At my age, I am of little use to you in a battle," Stavros said, watching Cirilo stow his flask and prepare to leave, "but if you were to fail—"

"I won't." Cirilo was one of the few men in the world who would dare to interrupt the Emperor, but it was still a bold move.

"*If* you were to fail," Stavros emphasized, "there is a contingency that requires my return to Ikrit."

Cirilo gave Stavros a questioning glance.

"I'll be a week behind you. Hold them off until I arrive."

"Lord Stavros, I must object. The people of Ikrit need you. You can't be put in danger. Not with the Necromancer's re-emergence in Jallfoss and Varanasi's army in full retreat."

"I've spent more time in that mountain than any man here." Stavros dismissed the Commander's concerns and changed the subject. "Do you have faith in me?"

"Unwavering."

"Then I need you to trust that this is necessary." Stavros held up a hand and placed his palm over Cirilo's heart. Pale green and yellow flames circled his hand and absorbed into the Acolyte's chest. At first, Cirilo felt nothing, but then his heart contracted, sending intense pain shooting through his body. Cirilo stepped back to catch his breath but forced himself to hide any semblance of agony from showing on his face.

Stavros saw the questions in his Cirilo's eyes. "In two weeks, that spell will take your life. I'm the only one that can remove it."

Cirilo furrowed his eyebrows, but then the realization of the spell's purpose occurred to him, and a smile parted his lips. "At least I understand this part of your contingency, Lord Stavros."

"Until the next sun, my friend," Stavros said, dismissing the Commander.

"Until the next sun," Cirilo replied, turning from the Emperor and walking briskly to the waiting horses. Four of the strongest remaining Acolytes in the Bastion would join him. Any more, and their presence would attract hordes of undead and hinder their progress.

The pyre had started to die, and the remaining Acolytes began returning to their barracks. Training had been suspended that day for the funeral, but it would resume in a few short hours, just before dawn.

Stavros took a deep breath of cool autumn air and surveyed the gathered soldiers. The life of an Acolyte was dangerous and uncertain on its best days. Few retired from the elite service, and fewer still departed unscathed. However, one man that had survived and left the select group of warriors was Risto Vasilios. Risto was one of the first Acolytes Stavros had blessed with a Drift Amulet. The man fought loyally at Stavros' side for many years, braving harsh climates and savage monsters at every turn.

Risto had retired shortly after finding out his wife was pregnant with their first child. Almost fifty years later, Risto's grandchild, Koş, lay buried in the Bastion's cemetery. The boy was nearly dead from an infection from several wounds when a farmer had dropped him at the Acolyte's front door. He probably only had hours to live when Stavros sapped the last bit of his life force to add to his own. By killing the boy, Stavros had been able to delve into the mind of one of the sentient skeletons. The undead believed it was on its way to restore the dead Empress and rescue the mountain.

Cirilo had to stop them. If he didn't, Stavros would go there himself, and the results would likely be catastrophic.

"Thank you, Koş. May I make the most of your sacrifice," Stavros whispered before turning from the fire's dying embers. He needed to make his way back to his enclave in Ikrit City and secure his most powerful weapon. First, there was one more person he needed to talk to.

He heard the thunder of hooves as five mighty Acolytes sped into the darkness on their mission. Dust and moon-lit shadows obscured their departure, leaving an ominous stillness as the dirt dispersed and settled. A single wooden cart was left on the road, illuminated by a dim lantern. Two heavy draft horses stood tied to its yoke, drooping their heads at the late hour. Either from the gloomy light or the effect of age on his eyes, Stavros couldn't quite make out their color.

A man in a vest and checkered shirt attended to the cart, strapping down the contents of large sacks and tying them securely. The man was well-aged but still looked decades younger than the Emperor. However, the man's common appearance didn't fool Stavros. He could tell the posture of a battle-hardened man when he saw one. This man was no Acolyte, but from what Stavros had been told, the farmer regularly traveled over the mountain passes by himself. That alone proved the man was resourceful and sturdy, a true hearty citizen of Ikrit.

"Are you Yeorgious, the farmer?" Stavros asked as he approached.

"The one and only," Yeorgious responded, not looking up from his work. "But the misses simply calls me *the love god*."

Stavros didn't expect such a forward response, but he found the man's comfortable demeanor rather refreshing. "I wanted to thank you for returning the boy to us," Stavros replied, barely hiding a laugh.

Yeorgious finished securing the final strap on his cart and turned to address his visitor. Finally recognizing the Emperor, he bowed deeply. "Apologies, Lord Stavros. I didn't know that was you." Stavros had gotten used to most men trembling before him, but this farmer remained calm and polite. "I only wish I could have gotten the lad here sooner and saved his life. Tough little fella, that boy. Didn't expect him to hang on as long as he did. I've seen some strange goins-on in that mountain, but the lad's stories had me scratching the ol' noggin."

Stavros's sharp Perception noted that the farmer said, *in the mountain,* not *on the mountain,* but he chose not the address the preposition. "Koş's resilience is a model for all Acolytes, from Junior to Master. His loss saddens me greatly."

"I'magine it does, m'Lord. Though it's unexpected the Emperor himself would come all the way out here for a Junior Acolyte's funeral, especially with a war wrappin' up. I take it you believe the boy's fever ramblin's were true?"

After so many years as an Emperor, Stavros could tell when someone knew more than they were letting on. The farmer's lax demeanor would have fooled most, but veiled intellect always showed itself. "The war with Varanasi is over, and this piqued my interest. The mountain has many secrets, and whatever happened to the Acolytes needs to be revealed. We all have things we're trying to hide."

Yeorgious watched Stavros carefully as the Great Lord ran a hand through the thick mane of one of the dozing horses. Faint streaks of magic followed Stavros's touch, revealing smooth red scales that quickly faded back to brown hair. "I haven't seen a grulvorg in many years. And never so docile. How did you manage to tame such beasts?"

The farmer knitted his eyebrows together, then pursed his lips and nodded his head in approval of the Emperor's ability to see through the illusion. "Found the pair about twenty years ago when I was foraging for schneeple nuts in the Karalki steppes. Their mother had abandoned 'em. Their little squeaks struck a chord in my heart, so I had to take 'em in. Almost lost a hand to the buggers more than once, but that's nothing compared to what they can do to a tribe of goblins."

Grulvorgs were vicious predators usually found in the Northern Highlands. They were solitary creatures that avoided civilized areas. The fact that the farmer had tamed such hellions was no small feat, as was his ability to disguise their nature. Such capabilities were exceptional among the farm folk of Ikrit. Stavros briefly entertained various possibilities of the man's origin, but decided not to pry beyond what the man would voluntarily divulge. "I've heard you're one of the few that ventures through the mountain passes. I can tell from these beasts, and your fine collection of snodbells and napunias, that is no exaggeration." Stavros patted a secured sack on the wooden cart.

Yeorgious accepted the opportunity to change the subject. "That's true, m'Lord. The misses uses every bit to make her potions and salves." The farmer bobbed his head from side to side and changed his voice to a higher pitch, "'*I told ya last time to bring me more chimerosas and brown flattersmills. Don't ya ever listen to me, Yeorgious?* she's always yellin'. The grouchy woman knows those only grow near Ghara's cave, and I'm not too keen on dyin'. She's lucky she owns to plumpest backside in all Ikrit, or I'd give her a piece of my mind instead of a piece of somethin' else, if ya know what I mean, m'Lord."

"I do," Stavros chuckled, enjoying the conversation with someone who wasn't intimidated by him. "Speaking of Ghara, what can you tell me of the conditions up there?" He left the question open-ended to see what the farmer would say about the elves' forest god.

God was an overstatement, but Stavros knew Ghara was a powerful Primal, nonetheless. Similar in origin to dragons and giants, Ghara was an ancient spriggan, likely emerging from the calamity that first formed their world. The Drift Amulets, flawed as they were, had ben been modeled after the power a Primal could bestow on their chosen emissaries.

"Getting worse." Yeorgious shook his head. "The elves are having a hard time holding back Ghara's monsters. One'a them buggers almost took a bite out of Truffle." The farmer motioned to one of his draft horses. "But luckily, my Papi taught me a thing or two." He patted the blade that hung sheathed on his belt.

"They're keen to trade," Yeorgious continued. "Always looking for a good weapon. Tight-lipped about their strange religion, but I could see it in their eyes—if they're winning the battle, which I doubt, it's not by much."

"As I sensed." Stavros enjoyed talking to the man, but there was little else he felt he could glean from his knowledge. "Safe and swift travels to you, good farmer. Until the next sun."

"Safe travels, m'Lord." Yeorgious climbed into the seat of his cart and shook the reins a few times to rouse up his sleeping ponies. "Come on, Truffle! Wake up, Butternut. We're late, and the last thing I need is the wrong version of a tongue-lashin'." The cart began rolling, and Yeorgious turned to the Emperor. "I wish you and your men luck. Er'be things much more dangerous than a ragin' forest god in that mountain."

Primal . . . Stavros corrected, though only to himself. *Not a god, but close.*

CHAPTER 7

Jacoby hurried through the streets and back alleys, trying to distance himself from the soldiers as much as possible. The dwellings were tightly packed together, obscuring his full view of the immense underground city. He frequently caught glimpses through the staggered roofline of a tall building at the city center, and the several massive natural stone columns that held up the cavern's ceiling hundreds of feet above him. The dim light percolating through the city came from dozens of globes embedded in the stone canopy. He could see just fine in the dull illumination, but it was little more than would be expected on a very cloudy day.

The roads curved and intersected in a seemingly random pattern. Some even doubled back on themselves, slowing his progress and forcing him to cut through the red sandstone buildings to keep moving toward the city center.

He jogged cautiously, impressed by his ability to move quietly even with the heavy armor weighing him down. His body knew how to shift his movement to avoid scaping metal plates or jostling his weapons. He moved steadily through the skeleton-infested city, but he couldn't help noticing black scorch marks as he passed, both inside and outside the buildings.

The marks were faint as the damp, stagnant air had likely encouraged their degeneration. Small splotches of mold had grown over several scorch marks inside the buildings where the direct light from the globes couldn't reach. Some of the buildings had even been burned from the inside out, leaving nothing but the charred timbers of their roofs behind. The stone walls of the buildings and the damp atmosphere must have been the only thing that kept the blaze from spreading through the entire city.

Something destructive happened long ago and was likely the event that turned everyone here into skeletons . . . lots and lots of skeletons. Jacoby thought, a shiver crawling down his spine.

The first few startled him, appearing unexpectedly in his path as he darted around corners or through doorways. Most were human, but some were dwarves and even a few orcs. Each had a unique green aura, of which the shade, intensity, and structure varied wildly. Some were light wispy clouds that hung drearily around their host, others were dark and looked like solid encasements, and every imaginable variation in between.

Strangely, Jacoby noted, there were few smaller skeletons and almost none that he would have called adolescents. If this were previously a populated city, he would also expect children to have been here. Jacoby wondered if the skeletons were summons, instead of former living beings. Maybe the men in red tunics he assumed to be his allies were fighting the undead, but that didn't help explain the two corpse-like men he'd woken up next to.

A small bit of pressure, like a mild tension headache, barely noticeable at first, formed in his head as he sorted through the memories of the encounter. *I couldn't control my rage, and I attacked the soldiers as the skeleton and dead soldiers did.*

Something had brought the dead back to life, but whatever this curse was, at least they weren't attacking him. The fact that the skeletons weren't aggressive toward him wasn't much of a reassurance in the dreary city crypt, as it implied a connection between him and the undead. *This is not a fitting way to die, either for me or all these people.*

Jacoby struggled to focus as he jogged along the sandy streets. His headache had become more noticeable, like something was tugging at his mind. He tried to logic his way through the details, but there were too many questions, and his mind was quickly spiraling into disarray. *The skeleton from my thoughts and the old man; they were trying to get to a ghost at the top of this place. I guess I'm in a mountain, but I need to gather more information to figure out what's happening.*

The buildings around him blocked his view. All he could see were dozens of massive pillars holding up the ceiling and the single, circular structure looming over the other rooftops. He knew the towering construction would be the best place to get a vantage point, but first, he needed to gather his thoughts.

When he felt he'd made enough distance between himself and the soldiers, he ducked into a small dwelling. The home was a single story, and on the outside of a curve in the road that had a good view of either side but would also provide him with cover. Unfortunately, the door and window coverings had long rotted and fallen off their rusted metal hinges. Inside was sparsely furnished apart from more rotted wooden furniture, a stone hearth, and some rusted pipes that jutted from the wall.

The remains of a broken wooden chair lay covered in sand near the entrance. Jacoby accidentally kicked it with his foot as he entered, sending parts of it skidding across the floor and coming to rest at the feet of the two skeletons that occupied the home. They didn't react, but Jacoby noticed the wood he'd kicked had been blackened and left behind charcoaled timber as it rolled.

Jacoby sat heavily on the stone and sand-covered floor, just out of view of the street. His body and mind were tired, and his headache was quickly developing into a migraine. He'd been on alert since the fight with the soldiers, not allowing his heightened awareness to subside. He pulled the water skin from his belt pouch and noticed that the wound from the soldier's blade had not only stopped bleeding but had sealed itself and was now little more than a scar.

He thought the accelerated healing was peculiar, but he didn't have the mental stamina to delve into that at that moment. Instead, he pulled the cork from the waterskin and took a few heavy chugs. The stale liquid abated his thirst, but it didn't seem to help with the pressure building in his skull. Glyphs flashed on the right side of his vision. Their incessant pulsing only made his headache worse, so he forced them from his view.

Jacoby hoped that a few moments of rest was all he needed. He shut his eyes and leaned his head back against the stone wall. He took a deep breath through his nose and caught the heavy scent of mildew masking a smell of ancient decay. As he released the breath through his mouth, a wave of energy cascaded through his body, starting in his chest and washing down to his fingers and toes. The pain in his head dissipated, and he found his focus had instantly sharpened. Instead of waiting for him to acknowledge, a new glyph forced its information in front of his eyes.

Status Effect Subdued: Necrosis Dismissed

He opened his eyes and looked at his hands. The cut had healed entirely, and his pale skin was now flush and full. His muscles no longer hung droopy and unresponsive. Instead, he brimmed with newfound vigor.

Jacoby instinctively reached for the silver chain around his neck and fished out the Amulet. Seeing that the Amulet had changed shouldn't have surprised him, given the day's circumstances, but he still marveled at the jewel. The blue half remained unchanged, but the other side was no longer clear. Instead, it had been filled with the dark red color. Even more strange was the number. The black **1** had been replaced with a half-translucent **2**. Again, he rubbed his thumb on the number, but it held firm.

A moment earlier, he had felt a buildup of energy being released in his body. Now he felt great, amazing even. He could almost feel his blood flowing more smoothly and his heart rate settling. His body had been rejuvenated just before he had noticed the change in the Amulet. Were the two somehow connected? He activated the Amulet's Ability and allowed the glyphs to display their information.

Status

Human Killed x2, Soul Essence Claimed, +1 Tiers:
STR +1, MOB +1, FOR, +2, ACU +1, PER +1, RES +2

Name: Jacoby

Race: Human

Tier: 2

Health: 28/28

Unknown: 32/32

Attributes:

   STR: 16

MOB: 15
FOR: 14
ACU: 11
PER: 13
RES: 16

The Amulet offered him no further explanation, but he was ready to continue with a renewed body and a clear head. He tucked the Amulet back into his collar and stood up.

With his senses no longer occluded, he noticed two distinct scorch marks on the far wall of the tiny dwelling. He ran his fingers over the faded black soot and found that the stone underneath had slightly deformed, probably melted from whatever flame left the marks. The wooden roof just above had also been singed. Only an intense but short-lived blaze could have melted stone without igniting the wood a few feet away. Though the current home hadn't been destroyed, there were still several others throughout the city that were completely burned from the inside out. Whatever had caused the fires was likely the same source that turned the inhabitants of the city into skeletons.

The skeletons presented him with another mystery. Their bones were pale and completely stripped of flesh. If they had been killed with fire, they should have the same scorch marks on their bones, unless they hadn't been skeletons when this happened.

I'm wasting time. I have to get moving. A quick glance out the door revealed the streets were still clear, apart from the masses of undead and their green auras. Jacoby set off toward the city center, plodding through the sandy roads. His feet were silent, but his mind roared with so many questions and very few answers.

He trapesed through more back alleys and building remains, but it wasn't long before he came to an open circular plaza. He stopped and cautiously peered from behind a stone building corner. More stone houses ringed the plaza, but the only distinguishing feature was a giant statue in the center. The sculpture was of a man in long ornate robes holding an open book and staring at it intently. It was made of a much lighter stone than the red that composed most of the buildings. It could have been marble, but Jacoby was too far away to tell.

Near the exterior houses on the far side of the courtyard, Jacoby saw four figures with green auras standing quietly. They were a few hundred feet away but clearly sported the same armor he now wore.

He cautiously made his way along the peripheral until he got near them. Nothing had stirred in the area since he'd circled the plaza, so he felt safe enough to approach the men.

One of them, likely the former leader, was a massive soldier, a head over six feet and full of muscle. His armor was charred, and he had wounds on his face that could have been burns, but they'd nearly healed. Despite the signs of recovery, his skin was pale and sagging, and his milky eyes stared blankly ahead. His heavy platemail was of very high quality, and Jacoby briefly considered liberating it, but it was much too large for him. Even if it would have fit him, the leather straps that held it together had been burnt and nearly destroyed.

Two of the other men showed similar signs of burn damage, while the third was covered in dried blood. The few minor signs of trauma on their bodies had mostly rejuvenated, but their skin looked sickly, and their eyes shared the same blank expression as their leader's.

The first three had burnt shards of cloth clinging to their armor. Even though the fabric was nearly destroyed, Jacoby recognized it as the same red tunics of the soldier's he'd killed. Curiously, the fourth dead soldier wore nothing over his plate mail besides rivers of dried blood that looked like it had been his own. Just like the two soldiers that had died at his hands, Jacoby felt these men must be on his side as well . . . *if there were any sides to this situation at all.*

Jacoby went through their packs and weapons, but he found that anything worth taking had been destroyed, or already taken, except for rations and water on the one bloody man. This was the second time he'd found signs of previous looting. Whoever had killed these men had use for their equipment. Now he was on a trail, with these soldier's murderers being the best chance for answers he'd found so far.

There was nothing more he could do for the undead men. He took the one intact sheath he'd found and secured it to his belt, discarding the chipped sword it held and replacing it with his current one of much better quality. He strapped the heavy metal club across his back with leather lashings from the unburnt soldier's armor so he could quickly access the weapon if needed.

He looked toward the city center and up at the big arch-covered building. He was close enough to make out that it was curved and built with pillars of a lighter stone. Jacoby gave the dead soldiers one final glance, then set off, resolving to bring their murderers to justice. Whatever that retribution might look like.

CHAPTER 8

Jai ran for miles, scaring nearby wildlife and bounding through the snow. He stopped running when he felt he was a safe distance from the worship hut, then pulled out Mayur's circlet and Drift Amulet. He studied them closely, admiring the magical items.

Over the past several months he'd frequently followed Talji's group, trailing the Sentinels through the Sprig-infested cities of upper Jallfoss. Jai had become familiar with the inside of the mountain nation's cave system and had even followed the Sentinels as far as the first ridge of exterior castles. He didn't mind the danger, and his skill in stealth had significantly grown over the years. Mayur was the only one Jai thought had ever noticed him, but the elf never gave they boy away.

The previous day, Jai followed them into the mountain. Within a few hours, the four Sentinels encountered a pair of Sprigs. The monsters were terrifying to behold but not the scariest that Jai had seen. Ghara's creations were always twisted and deformed versions of normal animals. These were no different.

The cavern they were in that day was one of the larger ones

just above the central city of Ammerthall, with walls of light stone and square buildings made of the same material. It had once been a housing district for upper-class citizens, but Jai couldn't recall its name.

Jai preferred to observe the Sentinels from the safety of a series of ledges as most Sprigs were ground-based. Most of them, anyway. He crouched low and watched the Sentinels send forth their Guard to confront the monsters.

The first Sprig was a birdlike creature the size of a small horse with orange plumage on its back and black and green frills on its head. It had black eyes, like most Sprigs, and a jagged black beak that hooked sharply to one side. It had no wings and supported itself by four yellow-brown avian legs tipped with black talons. The Sprig released a screeching trill when it saw the Sentinels and charged the group. The legs of the abominate were slightly different sizes, causing it to wobble in an exaggerated limp as it ran. Still, it overcompensated with raw power as it bound through the sandy street.

The second creature looked more like a pile of rotten vegetation than an animal. Much smaller than the other, its bulbous body was covered in green algae-like skin with brown sores that oozed a muddy substance. Its limbs were little more than thin branches and looked far too flimsy to hold up the Sprig's mass. It had two rows of even flimsier sticks jutting from its back. Jai couldn't make out its eyes, but a slit in the algae on its head opened wide to reveal black, pointed teeth jutting sporadically in every direction.

The feeble limbs on its back started twitching, and Jai realized that the branches were the structures of transparent wings. With a visible effort, the algae Sprig slowly lifted into the air. When it got high enough, it started pulling globs of green and brown muck from its body and throwing them at the oncoming skeletons. Most of the chunks missed and landed in the sand or on the stone buildings, sizzling and releasing whisps of steam.

The bird Sprig collided with the center mass of the twelve charging skeletons. It crushed the first two with its talons and sent several others sprawling, but the remaining skeletons surrounded it and began stabbing it with their swords. The Sprig screeched again, but this time with a pain-filled warble in its cry as it snapped at Talji's champion. Its beak crunched into the skeleton's round shield, but the Guard thrust with its sword and stabbed the Sprig in the neck.

The algae Sprig flitted toward the battle, slowing gaining height and increasing the accuracy of its attacks as it drew near. Finally, one of the globs hit a skeleton in the shoulder. Its arm dropped to the ground as the glob ate through its bone in seconds, but the skeleton didn't seem to notice; it just changed from sword strikes to shield bashes.

The algae Sprig prepared another attack when an arrow from Lata caught it and sent it spiraling. It dropped a few feet and tried to recover, but before it could right itself, another arrow hit the Sprig just as two red fireballs from Surat engulfed the flying creature. It flailed its arms and hit the ground, sending burning globs in all directions. Its body hissed and popped as it slowly stopped moving and turned black from the flames.

The bird Sprig hadn't fared much better. It tried to bite and claw its way out, but it was quickly overwhelmed by the skeletons' attacks. Its talons grew weak and it dropped to the ground in a growing pool of its own dark blood.

Talji smiled and began to say something until a loud shudder cut her off. A nearby wall exploded, sending chunks of rock and debris flying toward the elves and knocking her to the ground.

Long clawed toes gripped the edge of the hole that had just

been smashed in the side of the building. A long, hairy snout with jagged black teeth protruding from all around poked out from the billowing dust. A Sprig the size of a draft horse pulled itself through the crumbled stone and stood on the rubble. It looked like a giant rat, with grey, loose skin and intermittent patches of black fur.

Talji tried to push herself up, but her arm slipped, and she fell to the ground. The movement caught the rat Sprig's attention, and its black eyes narrowed on the vulnerable elf. It launched with enough force to crush the rocks below its legs and pounced on the elf with a gaping maw. The elf held up her bare hands in an attempt to stop the massive Sprig from crushing her, but just before it landed, Mayur plowed into the monster. His shoulder sunk into its ribs, making the rat Sprig contort in the air and its eyes bulge. They tumbled in a ball of grey skin, black claws, and white armor.

In the roll, Mayur managed to drive his lance deep into the Sprig's side, but the monstrous rat twisted its head and clamped its mouth around Mayur's neck. It bit through the armor with a grating crunch while Mayur drove his lance deeper into its belly. Blood sprayed from both, but the bite was deeper than the spear. With his hand still gripping the shaft of his lance, Mayur succumbed to his injuries.

Talji covered her mouth and stifled a scream of horror, but the creak of skeleton bones behind her pulled away her attention. The second Mayur died, two of the standing skeletons turned their heads toward the prone elf. There was no hesitation when their deathly gaze caught sight of the her, just reaction. They sprinted toward Talji with raised swords and gaping jaws. The third member of Mayur's guard, the skeleton that had been crushed under the bird Sprig's talons, now lay below its body, frantically claw at the sand to free itself. The attacking skeletons proved that Mayur was dead, and nothing could be done to save him.

Mayur's Guard was now an enemy, and they wouldn't stop until the elves were dead or out of sight. With a corrupted rat on one side and charging skeletons on the other, Talji had no choice by to run—an injured elf, even a Sentinel, wouldn't last long against such odds. Holding her lame arm, she sprinted for safety.

A volley of arrows and two fireballs struck the behemoth rat. It screeched and hissed, but the spear, fire, and arrows had done significant damage, enough to give Talji the space to maneuver around it. She fled past the monster, ignoring her mauled companion beneath its black claws.

Jai couldn't look away from the parade of horror. Two skeletons and a rat Sprig were in close pursuit of the three Sentinels, followed by the eight remaining skeletons still under their control. Finally, two smashed skeletons clawed their way from underneath the fallen bird Sprig. It had started to dissolve into ash and release a black, oily smoke, common to every slain Sprig Jai had seen before, allowing the broken skeletons to worm their way from underneath it. The scene would have been comical if it weren't for Mayur's mangled body in a growing pool of blood.

One of the broken skeletons continued dragging its body toward the direction its attached Sentinel had fled. The undead would keep clawing back to its owner until receiving a different order.

The other skeleton had been Mayur's guard. No longer under the effect of the circlet's hold magic, it had stopped moving when the elves had run beyond its vision. With no elf in sight, it would stay there and regenerate until it saw another target. After months of following the Sentinels, Jai was familiar with the behavior of the skeletons. Still, he had always thought it strange how the undead would attack on sight any being from outside the mountain, but nothing else could stimulate them to even react. *It's a strange evil magic,* Jai thought, *both the undead and Ghara's Sprigs.*

An eerie calm settled on the abandoned city. Jai heard rustling cloth, and he realized that he was shaking. "Focus. Focus," the elf repeated, steadying his nerves as the situation sank in. Mayur had sacrificed himself to save Talji, Lata, and Surat, and they abandoned him without a second thought. Jai knew Mayur was dead, but an empty feeling in his stomach emerged when he thought of leaving Mayur as the others had.

Jai carefully surveyed the area. It was early morning, and the sun globes in the high rocky ceiling cast light throughout the cavern equivalent to a foggy day. This mountain city wasn't as near the top of the mountain as some others, so it wasn't as bright.

He was high enough on a ledge to see the city's layout. One quarter of the cavern's edge was an opening for a ramp that led to another, more enormous city cave below. Half a dozen smaller tunnels exited the city and sloped gently upward or curved out of sight. The rest of the city was laid out like a tide pool, with streets swirling toward a collection of large, ornate buildings in the center. The humans of Jallfoss had a funny way of living, and Jai had often wondered if the high elves were closer to humans than they were to forest elves.

The dust settled where the rat Sprig had burst through the wall and ambushed the Sentinels. The Acolytes had long ago cleared main pathways to allow for easy transit. Because of that, the only entity that Jai could see was the broken skeleton lying just beyond the decaying body of the bird Sprig.

Jai pushed himself to his feet, willing his legs and arms to stop shaking. He cautiously made his way to the streets below, careful not to alert any lurking danger. It wasn't common for Sprigs to hide and ambush, but Jai didn't want to risk a getting caught unaware like Talji had.

On the street, he saw Mayur's body. He could make out claw marks in the Sentinel's armor and the red pool of blood that had soaked into the brown sand. Jai had an idea, but he had to be quick.

He darted out of the cover of the alleyway and ran to Mayur's body. As soon as he entered the street, the broken skeleton locked onto him and began dragging itself toward the elf. Its legs were still under the decaying bird Sprig, but it clawed its way through the sand as quickly as it could manage.

Jai tried not to spend too much time analyzing Mayur's dead body, finding it tough not to give him the homage the elf deserved. Mayur's circlet was soaked in red blood from the elf and black ichor from the rat Sprig. Jai pulled it from the elf's head and tied it around his own.

The skeleton had dragged itself within a few feet. Jai opened the palm of his hand toward the undead and spoke firmly. "Hold!"

Nothing happened. If anything, the skeleton picked up speed and clawed more aggressively. "Hold!" Jai shouted again, willing the spell to take effect as he stepped backward. "Hold!"

Jai focused so much on the skeleton that he forgot his surroundings. As he backed up, his heels caught on Mayur's body, and the elf tumbled over backward and thudded heavily into the sand.

Jai scrambled away, but the skeleton had already reached Mayur's body and clambered over it, reaching for Jai's feet. The elf kicked with his boots, failing to halt the clamoring undead.

A boney hand wrapped around his ankle, and Jai planted a

boot in the skeleton's face as it snapped its grizzly white teeth. It gripped onto his calf with its other hand hard enough to draw blood, and waves of pain shot through Jai's leg.

Why isn't this working? Jai panicked as he kicked hard to free himself, but the skeleton had a firm hold. He realized that he had never asked Mayur how the circlets worked. He just assumed that it happened.

The Guard is only as strong as its Sentinel's ability to control it. The circlets gain their power from the wearer, not the other way around. Those were Mayur's words. Jai didn't have time to contemplate them, just time to trust.

He pulled magic for his core, envisioning a turbulent waterfall crashing through a vine-covered jungle. Sunlight forced its way through the thick canopy and lit up the falling river with a brilliant golden luster. He focused his Guile, watching a surge of water blast over fall's edge and drop into the misty forest below. Instead of directing the magic toward his hands for a spell, he pushed it into the circlet's flow crystal. Jai would have felt a warm hum if he hadn't been scrambling for his life away from the skeleton.

He released the magic and shouted again. "Hold!"

Command Link Established 923/1200: Skeleton added to Guard. 1 skeleton available to command. (RES +1)

The skeleton stopped moving, frozen in place. Its tight grip on his legs remained, but it was no longer trying to kill him.

"Let me go!" Jai kicked again, and to his surprise, the skeleton released its grip. Jai quickly pulled himself to his feet, wary that the skeleton would decide to attack him again. He circled to the other side of Mayur's body to put a bit of space between him and the undead.

He eyed the skeleton with justified suspicion. He felt a tint of rage, but it was coming from outside his mind. Jai realized that there was a mental connection between him and the skeleton. He could feel its dead mind fighting the spell, but he knew it didn't have the Resolve to break free. The Hold spell was . . . Holding.

I held Mayur's Guard. No . . . my *Guard,* he thought. Excitement washed over him and mixed with his fear and adrenaline. Then he looked down and saw Mayur's body.

Vicious Sprig teeth had pierced the elven armor and dug trenches in the Sentinel's neck, but there was something else. Jai could see a broken chain in the gore. He reached down and grabbed the metal, pulling it gently. It resisted at first, then broke free and slid from the elf's mangled neck.

Jai had never seen a Drift Amulet up close, but every young elf was familiar with the magical items. He wiped the blood off to reveal a large flow crystal inlaid in steel. An almost clear **1** was displayed on the Amulet. One half was a deep blue, and the other was mostly full of red with the top portion clear. Jai looked down at the bloody claw marks on his leg. *Is this my Health?* he wondered. He activated his Status and confirmed the red and blue bars and the Attributes matched, even though the numbers were less than he expected.

Status

Name: Murenjai

Race: Forest Elf

Tier: 1

Health: 20/24

Vitus: 15/15

Attributes:

    STR: 6

MOB: 14
FOR: 8
ACU: 12
PER: 12
RES: 5

"SKREEAWW!"

The sound of an approaching Sprig stopped any further analysis. Jai took one last look at his Guard and sprinted for cover.

The encounter had occurred just the previous day, but Jai knew he would remember that experience for the rest of his life. Mayur sacrificed himself to save Talji. The only high elf that had ever been kind to Jai was dead, and in his passing, Mayur had given him what he needed to become a Sentinel, and Jai wouldn't squander the gift.

Now alone in a forest clearing, he committed himself to training. He had the tools to become a true Sentinel, he just needed to get stronger.

He untied the cord around his waist and loaded its pouch with a perfectly weighted stone. The sling had been the only thing he had ever been good at, and he was happy to focus on anything but what had happened to Mayur. Jai spun the strap hard and focused on the tree a hundred feet away. He released one end of the cord and sent the stone flying. With a heavy smack, it splintered wood from the pine right where he was aiming. Fragments of wood shot from the bark as Jai settled into his daily practice.

———

"Is this what *dirt elves* do to pass the day? Throwing rocks. No wonder you're all so helpless," Surat taunted.

Jai froze, and the stone in his sling flew from its pouch, skidding across the ground and burying in a patch of snow. He had become so engrossed with practicing his sling and trying not to focus on the previous day's events that he'd lost all sense of time and his surroundings. They'd found him. This was bad.

Jai spun around, failing to pretend he hadn't been caught by surprise.

"I saw you at the ceremony," Talji said softly. Her voice was nonchalant, slightly low and raspy, but in a melodic sort of way. That didn't stop Jai from picking up on the threat it held. Talji was renowned for her beauty, even above her talents as a Sentinel, but Jai could never understand how such a pleasant veneer could hide her wretched soul.

"You know you're not allowed near the worship hut," she chided. "You're lucky Bharat doesn't banish you from the valley entirely. Your presence is insulting enough without you thinking you'll ever be a Sentinel."

"Wh . . . why? Who says I ca . . . can't be a Sentinel?" Jai stuttered, searching for an escape, yet knowing he could neither outrun nor outfight any of them. He wouldn't stand a chance against a single one of their Guard, let alone nine armed skeletons. Panic shook the boys voice, but he refused to back down. Hopefully, they would get bored and move on.

"Bharat says so." Lata laughed. "And every other elf with a bit of sense in their heads. A smile spread across Talji's face, but Surat only narrowed his stern expression.

"Why do you hate me?" Jai responded, hoping for a bit of sympathy.

"Hate is a strong word," Surat said, "but it's hard to trust the brother of a traitor with anything beyond cleaning muck from chamber houses."

Jai fumed. He knew he was being bated, but it made him livid whenever someone brought up his sister in that way. "One day when I defeat enough Sprigs you can leave this forest forever," Jai spat before he thought to control his words. "You cater to the villages that shower you with gifts and ignore the poor ones. All you really do is galivant at the Theater while Ghara keeps making stronger Sprigs."

Now was Surat's turn to fume. "You think fighting a god every day is easy?" the Sentinel shot back. "Those peasants don't know how good they've got it, lounging around and being lazy. And you, Jai, are the worst of all. After what Harshmira did, your whole family should have been banished from Amera," Surat barked, and his Guard loomed forward. Jai took a step back, squeezing his sling even tighter.

Talji, who was much better at keeping a cool head, patted her companion gently on the shoulder. "Everyone has unrealistic dreams as a child. I thought I was going to be an herbalist. I loved making potions and salves of all sorts and I became quite good at it. Unfortunately for my aspirations, the Turning happened—Harshmira's betrayal killed the mountain and corrupted Ghara. She was probably in league with the Necromancer the whole time."

"I'm not her!" Jai shouted. He knew Talji wanted an excuse to beat him, but after saying something like that, he was ready to give her a reason. "I'll save Amera. Even if I have to fight you to do it!" He dropped his sling and focused all his Guile through his hands and toward a point on the ground just in front of Lata. An amber circle, the size of a large melon, formed on the ground between them.

The three Sentinels stepped back, and their Guard of nine skeletons moved forward. Talji wasn't afraid of the boy's sling, even though she knew he was skilled with the ranged weapon.

This, however, caught her by surprise. She had no idea the boy had any magical skills.

Jai forced his Guile through his hands and into the amber ball of swirling magic, struggling with his mind to reach through and grab anything that would respond to his call. He had never been sure where he reached and never knew what would answer. The stronger ones were nearly impossible to control, but in this case, he didn't need to direct it. He only needed to unleash it on the Sentinels.

Beckon

Jai struggled to focus through his anger, and several times he nearly lost the mental grip as he pulled, not quite sure what he was contacting. Finally, the amber sphere expanded then blinked away, revealing his summon.

As the focus returned to Jai's vision, he saw a smile creep across Talji's face. She wasn't fighting his summoned creature. He looked down to see what had appeared. *Oh no,* he thought, *anything but this.* He could barely control the actions of his summons and never *what* he would summon, but he'd hoped for something good this time.

A brown and yellow slug lay in the snow, barely moving from the cold. It was about three feet long and as round as his waste, with long yellow eyestalks and brown, milky eyes. Its body had a few dull spikes protruding, but the small flanges seemed utterly harmless.

"What in Ghara's name is that?" Surat laughed.

"It's almost as ugly and useless as Jai," Lata hissed.

Jai reached toward the ground for his sling, then jerked his hand back when a long thin dagger buried in the dirt in front of him.

"No you don't," Lata said, pulling another dagger from her belt.

Talji's champion Guard stepped forward and extended a foot. It stepped on the slug and slowly crushed it. The summon hissed in pain as yellow and brown goo squirted from beneath the heavy boot.

Jai was so distracted by the death of his summon that he didn't see the skeletons move. He did, however, feel the heavy blow of a skeletal fist to his face. He fell to the ground as the Guard pummeled him. They didn't use weapons, but at one point, Jai wished they had. Bone and boot rained down as Jai covered his head. It only lasted a minute, but each blow hurt and drew out the experience.

In between thuds from the Guard, Jai heard Lata giggling in joy. When he managed to peer out between blows, he saw Lata and Surat with wicked smiles on their faces, but Talji wasn't smiling. Instead, she looked stern and almost . . . sad.

"That's enough," Talji said, her voice just above a whisper though nonetheless commanding.

"No. We need to make an example out of him," Lata shrieked. One of her skeletons drew its sword and lifted the weapon for a strike.

Jai covered his head and prepared to die. He always figured a skeleton would kill him, just not a Guard. It was ironic and almost made him laugh.

He heard a loud *crack*, but no sword pierced his body. Boots crunched in snow. Moving toward him.

"Give up." He heard Talji's voice coming from right above him. "You'll never be a Sentinel." She turned and walked away. Lata and Surat followed her. Jai opened his eyes and thought he saw Lata wiping blood from her face.

The wounded elf lay on the ground, covered in snow, mud, and blood. He watched the Sentinels and their Guard fade into the forest. He pitied Lata and Surat. They were evil by nature and couldn't be blamed for their actions, but he hated Talji. She had the power to do good, but she was nothing more than Bharat's puppet.

That encounter forced him to realize one thing, however. Even though the summon was useless, it was the first time he'd pulled off a conjuration during a fight. He had a weapon in his sling. He had spells in his summoning. And he had a Guard. He was already a Sentinel, just a weak one. The guilt he felt from taking the circlet from Mayur was gone, replaced by the warm glow of angry determination.

Jai balled his fists and vowed to grow his power until he became strong enough to protect every forest elf in Amera. He would save the elves from the corrupted god.

"I don't worship you, Ghara," he spat, "I'll destroy you."

CHAPTER 9

The coliseum was a marvel of engineering, as impressive on the inside as it was on the out. It could have easily held thousands of spectators on the tiered stone seats and an entire army of contestants in the sandy oval pit below.

Jacoby had wormed his way through the various passageways and inner rooms of the stone building and now sat about halfway up the seating and looked down into the arena. It was a massive structure, over a hundred feet tall, but where one would typically see gladiators and wild animals, he witnessed something truly confusing. Another group of dead men stood in the arena, one of them obviously a mage in red robes. The man's green aura was the most unique Jacoby had seen thus far. It was a perfectly uniform sphere of a dark green hue. It didn't shift or flow like the others, but it still seemed to radiate from the man as though it were agitated or impatiently waiting to expand further.

Most strange, however, was his behavior; he was moving, walking around almost aimlessly. This was the first time Jacoby had seen anything with a green aura stir without the incentive of the rage-inducing red auras. The other three men were as still as would be expected from the undead.

His last thought troubled him. He'd just considered the skeletons and the soldiers as the same undead beings. Their behavior was the same, but how the soldiers healed their wounds and decayed simultaneously disturbed him greatly.

He turned his attention to the edges of the sandy pit. The high stone walls of the lower arena were lined with barred cages. As he sat and looked, he could have sworn that he saw puffs of green aura inside them. There were two main tunnels on either side of the oval-shaped pit. Near one, several chunks had been blasted from the walls; very recently, from the look of the rubble strewn about the arena and stone seating, and much different than the huge sections of destroyed seating higher up in the coliseum.

Before he could investigate the area below him, he needed to orient himself. He made his way to the top of the coliseum, where the final row of arches was solely decorative, allowing him to stand under them and observe his surroundings. Nearly fifty massive stone pillars partially obstructed his view of the city, but for the first time, the winding and curving road system made sense. Most of the roads spiraled toward the city center like a giant whirlpool, with smaller spirals twisting around the massive columns like small eddies in a more significant, fast-moving stream.

On the far side of the city from where he had entered, an enormous stone ramp led to an opening in the cavern's ceiling and up to a much brighter area. He thought he could make out another ramp that went down, but it was too far away and obscured by other buildings. The second ramp didn't matter. He'd found what he needed to continue his journey to the mountain tops.

A glance back to where he thought he had woken almost brought his excursion to an abrupt end. A handful of red auras flitted in and out of sight. They were far away, still near the tunnel exit, but their effect on his mind was no less powerful.

Status Effect: Enraged

Fury blinded him until all he could see were the red blazes. He shifted his weight forward, prepared to launch himself directly at them. He put his foot on the stone lip of the archway, and the edge broke free. The slip forced him to break his vision with the red auras long enough to regain his senses. He reached out and caught the edge of the archway just in time to stop himself from falling.

Status Effect Subdued: Enraged Dismissed

His rage quickly dissipated, and his focus returned to his body tilting dangerously over the stone lip. Nothing but open air stood between him and the ground a hundred feet below. He hauled himself back in, careful not to look back in the direction of the red auras.

So, the influence of the auras is wholly based on sight. They were far away, over a mile, and he was happy the path to the ramp was clear. Their distance gave him a bit of leeway, allowing him time to explore the arena. The first thing he wanted to check out was the image and the area of the pit that had been damaged.

The stone seating made for a quick descent as he circled toward his target, avoiding the larger destroyed areas that looked like they could cave in at any moment. The arena's lower seating levels were slightly nicer with stone backrests, and he stopped at a group that was likely seating for nobles to observe the happenings below. Two ornate chairs carved of marble sat on a small open platform. Rotted wooden remains hinted that a pergola or tent once stood over the area, but their form was too degraded to define their original structure.

He turned back to survey the arena. Now that he was lower, he could make out more details. The metal bars inside the stone archways in the arena's walls were portcullises that barred dark rooms and looked like they could be lowered from their positions to let something in . . . or out. Above each hole were words carved in the stone blocks above the arches. *Butcher, Fang, Havoc*—those were a few of the words he could make out. If this were indeed a combat arena, it would make sense to give the contestants names that would stoke fear in the audience. As he peered into the darkness behind the metal bars, he thought he could see flashes and swirls of green, but they would disappear before he could focus on them. He wanted to get closer to check it out.

A stone stairwell led below the nobles' platform. Dust on the steps had recently been disturbed, and Jacoby could make out at least three distinct boot prints. He followed the steps to a landing that took a sharp turn down to one of the two main tunnels.

The tunnel below was dark, but still had enough ambient light for Jacoby to make out passageways and a stone carving above a door near the back of the tunnel that said *Armory*. The tunnel showed signs of a recent battle; boot prints, a wake probably from a magical blast, crumpled stone along the tunnel's edge, and even a few hand and body prints in the sand. A closer look revealed the handprints to be skeletal.

Across from the stairwell, he saw a series of switches in an oval pattern; twelve small ones in the down position and two large ones in the up position. He touched one of the smaller ones, curiously checking it out, and accidentally clicked it into the up position.

The flick startled him, and he immediately heard gears grinding deep within the arena and the scraping of metal against stone. He tried to reverse the switch, but it wouldn't budge.

He didn't have much time to react. A howling of a dozen different beasts filled the arena; grunts, roars, bone scraping against metal, but most prominently, the sound of something heavy running on the sand.

Jacoby pulled his head back to peer around the stone lip of the tunnel and out to the arena. One of the metal portcullises in the surrounding wall of the pit had lowered, and a creature charged out. A massive skeletal lizard, nearly ten feet long from nose to tail with long boney claws and sharp teeth kicked up sand as it rushed toward the undead soldiers. A green aura blazed around its body and looked as though it were pulling the monster forward instead of being dragged behind by its charge.

"Ready arms!" Jacoby's shout came instinctually to warn the men of the incoming danger. The undead soldiers and the mage didn't react to his warning as the massive skeletal lizard plowed into them. It had no muscle or soft tissue, but it still hissed and growled as it shredded the men. It pushed them to the ground, snapping at their heads and clawing into the parts of their bodies that weren't protected with armor.

It didn't stop until the soldier's green auras sucked back inside their bodies. The lizard paused, dipping its head slightly and angling it toward Jacoby. The skeletal lizard had no eyes, but Jacoby felt it was staring directly at him. The creature let out a low guttural sound, a combination of a hiss and a growl. Then it charged.

With the giant lizard barreling toward him, Jacoby only had seconds to prepare himself. He didn't know what was further back in the tunnel, but he didn't want to fight in a place that may not offer a retreat. He saw the stairwell on the other side of the tunnel's opening and decided that was the best position he would get. He drew his sword and sprinted across the opening, baiting the lizard with his movement. The monster was close enough to take a swipe at him as he ducked behind the stone lip.

Sharp, boney claws gouged into the stone as the monster's momentum carried it into the tunnel, but Jacoby had already prepared his attack. The momentary break in sight from the creature allowed him to spin around and lift his sword. The lizard shot its head around the corner, and Jacoby brought down his blade on its skull in a heavy downward blow.

Klang! The blade shook in his hand as the sound of metal on bone rang through the stone tunnel. Bone chips flew from the impact, but the lizard's skull held strong. The blow staggered it, but only briefly before it resumed its attack.

Claws lunged at him, and Jacoby parried diligently and backed up the steps. One heavy swipe missed him and dug into the stone between his feet. He brought down his sword, hoping to sever the limb, but the lizard grabbed the sword with its mouth and tugged, pulling the blade from his hand. Another quick swipe from the lizard caught Jacoby along the chest. It dug rivets into the heavy armor but left him uninjured.

He stepped back, retreating around the corner bend in the stairwell, but he lost his footing and fell backward. The lizard forced its way around the turn, its size preventing it from scrambling up the passage and overwhelming Jacoby as the man dropped heavily. Only when he landed on the club strapped to his back did he remember he still had the weapon.

He struggled to his feet, taking claw swipes to his legs as he unslung the club. The lizard had rounded the corner and now had a clear shot at him. It lunged forward with a gaping maw wide enough to swallow his entire head. Dagger-like teeth as long as his fingers lined its jaw and dripped with the dark congealed blood of the soldiers it had just shredded.

Jacoby gripped the metal club in both hands and swung as hard as he could with a rising attack. The metal end caught one side of the lizard's jaw, shattering the bone and sending the creature sprawling to the side. The lizard landed with a heavy *thud* but recovered instantly, lashing out with another strike. Jacoby back peddled further, now standing on the stone platform at the top of the stairs. The impact from the club had been far more effective than his sword against the creature's bone, but it would take much more damage to bring down the monster.

He lifted the club for another strike, willing the Strength in his muscles to increase its damage, but a slight tug at his gut directed his awareness inside his body. It felt like a gust of wind grew from the intent in his mind and rushed across his skin, settling in his belly and swirling around. It wasn't like it stopped in his stomach, but rather somewhere intangible at the center of his soul—like discovering a room in a house that he never knew was there.

It felt like the core of his being that held everything that he was. He allowed his awareness to pull him through the fog of his mind. The blank space where his memories should have resided swirled around him, but for some reason, he trusted his subconscious to pull him in the right direction.

The fog continued to churn until suddenly, he broke through. Warm golden light cascaded over his mind's eye, filling him with a soothing glow and sense of ease. He also felt a hint of power. He reached out to his core, and the glow reached back, surrounding his arm. The gold color had swirls of earthy brown and vibrant green, and it reminded him of a wheat field. It even pulsed like the wind was blowing over a field of crops. He grabbed ahold of the glow as his will pulled him out of his core and back through the fog of his mind. His core disappeared, but he still held the pulsing glow in his hand. He forced the golden energy through his palm, directing it to the club's metal and willing his power through it.

As he brought down the heavy weapon, a faint golden light emitted from the dark metal. It was much dimmer than the monster's aura, but as the weapon descended, Jacoby thought he saw the energy flow through and disrupt the radiance like a paddle through water.

The blow caught the lizard in the shoulder. Bone crunched and shattered from the force of the impact as a blast of golden light discharged. The monster's arm separated from its body in an explosion of bone shards, and the creature sprawled to the ground. It flailed its legs, trying to get back to its feet, but Jacoby didn't give it a chance to recover. He dropped blow after blow on the giant lizard, crushing bone until its green aura sucked back inside its body and disappeared.

The emotions hit him like a battering ram. A deep hunger that went beyond the need for nourishment drove the monster to fight, but there was something else. It was threatened by him, driven to attack like an animal defending its territory. The exchange of emotions was similar to the exchange with the men after he had killed them, just bestial in nature.

Jacoby lowered his body to kneel on the stone platform near the nobles' chairs. He gasped in heavy breaths as he eyed the dead lizard, hoping it wouldn't spring back to life. He was drained. His muscles ached from the exertion of the unexpected battle. The pull and discharge from the energy in his core, as well as the lizard's final emotions, had staggered his mind.

He had a few minor cuts from the claws on his arms and legs where the armor didn't completely cover, but for the most part, he was uninjured, though he wasn't ready to stand. As he rubbed the back of his neck, his fingers brushed the silver links of chain. He tugged on the chain and pulled out the Amulet, this time expecting something to have changed. Before, he had a hunch that the crystal was communicating something to him, but now he was sure of it. The dark red portion of the gem had receded so that a quarter of it was now clear, but the other half was almost empty, with just a small sliver of dark blue showing at the bottom. Jacoby was more concerned with the **2**. It was no longer translucent but had turned black and was pulsing, almost like a beating heart.

He took in a few deep breaths to calm his mind and body. As he relaxed, he felt a wave of energy pour through his veins. Once again, vitality filled his body, and despite the rush, he still focused on the Amulet. The **2** faded, and a **3** took its place, swelling from the bottom until it was half black. Like pouring wine into a glass, the red and blue portions of the Amulet both filled completely as the cuts on his arms and legs instantly healed over, and his exhaustion fled from his body. His muscles bulged, boasting increases to Strength and Fortitude.

The experience felt so familiar to him, like he'd done it a dozen times before. He focused on the sensation, but the harder he tried to force his mind to remember, the further it slipped from his grasp.

He reached past the swirling mist of his mind and pulled on the golden light in his core. He wrapped the fingers of his open hand around the hilt of the metal club, willing his energy into the weapon.

Bolster

Golden light poured into the metal, and a sheen emitted

from its surface, slightly brighter than the first time he'd performed the skill. At the same time, he noticed the blue half of the amulet dip by a third.

Red and blue; body and mind; he knew the connection. He didn't understand how that knowledge existed within him, but he was confident the Amulet was the key to absorbing his enemy's power and strengthening himself. Glyphs had been assaulting his vision since the battle had ended, and Jacoby finally acknowledged them.

Skeletal Salamander Killed, Soul Essence Claimed, +1 Tier:
STR +2, MOB +1, FOR +1, ACU +3, RES +1

Ability Discovered: Bolster I. Imbue a weapon with magical energy

He walked over to the broken skeleton of the lizard and down the stone staircase. An idea began forming in his mind as he weighed possibilities against his situation. From the open tunnel, he looked at the soldiers' shredded bodies. Tiny swirls of green aura had formed over their corpses, much smaller than their previous form, but still there, all the same. A glance back at the skeletal lizard showed that a tiny version of its aura had returned as well. He took a step closer to the pile of bones as a cracked rib that hung at an odd angle clinked back into place. Just like his wounds, the skeletons and the soldiers were regenerating.

Time was working against him, and he didn't have much to waste. The sounds from the animals in the cages would have alerted the soldiers near the city's exit. The green skeletons would slow their pace, but if he wanted to make use of the arena, he would have to hurry. He'd opened one of the twelve cages, but up to eleven more creatures still waited for him.

There was no telling what dangers lurked above, but he'd need all the power he could get if he wanted to make his way to the top of this mountain, and he knew how to acquire it.

But first, he looked down at his bulky platemail and then to the armory at the back of the tunnel, *I'm going to need some better gear.*

CHAPTER 10

Three spiked appendages grazed Henry, reminding him why he had named the creatures *armor tongues*. The muscular red spindles that shot from their mouths were covered in black serrated barbs and no small amount of globby white saliva. The attack pierced the space that Henry had occupied only a split second earlier, crumbling the rocky wall behind him. He dodged with ease as each barrage seemed to move slowly through time and space now that Henry's new skill allowed his body to keep up with his Perception. The skill's demand on his Vitus was immense, but if he used it in short bursts he could keep up with the progress the other three skeletons had made.

After felling Smyrna's Golem, they had all made considerable gains with the accompanying Tiers the Drift Amulets had bestowed upon them. Buddy's magic had expanded, Beast's mastery of teleportation had increased, and Ox could take more damage than Henry thought possible. Even Muji seemed faster. The furry trogold hadn't bothered to get into the fray of battle, but he scurried with ease over the walls, almost as nimbly as the armor tongues they now fought.

The legions of monsters that had nearly killed them a week

earlier now seemed little more than minor challenges. Torgga's illusion rings gave them a significant advantage in stealth, and Henry had found a decent weapon in the extremities of the dread claws. Trading in his wooden javelins for the iron-hard spikes salvaged from the monsters' hands gave him four light but resilient throwing and stabbing weapons. Still, the Acolyte kite shield he'd found was far lower quality than the Gladiator Supreme shield that had been destroyed in the fight against the golem. He longed for a decent sword but had yet to find a suitable replacement.

Henry dodged past the ugly creatures' barbed tongues. The cave monsters looked like hairless dogs, covered in spikey black plates with clawed feet that allowed them to travel along the walls and ceilings as deftly as they did the floor. They had no eyes, but their sense of smell and hearing allowed them to somewhat counter the muffle enchantment of Torgga's rings. What acted as their mouths folded back in four parts like a putrid flower blossom, revealing rows of pointy teeth that dripped with globs of drool. Their ugly green auras matched those globs and cascaded from their hides like mud rolling from a hillside in the rain. The barbed spears that gave the armor tongues their name retracted back toward their mouths as they prepared for another assault. Henry was too fast to allow them time for a second strike.

Blitz

The newly upgraded Ability allowed Henry to rapidly increase his Strength and Mobility for a short time. The marked improvement greatly increased his precision and allowed him to cull through enemies both weak and strong, at the cost of substantially increased Vitus consumption.

He stepped to the side and skewered the nearest creature between the thick plates on its neck. The dread-claw javelin had no trouble piecing through its carapace-like armor. Its aura dropped from its body and dissipated before hitting the ground, telling Henry he had severed the monster's spine.

He pulled his spear from the limp body while dodging the attacks from the other two. Then, he channeled his Vitus through his body and launched the javelin at the far attacker. The weapon hit the creature in its open mouth and shot out the back of its skull, killing it instantly.

Henry didn't bother pulling another spear from the ties on his back. Instead, he focused Vitus into his wrist and balled his hand as he dodged to the armor tongue's side.

Harden

He threw all his force into the blow, and it connected with the creature's head. He felt the bones of its skull crunch as his fist sunk into the brain matter below. He'd intended to use his defensive magic to prevent his hand from shattering during the strike, but the magic had reinforced his body enough to multiply the damage.

His Harden Ability was much different from Ox's Health Regeneration—it allowed him to expend Vitus to preserve his body instead of restructuring damaged bone. Apparently, it could also be used to reinforce his fists and deal a much more significant amount of damage. He was nowhere near as strong as Ox, but it was a start.

STR +1

The Attribute gains were hard to earn. Henry found that pushing himself to his limits and finding new ways to utilize his Abilities was the only way to make his body and mind stronger. However, the *Second Path of the Desert* Status Effect troubled him every time he saw it in his display.

The two visions he'd had of the desert had mildly hampered his Strength and Mobility and made him weak to fire. Even so, Henry marveled at the physical and mental clout he'd gained in the short week since he'd woken up underneath a dead Acolyte. Each Tier he gained added to every aspect to his being. Henry liked that his body could finally keep up with him, and he could kill enemies instead of just weathering attacks with his Vitus-fueled defensive boost.

Even without his memories, Henry felt he'd awoken with an innate aptitude for almost any weapon. Mace, sword, spear, it didn't matter. Any weapon that Henry picked up, he not only knew how to use, but all its strengths and weaknesses and the best way to use it against each and every enemy. The problem was that his body could not keep up with that knowledge.

However, his Strength and Mobility grew with every bit of Soul Essence his Drift Amulet harvested. His attacks caused more damage, and he could strike and evade more accurately. Most remarkable was the ability of his bones to resist damage. Buddy had explained that the crimson half of his Drift Amulet represented his Health, or how much damage he could take before his body gave out, likely resulting in a second death. An attack from an enemy that would have torn him apart at earlier Tiers now only took a portion of his Health, and his bones held firm.

The power of his mind had grown significantly as well. When he'd first awoken, he felt as though his mind and body weren't synchronized. Not that his mind was faster, but he had trouble getting his body to match the speed of information his Perception relayed to him. However, with each Tier his Attributes increased, speeding up his reactions and reducing the delay between thought and movement. What's more, his Vitus had grown significantly. According to Buddy, Vitus was his mind's capability to process magic. It was represented by the blue half of his Drift Amulet, and it was what allowed him to execute his Abilities. Buddy had tried to lecture Henry on magic, but the warrior couldn't keep all the terms straight in his head. *What was the type of magic Buddy said I can use?* He wondered between stabs at the armor tongues. *Tree monkey magic? No, that couldn't be it. Tranquilizer magic, maybe?* Buddy would scold him later for not remembering. The mage would often act annoyed at Henry's lack of magical knowledge, but Henry could tell Buddy enjoyed any chance to talk about his craft.

From what Henry had observed, he had a much smaller Vitus pool than Buddy or Ox, but he could still perform an increasing number of skills. Unfortunately, his Abilities ate up a considerable amount of his Vitus, which also recovered much slower than that of his companions.

Further down the narrow tunnel, Ox and Beast tore through another dozen armor tongues like they weren't even there. Beast filleted them with expert precision, driving her daggers between the small joint seams in the natural armor. Ox, on the other hand, didn't bother to pick an exact spot on his enemies to attack. Instead, he struck them with such force that they exploded on impact in a spray of blood and black carapace chunks.

Buddy cleaned up the last few stragglers that tried to surround them by sending his blue fire men, *elementals*, as he'd repeatedly scolded Henry, to chase them down. Buddy had even learned to have them shoot fireballs of their own. Henry didn't know the reason, but he preferred it when Buddy used his own magical attacks instead of having the elementals do it. The elementals unsettled him, and he didn't understand why. He just knew they gave him a strange apprehension.

"Another victory," Ox boomed, whipping his forty-pound

hammer like it was a child's toy, flinging blood and globs of gore onto the walls and floor of the cave.

A group of nearly twenty armor tongues had tried to ambush them, but the skeletons' Perception was getting so high that they had no trouble spotting the assault. Henry held up his Drift Amulet. The number **10** was barely filled, indicating he had gained only a single Tier in the few days since their encounter with the golem, and almost all of that had come from the dread claws. The armor tongues had once given him a huge boost of Soul Essence, but now it was minuscule in comparison. How many creatures would he have to defeat to keep Tiering up? And if he was so much more powerful at **10**, how strong was the leader of the dwarves, Thorodd, at Tier **42**?

Haruspex

Name: Henry

Race: Human Skeleton

Tier: 10

Health: 64/72

Vitus: 52/99

Attributes:

    STR: 24

    MOB: 34

    FOR: 24

    ACU: 20

    PER: 33

    RES: 33

His Strength and Fortitude were hampered by the *Skeletal Body* Status Effect, but his Mobility, Perception, and Resolve all received a huge jump after they reached what his Haruspex called the *First Threshold*, an experience the other three skeletons confirmed with their own Statuses. However, his Strength and Fortitude were at **24**, just one point short of the threshold. Henry wondered what would happen once all his Attributes reached that level, but since Ox had already passed his Second Threshold in Strength at **50** points, Henry didn't have high hopes of regaining his flesh through Attribute increases.

"Must you insist on liquifying them? Do you know anything of finesse? Your excessive force is not necessary, and I hate being covered in blood," Beast lambasted Ox.

"Ghakk," Gator clacked from Ox's shoulder. The amalgamator skull had stopped trying to attack Ox and had occasionally made the sound, but they couldn't tell if that was intelligence or acclimation to his new home on Ox's shoulder plate.

"Good point, Gator." Ox patted the amalgamator skull next to his own. "We don't decimate our enemies out of necessity. We do it to send a message . . . and because it's fun." The shoulder plate was the last bit of armor that remained on Ox's giant skeletal frame. The dread claws had destroyed the rest, and Ox had left it behind without a second thought. Luckily, the Strength and size of his bones, as well as his increased capacity for healing magic, had made that armor less of a necessity.

Beast glared at the skeleton that was nearly twice her size, not taking her eyes off him as she shed blood and gore from her armor and cloak. Henry did the same, shaking his shield and javelin as the meat and blood splattered to the ground.

They'd been traveling steadily uphill on one of the main cavern tunnels for almost three days since they'd fought the dread claws. At least it felt like it was three days since they'd gone through three wake and sleep cycles, but it was impossible to tell this far down in the mountain. None of the sun globes that routed the solar energy from above the mountain were installed that deep into the cave system. Henry also had no idea if the sleeping habits of an underground skeleton matched those of an above-ground human. Until he had more insight, he would go with his premise of time.

Back at the dwarven stronghold of Hjardharfell, Henry had gotten a good look at the mosaic map of Jallfoss' tunnel system on Thorodd's giant dinner table. Thousands of miles of tunnels honeycombed throughout the mountain like an ant colony. Those pathways had evolved from natural fissures in the rock, dwarven mining tunnels, and both natural and man-made voids that housed entire ecosystems. Unfortunately, only a tiny portion of that was accessible without venturing into the deadly domain of abominable creatures affected by the Necromancer's magic.

Luckily, the path from the golem's lair in Lundarbrekka had kept them in one of the largest tunnel systems that made up a main thoroughfare to the depths below. Hundreds of tunnels branched off the main path that went into different places. Some were immaculately carved, lavish structures, others were little more than hand-chiseled tiny openings, but most were some combination of the two. If Henry had more time, he would have loved to explore each one. *What an adventure,* he thought, still wiping off blood and gore from his armor.

That's what the human Acolytes had been doing—trying to make it all the way down to the Source Crystal in the hopes of finding treasure. Henry remembered the first memory he had taken. The human's dying emotion was regret. The Acolyte imagined his ancestors being slain by monsters in the catacombs below. There was a vision of a gigantic crystal jutting from the floor of an open cavern, glimmering with all the colors imaginable, reflected from a light source that seemed to originate within the shining geode itself. These weren't memories the human had experienced but rather something he had mentally created and latched onto in his dying moments. Apparently, no Acolyte had ever made it all the way to the bottom of the dwarven Underdeep—a likelihood that Henry found completely plausible based on the labyrinthine nature of the tunnel system and the danger of lurking cave monsters.

The tunnel they were currently in was a huge circle opening, nearly thirty feet in diameter. A giant, rusty chain on a series of gears ran down the middle of the corridor. The dwarves had once used the mechanism to haul their carts up and down the steep passageways. The chains were heavily oxidized and covered in layers of dirt and spiderwebs after nearly a century of neglect. They looked more like the roots of an ancient tree than a mechanical system. The main tunnel was sturdy, but a sizeable off-shooting shaft near them had caved in long ago. Huge boulders and rubble now clogged its way.

Buddy approached Henry with his elementals flanking him. Their bodies were pillars of fire, and their limbs flowed together. They didn't pack much of a physical punch, but their blue flames were hot enough to melt the stone on which they strode. Without nerves, Henry lacked much of a sense of feeling and pain, though he could still perceive the intense heat radiating from their incorporeal bodies from half a dozen paces away. Buddy seemed impervious to their emissions, but none of the other skeletons had dared to venture too close to them.

Henry eyed them as Buddy drew near, not realizing he was staring until Buddy addressed him. "My elementals cause you angst," Buddy said, more of a statement than a question.

"Yes," Henry admitted. "Almost in the same way the black auras elicit fear. It's controllable but unnerving. The fact that it bothers me is more unsettling than the feeling of unease itself. Maybe the feeling comes from my recent susceptibility to fire."

"Interesting," Buddy mussed as the elementals swirled and

died out, leaving behind a cooling pool of molten rock. "I am no enchanter, so I am unable to add mind-altering Effects to my magic." He plucked a clear flow crystal from the leather bandolier that crossed his chest and held it below his waist, then somehow made a clicking sound with the tongue he didn't have.

Muji emerged from Buddy's pack and crawled down the mage's robes. The trogold landed softly on the ground. His long limbs absorbed the energy from the short fall, but Henry had witnessed the tiny creature land as gracefully from a twenty-foot drop. Muji stood on his back legs and stretched his little clawed fingers to grasp Buddy's hand. A white sheen enveloped the crystal and sucked inside it, filling it with a deep swirling blue.

"Beak," Muji chirped and scurried away, likely searching for a bug or lizard to chase now that the battle was over. At first glance, the trogold was a simple creature, highly motivated by food, with strong instincts to pounce on any animal smaller than itself. However, his obsession with Buddy and his proclivity for interacting with magic items added a curious element of intelligence to its otherwise wild nature.

Buddy examined the crystal for a moment, then tossed it to Beast. She caught it and whispered a word of gratitude before turning and walking away. When she'd found a piece of high ground that wasn't covered in armor tongue chunks, she held the flow crystal over her head. A spray of water shot from her hand, drenching her body, and rinsing blood from her cloak and armor until a red river flowed down the gentle decline of the main tunnel.

The spray of water stopped, and she analyzed the crystal that was now a much lighter blue. She tucked it safely into a pouch on her belt and gave Ox an evil stare. "I'll save the rest for our next battle, unless *his majesty* can learn to control his attacks," she snarked.

"We can only hope—" Henry started to say, but a distant rumble reverberating through the cave walls interrupted him. The rumble grew in intensity until the walls shook and dirt crumbled from the ceiling. A puddle of armor tongue blood near Henry rippled and splashed. Henry unstrapped a dread claw javelin from his back, and Muji scurried up Buddy's blue robes and climbed into his pack, peeking out from beneath a leather flap.

The skeletons looked down the shallow decline of the main cave road. Rolling black smoke flooded the tunnel and rushed toward them, filling them with fear and the urge to run.

Status Effect: Fear (Moderate): STR -10%, RES -30%, HAR -10%

Armor tongues, lizards, giant scorpions, and dozens of other creatures, both alive and skeletal, flooded into the tunnel in a panicked frenzy just ahead of the billowing aura. The live animals had wide eyes and open maws, gasping for air like they were fleeing for their lives. The undead creatures were unable to show physical signs of distress but still fled with the same sense of urgency.

"Another black aura. More spikey fiends, perhaps?" Ox gripped his hammer and shook his head, trying to dissipate the influenced tear from his mind.

"Whatever is approaching sounds much larger than the . . . what did you call them, Henry?" Blue fire engulfed the mage's hands as he prepared his attack. Henry was impressed that Buddy could ready his spells, fight off the aura, and talk simultaneously.

"Dread claws. Because of their dreadful auras . . . and their claws."

"We need to work on your monster taxonomy," Beast chided. She tried turning her back on the black billowing smoke, but the Effect faded much slower than that of the fiery red auras of the Acolytes. Teasing Henry seemed to help, however.

"Agreed, Harvey. You have many talents—naming monsters is not one." Ox stepped forward, preparing to meet the incoming cave creatures.

Status Effect Subdued: Fear (Minor): STR -5%, RES -15%, HAR -5%

Henry chuckled to himself, unable to defend his naming conventions as the stampeding animals threatened to quickly overwhelm them. Individually, the rushing horde was much weaker than the skeletons, but their sheer numbers were a considerable threat. More importantly, however, they needed to handle the onslaught before the dread claws could initiate battle.

CHAPTER 11

Beast fired arrows in quick succession, and Henry threw all but his last javelin, skewering half the stampede before they even reached the skeletons. Most effective, however, were the dozens of magical bolts that Buddy launched. Frost, lightning, force, and of course, blue fire decimated the charging horde, leaving destroyed flesh and bone in its wake.

Dozens made it past, seemingly unphased by the skeleton's attacks. Ox made quick work of the creatures, culling their mass so that the frenzied swarm that passed was small enough in number to not pose a threat and was easily avoided by the others.

They killed many fleeing creatures as they rushed past, but the cave dwellers were more concerned with evading the black aura than fighting the skeletons. Most kept running without a passing glance.

The rumble grew louder and drew the skeleton's attention away from the fleeing animals and back down to the tunnel. A hulking shape took form in the billowing smoke. It looked a bit taller than Beast at the shoulder and nearly that wide. It bounded on all fours, and the shaking grew louder each time it landed. The black aura obscured it from such a distance, but more details of the creature emerged as it neared, and each skeleton began prepping their attacks.

Under Henry's leadership, they had developed a series of tactics based on their strengths and weaknesses, and those of their enemies. Because this was a single attacker, Ox took the front to draw in their enemy while Henry and Beast prepared to surround it from the sides. Buddy stepped back and formed more blue fireballs around his hands.

"That's not a dread claw," Henry said. It looked like a bull-dog with muscular front legs and a protruding lower jaw, but it must have weighed a thousand pounds. It had thick bones wrapped in bulky muscles but no skin, just like the previous black-aura enemy. However, it lacked the quiet subtlety with which the dread claws had entered and attacked.

Ox took his position in the center of the tunnel. He faced the charging monster and brandished his war maul. The flow crystals on either side shone with a pale light, indicating that he had activated the force magic in his weapon.

Now within a hundred feet, Henry could clearly see the monster's features through the billowing aura. He saw dark maroon muscles lumped on its massive skeletal frame in ways that didn't seem natural. Two thick curved horns sprouted from its forehead and circled around to sharp points near its chin. It dug into the ground with clawed feet and propelled itself forward with an unnatural agility.

Like the dread claws, strands of dark muscle fibers connected a spike-tooth jaw to a thick skull. The jaw protruded forward and had two pointy tusks that jutted up with a slight curve back toward the skull. Without any other muscles or skin on its face, the white eyes with dark pupils made it look enraged and insane. The thick muscles on its shoulders left little neck to make out, alluding to the capability of dealing a heavy blow with its ram-like forehead. *Dread ram*, Henry mentally noted.

As the monster drew closer, Beast Blinked behind Henry and grabbed his arm, then teleported both of them behind the charging enemy.

This was the first time Beast had used her teleport magic on Henry. Buddy had called it something like *cobleration magic,* but that was all he could remember. The experience wasn't as unnerving as he would have imagined. One second, he was facing the charging monster, and the next, he was looking at its heavy hindquarters. He felt no movement at all from the transport.

From behind, they could see mighty back legs that sent loose rocks flying behind it and a thick stubby tail covered in small bony spikes. Black, smokey aura poured out of its body, forcing Henry and Beast to hesitate their attack.

Ox lifted his maul above his head, preparing to smash the monster's skull to pieces. "I hope you're stronger than you are fast," he bellowed.

Almost as if in response, the ram shot forward, covering the ground between it and Ox in a flash. Henry recognized the attack as something like the Blitz he used to bash with his shield or thrust with his sword. He wasn't expecting the creature's sudden increase in speed. Neither was Ox.

The dread ram slammed into Ox's chest as the skeleton swung the hammer forward. Ox didn't land the attack; instead, the force of the impact made him release the hammer and send it flying forward, landing between Henry and Beast. Unfortunately, they realized too late what had happened. As the hammer impacted, it discharged the activated force magic, sending an invisible wave in all directions and blasting Henry and Beast into separate sides of the tunnel.

The good thing about not having lungs was that it was impossible to knock the air out of them. That didn't stop bones from cracking as Henry smashed into the tunnel's rocky wall. He was thankful for the physical resilience that accompanied his Tier gains, allowing his Fortitude to prevent his bones from completely crumbling against the stone.

Henry tumbled to the hard ground of the tunnel and quickly regained his senses. The force from the hammer had damaged him, but it had also helped him shake the fear from his mind.

Status Effect Subdued: Fear Dismissed
Status Effect: Broken Ribs (Minor): MOB -10%

He focused his senses and looked up in time to see Ox tumbling a hundred feet up the tunnel, not stopping until he smashed into a dwarven cart.

Henry recovered the javelin he had dropped, then pulled himself to his feet as chips of his broken ribs clinked down his chest cavity. The resurrection magic would slowly repair the damage, but he didn't have time to wait.

Ox pushed the broken cart off his body and pulled himself to his feet to find the dread ram had selected a new target. It had stopped after launching Ox up the tunnel and reoriented itself to start a charge at Buddy. The black smoke that made up the dread ram's aura surged into the tunnel and obscured Henry's vision, but he could clearly see Buddy summon two blue fire elementals.

The monster rocketed forward, impacting the blue humanoids and destroying them in a burst of flame. It would have leveled Buddy, but it stopped just before the mage with a bone-crushing *thud*. Buddy held out his hands and sent as much magic as possible into the force wall, ensuring it could withstand the force of the dread ram. The monster stepped back, shaking the impact from its head, then charged again and again. Each bash made the invisible barrier shimmer and likely drained a massive amount of Vitus from the mage. Henry didn't know how much more Buddy had in reserve, so he lifted his javelin and sent a surge of Vitus through his legs and arms, powering his own accelerated attack.

Blitz

The force from his Vitus-fueled throw blasted the weapon through the air, burying it deep into dark muscles on the creature's back. It reared up and opened its jaw in a silent scream of rage that was more daunting than if it had released a sound.

Beast had recovered from the force hammer's impact as well. From the corner of Henry's eyes, he saw the elven skeleton disappear in a tiny puff of green aura and reappear on the dread ram's back. She buried her two razor-sharp frost daggers into the dark muscles along its spine. The dread-ram spun and tried to swipe its massive claws at Beast, but its arms were too bulky to allow it to reach her.

Henry retrieved another javelin from the body of a dead cave lizard and charged. The frost daggers had gotten the monster's attention, and Henry wasn't one to waste a distraction. The dread ram bucked and spun, trying to remove the elf from its back, but Beast held tight, slicing deeper into the thick muscle-like masses of flesh.

Henry channeled Vitus through his body and launched himself forward.

Blitz

The tunnel walls blurred around him as he thrust with his spear. The dread ram reared on its back legs and dropped its mighty horned skull toward the attacking skeleton.

Henry had his shield raised, but his body wouldn't react fast enough to avoid the crushing blow. His mind, however, was up to the task. He redirected the flow of Vitus from his legs to his arm and shoulder, reinforcing it with what he hoped was enough magic to counter the incoming blow.

Harden

The dread ram impacted him with the force of a train. His shield crumbled, and Henry expected the same from his bones under the force of the dread ram's skull. Surprisingly, both his bones and his Vitus held strong, even though the bash sent him tumbling back a dozen paces, chunks of broken shield scattering in his wake.

The dread ram reared again until the weight of Beast on its back caused it to overbalance and topple backward. Beast tried to jump as the monster rolled, but a heavy swing from its massive arms caught her legs and sent her spinning.

They both smacked to the ground simultaneously, and the dread ram recovered just a split second faster than Beast. It turned and brought down a heavy claw, intending to crush the elf before she could roll clear.

The claw impacted the stone of the tunnel floor, just inches from Beast's head. It dug rivets in the rock as it righted itself and tried to claw its way toward her, but it couldn't move forward.

"It's not nice to clobber a lady, even a grumpy one." Ox gripped the dread ram's stubby tail and pulled it further back. The dread ram's neck was short and balled with maroon muscles, forcing it to turn its whole body before it could cast a menacing glare at Ox.

"That's right. I'm not done with you," Ox admonished the monster.

The dread ram opened its jagged maw and spun its massive body, ripping its stubby tail free from Ox's grip. It thrust with its skull, and Ox grabbed both of its giant horns, halting the force of the blow.

Ox dug his feet into the ground as the dread ram clawed at the stone floor and tried to force him back. It was a stalemate, with neither side gaining ground until the monster activated its version of Blitz. The dread ram pushed with four legs against Ox's two, quickly forcing the skeleton backward. They picked up speed, and Ox lost his footing. Another lunge sent the two flying directly into the collapsed tunnel. Rocks exploded, dust billowed, and the two impacted the boulders that blocked the tunnel.

Ox held firm to the monster's horns as it continued to discharge its bash. Ox sent waves of Vitus through his body, likely wishing for a set of armor that could offset some of the damage. The monster forced them deeper through the rubble with each thrust, but Ox held strong. Then, with a final crunch, the debris gave way, and they tumbled through.

A bright green-blue glow shined through the black fear aura and billowing dust from the debris as Henry, Beast, and Buddy raced toward the sound of the fight. They dodged falling rocks and jumped over shifting boulders and through the hole that Ox and the dread ram had made.

Henry ran into a huge chamber, bright from layers of abundant lumimoss. Ox and the dread ram struggled in the middle of the room, still locked together in a contest of Strength.

The chamber was a hundred feet across, with a pile of boulders at the far end. The open expanse was littered with towering ore piles, organized in the familiar dwarven hoarding fashion. However, the mineral collections were much more unique than simple iron or copper. Most of the mounds were of a shiny, black rock, though some were gold, and one was a silvery metal that had a prismatic sheen to it.

Ox and the monster struggled in the center of the chamber. He still held its curved horns as the brutes spun, sending ore flying in all directions. Each vied for ground as they maneuvered for better leverage. Wooden carts filled with ore crumbled below the force of their battle and splintered apart.

The dread ram slipped on the loose ground, and Ox struck with a knee, catching the monster under the chin and lifting its head. Ox pushed up, forcing the monster's front legs off the ground and preventing it from pushing him back. However, that didn't stop it from attacking. It swiped heavy claws and tore into Ox's ribs, sending chunks of bone flying. Tendrils of white magic shot from Ox's body and caught the bone chunks, returning them to their rightful place as fast as the dread ram could deal damage, but Henry knew Ox was running low on Vitus.

Buddy summoned two blue balls of fire and launched them at the monster. They impacted it in the side with a thud and a sizzle. The dread ram reeled from the heat, and Henry could see burning flesh and charred bone at the point of impact.

It flailed in anger, reaching forward and raking against Ox's chest. Ox refused to let go until the force of the dread ram ripped his arms from his torso. The monster dropped its body and thrust with its skull, butting Ox hard and sending him tumbling through the ore piles.

Now close enough to analyze the monster and successfully resisting the fear Effect, Henry activated his divination.

Haruspex

Type: Dread Ram
Health: 102/205
Vitus: 9/36
Attributes:
    STR: 52
    MOB: 28

FOR: 48

ACU: 12

PER: 11

RES: 8

Resistances: Physical, Mental (Immune)

Lore: A sturdy cousin of the dread claws, the dread ram is a pow-erful addition to the Necromancer's evil army. Avoid its direct attacks at all costs

Ox was down, but he had given them time to regroup. Three bucklers shot through the air, each engulfed with Buddy's blue flame. They struck the dread ram in the head and side as Beast Blinked to its back and resumed shredding the muscles along its spine. The monster shook its massive head, flinging Ox's arms from its horns.

Henry had discarded his broken shield, so he could only use his shoulder for his attack.

Blitz

Harden

The impact lifted the dread-ram and dumped the monster on its side before it could recover its base. Henry felt the bones in his shoulder crack, but he was still able to thrust a dread-claw javelin into thick slabs of muscle on the monster's chest. The maroon flesh gave way to the iron-hard bone of his spear. Henry ducked below a heavy swipe before thrusting again. The monster was injured but was still mobile enough to present a substantial threat. Henry dodged another massive claw, his Vitus keeping him just outside the range of its attacks, but he knew he didn't have the magic remaining for a decisive blow.

Sacrifice

During his fight with Smyrna's Golem, He'd learned to pull Health from his bones and restore his Vitus. It was a dangerous

Ability and the exact opposite of Ox's regeneration. It would lead to his death if overdone, though he hoped never to use it to its extreme unless he was protecting his companions.

Blue streams of lightning pulled magical energy from his bones and into his core. The tempest spun, doubling, then tripling in size. Waves of nausea threatened to falter his movements, and he felt his Health drop by a third, but the rush of Vitus steadied his footing as he dodged another blow and searched for an opening.

Beast Blinked near the monster, materializing just long enough to slice into dark flesh before transporting herself to another point of attack. Black muck oozed from the wounds in the dread ram's clumps of muscle, and with each cut it seemed to lose a bit of Strength and Mobility.

The dread-ram thrashed and clawed at Henry and Beast, enraged by the painful combination of blade and fire. Henry pressed the attack as a shiny mist swirled around the dread ram. The mist spun into five balls of light that quickly manifested into dwarves in full bronze plate armor.

Bright red auras surrounded the dwarves as they attacked the dread ram. They weren't hurting it, but they succeeded in driving it into a distracted frenzy. Rage from the auras pulsed through Henry's mind and urged him to attack the dwarves, but he quickly recognized the illusionary magic from Torgga and forced the emotion aside. The dread ram didn't.

It swiped at the dwarves, but its claws passed right through them. More balls of fire hit it in the side and chest, charring muscle and bone.

Sacrifice

Henry pulled more magic from his bones. Again, he felt the sickening weakness that accompanied his skill, but he only needed one clear shot.

The dread ram reared once more, and Henry blurred forward. He thrust hard with his spear, sending it under the monster's jaw and into its brain. The monster thrashed and flailed until its Strength gave out, and it toppled. The floor shook with its impact, and small chunks of ore clinked and fell as the surrounding piles shifted. The black aura dissipated, and the dwarves faded back into the shining mist, taking their red auras with them.

Henry relaxed, finally free from the mental drain of the different auras, and still slightly nauseous from his Sacrifice Ability. With a shake of his head, he dismissed the empty feeling of the monster's emotions as Soul Essence flooded into his core. A quick glance at the top of his display showed a nearly-full **11**. He was almost at the next Tier, but his Vitus was nearly gone, and his Health was dangerously low.

Another close battle had ended, and it was time to get some answers from Torgga.

CHAPTER 12

The muscle on the dread ram had already started to turn to ash when Henry heard Buddy's strained grunt.

"Uggghh . . ." Buddy's arms were pinned tightly to his sides as he hovered in the air and kicked his legs. More shiny mist formed and spun around him, and suddenly Henry saw a short figure in dwarven half-plate lifting the mage with a massive bear hug.

"Buddy! You're alive!" Torgga squealed beneath her bronze helmet.

"Uggh, ugh," Buddy grunted as the dwarf set him back on the ground.

Torgga spun the mage around to face her and gripped his forearms. "Oh, I'm so happy. When the monsters started coming in waves I thought the worst, but now you're back and you're safe. And you've found a treasure trove. Oh, I knew you were a hero."

The sudden movement and the sound of Torgga's cheerful voice summoned Muji from the perceived safety of Buddy's leather pack. The trogold sprang from Buddy's back and onto Torgga's shoulders, scrambling for a hold until his tiny claws found a grip on the dwarf's armor.

"Oh, Muji. I missed you too," Torgga cooed. She gave the trogold a series of aggressive scratches that sent a small cloud of dust into the surrounding air. Muji returned the affection by playfully biting at her fingers until a scurrying cave lizard caught his attention. He squirmed from the dwarf's grasp and landed with a less-than-graceful thud before chasing the unfortunate lizard behind one of the ore piles. The spectacle elicited a round of giggles from Torgga before she turned back to Buddy and began assaulting him with rapid-fire questions.

Ox had recovered from the battle, though he was still missing his two arms and had began searching the ore-filled room for them. He leaned over and quietly said to Henry, "I believe it was me that found this place, but for Bertie's sake, I'll let him take the credit."

Henry chuckled but kept his focus on the dread ram's body. Like the pack of dread claws from earlier, its outer muscles were turning black and dissolving into ashen whisps. Without the dark tissue to hold them together, its structure crumbled, leaving behind a pile of dread bones and what looked like an armor tongue skeleton.

This monster was another shell over a once-living creature. They needed answers, and hopefully, Torgga could provide them.

"Torgga," Henry shouted, trying to overcome the sound of the dwab's voice, "what do you mean by *waves of monsters*? And what do you know about this dread ram?" Beast gave him a quizzical look that said she disapproved of Henry's name for the monster.

Torgga had pulled off her helmet but still wore her single-lensed goggles as she talked excitedly to Buddy a mile a minute. Henry's question caught her off guard like she had forgotten he was there. "Oh, Henry, of course. A few days ago, hundreds of cave creatures, alive and dead, began flowing into Hjardharfell from the tunnels below. They're killing our citizens and damaging our cities. We've rallied a defense, but it's quickly failing. Our arms and armor aren't what they used to be, and we can't make more.

"That's kind of why I'm here," she continued, giving Buddy a sideways glance. "I was praying to find you. We need help."

"Have you seen other creatures like this with black auras that induce fear instead of rage?" Beast joined Henry examining the dread ram's remains.

"Beast! Thank Minoa's sugared muffins." Torgga's pleasant voice rang with excitement but failed to cover up the shake of uncertainty. Understandably so. Hjardharfell was her home. Monsters had threatened it her whole life, but now it was under siege. "Only rumors. I've heard stories from scouts that had explored too far past Lundarbrekka. We call them the *Silent* since you don't get memories or emotions if you manage to kill one. They're considered the front-line soldiers of the Necromancer's evil forces, though I've never heard of one venturing up this far.

"Good eye, Gator." Despite the damage Ox had received from the battle, the amalgamator's skull still held firm to his shoulder plate. The massive skeleton knelt and awkwardly lowered his body to the ground until white whisps of magic reached from his shoulder and pulled his detached arm back into the socket with a *thunk*.

Torgga continued to talk but now had a confused look on her face as she tried to grasp why Ox had a second skull on his shoulders. She managed to formulate a response to Beast's question but couldn't pull her eyes from the sight of the double-headed giant skeleton. "Dwarves can't normally see auras, and we don't experience the rage from the red ones, but the stories say that even the strongest scouts have been sent running in fear from the Silent. I'm ashamed to admit that I would have helped you sooner if this monster hadn't left me quaking in my greaves."

The dwab took a deep breath to steady her nerves. "My father sent warriors to block the tunnels to Hjardharfell, but they're not prepared for this." She pulled out a parchment and quill, and hurriedly scribbled something, then folded the paper in half. A small wooden cylinder covered in dwarven carvings hung from her waist by a braided cord. She twisted a cap from its end, then pushed the folded paper inside. The wood shimmered for a second then faded, and even Henry could tell the item was enchanted. "I just used the last charge to tell them you're coming. I wouldn't want them to accidently attack when we arrive."

Buddy and Beast both started to ask about the nature of the magical device, but Henry interrupted them. "We encountered a group of similar monsters earlier. They were just as deadly but smaller and used these as weapons." Henry held up his dread-claw javelin. "This dread ram, or Silent, as you called it, was extremely powerful. It also used translation magic, similar to my Blitz."

"*Translation* magic?" Torgga gave him a questioning look.

Buddy held up his hands and signed. "*Transmutation*. It's called *transmutation* magic . . ."

"Of course," Henry said, shrugging as Torgga giggled, though the worry still hung in her voice.

The dwarf walked away from Buddy's side and joined Henry and Beast at the remains of the dread ram. "If the Silent have fear auras, then maybe that's what is forcing the cave creatures to swarm our defenses. No wonder our illusions haven't been effective against the onslaught."

"Torgga." Beast's voice was calm but stern. "We don't have

time to waste. Henry discovered that Lord Stavros of Ikrit is the Necromancer, and he knows we're headed to the Empress. That must be why the Silent are broiling up.

"Stavros?" Torgga's worried expression grew. "But how? What all happened down there?"

"A lot." Buddy had used his force magic to pull Henry's pack through the fresh passageway and over the scattered boulders. The leather satchel dropped softly at his feet, and Buddy opened it, pulling out the dwarven treasure. "We destroyed Smyrna's golem and found the Magma Blaster—"

"What?" The dwab rushed Buddy, nearly bowling him over in excitement. "You should have said that first. Hand it over, Mr. Bones." She squealed as she pulled the item from the mage's hands and marveled at the magical tool. "This is exactly what we'll need. My father is rallying every able-bodied person in greater Hjardharfell to repel the cave creatures, but they're not equipped for the fight. Now that you're here, and you've recovered the blaster . . ." She held up the rod, then motioned to the piles of ore in the green-lit cave. "And discovered a whole treasure hoard, we've got a chance."

Ox had found and attached his other arm and wasn't paying much attention to the conversation, but Torgga's words grabbed his interest. "Treasure, you say? What kind of treasure would that be?"

"There are enough rare metals here to outfit an entire army of dwarves." Torgga picked up a black chunk of rock from a nearby pile. "The smiths call it *molybdenium*, but most just refer to it as *golem steel*. When smelted with iron and hammered into plates it becomes nearly impervious to any heat less than Jallfoss's lava flows. It's heavy but highly resistant to magic."

"Would it be correct to say that Smyrna's Golem was built from this steel?" Buddy asked.

"Very likely. Most golems that worked closest to the lava fields were shielded with the material. After Ortegus Oxendine brokered peace between dwarves and humans, we stopped building golems for combat, at least until Smyrna decided to protect our treasure stores from the Acolytes."

Henry picked up a chunk of the heavy black ore. Silver veins ran through the obsidian rock, and tiny specks of metallic green glinted in the faint light.

Haruspex

Item: Molybdenium (Epic)

Description: Component, ore. Also known as golem steel, this material is highly resistant to heat and is commonly used in the construction of dwarven golems.

Torgga continued her explanation as she picked up a chunk from the single pile of prismatic ore. "This, on the other hand, is called *eversharp*. It's one of the rarest metals in the world and almost as magically conductive as the flow crystals themselves. It's often mixed with copper and gold to form weapons that are impossibly sharp and nearly indestructible. What's more, even if damaged, with the application of a bit of Steam, it will return to its forged shape. Only my father and a few of his strongest warriors have weapons made from eversharp. This pile, however, is ten times the amount that exists in all Hjardharfell."

Haruspex

Item: Argonalite (Legendary)

Description: Component, Ore. Mages, warriors, and smiths throughout the world dream of incorporating this rare ore into their kit. Depending on the base metal with which it is combined, it will

contain various magical properties. The most common alloy is dwarven eversharp.

"Now that you have the Magma Blaster, can you relight the forges and make use of this ore?" Beast asked.

"Absolutely. We're only a few miles from the front lines. Once the forges are blazing, the chains that run along the center of the main tunnel should reactivate and we'll be able to start hauling it up. Unless . . ." she trailed off, looking apprehensively at the pile of boulders that indicated another caved-in tunnel.

"Unless the Silent break through to Hjardharfell first." Buddy finished her thought. His voice seemed nearly as worried as Torgga's.

There wasn't much to think about for Henry. The way ahead seemed obvious. "I say we join the dwarves and fight off the Silent long enough for them the light their forges," Henry said, mainly to Torgga. "But once that's done, we have our own mission to finish. Stavros is still coming, and we must get to Lady Destria before he does."

"Agreed, Henry," Buddy affirmed. "Assisting the dwarves is the most prudent course of action." Torgga's face flushed with red, her mouth slightly agape as she beamed at the mage.

Beast nodded, and Henry felt she would be smiling if she had lips. "I suppose since you've led us this far, Henry. We might as well keep going until you get us completely killed."

"Thank you, thank you." Torgga wrapped her arms around Henry's waist. Henry felt his bones creak under the Strength of the dwarf and was grateful she directed most of her affection at Buddy.

"My minions have a knack for words. If only their prowess in battle matched that of their tongues." Ox had picked up the dread ram skull, curved horns included, and placed it over his own like a ghastly helmet. It wobbled loosely as he posed, but Ox's frame was large enough that Henry thought the look suited the giant skeleton. Beast, however, did not.

"You idiot, take that off, and let's get moving," the elf scolded, crossing her arms over her chest as she did every time Ox annoyed her.

"I will keep this skull as a trophy. The unnatural way its flesh controlled its bones bothered me more than how it used me to open the tunnel. I can forgive it trying to kill me, but wearing muscles where it shouldn't is unacceptable." Ox then pointed to the exit at the far end of the cave. "Also, instead of arguing with your emperor, you should be more like Muji and finish searching the bodies."

"Beak." Came a distant chirp, almost in response to Ox's statement. Beast scowled at Ox, but the warrior ignored her and instead picked up the dread ram's massive claws and waived them around like a child playing with a new toy.

Too much had been happening to take notice, but as Henry surveyed the far end of the bright cavern, he saw a huge number of scattered bones near the source of Muji's beak. All but Ox walked over to survey the scene. Two mostly-whole dwarven skeletons lay near the blocked exiting tunnel. Their flesh had long rotted off, but they still wore their leather miner's gear, with a few strips of tattered cloth clinging to their bones. The strangest aspect of the skeletons was that no green aura wrapped around their lifeless bones, an aspect that Henry was quickly beginning to associate with danger.

Bones from at least two other dwarves littered the area, but scattered amongst them were the unmistakable shells and spears of dread claws. Henry picked up one of the long boney shafts and examined it closely, allowing Haruspex to confirm it was from one of the Silent.

Torgga, however, was more interest in the exiting tunnel. She ran her hands over the wall and the fallen boulders that blocked the opening. "This cave-in was intentional. You can tell by the way the boulders are marked that they placed charges. However," Torgga motioned toward the tunnel that Ox and the dread ram bored through. "That looks like an accident that was caused by the first blast, judging by the fissures in the ceiling."

"They blew themselves up while fighting dread claws. These dwarves sacrificed themselves to seal this cave," Henry could tell by the arrangement of the scattered bones that some sort of explosion had ended whatever confrontation had taken place in the damaged cavern.

"Heroes," Beast added, but Henry felt her tone was more admonishment for fool hearted courage than admiration for bravery.

"That's the only explanation I can think of. It's rare for a dwarf to seal up any tunnel without a good reason," Torgga said, turning her attention to the dwarven skeletons, "I think humans feel the same way about burning bridges."

Near one of the whole dwarven skeletons, the furry backside and bushy tail of the trogold wiggled its way inside a leather sack. The little creature grunted as he squirmed in the pouch.

Beast, Buddy, and Torgga gathered around as Muji pulled himself from the pack. His tufted ears twinged, and he beaked in excitement, holding a flow crystal the size of an apple in his tiny hands. When he realized the group's attention was on him, he rolled onto his side, biting the gem, and kicking at it with his back legs.

He growled in feigned aggression when Torgga reached to take it from him. "Yes, Muji, I know you're cute, but you need to let us see what you've found."

Buddy ignored the interaction and picked up the bulging sack. It was a hefty leather pouch of high quality that had held up well over the years. Its contents clinked as Buddy lifted the sack and looked inside. "Flow crystals," he said, pulling out a gem just slightly larger than the end of his thumb, "and of extremely high quality."

He tossed the crystal to Henry, who caught and examined it.

Haruspex

Item: Flow Crystal (Transcendent)

Type: Component/Accessory

Description: Flow shard from beyond the dwarven Underdeep

Torgga pulled the sack down to her level and retrieved a handful of different-sized crystals, "Amazing. I can't even sense resistance to their channeling. The artificers will lose their shrooms over these."

"Transcendent? Is that how you can tell it's high quality?" The flow crystals were completely transparent and glistened brightly in the green light of the lumimoss, but Henry didn't notice anything remarkable about their appearance.

"Transcendent is a step above legendary, but I don't rely on the human Drift Amulet's divinity. Some mages have the Ability to sense the flow of magic. It's almost like vision, but more . . . speculative." Torgga waved her hands in excited circles as she explained. "At higher Tiers, it can be more effective than normal sight."

"I can feel eddies in the streams of magic as they circulate through flow crystals, but with these, it's more like an unhindered waterfall. I sense no impurities whatsoever. If these were used in Ox's hammer, he would get nearly fifty charges." Buddy mimicked Torgga's excitement as he pulled more shards from the leather satchel.

"Or one big charge, judging by the outflow potential," Torgga added.

"Yes, and he'd probably kill himself in the process," Buddy continued without a hint of sarcasm in his voice. "The only crystal of similar quality we've found is the one in the hilt of your sword, Henry. That's probably why you were able to drain the golem enough for the Blaster to finish it." He filled the open spots in his bandolier with the pure crystals and put another handful into a pouch on his belt.

Beast had been watching the interaction between Buddy and Torgga with a hint of amusement until she lost interest in the intricacies of their talk about magic and flow crystals and started searching the surrounding area. Scattered on the floor and piled in wooden boxers were small, cigar-shaped objects that looked like candles wrapped in paper with small strings sticking from one end. "What's this?" Beast picked one up and showed it to the dwarf.

"Oh, don't touch those!" the dwab exclaimed in alarm. "They're *solofurnos*. Miners use them to blast away rock, but they become extremely unstable and dangerous after a while. Better known as *Minoa's monthly temper*, if it goes off, it'll take you with it."

"Could the dwarves have used these to cave in the tunnel?" Beast asked, suddenly wary of the item she held.

"That's exactly what they did. Most dwarves don't have magic, and even if they do, it's not evocation. So we drill holes in the rock and use solofurnos to blow it up." Torgga smacked her hands together to mimic an explosion. "Much faster than a pick and hammer, but way more dangerous."

Beast set the solofurno down cautiously but continued to

eye the devices with curiosity. "Where can I find some that are stable?"

Torgga gave the elf a wink as she took the sack of crystals from Buddy and Hefted it over her shoulder. "I'll introduce you to the alchemist when we get back to Hjardharfell."

Henry quickly riffled through the rest of the dead dwarves' possessions, careful not to disturb the solofurnos. He found some quality yet old mining tools, some long-rotted leather, and a strange device. A metal cylinder, about the size of his fist, was filled with an array of shattered flow crystals. Poor-quality crystals would crumble when exposed to too much magical energy, so he assumed it was a broken magical device. Haruspex was just as uncertain and told him little more than he was able to observe.

He asked Torgga what it was, but she had no idea and was far more interested in getting back to Hjardharfell. Nevertheless, she suggested bringing it back for the artificers to examine, so he stowed the device in his pack.

Henry had to stifle his inclination to continue exploring. The impending danger of the Silent and the accompanying flood of cave creatures into Hjardharfell urged him and the other skeletons to hurry from the location. They gathered their remaining weapons and equipment and followed the dwab through the freshly dozed tunnel.

CHAPTER 13

Two scorpions, each the size of a small horse, skittered up the slope of the main tunnel, one on either side of the rusty dwarven chain running along its center. Their black carapaces glistened under the blue-green hue of the lumimoss, contrasting with purple splotches at the tips of their thick claws and hooked tail stingers. Streams of green aura emitted from the frightened cave creatures, a sure sign the influence of the Silent prevented them from masking their presence as they exchanged stealth for speed. They paid little notice to the skeletons and dwarf watching from the strewn rubble of the recently opened tunnel.

Lizards, armor tongues, and several other creatures that Henry didn't recognize, both alive and dead, clawed their way up the sloping tunnel in a panicked frenzy. They came one or two at a time, not in the stampede from before, but they all had the same fear-filled urgency of prey fleeing for its life. Henry knew all too well the impact that an aura could have on emotions. He'd grown more resistant to their effect on his mind as he'd been continually exposed to their influences. His Resolve had grown substantially with each Tier, but it was still an unpleasant feeling that he had to power through, lest it force his actions.

Buddy had explained that the auras were an intangible manifestation of one's soul. The mage's blazed around him like a fiery tempest. Ox's was huge, nearly thirty feet across and towered high like a mountain. Beast's was a series of barely noticeable tendrils that snaked their way over her bones. Henry couldn't see his own, but he'd been told it looked like a crystalline shell that surrounded his body like the carapace of a beetle. Luckily, Torgga's illusory rings hid their auras at the cost of a few Vitus points and gave them a huge advantage against the cave monsters of the Underdeep.

Most agreed that auras had something to do with the Necromancer and Lady Destria, but that didn't explain the influence they could have on a psyche, or even why they were different colors. Green auras, for those from inside the mountain nation of Jallfoss, had no effect on the skeletons, but seemed to provoke attacks from threatened animals. Torgga had connected the response to animalistic instinct, though Henry felt magic was more of an art than a science, regardless of how many times the mages tried to educate him.

Red auras marked those from outside Jallfoss. They would send the undead into a murderous frenzy. Living intelligent beings couldn't see auras, but the dwarves seemed convinced that auras were part of Lady Destria's spell to protect the mountain from the invading Acolytes.

And now, there were black aura's that came from the Necromancer's Silent. The smog sent all beings, alive or dead, fleeing in fear. *Were there other auras left to discover?* Henry hoped not. He wanted to ask Buddy, but the discussion would have to wait until they reached the dwarven stronghold.

The skeletons and the dwarf had gathered as much of the

rare ore as they could carry and started the last leg of their return to Hjardharfell. The treasured components would be a boon for the dwarves, but only if they could start their forges and use it before being overwhelmed.

In a lull between rushing cave creatures, the group began to run, but they only made it a few steps when they heard the sound. It was distant but unmistakable. The heavy thrum of dread ram footfalls mixed with the high-pitched squeal of dread claw fingers rubbing against each other. There was something else; a low hum, almost a vibration that pulsed with ominous intent.

"A war song from the Silent . . . are you ready for another battle, Harry?" Ox ran closely behind Henry. He could relate to the huge skeleton's desire to engage in combat. Even bound to their mission to save Jallfoss, Henry felt himself pulled toward the encroaching dread monsters, if only to test his metal against their evil. He knew he wasn't yet strong enough to face whatever was coming, but the thought of battle excited him.

"I don't know how many we can take, but I feel it's less than what's coming," Henry replied over his should to Ox. He saw Torgga's worried expression and felt the mix of concern and hope radiating from her eyes. The Silent were still far away to sense their black auras, but their sound indicated their numbers were much more than in the previous battles. Urgency set their pace as the group tried to put distance between themselves and the incoming threat.

The sound diminished but never completely faded behind them. Aside from a few crazed fleeing cave monsters that were quickly dispatched, the run was uneventful, and they made good progress. Nearly at Tier 11, their Fortitude was high enough to allow them to exert themselves for much longer before becoming exhausted. The fact that his skeletal body had any stamina at all without muscle still seemed odd to Henry; even more so that he could feel fatigue and not pain. He made a mental note to ask Ox about that later. For the moment, he had more important things to consider.

Henry dropped back in the formation to gather information from the dwab. He hadn't noticed any physical defenses during their approach, so he wanted to understand what to expect. "Torgga, you said the dwarves were rallying. What kind of fortifications are they setting up?"

"We've tried a few things over the years: walls, anti-siege weapons, traps, but without our forges and resource resupply we have no way to maintain them. Until now, the illusions that our Geists create have been the most effective defenses against both the cave creatures and the Acolytes."

"Why didn't you just use the solofurnos to block off the tunnels?" Beast asked.

"Politics and tradition, mostly," Torgga stated simply. "We've been digging for thousands of years, and there's a high degree of investment in the lower reaches. Sealing the depths would have been prudent, but dwarves are stubborn, and, like I said before, there's a stigma about closing a path you've already opened. That's for a single tunnel. Most dwarves couldn't fathom blocking off thousands of years' worth of progress."

"So, illusions are your only defense?" Henry asked, not intending to offend the dwab but still wanting to understand what they had to work with.

"No. My father was never a fan of illusions, though he saw they could be effective in the absence of armor, weapons, and other supplies. With the illusions failing, he'll go back to what he knows best." Torgga replied, not showing any sign of fatigue despite several miles of uphill running with her heavy armor.

"And that is?" Buddy gasped under the load of his pack. His Strength, Mobility, and Fortitude were significantly lower than the other skeletons, and the strain from the run's exertion was showing in his voice.

"The most impenetrable force known to the world," Torgga said, beaming with pride. "A wall of dwarves and steel."

"I would expect nothing less from the minions of Ortegus Oxendine," Ox added over the hefty pad of his own foot falls.

"A handful of heavily armored dwarves could hold off an army of thousands, but sadly, our soldiers aren't what they used to be. We only have a few hundred inhabitants that can act as defenders. Fatigue, along with the lack of current training will force us to rotate them out, cutting those numbers to a third. Our smallest combat element is called a cell and is made of nine soldiers. Three heavily armored dwarves with tower shields and swords hold the front line. Second, two spearmen, usually orcs, will surround and defend a center artificer. Finally, two heavy crossbows will flank a mage, usually a Geist, but sometimes an evoker or transumer."

"Only nine?" Henry asked.

"Yes, but for bigger tunnels, we combine cells into clusters. Usually there's a Captain and their Lieutenant in charge of a cluster, and they'll fill the front line where needed. That allows us to break up and defend whatever tunnel we're in."

"But there are thousands of miles of tunnels. How do you cover that with three of four clusters at the most?" Henry asked, happy that Torgga was much more patient with his questions than Buddy.

"That's why we had to switch to illusions when we ran out of troops and supplies," The dwab replied. "Luckily, the dwarves of yesteryear had the foresight to create convergence points where all the tunnels rejoin before proceeding to a lower section."

"Interesting," Buddy responded, but the single word was all he could get out between labored breaths.

"Lundarbrekka is the main one," Torgga continued. "It's a single bottleneck for the entire system, but just before Hjardharfell, there are three parallel junctions. If we can block all three, there is no other way around."

"But if one goes, then the others will get surrounded?" Henry was beginning to understand the tactical disadvantage the dwarves were fighting against.

Torgga nodded. "That's only part of the problem. What makes defending so much harder is that the monsters keep resurrecting. If we don't take the bodies and skeletons and dump them in the airshafts, they'll resurrect after a few days and keep attacking. We can't win a war of attrition against a foe that keeps coming back. After fifty years we ran out of arms and armor and couldn't afford the heavy losses. That's when we started experimenting with illusions. It took decades for my father to fully buy into using Geists instead of armored warriors. It's much more efficient to use magic to ward off the monsters of the Underdeep, but because the auras of the Silent are overpowering our spells, my father went back to what he knows best, a wall of dwarves.

"Sadly, we're out of reliable weapons and armor. Worse, we're out of practice; our smiths and artificers, our miners and even our beer makers. Without the forges, we've become little more than mushroom farmers."

"This travesty must be rectified." Ox hadn't been paying much attention to their conversation, but the mention of beer piqued his interest. "Those that practice the fine art of brewing and distilling must not see their precious craft atrophy. I will rescue you from a sober existence."

"That would be much appreciated, Lord Oxendine. All

of Hjardharfell would owe you a debt of gratitude." Torgga's smile grew under her bronze helmet.

Henry had more questions for Torgga, but he felt they were drawing near the dwarven stronghold.

The tunnel twisted and doubled back in a shallow incline. Torgga explained that the feature allowed for the largest gain in altitude over the shortest distance and mitigated the potential for loss of control of precious mining equipment.

Brilliant red auras assaulted them the moment they turned the corner. Henry was used to the exaggerated form of the dwarven illusions, but it was no less offensive to his senses. The auras surrounded monsters of various makeups along the sides of the expanding tunnel and were probably meant to distract oncoming creatures to the sides of the passage. Henry engaged his Resolve and forced the emotion to the back of his mind.

Status Effect Resisted: Enraged

Just past the red illusory auras was a solid wall of stone, but Henry knew better. He heard the twang of bow strings and saw arrows, bearings, and bolts of varying magical types pour through the fake wall and fly toward them. The attack faltered harmlessly on Buddy's force wall as they slowed their approach.

"Stronct!" Torgga bellowed in a thick dwarven command. The assault halted and the illusions burst into a white mist.

With the passage no longer obscured, Henry could now see another wall. This one was made of bronze-armored dwarves. Eleven warriors stood shoulder to shoulder, completely blocking the thirty-foot-wide tunnel. They had picked a point to defend with flush walls on either side beneath a dipped portion of ceiling that only left a dozen feet above their heads.

In front of the defending line, piles of slain cave creatures lay strewn about the ground, including the black and purple scorpions they had seen earlier. When the dwarves heard Torgga's voice, they relaxed their defenses and allowed workers to pass by. The workers began loading the corpses onto wooden carts, dragging them back behind the line, likely to be dumped down various air shafts.

"It's them. I told you they'd be back." A dwarf on the front line pushed back the visor on his helmet and Henry recognized the neatly braded beard that belonged to Einar, the first dwarven guard that had stopped them at the Hjardharfell city gates just a week earlier."

"They look almost as rough as us." A spearman just behind Einar replied. Henry recognized Floks with his unkept beard that looked like an unpruned marserial bush. The two dwarven guards, as well as the rest of the front line, carried exhausted yet hopeful expressions. Their armor was of ill repair and covered in blood and scratches. The front line was mostly equipped with bronze armor, but the spearman just behind had very little protection. They were doing the best they could with the sparse materials available, but the defenders were hurting.

Ox approached to a chorus of applause. The back line of gnomes pushed through the armored dwarves and surrounded the giant skeleton. "Ortegus! Ortegus! Huzzah!"

"Huzzah indeed my loyal minions. I have returned victorious!" Ox removed the dread ram skull from his own and handed it to his tiny supporters.

"Oooooh . . ." They collectively reached for the makeshift helmet, examining it and excitedly chattering among themselves.

"Troops! Lock it up. We don't have time for social hour." Another dwarf, whom Henry recognized as Craggitt, the Captain of the Hjardharfell city guards, stepped forward and impeded the skeletons approach, then addressed Torgga. "Lady Torgga, we're glad you're safe, but you need to get back to the city. We've nearly been overrun several times, and scouts are reporting something far stronger is headed our way. We're standing by for your father's order to abandon Hjardharfell." Dried blood stuck to Craggitt's head and Henry couldn't tell if it came from the sturdy dwarf or the dozens of dead cave creatures that lay before them.

"No, we can't abandon—" Torgga protested, but she was interrupted before she could finish the thought.

"Yes. We can." Thorodd's booming voice shook the cave and silenced everyone as the dwarven Elder approached from the rear of the formation. "We'll hold the lines until the city is evacuated while we still have the option. Torgga, you will return to help clear Hjardharfell."

"Lord Thorodd, you've arrived." Craggitt bowed as his leader approached. The dwarven line parted, revealing a stout dwarf with a white braided beard. He wore black plate mail and carried twin axes that glistened even in the dim light. *Golem steel and eversharp,* Henry thought, eyeing the dwarven leader's impressive gear.

Thorodd nodded to Craggitt, then turned to Henry. "You're too late for anything but a fight, skeleton."

"Then we'll settle for a fight." Henry retrieved a dread claw javelin from the leather ties and turned to look back down the sloping tunnel. The ominous ballad of the Silent made every warrior focus on the winding stone passage. It was weak and distant, but they knew it was moving closer. The beat of a dread ram's heavy claws was soon overtaken by the sound of stampeding cave creatures. Snarls, growls, hisses, and several other frantic animal cries echoed off the rock tunnel walls.

"We must have been just ahead of the flood," Beast said,

unsheathing her daggers. Henry was certain the skeletal elf was smiling.

"Here they come!" Einar shouted and lowered his visor. The dwarven wall followed suit as they steadied themselves for the wave of monsters.

Hundreds of creatures poured around the bend in the tunnel. Armor tongues, giant insects, skeletal animals, and myriad other monsters clawed over each other to escape the fear aura that spurred them on.

"Ox, Beast, Buddy," Henry said as he looked to Thorodd. "What do you say we give these tired dwarves a rest?"

"To arms, Harvey!" Ox cried in excitement and powered the flow crystals in his hammer. Thorodd squinted his eyes at Henry before a faint smile creased the dwarven elder's beard.

"Einar, may I borrow this?" Henry gripped the top of the dwarf's tower shield. The guard nodded his head in a quick affirmation before unstrapping and relinquishing the curved metal slab. Henry turned and addressed the skeletons. "Ox and I have the front. Buddy, slow the tide so we don't get overwhelmed. Beast, thin their numbers and finish off any that get past."

"Men and their orders . . ." Beast replied, but the gusto with which she twirled her daggers betrayed her feigned annoyance.

Ox and Henry took their place thirty feet in front of the dwarven lines. The ceiling sloped higher there and expanded to a much wider portion of the tunnel. A tsunami of flesh and bone rushed toward them. The frenzied creatures clawed over each other, ripping armored skin and sending bouts of blood into the air like whitecaps from storm-swept waves. The sounds of the approaching horde blended to form a deafening howl that drew closer by the second.

Then Henry saw it. Billowing from far back in the tunnel,

the black smoke of the Silent began filling any space that wasn't occupied with cave creatures. The oily smog swelled with an intensity that dwarfed their previous encounters.

Status Effect: Fear (Severe): STR -20%, RES -50%, HAR -20%. Healing effects reduced by half

Fear gripped Henry. There were hundreds of creatures rushing them, and Henry didn't know how many Silent would follow behind them. He couldn't protect himself, let alone his friend and the dwarves, and this was only one tunnel. He would fail, he had to get away from the black aura. He had to—

"It's rude to take all the fun for yourselves, skeletons." The dwarven Elder, who resembled a boulder more than a soldier, stepped between Henry and Ox. Thick golem steel plate covered his body and legs. His arms were bare, revealing bulky muscles coiled beneath the rugged flesh of his arms like pit vipers poised to strike. He held his ax-hammers low, but they shimmered with a prismatic gleam that held more than a hint of magical power. His white beard hung from the open face of his black, ornate helmet, and his broad shoulders glistened with sweat.

Thorodd, Dwarven Elder and King of Hjardharfell, had come to fight.

CHAPTER 14

The living wave of cave monsters rushed forward, cresting to a mass of bodies that threatened to collapse on the dwarven resistance just a few hundred feet away. Henry could feel his own fear echo through the dwarves behind him. Their voices quivered, and questions of retreat hung in the air.

Thorodd only rolled his shoulders back and closed his eyes. He flared his nostrils and sucked in a huge breath, then started to hum. Golden light radiated from the dwarf, faint at first, but it grew in intensity along with the volume of his tone.

Henry felt the sound from the dwarven elder vibrate through him, much louder than either the stampede or the Silent song that followed. It reverberated through his body, shaking past his bones and into his very core. The lightning tempest beyond Henry's mind swirled and sparked, almost as if in response. Thorodd began to sing.

A thousand years of stone and fire
Forge my hammer with the steel in my heart

Break their bones below our mountain
Hjardharfell

Henry's core picked up speed, sending blasts of lightning through the fog in his mind and chasing away the feeling of dread. He realized Thorodd wasn't just singing, he was casting a spell that was breaking the influence of the black auras, and it was working on more than just him.

Status Effect Subdued: Fear Dismissed

Status Effect: Broken Aura of Balance (Damage Resistance: All +1)

Henry's core pulsed to match the growing intensity of Thorodd's glowing light, and Henry realized it was more than a spell. The gold emission was Thorodd's aura. In unison, the dwarven line responded.

Oh, oh, oh
Hjardharfell is calling me
Oh, oh, oh
For glory I live on

His thoughts clear, Henry no longer saw a wave of approaching doom. Instead, his Perception picked out weak points; kill spots on each individual creature that rushed toward him. Excitement filled his mind as the fear dissipated. The cave creatures plowed their way ahead, now within a hundred feet as Thorodd's voice increased in volume.

Cracks and fissures in the mountains core
Fire blasts and Jallfoss roars

Flowing lava fills my veins
Hjardharfell

Henry felt the song flooding through him, and he steadied his nerves, preparing his attack. Behind him, crossbow strings pulled taut and leather gauntlets gripped spears and swords. The wave drew within a few feet as the voices of the dwarves rang out, reaching a crescendo that matched the approaching tidal wave.

Oh, oh, oh
Hjardharfell is calling me
Oh, oh, oh
For glory I live on

The cave monsters crashed into the defending skeletons, and the tunnel erupted into chaos.

Thorodd's axes lit up brighter than his aura, illuminating the encroaching horde. The dwarven Elder crossed his weapons in front of his chest, then whipped them to his sides, fully extending his arms and releasing a loud *whoosh*. An arc of golden magic launched forward and barreled into the swarm sending them tumbling backward. The creatures in the front were pushed back, but the rushing mob met the force from behind and it rose like a monstrous tidal wave, threatening to crash down on them.

Buddy matched Thorodd's magic with a force wave of his own, releasing an invisible blast that rushed over their heads and impacted the rising mass of creatures. Bones splintered and bodies ripped apart, sending a mist of blood and broken limbs flying back.

Not to be outdone, Henry and Ox joined the fight. Ox powered his massive hammer and swung with every point of his Strength. The weight of the weapon coupled with Ox's vigor would have been enough to sunder almost any foe. Combined with Buddy's force magic, it pulverized every animal withing his reach.

Henry forced Vitus into his legs and launched himself forward, bashing the oncoming enemies against the heavy shield. He would slam himself forward two feet, then step back one, giving him enough space to kill anything within reach with his dread javelin before pushing forward again. The wave stopped him from moving very far, but the creatures before him died en masse, crushed by his tower shield or impaled by his spear.

Henry took a moment between attacks to glance at Thorodd and for the first time, he saw what a dwarf at Tier **42** could really do. Thorodd wasn't a dwarf, he was a machine; a death golem all his own. Henry's Haruspex had failed the first time he'd activated it on Thorodd, but now he could see the elder's status. At **49** points each, his Strength and Fortitude nearly riveled Ox's, but when mixed with blinding speed and overwhelming magic, the creatures before him were shredded to bits. The dwarven Elder spun like a buzzsaw, cleaving his way through the endless monsters and leaving a bloody wake in his path.

Henry and Ox struggled to keep their footing in the growing lake of gore. They had to move forward or risk allowing the flooding creatures to climb overtop the piling dead bodies. Buddy lobbed balls of elemental magic to thin out the onslaught, but crazed animals wormed their way past by the dozens. Luckily, Beast hunted them down with lethal efficiency, leaving only a small number for the dwarves to clean up.

As quickly as the assault started, the horde thinned and eventually stopped. Henry thrust his javelin between the chelicerae of a final giant scorpion. Its stinger and claws flailed harmlessly against his tower shield for a moment before it burbled up black goo and died. He surveyed the carcasses strewn about the battlefield and saw Thorodd had taken a knee and was coughing up blood. The dwarf's brilliant aura held strong, but Henry could see the Elder was in pain.

Haruspex

Name: Thorodd the Broken

Race: Dwarf

Tier: 42

Health: 230/230

Steam: 42/189

Attributes:

    STR: 49

    MOB: 38

    FOR: 49

    ACU: 45

    PER: 32

    RES: 42

Resistances: Physical, Slashing, Environmental, Light Magic, Mental

Weaknesses: Dark Magic

Henry wondered how Thorodd could be injured yet still show full Health. He stepped toward the dwarf to help, but an earthquake stopped him in his tracks. A deep hiss and the scrape of huge claws accompanied heavy footfalls, much larger than that of the dread ram.

A giant lizard rounded the bend. Henry recognized it as the Greybeard Salamander they'd killed several days earlier. Its milky eyes gave it a sense of distracted fury, and the once red-brown scales on its back had lost their sheen and now looked dull as the grey plates on its throat that gave the goliath its name. Globs of thick saliva dripped from its horrid jowls between teeth as long as swords.

The giant salamander ambled toward them, fighting against the lifeless muscles that surrounded its bones.

Henry and Ox charged forward and separated to opposite sides of the tunnel, hoping to draw the salamander's attention, but the monstrosity drove forward, straight for Thorodd.

The dwarven leader stood and Henry expected him to run, but the black-armored warrior held his ground.

"Move!" Henry shouted. Thorodd only tightened the grip on his axes. Henry and Ox tried to attack the salamander's legs and body, but they couldn't even slow the giant beast. The colossal lizard opened its jaws large enough to swallow Ox whole and lunged at the dwarf. Thorodd refused to move.

The distance and the fury of battle obscured Henry's vision, but he was certain the corners of the dwarven Elder's mouth curled into a ruthless smile. It was the countenance of a true warrior in his element—in the literal jaws of combat.

Thorodd lifted and swung his twin axes in wide arcs just as the monster chomped down on him. With a sickening crunch, eversharp spikes erupted from the lizard's snout and lower jaw, along with bouts of congealed blood and splintered bone.

The monster writhed in pain. Every twist and jerk dug Thorodd's axes deeper into its flesh. Several jagged teeth cracked and broke against the dwarf's heavy armor. The monster braced its forelegs and strained to pull away, but Thorodd had somehow anchored himself to the ground, or perhaps the Elder was holding the Greybeard Salamander in place through sheer grit.

"Father!" Torgga shouted. She waved her hands in intricate circles and ropes of white mist encircled the lizard's head and body. The ropes solidified into red clawed tentacles and began to squeeze. The salamander hissed and wrenched its head, still unable to pull away from Thorodd's axes. To Henry's surprise, he saw the lizard's skin bulge under the pressure of Torgga's illusion-turned-real. The wriggling arms wrenched the lizard's head back and pulled its jaw open, ripping free of Thorodd's axes and showering the area with thick lumps of coagulated blood and saliva. Thorodd dropped to a knee again as the tentacles yanked the monster's head once more and pulled its mouth open even further. Bones cracked and tendons snapped as the creature's jaws folded back.

The lizard flailed and dug at the red arms ensnaring its head, but the squirming mass only grew thicker and squeezed tighter. Once again, Thorodd raised himself to his feet. He cocked his arm back and sprinted forward, spinning the axe in his hand and attacking with the blunt hammer end. The attack caught the salamander in the chest. Multiple ribs shattered on impact, and the force sent the undead monster reeling backwards.

The salamander flailed and crashed against the side of the tunnel, losing its footing beneath the mangled bodies of the smaller cave creatures. The tentacles pulsed and contracted. With a final squeeze, the lizard's skull crumpled, and the monstrous body slumped to the ground.

The tentacles disappeared in a flash of white mist, and Torgga ran to her father's side. Thorodd smiled and wiped blood from his mouth as his daughter steadied him.

"You old fart!" Torgga scolded. "You know better than to overdo it. And now you're covered in stinky dead lizard muck."

Henry approached the two dwarves and addressed Thorodd. "You're not injured, but something brought you down?" Thorodd's golden aura dimmed then faded completely.

Status Effect Subdued: Broken Aura of Balance Dismissed
Status Effect: Fear (Minor): STR -5%, RES -15%, HAR -5%

The boost from Thorodd's aura slowly diminished and the fear Effect crept back into his consciousness. The black smog billowed higher, though Henry's Resolve allowed him to resist most of it.

"You're a smart lad. Read my Status and tell me what it says," the dwarven elder spat.

"Thorodd the Broken . . ." Henry read aloud.

"The gods don't smile upon failure," Thorodd replied, perking up slightly after the sheen faded from his skin. "The aura comes at a cost for me. Though I may be old and broken, I'm still the strongest we've got."

Henry wasn't given the time to ask a follow-up question. Another rumble of heavy footfalls sounded from the tunnel and a dread ram rounded the far bend. Black oily smoke poured from its body as it galloped toward the group. Henry could make out its cruel smile from a hundred yards away.

CHAPTER 15

"Torgga, get him behind the lines, we'll take this one," Henry ordered the dwab. She nodded and helped her father through the parting wall of dwarves. Henry briefly considered asking Buddy if they should use the Magma blaster to melt the enemies in the narrow tunnel. He dismissed the idea, not wanting to accidently cause a cave in, or damage the ancient device before it could be used to restart the dwarven forges.

Henry readied his javelin and prepared to fight, but Ox stopped him. "This one is mine, Herbie." Ox stepped forward to the portion of the cavern with the highest ceiling. The dread ram's heavy claws pounded against the stone floor as it approached. Henry heard whispers of trepidation from the dwarven line as the fear Effect began to retake its hold.

Instead of preparing his hammer for an attack, Ox flicked the heavy weapon high in the air. The monster ignored the spinning metal as it bounded within a dozen paces of the skeleton. Henry fought every urge to join the fight and trusted Ox had a plan.

As before, the dread ram activated its Blitz Ability. Ox

stood his ground, and the bull-sized creature blurred forward. Just before catching the bash to his chest, Ox kicked his feet out to the side and dropped to the ground.

Unable to affect its momentum, the dread ram flew over the prone skeleton. As it crested him, Ox reached up and grabbed its lower jaw. He called on every point of his Strength and with a mighty heave, pulled the dread ram's skull into the stony ground. The monster's inertia and Ox's monstrous Strength forced the creature to smash face first in the rock floor and tumble to its back.

Still holding the ram's jaw, Ox leapt to his feet and extended his other arm to catch the falling hammer. He brought down the steel maul directly on the underside of the monster's skull. Force magic detonated and sent black chunks of brain streaming from every orifice in the bones. Henry knew the dread bones were sturdy, but he was still amazed they held up to the mighty blow.

Thick black blood dripped from Ox. The dread ram's body slumped, and all was quiet for a moment, until the party of gnomes erupted in a raucous cheer. "Huzzah, huzzah!" Ox pulled his hammer from the dead monster's body and raised his chin, smugly staring into the distance.

"We're not done yet," Buddy said, gesturing toward the tunnel's bend. Henry saw three more dread rams round the curve, followed by several dread claws. Strangely, the monsters held their position, as if studying the carnage before them.

"If you've got one ready, now would be a good time to Tier up." Henry shouted to the others. Without waiting for their response, he took a deep breath and allowed the Soul Essence to flow through his body as he acknowledged several flashing glyphs.

Haruspex

Cave Creatures Killed x45, Soul Essence Claimed, +1 Tier:
STR +1, MOB +2, FOR, +1, ACU +1, PER +2, RES +1

Strength surpassed first Threshold. Attribute bonus applied (STR +10%), Damage Resistance: All +1
Fortitude surpassed first Threshold. Attribute bonus applied (FOR +10%), Health +1 per point of FOR, +1 Health Regeneration per hour

Henry winced as something resembling pain sparked in his core. Immense power filled his body, and he could feel his bones charging with energy. He'd finally gained enough Attribute points in both Strength and Fortitude to overcome his Skeletal Body Status Effect and push those Attributes past the first Threshold.

Since he gained a Tier, his Health and Vitus filled to the brim, and as he checked his upper display. He noticed that he was already well into Tier **12**. He looked around to see the other three had also Tiered, but kept his attention on the mass of Silent that loitered at the bottom of the tunnel.

"What are they waiting for?" Henry asked.

"They're smart, likely planning their attack?" Beast offered.

"If they're smart, the cowards are contemplating their surrender." Ox stepped forward and bellowed at the gather Silent, taunting them to press their attack. "Are you afraid, or are you having trouble seeing me through your smoke? Maybe this will help." Ox pulled Torgga's muffle ring from his finger, and Henry expected a green hue to fill the chamber, but instead, a blizzard of white shrouded his view, expanding to either edge of the tunnel.

Status Effect Subdued: Fear Dismissed

**Status Effect: Temperance Aura. +5 Health Regeneration per hour,
STR +5**

Buddy stood beside Henry and they both marveled at the provoking skeleton. "Are you seeing this too, Henry?"

"Are you referring to the blizzard, or Ox's huge balls?" Henry asked.

"The idiot is going to get us killed. I just hope he dies first," Beast grumbled.

Buddy didn't respond, but the Silent took notice. The three dread rams charged in unison, and the dozen dread claws glided behind.

"Their bones are strong," Henry shouted to the line of dwarves, "but their muscles power their movements and are vulnerable. Maim them if you can. Ox, Buddy, hold off the dread rams until Beast and I thin out the others. Ready? Go."

Henry launched toward the charging dread rams with Beast holding his pace. The added Strength that came from advancing past the first threshold was unbelievable, and coupled with the boost from Ox's aura, his new power allowed Henry to fling himself forward at an incredible speed. He bolted straight between two of the dread rams, almost begging them to attack.

Blitz

One swiped for him with a massive claw, but Henry ducked under the arm and stabbed hard at a dark patch of muscle near its chest plate. The stab didn't cause much damage, but it gave Henry a chance to calibrate his new Attributes as he continued his rush toward the dread claws. Beast took the opportunity to attack as well, slicing the meaty portions of the dread rams then teleporting past.

The rams paid them little attention and seemed focused on Ox and his blizzard aura. Henry knew, or at least hoped, that

Ox and Buddy could handle the three brutes. Henry pressed forward and targeted the dread claws. There were twice as many as before, and as they neared, the line of Silent aimed their claws at the approaching skeletons and released a barrage of bone spears. With his boosted Strength and metered Blitz, he managed to counter the web of expanding claws.

His tower shield did little against the attack, but he didn't use it for defense. Instead, he waited for the claws to penetrate the metal then twisted it sideways and pulled.

Harden

Henry used the Perception Threshold perk to transfer his Ability to the metal shield. The claws became locked in the metal and Henry activated Blitz to change directions, then used his increased Strength pulled half of them off balance.

Beast took advantage of the distraction and Blinked to the middle of the gaggle before unleashing her Shriek. Henry was far enough away to avoid the brunt of the shock, but the sound still rattled his head. The dread claws near Beast fared much worse. Black blood spurted from the bulbous skulls of the monsters nearest her, while the others struggled to distance themselves from the elf.

Henry could tell that Beast's power had grown. She was faster and her magical movements iterated much more rapidly than before. Beast sliced the swollen patches of muscle on their arms, reducing their ability to activate their claws, then she jammed her frost daggers through the bottoms of their skulls.

Henry dodged bone spears with lethal efficiency and aimed his own spear either below their jaws or through their eye sockets, targeting what he perceived as their only weakness—their brains. He remembered the lesson from his previous fight with the dread claws and kept an eye on his Vitus. If he ran out of magic or got caught with a direct hit, the monsters would pin him down and tear him to shreds in seconds.

Blitz

Magic poured through Henry, allowing him to avoid all but a few glancing blows to his shoulders. His Fortitude and timely applications of Harden allowed him to shrug off most of the damage from the spikes. However, the dread claws were still remarkably fast, and their coordinated attacks left Henry few openings to land a strike. Luckily, Beast was just a bit faster. Henry saw little more than an afterimage of the deadly elf as she wove through the monsters. She only needed a split second to appear out of thin air, slice the robe-like muscles on their legs or the pulsing lumps on their arms, then vanish before the enemies could retaliate. Her subsequent attacks were well on their way before the previous victim even knew they'd been hit.

At one point, the interval between her attacks slowed and she stayed in place for an extra swipe of her blade. Dozens of spikes rushed toward her. At the last possible moment, she vanished, and the spears impaled the dread claw that Beast had been attacking.

She's toying with them again, Henry thought as the Silent tore through their own ally. Bone snapped under the force of vicious claws. Watching the horror before him, Henry realized the only thing that could pierce dread bone was more of the same foul structure.

Beast reappeared between the outstretched arms of another monster and sliced her blade clean through the dark tendons on either side of its jaw, leaving the lower teeth hanging and exposing a black brain underneath.

Beast vanished again, and Henry launched himself at the black pulsing flesh. He thrust with his javelin, blurring forward and skewering the vulnerable organ. The tip of his spear hit the back of its skull and burst through, sending bone shards and globs of brain flying. Ox's force-powered hammer hadn't been strong enough to crush the dread-ram's skull from underneath, so Henry was surprised to see the bone give to his javelin, even if it was the same material.

With their flesh flayed and useless, the dread claw's strafes and attacks became much less of a threat. Beast and Henry made quick work of the last few, but Henry knew if there had been any more his Vitus wouldn't have lasted. His added Strength and Fortitude had carried him through the fight, but he needed more than boosted Attributes if he wanted to finish this battle and make it to Lady Destria before Stavros.

Henry turned back to the dwarven lines to see Ox and Buddy's battle had been a success as well. Ox's white aura still spun like a raging blizzard, but when the massive skeleton returned Torgga's ring to his finger the gale vanished, and the Status Effect faded.

Status Effect Subdued: Temperance Aura Dismissed

All three dread rams had been killed. Buddy and three of his elementals stood around a blue pyre with a mass of dread monster at its core. Another lay scattered about the tunnel floor. Its limbs had been torn from its body and its remains had already begun to turn to ash with Ox's stoic form towering over them. Henry couldn't see the third as its body was encircled by dwarves, but it looked like the contingent had surrounded the monster and overwhelmed it.

"Ox, where did that come from? How did you change your aura?" Henry asked, approaching the huge skeleton.

Ox didn't respond at first, seeming lost in thought, and even Gator had stopped clacking his jaw. Ox spoke without looking at Henry. "I found a memory, though it wasn't my own. It seems I *have* traveled down a path similar to yours, Henry." Though cryptic, Ox's response was the first straight answer Henry had ever received from the brute, and also the first time Ox had used his correct name. Something hung on the tip of his mind, and Henry felt he and Ox were on the verge of an answer, but Thorodd's loud voice interrupted the thought.

"No time to waste, skeletons." The dwarven leader approached with two heavy breathing gnomes on his flanks. "The other two choke points are under siege. I hope you've got some extra Steam in your tanks."

Henry was annoyed that he would have to hold his questions for the time being, but the dwarf's query implied their help was still needed. The battle had drained him, though it wasn't enough to push him past his limits, and he repressed a twinge of excitement at the prospect of continuing the fight.

"How far away, and how bad?" Henry asked the dwarven leader. Thorodd looked peckish but seemed to have recovered from the aftereffects of his own magic.

"Cluster three's defense point is under a mile. We're holding off the big uglies, but our shields won't last forever. Some of the dwarves have started to flee," one of the gnomes responded.

"Cluster two isn't far, but it may be too late," a second gnome added, and Henry recognized him as Olafur, the bearded transmuter that had first welcomed the male skeletons to Hjardharfell. "Three big flyers with razor claws."

The other skeletons had joined the conversation and waited for Henry to respond. "Ox, Beast, follow him." Henry gestured to the first gnome, "and handle the dread rams. Torgga, Buddy, come with Olafur and me to take down the flyers."

The gnomes looked to their Elder for confirmation. Thorodd gave them a nod and they took off without another word, not looking back to see if the skeletons were following.

"Thorodd, can you hold this tunnel until we return?" Henry asked.

"Craggitt and I can handle any late arrivals," Thorodd replied, failing to hide a smile. "We'll send scouts to see if anything is still on its way, then we'll meet you at Lord Oxendine's tunnel."

"Just Ox is fine," Ox replied with a sullen tone. Everyone looked at the huge skeleton. His blank expression left the response unable to be interpreted. Henry wanted to ask, but knew they were running short of time. Instead, the skeletons gathered their gear and followed close behind their respective guides.

"Henry," Thorodd yelled behind the departing group. He stopped and looked back at Elder. "You need a better weapon." Thorodd tossed one of his eversharp axes. It spun in the air, glinting off the green light from the lumimoss. Henry caught the axe-hammer with a quick word of gratitude, then took off after Torgga and Buddy.

Craggitt stood beside his leader as they watched the skeletons disappear around the tunnel's curves. "You trust these monsters, Lord Thorodd?"

"That sounded like a question," Thorodd huffed.

"It was," Craggitt sighed. "Not only do you trust them with a treasured weapon and your daughter, but with the fate of Hjardharfell. We need you as our leader, not them."

Thorodd left his Captain's words hanging in the air for a long moment before responding. "My time to lead should have ended long ago. Torgga will soon take my place, but she can't be prepared to do so if we hold her back." Thorodd paused once more before finishing his thought. "And no, Craggitt, I don't trust those skeletons. I do, however, trust who they once were."

CHAPTER 16

The heavy axe-hammer felt good in his hands and a few mock chops showcased its masterful balance. The weapon's quality matched that of his melted sword and its heft would make great use of his upgraded Strength. Henry focused on the glinting steel of the gifted weapon as he followed Torgga, Buddy, and Olafur.

Haruspex

Item: Regnboga Tabar (Legendary)

Description: Weapon, Dwarven axe-hammer forged with eversharp.
Hardness 50, Structure 150/150

Lore: Fabled weapon of the Hjardharfell Elders, likely crafted by Solofur himself

Abilities:

Sunder IV: High chance to destroy any weapon or armor of Superior quality or below

Bypass III (Passive): Attacks ignore Physical Damage Resistance

Henry wished he'd had the tabar on the return journey

from Lundarbrekka. It would have made the battles much more manageable, and it would likely be useful against whatever they found at the next location. Olafur had said something about flying creatures with razor claws, and he could only hope the enemies weren't a new type of Silent.

The other gnome led Beast and Ox down a separate fork in the tunnel and out of sight. With a few quick strides, Henry easily caught up to Buddy and Torgga. The mage and dwarf were already deep into another discussion about magic while they ran.

"I was not aware illusions could become tangible. How did you do that? It must be more than merely increasing the influx of your Steam," Buddy asked the dwab as they trotted side by side.

"Well, I've been practicing, but I've never been successful with such a large illusion. The Ability is called *Manifest*, but I'm the only Geist who can cast it. I just got emotional and forced all my magic into the spell. It almost drained me, especially that last squeeze."

"Truly remarkable, Lady Torgga," Buddy said. "Is it conjuration?"

The dwab blushed and Henry could clearly see her grinning beneath her bonze helmet. "No. Strangely it's still illusion magic, though a highly advanced spell."

"What are you two talking about?" Henry interrupted.

"Torgga's magic." Buddy kept his attention focused on the dwarf as he responded to Henry. "She is pushing the bounds of a normal mage's capabilities."

"That *was* an awesome spell. But I need to know everything about your father's and Ox's auras. And why is Thorodd's broken?" Henry asked.

Torgga shook her head. "It's a secret that he refuses to talk about, but I've heard that an elf tricked my father, and he failed some trial."

Olafur interrupted their conversation. "We're almost there. I can still hear the fighting. We're not too late!" The gnome quickened his stride and continued to guide them through the winding tunnels.

The sounds of battle echoed off the stone walls, and Henry also heard the buzzing sound from earlier. This time, it was much louder and almost rattled inside his skull.

Status Effect: Fear (Minor)
Status Effect Overcame: Fear Dismissed

More concerning than the sound was the cryptic black aura oozing over the ground. Its presence confirmed that more of the Silent were forcing the attack. Curiously, Henry saw patches of white mist from the dwarven illusions throughout the smog. Henry expected the fear Effect to be much stronger, but the mist somehow suppressed it. He asked Torgga, and she theorized that one of the dwarven Geists must have figured out how to counter the Effect. That was likely the reason the dwarven line was still fighting and hadn't been sent running in fear.

"Though they can't perceive the black aura as we do, they've nearly countered its influence. When this is over, I will need to spend more time with these dwarven Geists." Buddy wasn't one for compliments, but Henry could tell when the mage delivered one. The dwarves were slowing winning the blue mage over with their proficiencies in magic—Torgga most of all.

They rounded a final bend to reveal similar carnage to the previous battle site and found this dwarven cluster had fared much worse. The tunnel was smaller than the other and only two cells of nine composed the defensive formation. Their lines were in shambles, barely holding, and some of the support dwarves fled the battle along with several cave creatures that had made their way through the shield wall. Two soldiers bled from deep lacerations as an orc dragged them away from the front line. They writhed in pain, but at least they were alive. Henry saw two other warriors who had succumbed to their injuries.

Stray salamanders and armor tongues were the least of their worries as Henry's fear had come true. A new type of Silent was wreaking havoc on the dwarves. Three horse-sized monsters zipped above the battlefield, held aloft by four pairs each of short, fat wings extending from purple muscle sacs on their backs. The wings buzzed too fast for Henry to make out their structure, but they were definitely the source of the resonance. Six claw-like legs hung from each cigar-shaped body made of plates of dread bone. Their heads were a horrifying human-like skull, but with extended jaws unhinged to reveal rows of curved teeth and two giant fangs extending down like a cobra. Narrow shoulders supported two mantis-like arms that sported jagged blades longer than most swords.

Dread-Mantid, Henry thought. *Beast is going to love that name.*

Though the creatures looked awkward, they were extremely agile in the air. They changed directions like hummingbirds as they dove and sliced at the row of dwarves, ripping into metal tower shields like scythes reaping a harvest.

Henry's group approached the rear of the soldiers, and he focused Haruspex on the monsters. The Ability resisted him at first, and Henry thought it would fail like it had with Thorodd, but he forced his Perception against the monster's Resolve and the information appeared in his view.

Haruspex

Type: Dread-Mantid

Health: 163/163

Vitus: 26/56

Attributes:

    STR: 32

    MOB: 43

    FOR: 39

    ACU: 14

    PER: 24

    RES: 20

Resistances: Physical, Mental (Immune)

Weakness: Magic, Fire

Lore: An advanced iteration of the Necromancer's minions, the Dread-Mantid's aerial agility is the bane of ground-based combatants

Ability Discovered: Haruspex IV (Divinity). Delve into shared awareness and access even more insight. Superior Perception may reveal concealed knowledge. (PER +7, AFI +7, HAR +1) Supersedes item Abilities

Henry didn't expect Haruspex to Tier, so he pushed away the notification, not wanting to figure out what *shared awareness* meant. It wasn't important at the moment, but the Dread-Mantids' Attributes were. With Mobility so high, it was no wonder they were devastating the dwarven resistance.

The sharp mantid blades sawed through the heavy dwarven tower shields and there were almost as many injured and dead dwarves as active defenders. A stout dwarf in the middle of the fray held the line together with what looked like magical shielding. Flashes of orange emitted from his hands as corresponding disks appeared before the dwarven wall, just in time to deflect slashes from the dread-mantids.

The dwarf's black, golem steel armor made Henry assume he was the Captain leading the cluster. The dwarf's swirling circles of magical defense were effectively repelling the mantids heavy attacks, though the creature's speed and relentless assault kept the Captain too busy to mount a counter assault.

The dwarven wall limited their Mobility and made them easy targets. Their shields prevented them from maneuvering in the tight tunnel, but Henry knew if they abandoned their defenses, they would perish just the same.

The only capability that seemed to damage the dread-mantids were two gnomish artificers flinging burning rocks from strange metal contraptions with surprising accuracy. One of the rocks impacted a flying horror and knocked it sideways. The mantid recovered before it hit the ground and buzzed back into the air. The artificers effectively held back the flying monstrosities, but a dwindling pile of skull-sized boulders near the devices indicated they were running low on ammo.

Henry only had a split second to analyze the battle. He formulated a quick plan as they neared the rear of the defending dwarven wall. "Olafur, I need you to start healing everyone you can," he shouted, sprinting past the gnomish transmuter.

"I'm on it," Olafur replied, halting to help the orc attend to the two ambulatories.

"Torgga, can you do the tentacle illusion again?"

The dwab responded by forming balls of white mist around her hands. The intensity in her eyes showed she was up for the task.

Henry knew this type of Silent was even more deadly than the dread rams, and he was thankful Buddy had come with him. He managed a glance back to address the mage. "Buddy, they're weak to magic and fire. Light 'em up!"

Buddy had already begun casting his elemental magic, allowing swirls of power to manifest in the air around him. Balls of lightning, ice, and blue fire filled the tunnel, streaming just over the line of dwarven helmets and careening toward the airborne horrors.

White mist enveloped the closest dread-mantid, manifesting into the same clawed tentacles Torgga used to finish the Greybeard Salamander, and wrapping around the flying monster. The ball of red flesh and white dread bone dropped to the ground with a heavy crash, splashing the carnage of slaughtered cave creatures on the tunnel floor in all directions. The mantid sliced and bit through the illusion, but Torgga manifested more tentacles as quickly as the monster could cut them. A second mantid dropped on its ally and chopped at the wriggling mass of tentacles, leaving only a single monster hovering in the air.

Henry pulled magic from his core and forced it into his bones.

Blitz

Coupled with his improved Strength, the Ability launched him over the line of soldiers and directly at the flying dread-monster. Unfortunately, Henry's plan didn't go beyond the initial attack, and he realized once he was in the air that he couldn't change his direction. The mantid capitalized on his mistake.

The flying monster ignored a blast of blue fire impacting its plated torso and swiped at the air borne skeleton. Henry was barely able to maneuver the Regnboga Tabar to block. The dwarven axe held up, but downward swipe rocketed Henry to the floor.

Mobility +1

He gained an Attribute point from a failed attack, and luckily, the mantid's counter didn't finish him. He landed on a giant dead beetle, and it softened the impact enough to only take his Health down by a quarter. Henry didn't have time to be grateful for the soft landing as the mantid stopped its wings and dropped on top of him.

Blitz

Harden

Six insectoid legs, all tipped with vicious spiked claws, as well as two bladed arms, jabbed and swiped at him, piercing into the rock below. Henry pushed off a mangled beetle corpse and rolled away, avoiding the deadly dread bones by an uncomfortably small margin. The monster stomped and stabbed at him. Henry swung his legs and spun to his feet, blocking a slicing claw with Thorodd's tabar but leaving himself wide open for the monster's second attack. The bladed bone sliced into his armor just as he poured enough Vitus into Harden to weather the attack. The mantid pulled back for another strike, and Henry activated Blitz to avoid the lightning-fast claw. Before he could dodge, three fire-covered bucklers smashed into the Mantid and engulfed half its body in a blue blaze.

Intense heat and pressure forced Henry to scramble away from the magical fire as his Health ticked lower. Henry realized his **-5** fire resistance was more significant than he had originally thought and made a mental note to avoid Buddy's attacks as much as possible. The dread mantid also reacted to the fire, and it was less than happy. The monster immediately lost interest in Henry and charged at the mage, plowing through the defending dwarves and ignoring their swords and spears.

The monster cleared the space between itself and the mage in a heartbeat and sliced with its jagged claws. Buddy's Mobility was low, but he managed to compensate with his magic. The mage extended his hands forward and unleashed a blast of force magic, launching the mantid back but also sending himself tumbling. One claw managed to hit Buddy, but it only cut into his robes and sliced the leather bandolier from his chest, scattering flow crystals through the rocky tunnel.

With his low Fortitude, Buddy recovered slowly, but the Mantid resumed its attack immediately. The monster raced toward the mage, scattering rubble and slain cave creatures in its wake. Henry forced the rest of his Vitus into Blitz and caught up to the charging mantid just as the dread monster reached Buddy. It raised its bladed arms to finish the dazed skeleton. Henry swung the tabar and activated its Ability.

Sunder

The axe's blade sunk into a purple flesh sack and buried in the creature's thick chest plate behind the pulsing flesh. Unfortunately, the Ability failed to penetrate the bone. Henry pulled on the axe, trying to free the embedded weapon, but the Mantid spun and sliced. Without enough Vitus to activate Harden, the dread-mantid chopped through his arm, leaving a skeletal hand and forearm dangling from the embedded tabar.

Injury: Right Arm Amputated (Severe): STR -25%, MOB -25%

The mantid eyed the damaged skeleton, blood lust filling its deranged eyes. With one arm and no weapon at the ready,

Henry felt the end was close. He refused to give up, frantically searching for a way to take down the huge insectoid.

The monster stepped toward him, slow and menacing, and it accidentally kicked one of Buddy's flow crystals with its spiked leg. Though Henry wasn't proficient with magically charged flow crystals, the item gave him the inspiration he needed. The mantid brought down both of its clawed arms. Henry rolled forward between the descending strikes and reached for the crystal with his remaining arm. The chance at victory and the hopelessness of his situation filled him with more adrenalin than fear. Though Henry doubted he would survive the next few seconds, he was almost enjoying himself.

He wrapped skeletal fingers around the crystal, not able to get a clear view of it, but when his bones touched the magical item, he instinctually knew what spell Buddy had put in the crystal and feared what was about to happen far more than dread mantid claws. A quick glance at his Status showed that he only had **3** Vitus points remaining—not enough to activate Blitz. His Health, however, was just below **50%**.

Henry's roll stopped as his feet hit the ground directly below the mantid's head. He heard the rush of wind from the monster's descending attack, but he could only push hard with his feet and extend his remaining arm above his head.

Sacrifice

Blitz

Henry pulled enough Vitus from his body to charge one last attack. The magic shot through his bones and launched him straight into the air. The dread blades impacted where he had been just a second earlier, and Henry buried his fist below the Mantid's jaw, deep in its brain.

Henry squeezed his hand and activated the lightning spell in the flow crystal. A flash of brilliant light filled his vision. The tempest in his core roared as massive arcs of electricity burned through his bones. Henry embraced the onslaught of magical energy and forced his eyes open.

CHAPTER 17

Rain pelted his face, and a chill wind swept across his body. Henry knew he was no longer fighting the Silent in Hjardharfell. He now stood in the middle of a jagged outcropping of stone.

Twice now, he'd appeared in this desert landscape, and he was starting to see the commonalities. Each time he'd been hit with lightning he'd been transported to this location. The first was from a discharge from Ox's warhammer while fighting a giant squid in Husavik. The second came from Smyrna's soul-eating golem, absorbing and reflecting Buddy's spell.

He'd been transported to a foreign landscape, and the experience was so real that it had left him questioning which reality of his was true. Now in the desert, his body had been fully restored; a powerful muscular physique seemed so much more real than the existence of a skeleton fighting monsters under a mountain.

On his first journey to the desert, he'd appeared in a wide-open sandscape, assaulted by a blistering sun and a driving sandstorm. He'd tripped on a yellow glass boulder and touching it had sent him back to the mountain with an electrical shock. On the second, he'd tried to unearth the rock. He'd revealed a few feet of what looked like dark yellow glass; marbled with metallic blue veins and other red and gold minerals.

After the intense heat forced him to abandon the excavation, he walked for miles in the harsh environment, until the sun and sand were replaced by a raging tempest and torrential downpour. He followed a shadow in the storm above him, and through lightning strikes he navigated to what he hoped was cover but was now looking unlikely to be so.

From miles way, the outcropping of dark grey stone looked like the spikey leaves of a cactus plant that jutted and crossed in random directions. He'd made his way to the center of the stone island, slipping on the wet, uneven surface until he came to a much larger version of the yellow, barely-opaque stone. Lightning silhouetted the rock to show that it towered twenty feet above him, but at the base of the monolith was a small cave; the height of a man and only slightly deeper. Jagged, yellow stone spikes blocked the entrance of the cave, like the clamped teeth of a giant beast, leaving barely enough space to fit an arm through.

Now he was back a third time, and what was inside the cave drew his attention and almost made him forget the screaming wind in his ears and pelting rain on his skin.

Lightning flashed and lit up the cave, alternating bright light and dark shadows from the jagged stone teeth that blocked the entrance. But there was another shadow that Henry saw deep within.

A man cowered at the far side of the cave with his back to Henry. He squatted on the ground and was nearly naked, save for a few tattered scraps of cloth that threatened to fall from his emaciated body at any moment.

The man's arms were wrapped tight around his torso, and

he shivered ever so slightly. The bones of his spine and shoulders poked beneath his sickly-purple stretched skin, making him look days away from being one of the skeletons in Jallfoss.

"Hey!" Henry shouted. "Hey you!" The man didn't respond—didn't even move—though the tips of his long, matted hair continued to tremble under his shivering, which seemed to grow more intense by the second.

The man must be deaf, Henry thought. The howling wind was loud, but the cave provided enough cover from the elements for the sound to make its way a few feet.

"Hey!" Henry shouted again, louder this time. The man's head tipped up slightly. His face was covered by shadow, but Henry saw his jaw move slightly as he whispered something Henry couldn't hear. "Are you trapped here? I was trying to get out of the storm when I found this place. You look like you need help."

The man turned his head slightly, but Henry still couldn't see his face. The wind had started to die down, and the lightning had moved further away, but the flashes were still frequent enough to light the cave every few seconds. Just above a murmur, the man croaked in a weak, tired voice, "Leave me be, specter. I haven't the time for your taunting today. Too much to do. Too much to do . . ." His voice trailed off, and he dropped his head again.

"Who are you?" Henry persisted. "And how did you get here? I'm lost and don't know where this is, but maybe I can help you."

"You toy with me, specter." His frail body continued to tremble, but he didn't even lift his head to respond. "I know all too well how dangerous hope can be for the mind of a prisoner."

Henry pulled off his tunic and threw it to the man. It wasn't much, but it would provide him more warmth than nothing at all. The tunic landed a few inches from the hunched figure. The man picked up his head weakly to take in the cloth, then slowly turned toward Henry. The skin on his face was pulled even tighter than that of his body and was crossed with black veins that pulsed as the man shivered. A few brown teeth hung from pale gums as the man struggled to breathe through his mouth. His sunken eyes were wide in a fearful expression, as though his skin were too tight to allow him to blink. His unfocused stare wandered over the tunic and around to Henry but didn't seem to take in anything.

His gaze drifted back over the cave wall, and he looked like he was going to bury his head again, but he paused, and his eyes widened even further. Joints popped as the man unfurled an arm and placed a palm on the yellow stone of the cave wall. With a shaking finger, he traced the blue veins, scratching at them with a long yellow nail. His mouth quivered, but Henry couldn't tell if it was from a shiver or another emotion.

"You are not a specter at all. No, no, you are not." His voice was still little more than a whisper, but now it had a hint of force behind it. His eyes traveled back to Henry and this time locked onto him. "You're a traveler, just like me, searching for answers." More bones popped. Muscles groaned and already-tight skin stretches as the man unfolded himself to stand. The movement was slow and looked painful, but the man's eyes never left Henry's. "I haven't had a real visitor in quite some time. Tell me what it is that you need, and maybe I can give it to you."

"You look like the one in need of help, my friend. Who put you here, and how can I get you out."

The man didn't answer Henry's query. Instead, he struggled

to lift a foot and take a step toward the front of the cave. He wobbled, his frame barely able to keep him upright, and Henry feared he would topple to the ground and die before he could be freed.

"Where are you from, young warrior, and where are you going?" Strange expressions fought their way over the man's face. Excitement, trepidation, fear, doubt; all obfuscated by the man's ghastly skin.

He has obviously been in the cave a very long time, of course his reactions would be strange, Henry posed to himself. "I don't know, I keep getting transported here every time I get hit by lightning—"

"Lightning!" the man croaked, more to himself than to Henry. His face stretched further as his mouth opened into a smile, but it looked more like a snarl than a reflection of happiness. "I believe we *can* help each other."

A roar tore through the dark sky. The wind howled and lightning flashed, but a rush came from the storm above that was much deeper than the wind. The stones around him shook from the sound and Henry struggled to keep his footing.

Henry felt something around his wrist and turned to see the man gripping his arm through the stone bars of the cave. The man's mouth was now truly a snarl and his eyes fully open in a fearful visage. Henry tried to pull away, but the man held with a strength that he didn't expect.

A sickening smell of rot and decay wafted from his mouth as the man shouted. "It comes for you, Remnant. Only I can save you."

Henry pulled, freeing himself from the man's grasp, but he stumbled and fell backwards, landing hard on the rocky surface. The man still reached at him from between the columns of stone, shouting and growling at him, but Henry could barely hear him over the raging wind and roar of the storm above them.

Henry heard the rush of a powerful gale and looked toward the sky. It was nothing more than a shadow hidden by rain until it opened its mouth. Electricity filled a maw of long jagged teeth, and quickly spread over its scaled body to the tips of its wings. The lightning was too bright for him to make out much detail, but if it wasn't a dragon, Henry had no other name for the monster.

It flew directly at him, its jaws opening into a deafening roar. Henry rolled as the dragon released a blast of pure electrical energy. He tumbled far enough to put a stone spike between him and the blast, but it did little. The stone shattered under the lightning bolt as Henry struggled to evade. Lightning spread through the ground, snaking along the rocky surface like deadly fingers searching for him.

There was nowhere to run. The lightning forced itself into his body, burning its way through his skin and boiling the blood in his veins. His insides felt like they were exploding, and his mind stopped functioning from the most intense pain of his life. But there was something more.

He felt himself starting to lose consciousness, but the lightning in him felt alive. Like it was a being attacking him from within. He followed it through his body as the pain intensified, threatening to rip him apart. Henry forced his awareness into the obscured consciousness of his mind, bursting through the fog and appearing at the thunderhead in his core. It had grown, and now spun like the raging storm overhead, throwing its own bolts of lightning. Henry opened the channels of his mind and felt Vitus flow from his core.

Like a school of meat-eating muscuda fish sensing wounded prey, the dragon's lightning let go of his body and poured into the billowing cumulus. The two electrical forces met, combining into a flash of blinding azure and white. His vision went black, as the sound of exploding mantid brains filled his ears.

CHAPTER 18

Status Effect: Third Path of the Desert. STR -7, MOB -7, Health -10, Fire Resistance -10, Lightning Resistance +10

Modified STR below first Threshold. Attribute bonus removed

Access to Remnant Attributes granted: Might +1, Affinity +1, Harmony +1

Ability Granted: Spark I (Evocation). Imbue gear with minor lightning effects. Chance to increase the Tier of weapon Abilities. Temporary Effect: -1 Max Health per use

The detonation from the lightning-charged flow crystal blew chunks of dread mantid brains across the entire battlefield and flung Henry thirty feet to the middle of the scattered dwarven line. He bounced along the rock floor but had enough awareness to review flashing glyphs in his Status display. His Vitus was nearly empty, but his Health was just below **50%**, a testament to his newfound lightning resistance. Henry rolled to a stop and quickly gathered himself to his feet, struggling to overcome the wobble in his legs from the massive decrease in his Strength.

Every head on the battlefield turned toward Henry, including the two dread mantid's recently freed from Torgga's illusion. The white mist where the tentacles had been quickly faded as Torgga's Steam ran out. All was still for a moment until a heavy thud from behind him indicated the lightning blast to its brains had finished off the first monster.

The tunnel erupted in a new round of chaos. The remaining mantids, spurned by their fallen comrade, charged directly at Henry. He needed to even the odds and quick, but without a weapon he didn't have many options. The mantids were fast, but they didn't have range, though neither did he. Their long, sword-like mandibles were too devastating to allow him multiple attacks, so he couldn't rely on his strategy of maiming them. He had to get close and kill them with one hit.

He knew he was too far away from Thorodd's tabar and too low on Vitus to reach it before they would overcome him, but he saw his javelins laying on the rocky ground, just between him and the approaching monsters. They were the only weapon sturdy enough to pierce the dread bone.

Four blue fire elements rose from molten rock in front of the charging mantids and unleashed a barrage of fireballs. The dread mantids slowed their approach to address the hail of searing heat, giving Henry the time he needed to reach his weapons.

He sprang forward, covering the ground between them as quickly as he could, but the detriment to his Strength and Mobility sapped the speed from his bones. The fire elementals dealt little damage to the mantids before razor-like claws banished them, but Buddy's summons gave Henry enough time to span the distance. The front mantid reached Henry and swiped heavy claws at the running skeleton. Henry ducked his head and tumbled forward, struggling to retrieve the weapon with his remaining arm, but the instant his boney fingers grasped the wooden shaft, he righted his body and thrust straight up, hoping to pierce the mantid's vulnerable skull.

The monster was too fast for his attack, and it caught him with a glancing blow, sending him tumbling to the ground between it and the other Silent. Henry recovered and thrust hard with his spear, hoping to take one of the monsters with him as two sets of deadly claws descended on the wounded skeleton.

Instead of dread-bone impacting dread-bone, both the mantids' and Henry's attacks rebounded off orange circles of magical defense. Henry recoiled from the impact as he heard the cry of dozens of dwarven voices. Like the dread mantids, the cluster had also rallied from Henry's victory over the first monster and reformed their line to charge at the winged horrors.

Fire cloaked bucklers, burning rocks, and dozens of dwarven spears crashed into the distracted Silent and sent them reeling. Henry looked around to regain his composer as the dwarven Captain rushed past him and summoned more orange shields to protect the attacking dwarves.

Buddy got to Henry's side and helped him to his feet. "You're slow again. What just happened?"

"Another vision," Henry managed. "I lost my Strength Threshold, but I have a new Ability."

"I hope it's useful," the mage said, turning his attention back to the battle.

Henry had no choice but to assume it would be, but he was too low on Vitus to try using Spark. He focused on the Health in his bones and activated his Ability to pull it into his core.

Sacrifice

Ability Discovered: Sacrifice II (Transmutation): The line between mind and body begins to blur. Trade a portion of your Health for a lesser amount of Vitus. Damage Resistance (Mental) +2, Max Vitus +5, +2 Vitus per 5 Health sacrificed

The Ability upgrade barely registered to Henry, but what he did notice was that even though his Vitus replenished, no Health was pulled from his bones. Instead, the spear in his hand shrank significantly.

That must be how they power their bodies, he thought. The purple sacks weren't muscle, they were Health stores. Henry reversed the flow of magic through his core, converting Vitus back to Health and pushing it into the spear, and sure enough, the spear shot back to a full-sized spear, just a few inches short of its original length.

Henry had a weapon and a source of Vitus, and not a moment too soon. The dread mantids had recovered from the dwarven rush and returned to the air on their buzzing wings. The shield line held, but the monsters were unbelievably agile in the air, and they easily avoided the barrage of fire and spears as they returned heavy clawed attacks. The dwarves were quickly losing their advantage and Henry feared they wouldn't last long.

"Can you get me up to one of them?" Henry shouted at Buddy.

The mage gave him a questioning look between launching fire balls. "Are you planning another heroic attack? They are faster than you in the air."

"They're not faster than your magic. Just get me on top of one of them." Henry pulled all the Vitus he could from the dread javelin, then did the same to his last three that lay scattered on the ground, keeping one in his hand. With his

Vitus full, he nodded to Buddy, and imagined he could see the skeletal mage smiling.

Henry turned and ran toward the battle, eyeing a hovering mantid that was engaging several dwarves. Trusting Buddy, he leapt into the air and felt a massive force launch him to the top of the tunnel. Buddy's magic took over and aimed Henry in a huge arc that sent him careening directly toward the hovering Mantid.

Buddy's aim was close enough, but far from gentle. Henry collided with monster, plowing directly in the center of its back between the four sets of wings. He grabbed onto the purple muscle sacks and held on tight as the mantid bucked and spun in the air, beyond agitated at the unexpected passenger. With only one arm, Henry had to clamp his teeth around the shortened dread spear so he could grip the bone and Health organs. Henry clawed his way up the monster as it spun through the tunnel, plowing into the stone walls and trying to smash him off.

Henry tightened his grip and squeezed his legs around the monster's bone plates, hugging his body close to avoid wild claw swipes as he waited for the right moment. Focused on Henry, the mantid smashed into a large outcropping of stone, sending itself, along with Henry, spinning through the air. It wasn't ideal, but it was the split second he needed. In a smooth motion he pulled the spear from his mouth, reversed the flow of Vitus through his Sacrifice Ability, and stabbed at the back of the Mantid's skull.

The dread bone pulled most of Henry's remaining Vitus from his mind as it grew ten-fold in an instant. The mantid's skull resisted, but with a loud *crack*, it gave way, and the spear broke through and impaled the monster's brain. The dread-mantid shuddered and spasmed, careening uncontrollably toward the ground.

Sacrifice

Henry pulled the Health from the dread javelin and shrunk it back down to dagger size, only retrieving a portion of the Vitus he had originally invested. He leapt from the monster's back seconds before it smashed into the ground. He landed hard, unable to cushion himself with only one arm, and felt several bones crunch against the stone tunnel floor. The impact forced him to release his hand, and the dread bone flew from his grip.

Injuries:

Right Arm Amputated (Severe): STR -25%, MOB -25%

Broken Rib (Moderate): STR -10%, MOB -10%

Broken Shin (Moderate): STR -10%, MOB -10%

Concussion (Moderate): MOB -5%, ACU -5%, PER -5%

Status Effect: Dazed (Minor): PER -5%

Henry was injured and a bit dizzy, but alive. He pulled himself to his feet, barely able to stand on his broken leg, and surveyed the battlefield. The mantid had landed far behind the dwarven defenses, dropping him nearly on top of the first corpse. Henry reversed his Sacrifice Ability and tried to mimic a healing spell for himself instead of pouring it into a dread bone.

Sacrifice

Ability Failed: No viable target

I guess I can only pump Vitus into dread bones, not my own, he thought. *I'll have to use Harden to prevent further damage.*

With only one mantid remaining, the fight had turned into a stalemate, but Henry could see the dwarven resistance faltering.

Buddy and Torgga had resorted to helping the artificers reload their strange catapults, likely drained of Vitus themselves. The dwarven Captain had taken several hits from the mantid's claws, and his shields were no longer protecting the other warriors.

Henry looked to the first mantid corpse and saw Thorodd's axe still imbedded into the thick bone. He hobbled over to it and pulled on the weapon. It took several tugs, but he eventually dislodged it. The resounding buzz from the final dread-mantid shook his broken bones and the cries of dwarves filled his ears. Henry lifted the tabar and staggered toward the chaos as quickly as his shattered bones would carry him.

Henry neared within twenty strides of the fighting dwarves as the mantid dove and sliced two fully armored defenders clean in half. Their screams echoed through the tunnels before fading to dying gurgles. Olafur ran to the downed warriors, but Henry saw the damage was too severe for the gnome to save them. The rest would soon follow if Henry couldn't end the battle quickly.

Henry tightened his grip on the axe and shouted as loud as he could. "Hey big ugly! I'm the one that killed your friends!"

Once again, every head in the tunnel turned toward Henry, including the final dread mantid's. The monster stretched its jowls open large enough to devour a gnome whole and charged the stumbling skeleton. Black smog poured from the monster, but Henry pushed the Effect from his mind and took inventory of his Status. His Vitus was below a quarter, and his Health down to **10%**. His broken bones would prevent him from dodging, so he only had the chance for one attack. He had to wait until the mantid was too close to miss.

The monster neared within ten paces as Henry cocked back his arm, pulling all the Vitus he could from his bones and powering his Abilities.

Blitz

Spark

The axe charged with lightning, and he threw it as hard as he could. His legs and ribs crumbled, and the tabar spiraled from his hand, sinking deep into the center of the mantid's skull with a heavy *thunk*. Without sturdy bones to carry him, Henry tumbled to the ground, his fall dropping him below the flying mantid's uncontrolled charge.

Henry smashed into the ground, unable to slow his fall. He heard the thunderous crash of the monster behind him but his empty Vitus and nearly matching Health left him spinning with vertigo. Soul essence flooded into his bones, and he could almost hear the quiet agony of the creature.

His vision blurred and he felt he lost consciousness. Several moments passed until his eyes slowly refocused on four heads hovering over him.

"Is he dead?" Torgga asked, frantically trying to piece together Henry's broken ribs.

Olafur pushed her hands aside, trying to prevent the dwab from doing further damage. "No, he's still with us, but I don't know how. I think I have enough Steam to keep him stable. Where's his arm?"

"I think it's over there. Elnodd, fetch the skeleton's arm," the dwarven Captain ordered a nearby defender. There was a flurry of action as they worked to heal Henry, but after a few moments he felt the gnome's magic flow through him enough to allow him to focus on the flashing glyphs.

Dread-Mantid Killed x3, Soul Essence Claimed, +1 Tier:
Tiers: STR +1, MOB +2, FOR, +2, ACU +2, PER +1, RES +1

FOR +1

ACU +1

MIG +1

Henry yelped as Olafur's magic, along with the Soul Essence from the Tier gain, knitted his body back together. He felt substantially weaker after the loss of his Strength Threshold, but his other four Attributes that had surpassed that mark had carried him through the battle. The effects from his desert visions were starting to have a dramatic impact on his development, but now he was certain that lightning was causing him to experience the strange journeys. Why was a dragon trying to kill him? Who was the man trapped in the yellow glass cave? Also, why had the man called him, 'Remnant', and what did that mean?

"Suicidal maniac. Ye saved us and likely all Hjardharfell. On yer feet, ye boney heimshkingi." The dwarven Captain grabbed Henry's arm and hoisted the skeleton to his feet. A quick Haruspex revealed the dwarf's name was Harraldd and he was nearly as strong as Craggitt.

Henry was still gathering his thoughts when he caught Buddy's stern gaze. "Another close call, Henry. There's no glory in a second death."

"You're right, but I couldn't think of a better option," Henry stammered.

Buddy dismissed his excuse. "What happened out there? Your Attributes dropped significantly after killing the first . . . *dread beetle* . . . I assume you're calling it."

"Dread mantid, but yes. The lightning from the flow crystal sent me back to the desert with a much stranger encounter this time. When I returned, the accompanying Strength reduction dropped me back below the first Threshold. I'm getting stronger and weaker at the same time."

Torgga gave Henry a heavy pat on the back. It was meant as a reassurance, but the jolt further loosened the tattered gladiator leather and chain armor hanging from his bones. "Your definition of weak must be different than mine. Killing three Silent almost by yourself is no short task."

"Luck is easy to confuse with skill when things work out in your favor," Buddy warned.

A loud hiss and a scratch of claws against stone drew their attention. With the black fear aura gone, one of the fleeing salamanders had turned around and now charged the group. Blue fire swirled around Buddy's hand, but before he could sear the attacking lizard, Muji sprung from the mage's leather pack and jumped to the floor with a heavy *hmmph*. The instant his furry body hit the stone he leaped toward the lizard with unexpected agility. The tiny trogold flung himself at the salamander and latched onto its neck.

"Beak . . . bea, mmph. Beak," Muji released a muffled squeak, and his tiny fangs tore into the lizard's neck. The cave creature raked at the fur ball, but its claws couldn't penetrate the matted pelt. Blood sprayed from the scaled neck and Buddy rushed to the flurry of skin and fur. The mage had surrounded himself with an intense blue flame, but before he got there, the salamander fell to the ground with a *thud*.

Covered in lizard blood, the tiny trogold stood on his hind legs, looked quite pleased with himself.

Henry and Torgga joined Buddy as Muji took to cleaning his fur. "I didn't know you were so concerned for the little guy," Henry chided the mage. "I guess now we know what a Tier 15 trogold can do."

"Tier 15?" Torgga raised her eyebrows as she used her Amulet's Assess Ability on Muji. "How did that happen?"

While Henry explained Muji's extreme Tier progression,

Harraldd approached and gave them an update. "I've sent scouts to see if any more of the Silent are comin'. So far, we're in the clear. Our Geists and artificers learned to counter the fear Status Effect and hold the monsters back, but we couldn't have brought the ugly things down without yer help. Never thought I'd be thankin' a bunch'a skeletons."

"We're happy to help, but if your cluster can handle the tunnel we need to meet up with the others," Henry said.

Harraldd agreed, then scribbled something on a sheet of paper, rolled it up, and placed it into his Farscroll. It was the same device that Torgga had used earlier. Henry eyed the magic item intently as it flashed, then he turned and made his way to the back of the tunnel with Buddy and Torgga.

Olafur was busy healing but looked up to wave to the departing skeletons. "I'm assigned to this cluster, so I have to stay here and get everyone healed, but Torgga knows the way. Go see after Beast and Lord Oxendine. I'll catch up with you later. Don't do anything stupid."

Henry, Buddy, and Torgga returned the wave, then set out to find Ox and Beast.

CHAPTER 19

Beast didn't need to taunt the rows of dread claws before them; Ox had that covered simply by wearing the massive dread ram skull as a makeshift helmet. The idiot had a way of infuriating his enemies to such an extent that could only be matched by his moronic charm. He'd won over the gnomes with whiskey and the dwarves with his undeniable battle prowess, but Beast was repulsed by his undeserved confidence and absolute surety of whatever thought popped into his mind.

However, their short run to join the dwarven cluster had been a different interaction than she was used to. Instead of his normal boasting and enthusiasm for battle, Ox had followed Ozler, their gnomish guide, in stoic silence. Deep in thought, it was Beast who found herself unexpectedly engaging him for the first time.

"What's on your mind?" she asked, her silent footfalls matching the pace of Ox's heavy stomps.

He looked over to her as though he'd just noticed her presence. After a long pause, he answered, "Regret . . . regret and loss, though I can't place the origin of the feelings. The empty memories are the same for all of us. My concerns can wait."

Short as it was, that was the first serious conversation the two had shared, and it ended with them running headlong into a fierce battle between the dwarven cluster and at least thirty dread claws.

Ox's confident demeanor had returned the instant he entered the fray. "I swear on Minoa's unbound chebblies, you are the weakest enemies I've ever fought. All of you, assail me at once, lest I die of boredom."

The dread claws swarmed the massive skeleton. Beast couldn't tell if Ox's goading had incurred their wrath or if he just appeared as the biggest threat, but it gave the elf the perfect distraction. She wove through the monstrosities, severing the vulnerable muscle sacks from their iron hard dread bones.

Ox's maul had long run out of force magic, but his impossible Strength still laid waste to waves of dread claws. The bump in her own Strength from Ox's temperance aura and the weakening Effect it had on the Silent was all the advantage she needed to slay them with ease. That didn't mean she didn't enjoy testing her skills on them.

Void

Her magic wasn't yet strong enough to hurt their bone spears and carapace, but the spell removed a perfect sphere from the bulging purple sack that powered the monsters' bodies. She'd stowed her daggers and now only had need for her fists. Every blow she landed removed a skull-sized circle of flesh from her enemies and sent it to whatever plane the magic's chaos chose.

Eight dread claws moved to surround her, but between her incapacitating strikes and Ox's aura, they were no longer a threat. Dozens of spears shot toward her, and she waited for the last possible instant to avoid the attack. She wondered if they could feel the hope of killing her just before she snuffed out their lifeforce with her superior skills.

Blink

Powerful dread talons shot through blank air and Beast appeared between two dread claws. She placed a palm on each of their bulbus faces and let the magic flow from her shadow core. They didn't stand a chance.

Void

Strands of muscle that held their jaws in place, along with their eyes and brains, vanished from existence, leaving behind empty skulls. The two monsters collapsed as another barrage pierced the space between them that Beast had occupied just a moment earlier. She reappeared on the other side of the battlefield with a knee on Ox's shoulder opposite the annoying amalgamator skull and wedged her other boot between the brute's ribs for stability. She was out of arrows, but those would have been ineffective against any of the Silent. That didn't matter, as the battle would be over shortly.

Only a hand full of dread claws remained and they all shot their deadly fingers at the two. Beast easily dodged, teleporting behind the attackers and delivering another barrage of lightning quick slices to their vulnerable points. Ox, however, took the attack directly. Instead of evading, he allowed the claws to pierce his bones. Before they could retract their weapons, he gripped their extended spear fingers and pulled.

The Silent could do little to resist Ox's Strength as he spun and smashed the lot of dread claws against the cave walls. Black and purple flesh liquified in a violent spray that painted a scene of carnage against the tunnel's rounded stone. The lump of bone and muck dropped to the floor and lay still.

The dwarven line stood in shocked silence at the massacre that Ox and Beast had delivered to the monsters, but after a still moment, all the gnomes erupted in cheers of unanimous admiration. Only Beast noticed that Ox's pompous demeanor had stymied slightly as the massive skeleton ignored his gnomish followers and smugly surveyed the heaps of crushed bodies on the tunnel floor. He replaced Torgga's muffle ring on his boney finger and the white blizzard that surrounded him faded instantly.

The dwarves set to work immediately. Under the guidance of their Captain, they sorted bodies and scouted for further danger. Beast let them know that the Silent were only shells and they would find permanently dead bodies inside the dread monsters.

The dwarven Captain approached the two skeletons and offered his thanks. "I've heard of yer lot. Glad ye came to help. Our shields were useless against them, and my defensive magic wouldn't have lasted a minute more. The eerie sound of their claws is gone, along with the thump and hum from whatever else was in these tunnels. I've sent the scouts forward, and their reports should be coming back soon." He tapped the wooden cylinder on his belt. "But for now, no news is good news. It looks like we're safe."

A quick Assess revealed the Captain's name was Jokull, but Beast was more interested in the magical item on the dwarf's belt. "May I see that?" She pointed to the wooden cylinder.

"Of course." He unstrapped the item and handed it to Beast. It was carved with dwarven lines and patterns with several flow crystals inlayed in the design. The container looked like it'd seen better days.

Assess

Item: Farscroll (Superior)
Description: Accessory. A dwarven communication device that can

transport small items over moderate distances. Hardness 5, Structure 14/20

Ability: Send. Use stored Conjuration magic to transport small items to a paired device

Beast handed the Farscroll back to Jokull and the Captain returned to his duties, but Beast knew that with a good artificer, she could improve the item's Abilities to suit her needs. That could wait. For now, she needed to talk to Ox.

"What's with the blizzard?" she asked the giant skeleton who had just finished repairing his skewered bones.

"Aura of Temperance, allegedly. But humility seems more accurate," he said flatly. "Henry hears a woman shouting his name, I only feel the breath of someone that I promised to protect. Anything beyond that is fog. As for the aura, I'm not sure how it works or where it comes from, but I have questions for the dwarven Elder."

The pad of feet from the back of the tunnel drew their attention and they saw Henry, Buddy, and Torgga making their way toward them. Torgga's cheerful voice rang through the tunnel when she saw them. "Beast, Ox, I'm so glad you're alive. I mean, not any more dead, I guess."

Beast returned the pleasantry, but Ox's vision locked on Henry and the smaller skeleton felt a strange sensation, like water flowing through his bones. It was intrusive and unpleasant. He realized Ox was using Haruspex on him.

"So, Hughie, I see you've unlocked your other Attributes. Have you figured out how to use them?" The incorrect names were back, but Ox surprised Henry with the direct question.

"Are you going on about that again? I only see the same six we all have." Beast's annoyed tone had also returned as she Assessed Henry.

"No, he's right. Might, Affinity, and Harmony. But I have no idea what they do," Henry affirmed.

Ox grabbed Henry's skull and twisted it from side to side like a jeweler examining a gemstone. The horns from his dread ram helmet stopped just inches from Henry's face as Ox spoke. "It took me a bit to figure out, but it seems I've had them for much longer than you. Answer me this, minion. Any unexpected Abilities?"

Henry freed himself from the huge skeleton's grasp and pushed Ox's hand away. "Yes, actually. I learned Spark. It lets me add a shock attack and increase the Tier of item Abilities. I think I got it from my desert path, but I have no idea why."

"From what I've gleaned, its power should be based on those new Attributes. Anything else you've discovered?" Ox prodded.

"Well, I modified Sacrifice to pull Vitus from my javelin. That made it shrink and I was able to reverse the Ability to make it grow again, but when I tried to heal my own bones, it didn't work."

"Your Affinity permitted you to modify the spell, and it can do quite a bit more than that. Harmony allowed you to understand how the bones work. Maybe that knowledge will be useful to the gnomes and dwarves," Ox explained, but Henry still had trouble understanding just what exactly the new Attributes did. Strength, Mobility, and Fortitude were of the body, and Acumen, Perception, and Resolve were dealt with his mind. If that was so, what were the other three connected to?

Buddy's frustration at not being included in the conversation about magic boiled over. "Now hold on. That's not how magic works. And why do I have no knowledge of these Attributes? I can't see them on your Status.

"Excellent question, skeleton, but I doubt Lord Oxendine

has the answers." Thorodd's booming voice echoed through the stone tunnel causing the working dwarves to snap to attention. Thorodd approached with Floks and Einar in tow. He waved a hand, dismissing the cluster's reverence and indicating they should return to their work.

"It sounds like you do?" The accusatory tone of Buddy's voice wasn't lost on the dwarven Elder, but he chose not to engage.

"Some. From what I hear, my warriors were in a sorry state before you arrived. Once again, we're in your debt. That boon will have to wait. We've stopped the flood of monsters, and I'm satisfied with the current state, but I doubt it will last. We're low on supplies and my defenders are out of schlitz. Another attack like that and Hjardharfell may be overrun. We'll need to start packing up and leave the mountain." Thorodd had expertly changed the subject as though his statement about Ox's knowledge required no further explanation.

Before Buddy could press the question again, Torgga accosted the Elder. "But father, we'll be at the mercy of the Ikritians, or even worse, the elves. I'll fight to the death, to my very last breath, to protect Hjardharfell."

"No. You'll live." Henry heard the hint of resignation in Thorodd's voice. "The humans and elves are hopefully more merciful than the Necromancer. I know every dwarf, gnome, and orc under me would die to defend our home, but if Hjardharfell is to live on, we can't do it in this dying mountain."

Buddy dropped the large leather bag from his shoulders and plopped it on the ground. The mage shooed Muji out of the way and pulled out the Magma Blaster. "If I may interrupt, it sounds like your shortfall is in logistics, not will. Could you defend Hjardharfell with this?"

Thorodd eyes grew wide. He shook his head in disbelief

before taking the rod from Buddy. "Unbelievable. You actually did it. Torgga, why didn't you tell me this with your message. This changes everything."

Torgga didn't even try to suppress her grin. "We were busy, and I ran out of charges on my Farscroll."

Thorodd's critical look at his daughter only lasted a moment before he replaced it with a smile. "Your message only referred to the golem steel and eversharp ore. The materials didn't matter when we were preparing for battle, but with the Blaster in our hands we'll need to get those components to the forges right away.

"Einar! Gather the smiths and alchemists and meet us at the forges," Thorodd ordered.

"Right away, Lord Thorodd," the dwarven soldier answered.

"Flokks! Take as many dwarves and orcs as Jokull can spare. Retrieve the golem steel and eversharp and bring it to the forges. The ancient smithy at Hjardharfell pales in comparison to the mighty machines in lower Hraunfass, but if Torgga's description is accurate, the store is more than enough to outfit every last cell." Thorodd ordered the other dwarf.

Henry held up his shortened dread javelin and powered it with enough Vitus to triple its length.

Sacrifice

The bone shot forward, startling Thorodd and drawing everyone's attention. "These Silent bones are of legendary quality. Your tabar couldn't even break them until I added my magic. I think they can make exceptional weapons and armor."

Thorodd held out his hand. "I'll have that back now that you're done with it." Henry returned the Elder's weapon, then Thorodd continued with his orders. "The bones too, Flokks."

"I'm on it, Lord Thorodd." Flokks snapped his body to rigid attention, then ran off to carry out the orders.

Thorodd kept his eyes on Flokks as he addressed the skeletons. "I want to ask you to stay and help, but you've done more than your part, and I can sense your urgency."

Henry nodded. "You've got what you need to save Hjardharfell, but you're right, our mission is pressing. We found out that Stavros is the Necromancer, and he's headed to Lady Destria's ghost. If we can get there first, maybe we can stop this whole curse. I can only speak for myself, but if we succeed, I'll return to help you recover your kingdom."

Thorodd's face turned pale at the revelation, but before he could stutter a response, Ox placed a massive hand on Henry's shoulder. "My minions will not face the dangers below without the emperor at their side. I too shall return."

Buddy stole a quick glance at Torgga before he spoke. Without his skin, the look was almost imperceptible, but it was there, nonetheless. "There is much to be discovered below. If it is in my power, I will assist." Torgga held back tears as she beamed at Buddy.

All turned to Beast, not wanting to force her hand, but waiting for her intentions. She was staring at Ox, but she hid the meaning of her visage better than Buddy. When she realized everyone was watching her, she crossed her arms and scoffed. "You'd all be long dead without me. I might as well keep helping."

Thorodd's forehead creased with heavy concern. "It is more than generous to offer your service once again, but how do you know Stavros is the Necromancer. If that is true, I would be foolish to lead my dwarves to his clutches."

Henry described the memories from the dying boy, the undead man, and the evil Lord as quickly as he could. When he finished, Thorodd beckoned them to the tunnel's exit and toward Hjardharfell. "You're stronger than I thought, but you won't stand a chance against Stavros with your current gear." Henry looked himself and the other skeletons over and knew Thorodd was right. Their armor was in shambles and covered in blood; Ox was naked minus his dread ram helmet and the single shoulder guard holding Gator. Their weapons were sub-par at best.

"Give us until the morning to properly outfit you," Thorodd continued. He didn't allow them the opportunity to argue. With the Magma blaster securely in his hands, the Elder led them back to Hjardharfell. "Enough wasting time. Accompany me to the forges. We've got much to discuss, and I want everything fired up before the next attack."

The four skeletons and Torgga followed Thorodd up the tunneling, leaving the toiling defenders to their tasks.

CHAPTER 20

Thorodd led the undead contingent through winding corridors, obviously in a hurry to activate the forges. Buddy and Torgga lagged behind, enveloped in another of their conversations over magic. Beast carried Muji in the crook of her arm while the trogold dozed softly.

Ox and Henry were eager to get something out of the dwarven leader, and it seemed Thorodd was ready to talk. "I still can't believe the Necromancer installed himself as Livadi's predecessor. For years Stavros has thrown his Acolytes at the Underdeep like a starving man casting for fish, but I never imagined he was actually the Necromancer."

Henry lowered his head. "It's my fault. I hit a young Acolyte with a javelin, linking us to my Drift Amulet. I thought I'd killed him, but he made his way back to Stavros. The Ikritian Lord ate the boy's soul so he could pry into my mind. I don't know how much information he got, beyond our quest to revive Destria's ghost."

Thorodd's heavy footsteps quickened as the dwarf took in Henry's story. "Your memory is still dustier than an abandoned quarry, so you probably don't recall the fairy tales about how Jallfoss was founded?"

Silence indicated their ignorance, so Thorodd continued. "It's a simple story. Malek Vik'Taus, the Archon King, as he's been called, battled the Oxendines and Degonharts at the very peaks of Jallfoss. After a bloody battle, Malek was slain, and the Oxendines secured their right to rule. There's a lot more fluff, but that's what we tell the children."

"A bedtime story filled with battle, there is no better way to lull a child to sleep," Ox said, more serious than sarcastic.

Thorodd chuckled. "I can't argue with that, but stories are only stories. However, we've got five thousand years of stories in our scroll storage here, and I've had nothing to do for a hundred years but read those scrolls and drink garbage sharinji swill."

"I take it your studies led to something?" Henry asked.

"It did. I know the whole story of Jallfoss. Well, most of the story, but it didn't matter until now. The mountain range of Jallfoss is named after the original god himself. We dwarves believe that Jallfoss was a master blacksmith and the lava below us is nothing less than the forge he used to create the world. Every hammer strike from the god would send sparks far and wide, spreading life and knowledge to the far corners of the land and seas. He's still down there, forging away and keeping the world turning.

"Our gnomes will tell you that Jallfoss carried all life in the form of jewels in a giant chest strapped to his back. He stumbled while traveling over the mountains and spilled his horde, scattering the jewels far out of his reach. The god was so heartbroken at his loss that he simply laid down and died. Then we have the damned elves, who think Jallfoss was a tree, or some nonsense like that, with fruit that fell and grew all life in the world."

"What do these stories have to do with the Necromancer?" Henry asked.

Thorodd's gruff response and side-eyed glance indicated the Elder wasn't used to being interrupted. "I'm getting there. Be patient. We've got a long walk. Every race has a different story for how the world began, but they all lead to the same thing. Something splintered off from Jallfoss at the start of the world. I believe there were eight splinters in total that became what surface dwellers call the *young gods*. Five of those gods went on to create beings known as *Primals*. The Primals became the shapers of the world and begetters of all existence today."

"Primals . . ." Henry and Ox each mouthed the word.

"Celestials and Archons. Dragons, Spriggans, and Giants. Those are the five elder races. There was also Veletos, who became the oceans, and Solaire, the firebird, who took to the heavens and never returned."

"That's only seven," Buddy said.

"Outside of Jallfoss, most humans worship the Raven, the mysterious god of wisdom. I have little more patience for the religions of men than I do for those of the elves. Now, stop getting me off topic. I've read through thousands of scrolls and books, and this is what I've pieced together. Whether Jallfoss was a god, a cataclysmic event, or creation itself, it doesn't matter. The Primals came from him then existed in this world for eons," Thorodd explained.

"However, over the endless expanse of time, almost every Primal has disappeared—killed from wars amongst themselves, eroded into lesser forms, or departed to another domain, perhaps. Most Primals interacted with the other inhabitants of this world; some even had their favorites and developed ways to bestow their power on select, lesser beings. These second-generation Primals were known as *Remnants*.

A Remnant is a mortal who has claimed the power of their Primal progenitors, and that's where the story of Jallfoss proper begins."

"Remnant. The prisoner from my visions used that word," Henry recalled.

Thorodd looked at Henry and the skeleton felt the uncomfortable sensation of Haruspex as the dwarf analyzed him. Thorodd snorted and shook his head, but only replied to Henry with a gruff, "should have known."

Thorodd took a deep breath and continued as though Henry hadn't said anything at all. "Malek Vik'Taus was a Remnant of the Archon Primals. He even went so far as to call himself the Archon King. He was obsessed with power and ravaged the world as he built up his army."

"Until?" Buddy asked, he and Torgga had stopped their conversation and now listened intently to Thorodd's tail.

"Until he battled two other Remnants. Raynott Degonhart, Dragon Remnant, and Osyrian Oxendine, Celestial Remnant. The battle lasted for a long time, some accounts saying it raged for over a hundred years and shaped the world as we know it. Eventually, it ended with the Archon King destroyed at the peaks of Jallfoss, miles above us."

"What does your historical account have to do with what's happening now?" Buddy did nothing to hide the impatience in his voice.

Thorodd slowed his stride then stopped and faced Buddy. "I don't think they killed Malek."

None responded while they waited for the dwarf to continue. The only sound was Muji's heavy breathing as the trogold slept in Beast's arms. "The Archon King allegedly had the power to bring the dead back to life and was said to have forced legions of the undead into his service. I think he was too strong to kill, so Raynott and Osyrian banished him, far into the depths of the mountain."

"We have a clear candidate for the Necromancer," Beast mused. "The other Remnants sealed him away . . ."

". . . only to have the dwarves release him a hundred years ago?" Henry finished.

Thorodd lowered his eyes. "Aye, much to my shame, it was my own dwarves that brought about our destruction. The genius Smyrna himself doomed us all. Livadi must have known. He pressed us to dig deeper, even funded our tunneling. He was hoping to steal the Archon King's power. Luckily, Lady Destria Oxendine was strong enough to banish both from the mountain. Malek was probably greatly weakened from his battle with Lady Destria, but the Archon King was clever. He didn't return to the source crystal like we all thought. The coward must have fled with Livadi, then took fifty years to regain his strength before taking over Ikrit. Now he's threatened by the only force to ever stop him: the Oxendines. More specifically, the Empress herself."

Thorodd turned away and resumed his trek. "I've read that the most powerful Remnants can ascend to their Primal form. If Malek, now Stavros, is truly the Archon King, then he can create his own Remnants.

"The Silent," everyone said, nearly in unison.

Thorodd nodded. "He's every bit of the Necromancer that we fear. A week ago, I would have called it all salamander shite, but now, Hjardharfell has no choice but to stop his army from boiling up from the fiery depths. That's where you come in, skeletons. I tell you this in confidence. You're our best hope to finally stop Stavros. You must bring back Destria, but you're going to need our help to get here. That's why we're going to the forges. Give us one night to get you geared up and on your way."

"Thorodd, what does your story have to do with your and Ox's auras?" Henry felt like he'd asked the same question a dozen different ways but never gotten a straight answer.

"Thorodd is a Remnant," Ox replied. He'd been strangely silent for the entire discussion, but the confidence in his voice convinced Henry he spoke the truth.

The dwarven elder chuckled. "No. A Remnant is one who had been blessed with the full power and none of the weaknesses of their Primal. I'm broken, and that ship has long sailed. However, Lord Oxendine, you *are* a Remnant. As for you, Henry, only time will tell. Sadly, that is all I can give you for the time being. The rest you must discover on your own."

That was only a partial explanation, though the tone of Thorodd's voice indicated that part of the conversation was over. Still, one more thing bothered Henry. "You said the Primals are *almost* gone? What did you mean, *almost?*"

They had followed Thorodd past countless turns and forks in the tunnel and through several illusory walls, until he brought them to a hidden passage. The Elder felt around the stone until they heard a *click*, and the boulder dropped to reveal the entrance to the Grunischwald and its massive mushroom trees. Thorodd led them through as he collected his thoughts. "I did say that. Dragons are gone. Giants have turned to stone, but the forests live on. At least one Spriggan remains. The elves used to worship it, but after the Betrayal, it was corrupted. Once it created wild creatures of the forest. Now it spews forth monstrosities. The elves fight them from above, as we now fight the Silent from below. To get past the Spriggan's monsters, you're going to need weapons and armor."

Torgga cringed at the mention of the forest Primal. "Oh Buddy, be careful, I've never seen the Spriggan's horrid creatures, but I've heard tales of their terrible nature."

"I match her sentiment, but Ghara's Sprigs aren't the most dangerous thing above us," Thorodd grumbled.

Though he dreaded the answer, Henry asked, "What is?"

"Fracking Elves."

CHAPTER 21

Broken stone bit into Jai's skin as he scrambled up the rubble. Blood poured from more than one wound, and his hands and feet struggled for purchase on the loose rocks. Minor injuries were the least of his worries. Higher on his list of concerns were the three chomping beaks from the Sprig trying to eat him. His training was not going as planned.

The Sprig's fat body, stubby wings, and taloned feet resembled a plucked chicken—and that was where the similarities stopped. It was the size of a large dog, and no feathers clung to its black and green skin. It scratched jagged wings on the unstable footing and stretched its three heads as far as it could, chomping in turn and hoping for a bite of the panicked elf. The Sprig was on the small side of Ghara's creations, but at that moment Jai realized it was probably more than he should have taken on.

Jai kicked, smashing the heel of his boot in one of the creature's faces. Its eyes spun and it let out a pained squawk, but another head bit at the elf's ankle and tore a chunk from the shoddy cloth of his pant leg.

The Sprig would have already been on top of him, but the

disfigured creature had a long spiny tail, and holding on to that tail for everything it was worth was Jai's Guard.

The frail skeleton under the Hold spell could follow simple orders—attack, follow, stay—things that one could train a dog. The command Jai chose to use for this particular encounter was, "Help!" Luckily, the magic in his circlet correctly conveyed intent to his boney follower, and the undead attempted to keep the Sprig away from its master.

The Sprig, however, quickly grew tired of the interference and turned on the skeleton. Ghara's monsters didn't typically interact with the undead, but in this case, preventing it from a meal was enough to draw its ire. The Sprig turned and launched itself at Jai's Guard, snapping bone with its beaks and rending ribs with its mangled talons. The Sprig ripped an arm and a leg from the skeleton and continued to attack. Jai knew the skeleton would only keep the Sprig's attention for a few more seconds so he didn't waste time. He drew the farmer's blade from his belt and leapt onto the monster's back.

He grabbed ahold of one of the creature's necks and squeezed hard with his legs around its bulbous body while jabbing the knife deep into a throat. The Sprig screeched in alarm and bucked hard, trying to throw the attacking elf from its body. The Sprig bounced, and Jai found himself tumbling through the air. He landed hard on his back, the air rushing from his lungs as his knife flung from his hand, landing too many paces away for him to retrieve.

One of the Sprig's heads hung limp, almost to the ground, and dripped with black blood. Wounded and angry, the vile creature launched itself at the vulnerable elf and Jai saw his death in its black eyes. The boy cocked back his leg and thrust as hard as he could, hoping to damage the monster before it could sink its beaks into his flesh.

His foot connected, and the monster stopped its advance. Jai thought his kick had made the monster reconsider its attack, but when the Sprig still tried to claw toward him, he realized the blow hadn't been effective—his Guard had. The skeleton was missing an arm and a leg, but it had bitten down on the Sprig's tail and was frantically pulling with its remaining limbs to keep the monster away from Jai. The elf could see his Guard was the losing battle.

Not wanting to waste another moment, he dove deep into his core and put all the Guile he could into his summon spell. He forced the magic out into the ether, hoping to get an answer from anything.

Beckon

A swirling amber orb formed just in front of the Sprig, and something answered Jai's call.

A fanged mouth, followed by a red, spiny frill and the scaled body of a snake shot forth and collided with the Sprig. The serpent's yellow and black skin glistened even in the dim light of the upper city. It was well over ten feet long and thicker than one of Jai's legs, and it struck the Sprig with enough force to send it plummeting down the rubble slope. The snake coiled around the Sprig and began squeezing even as the two rolled.

They stopped falling after a short tumble, writhing in a mass of scales and putrid plucked skin. Even though it was the biggest snake Jai had ever seen, it still struggled to control the corrupted fowl. Jai only had one weapon left and he wasn't about to let the Sprig have another go at him. With practiced form, he pulled the sling from his belt and loaded it with a rock in one smooth motion. It only took him a second to spin the weapon fast enough to launch the munition. His countless days of practice paid off and the rock hit true, cracking one of the Sprig's skulls and allowing the snake to take control of the battle. Jai shot three more stones in quick succession before the snake had the bird fully in its wrap. The Sprig's eyes bulged, and the elf heard its bones snap as it died with a final sickening squawk.

Jai slunk to the ground, exhausted from the battle but still trembling from adrenaline. His muscles burned and his hands shook. He was alive. He collected his senses and looked around to find that the snake had let go of the Sprig and now sat coiled. It lifted its head several feet in the air and stared at him with eyes betraying an intelligence the elf didn't expect.

"Thank you, Lord . . . Snake. I can tell you want something, but I don't think I have anything to give you," Jai said to the summoned serpent. He could have sworn that the snake squinted its eyes and shook its frill before an amber sphere formed around its scaled body. The snake swirled and stretched, then disappeared back into the spell.

An unnerving calm settled over the rubble of the destroyed city, and Jai realized the only sound in the immense cavern was his own heavy breathing. He focused on his heaving lungs, slowing their pace and clearing his mind. The Sprig's crumpled body lay further down the rubble. Its eyes still bulged and one had even popped from its socket and lay in a pool of thick black and green blood.

Jai surveyed the remains of the elven city. It had been one of the jewels of the high elves, second in beauty only to the Oxendines' upper spires. The houses were immaculately carved in stone, and everything was in perfect order. The rubble upon which he had fought the Sprig had once been Ghara's largest temple outside of her lair. Wooden scaffolding that had been set up to repair the destroyed holy site had long collapsed under the relentless ebb of time's decay.

Jutting from the nearby rubble were half a dozen rib bones

that stretched toward the sky like the outstretched hand of a giant skeleton. Each bone was as wide as a tree trunk, indicating that the long dead monster buried under the razed temple had been nearly incomprehensible in size.

Jai had been told that it wasn't the Turning that destroyed this particular city, but a battle between four outsiders and a very mean troll. As the story went, the foreigners, with the aid of the forest elf Sentinels and Lady Destria's court wizard, destroyed a troll with unbelievable powers. Much to the displeasure of the high elves—and Bharat in particular—Lady Destria commissioned the strangers instead of punishing them.

Ha, Jai thought, *serves the high elves right.*

The city's inhabitants had just started rebuilding before the Necromancer attacked, and Jai could even make out the fallen remains of partially built stone archways and wooden trusses. The stories the old elves told of the troll had kept him awake as a child, scaring him just as much as those of the Necromancer.

Just a few feet away, Jai's Guard balanced unsteadily on a single leg. With the Sprig dead and no further instruction to obey, it would remain there and heal until Jai gave it another order.

"That was way harder than I expected, but if we want to get stronger, we have to keep fighting Sprigs—little ones, of course," Jai explained to the mangled skeleton.

His Guard didn't respond, but at the thought of growing stronger, Jai's eyes grew wide, and he fished out the Drift Amulet from his sweat covered tunic. The **1** had filled and was flashing. As Mayur had described the experience, he relaxed and let the Soul Essence flow though him. Exhaustion drained from his body, and his mind cleared. He felt his muscles harden. A flashing icon caught his attention. He focused on the symbol and marveled as the information popped into his view.

Sprig Killed, Soul Essence Claimed, +2 Tiers:
STR +1, MOB +2, FOR +1, ACU+1

Ability Upgraded: Beckon II – Summon stronger creatures with a greater chance to determine their origin and control their actions. Max Vitus +5, ACU +1, RES +2

The power from the Drift Amulet was everything he expected. He was well on his way to becoming a Sentinel. *Just wait, Talji,* he swore. *I'll show you what a forest elf can do.*

CHAPTER 22

For the most part, Beast seemed unaffected by Thorodd's repetitive jibes at elven kind. She was much more interested in Torgga's Farscroll and cuddling with Muji than listening to the dwarven Elder go on about *pointy-eared-this* and *bald-faced-that*. If she had uncovered any memories of her past, she was doing a great job hiding it.

Thorodd led them through a series of tunnels and deep into the bowels of Hjardharfell. The city was a bustle of activity and Henry could see fear and apprehension in the eyes of its citizens as he passed. Dwarven mothers hurriedly stowed food and supplies into burlap sacks and yelled at their children. Many elderly inhabitants wandered in a daze, unable to come to grips with the urgency of an impending invasion. Their leader, however, was ready to assuage their trepidation.

"Stop packing and help with the forges," Thorodd shouted at everyone they met along the way. "Spread the word that we're staying to fight." Reactions were mixed, but for the most part the citizenry was eager to defend their homes instead of abandoning their livelihoods.

They traveled through more tunnels, and the activity picked

up. Dwarves, orcs, and gnomes scurried like ants in a colony as the word spread. The tunnel grew larger, and they came to a massive set of steel doors with dwarven carvings on them. Weathered scenes of dwarves fighting men adorned the portal, and Henry wished for a chance to learn the story that the metal depicted.

Thorodd pushed on the doors, and they opened in groaning protest under the heavy force of the dwarven leader. The skeletons followed him into a huge room with a high, vaulted ceiling lined with metal pipes thicker than Henry was tall. It was dimly lit, save for one giant sun globe high above them and a few splotches of stray lumimoss attached to the walls. Thorodd explained that by the time they'd installed the sun globes they had moved their production to the lower forges of Hraunfass and had no need for this antiquated chamber. Henry could tell that it had set idle for a very long time. Rust and a thick layer of dirt covered everything, and most of the implements looked worn and broken.

On the far side of the room, three holes the size of a gnome sat in the wall about twenty feet up. Stone troughs led down the wall below the holes and joined together on the floor before following a single path to the center of the room where a circular basin nearly ten feet wide was carved into the stone. Had water been flowing from the holes, it would have made for a beautiful fountain. A pedestal two feet high stood at the lip of the bowl. Strange handles, buttons, dials, and various other controls that Henry didn't recognize protruded from the pillar.

Various stone workbenches lined the room, each with its own huge metal anvil. Two chains, with their accompanying wheels led from the chamber and out through smaller doors on opposite ends of the forge. Several dwarven mining carts were attached to the chain and a few were even filled with black iron ore.

Empty armor stands and weapon holders were arranged sporadically throughout the chamber, the armaments long doled out to the defending cells. Half a dozen dwarves and orcs scurried through the room, setting up equipment and pushing in carts full of dull-colored ore.

As the group entered, a grizzled old dwarf with an angry look on his face approached the Elder. "Thorodd, you better not be pulling my chain. Einar tells me you have the Magma Blaster. If you're getting me worked up for no reason, I'll give you such a thump." The dwarf's voice creaked and wheezed as he spoke and his white beard, wrinkled skin, and hunched posture advertised his extreme age. His arms were thin and frail, but he approached with a determined confidence that said he wasn't ready to give up his will to the passing years.

Thorodd ignored the chastisement and responded with a grin and a laugh that one would give to an old friend. "Skeletons, allow me to introduce Torbball Ollastersson, Master Blacksmith of Hraunfass. He's one of the last living dwarves that worked the new forges, and he's spent the last hundred years teaching young dwarflings the fine art of pounding metal into submission."

"Hard to teach anything more than theory with a cold forge," the gnarled blacksmith grumbled. "And by *Master Blacksmith* he means one of the few that escaped alive. Now, do you have it or not, Thorodd? Don't keep an old dwarf waiting."

The Elder pulled the Magma Blaster from his belt and held it upright in front of the smith. Torbball's eyes grew wide, and a smile crept onto his weathered lips. "Never thought I'd see one again." With gnarled fingers, he gently plucked the device from Thorodd's hands and pulled it close. Expressions ranging from curious disbelief to childlike joy washed over his face as he rotated the Blaster. His brow quickly knitted before he turned to the scrambling dwarves behind him and shouted, "Lauggar, Gardhur, Hoffnur. It's your time to shine, boys." Three dwarves, busily organizing various implements, all perked up their heads at Torbball's command, then ran to the far wall to three respective panels full of levers next to the stone throughs. The levers reminded Henry of the set that controlled the cages from the arena in Ammerthall, though the forge contained several times as many mechanisms.

"Those are my three apprentices. Let's see if I've taught them well," Torbball huffed as he walked over to the pedestal at the edge of the stone pit. He lifted the Blaster and aligned it with one of the holes and held it there as he addressed Thorodd. "I can't promise what the business end of this Blaster will do to the forge after a millennium of sleep. Once we start this, who knows what we're going to wake up. Best case, the utilities through the mountain will have to be shut off manually, if they're not completely shot. Worse case, a supply pipe breaks and we flood Hjardharfell with lava. The tense expression on his face indicated the threat of a lava flood wasn't an exaggeration.

"Hjardharfell is lost without the forge. We don't have a choice at this point. Continue," Thorodd directed.

The blacksmith seemed pleased by Thorodd's guidance. He dropped the Blaster into place and adjusted dials on the pedestal. When his apprentices finished preparing their respective levers, he shouted, "All clear!" then clicked the ring on the Blaster's handle.

Dozens of orange light patterns spiraled down the pedestal, following carved lines and zipping down the troughs. The lights reached the far wall and followed the stonework up before converging on the dark holes.

Torbball clicked the handle a second time and the blaster

began to vibrate, filling the room with a deep hum. The lines pulsed from orange to yellow and a faint glow formed in two of the holes in the walls. "How's it looking?" Torbball shouted as he continued to adjust the controls.

Two apprentices scanned gauges on the walls and gave him a thumbs up, but the third shook his head and replied, "pressure is low." He pulled more levers and turned the dials and after a minute, the third hole lit up as well.

"Here we go," Torbball said and clicked the ring a third time. The humming intensified and a distant rumble came from deep within the mountain. Again, the first two dwarves held up their thumbs, but the third shouted, "Now the pressure is rising too fast. I'm shutting it down." After a few more inputs and a tense few seconds of rumbling, the glow in the third hole faded. Meanwhile, the other two holes got brighter. The first two apprentices looked at Torbball, waiting for his instruction. A quick nod from the blacksmith told them to proceed. Tension hung in the air as they exchanged nervous glances, then simultaneously pulled the largest levers on each or their panels.

The rumble increased and dust began to shake from the ceiling. A loud grating sound came from the bright holes and barely molten rocks tumbled out, silhouetting in front of the bright yellow glow. The glow and discharge grew until the dark rocks became a viscid, flowing liquid. Lava slowly dripped from the first hole, but violent spurts like a drunk vomiting cheap whiskey shot from the middle hole. Though Henry and the other skeletons couldn't directly sense the rapid increase in the rooms temperature, visible heat waves radiated from the lava, blurring the air and forcing nearby dwarves and gnomes to shield their faces and exposed skin.

Molten projectiles shot forward, and Torbball stepped back

to avoid the missiles, but Buddy had already erected a force wall that deflected the molten pellets and deposited them harmlessly in and around the basin.

"Too much, Lauggar. Bring it down. Gardhur, more from you." The apprentices complied, and after a few more adjustments steady streams of molten rock poured down the first two troughs. Molten yellow and orange blobs flowed over the stone. Cool spots on the flow turned black and tried to solidify, but the stream moved so quickly that they were absorbed back into the lava as it poured into the basin before spiraling down a tube in the center.

"Ha!" Torbball exclaimed with a trill in his voice that likely hadn't been there for decades. He slapped his palm on the pedestal's largest button and the grating sound of unlubricated sprockets filled the hall. Black metal shielding rose from slots on the edges of the troughs and met to form a dome over the lava rivers. Henry could tell by the rough mat texture of the metal that it was made of thick plates of golem steel. The heat in the room instantly reduced, but it was still much hotter than it had been. Between the domes riveted sections, Henry could see glowing holes that looked like windows on the metal.

Torbball turned and smiled with a grin at least half filled with teeth. "Now the fun starts." The chains on the floor and the gears on the walls must have been waiting for the blacksmith's cue, because just as the old dwarf finished his sentence, they sprung to life. Chains started pulling ore-filled carts and a whoosh of cool air blew from the room's entrances and rushed upward. Henry looked up to see hidden air shafts opening as they sucked out the fumes from the scorching magma. He instinctually expanded his ribs to suck in the air, but no breath pulled into his nonexistent lungs.

Torbball's apprentices rushed back to the old dwarf, beaming with excitement like puppies when their owner returns. "Now what?" Lauggar asked.

"What do you mean, *now what?* You know what to do."

The three dwarven apprentices exchanged unconfident glances but a raised eyebrow from Torbball made Gardhur pipe up. "Um, test the smelters and start forming ingots?"

"Are you asking or telling?" Torbball gave another impatient answer.

"Um, telling?" Hoffnur replied, nervousness quaking in his voice.

"That still sounded like a question, but yes. Get everyone organized and start smelting." With the master blacksmith's blessing, they raced to the growing piles of ore and started organizing the other dwarves and the few orcs to start wheeling carts over to the forges. Their efforts were chaotically unorganized at best.

Torbball turned his judging eyes away from his apprentices and back to Thorodd. "That'll keep them busy for a bit, but iron and copper will only get us so far. I hear you've got something else coming for me."

Thorodd glanced back to his daughter and raised his eyebrows. "Torgga said these skeletons found golem steel and eversharp. Lots of it, apparently. I've already sent teams to start the retrieval process."

Torbball looked over the skeletons as though he hadn't noticed them before, but his eyes shone with a light that Henry felt hadn't been there in a hundred years. If he truly was a master blacksmith, he had lived a century without working his craft. The joy at rekindling his passion must have felt great. His eyes went to his apprentices, and he smiled, "Golem steel and eversharp . . . the boys have got years ahead of them before they master either of those. Good thing my old bones still have the Strength to swing a hammer."

"Like I said, you dusty old fart, you don't have a choice. We either get weapons and armor to the front lines, or we start abandoning Hjardharfell." Thorodd replied with a forceful tone that could only be interpreted as an order from the dwarven leader.

Never one to be out of the center of attention for long, Ox took the opportunity to interject, "If you're going to outfit your soldiers, you'll need all the material we found. Luckily for you, I happen to specialize in lifting rocks, and I know I can do it faster than your chain carts."

Henry was surprised when Beast agreed with Ox's assessment of the situation. "The idiot is right. Your forces are stretched thin, but muscle will only go so far. I need to practice a few Abilities, so I'll help as well."

Torbball paused and stared at the skeletons, a reaction that Henry now saw as normal to hearing a voice reverberate from an animated skull. A nod from Thorodd reassured the blacksmith before he agreed to Ox and Beast's assistance. "I won't turn down willing labor. You can help them move the iron we've already brought up, then we'll send you down to get the golem steel and eversharp."

Buddy nudged Henry. "I have a feeling you and I are needed elsewhere, but if they're making armor and weapons, you should show him the other components you've gathered."

Henry had reduced four of the dread spears down to the size of small daggers. He retrieved one from his belt and presented it to Torbball. "I took these from the Silent we defeated."

Sacrifice

The dread bone shot to the length of a full spear. The master smith took the weapon and studied it closely. "Impressive material and quite strong, but what do you expect me to do with that? I've got no implements capable of shaping Epic-quality components."

Buddy looked slightly disappointed at Henry's lacking explanation, so he stepped in to help. "The Necromancer's forces power their bodies through Health-storing organs. Those organs are vulnerable, but the shells that make up their exoskeletons are of the same quality as this spear. We've killed several dozen of the monsters, and we think their bones could be turned into weapons and armor, with the right expertise. The dread bones, as we're calling them, can be shaped by a proficient transmuter with ample healing spells. Henry seems to be the only one with a skill that can translate Vitus directly into the dread bones, so I recommend taking advantage of Ox's magic, or having several healers handy if you're going to work them as components."

"Epic quality with a hardness of **30**." Torbball tugged on his beard as his mind toyed with various designs. "And all we have to do sacrifice our Health to turn it into weapons, what could go wrong."

A crash interrupted Torbball's skeptical thought. An orc had pushed a cart into another, and ore spilled all over the floor. While they'd begun talking, the chaos in the forge had gotten worse, and the three apprentices were running around shouting at each other. Workers were hammering, smelting, and shoveling, but nothing seemed to be working quite well. Once again, Torbball's brow knitted together, and he raised his voice. "What do you think you're doing? Who taught you how to run a forge?"

A cast of melted ore hit the floor, scattering slag across the room. Frustration erupted and Lauggar shook two hammers and shouted. "We're working on it, Master Torbball."

"No, you're not," Torbball snapped. "What are you missing right now?"

Three dumb-founded looks were the only response the blacksmith received from his apprentices until Gardhur's eyes widened and he exclaimed, "Oh yeah!" He grabbed a hammer from Lauggar and started pounding in a slow rhythmic beat. He raised his head and began to sing in a voice that was both rough and pleasing to the ears.

Morning rise and to the forge

The entire forge froze and looked at him, but he kept pounding and repeated the line, much louder the second time.

Morning rise and to the forge

Lauggar and Hoffnur seemed to realize what their fellow apprentice was doing, and both replied in unison.

Fire and anvil, fire and ale

A wave of recognition rolled over the workers as Gardhur continued to hammer and sing. A chorus of voices spread through the cavern, echoing off the stone walls and amplifying the reverberance to create an ethereal chant.

Drink a pint and then one more
Fire and anvil, fire and ale

Torbball stood beside Thorodd with a smug look on his face. "I was wondering how long it would take them. You can't run a forge without music. Every dwarf should know that."

As if the chant had cast an *organize* spell over the forge, the chaos died immediately. Orcs, dwarves, and gnomes all began to move as one at a steady, rhythmic pace, all following the beat of Gardhur's hammer and the dwarven song. Ox began nodding his head to the forge workers' chant.

My lady said don't come home drunk
Fire and anvil, fire and ale
If she gets mad, I'll sleep at the pub
Fire and anvil, fire and ale

"Not the song I would have chosen, but it's getting the job done," Thorodd ribbed.

"No, dwarf boss, the song is perfect. Drinking and pounding; two of my favorite things." Ox detached two carts from the floor chain and carried them over to the covered smelter. Beast assisted by teleporting larger chunks of ore from one spot to another.

Thorodd watched them with an amused expression, but soon his glare turned to stone and serious tenor grew in his voice. "The creatures that came from the deep were powerful, and I fear the worst is yet to claw its way from the depths of the mountain. Hjardharfell doesn't have much time, Torbball. However, the skeletons have a mission at the peaks of Jallfoss that may be more important than our own. Your priority is to get them outfitted by morning with the finest arms and armor you can create."

"Then we'll need to get started. Leave your weapons and armor here." Torbball pointed to an open stone bench.

The blacksmith gathered a contingent of gnomes who surrounded the skeletons and took their measurements with strange metal implements. Henry removed his Gladiator Supreme armor and the Acolyte chain mail, then sat down his dread javelins and the hilt of his melted sword. Buddy left behind his robes and bronze bucklers, but he kept his bandolier and pried out the flow crystal from Henry's sword and placed it in his pack. The gnomes swept up the gear as soon as they could, taking more measurements and drawing sketches on parchment paper.

While Henry and Buddy stripped their gear, Ox and Beast dove into the action. A few of the workers initially gave the undead concerned looks, but their trepidation faded quickly when they saw how efficiently the two could move material. Within minutes, Ox and Beast seamlessly integrated into the lines of forge workers.

Thorodd watched the bustle in the room until he was satisfied Torball had the forge under control, then he turned to Buddy and Henry. "I didn't think you had it in you; didn't expect to ever see you again. You did what I never thought possible. Hjardharfell owes you a great debt."

"Not bad for some undead tourists," Henry replied.

Thorodd ignored Henry's quip. "I have another job for you two while you wait. New armor and weapons will go a long way to protecting our clusters, but without enchantments we'll still suffer too many losses."

"How can we help with that?" Henry asked, as much to Buddy as to Thorodd.

"Our gnomes are great with engineering and even better with artificing, but they're garbage at evocation. That's where you come in. We're going to use your Abilities to augment out armaments, but there's plenty in store for you in return, and you'll need all the help we can offer to get past the Sprigs."

"Sprigs?" Henry and Buddy asked in unison.

"Torgga will explain. Now get your dead rumps out of my forge. There's much to do and we're out of time."

CHAPTER 23

The mountains of Jallfoss loomed over the approaching Acolytes. The sun had just begun to set behind the snowy mountain peaks miles above them, sending jagged shadows racing across the plain to meet the warriors. The greeting was neither pleasant nor welcome. Cirilo's body was far too tempered to be fatigued by a few days in a saddle, but the sweat gleaming on his horse's hide testified to the hot march in the summer sun. They'd made good time but had to press their mounts nearly to the breaking point to hold the pace.

As the sun began to set, the heavy, humid air turned to a slightly cooler breeze. Cirilo was always captivated by how the flat plains of Ikrit ended so abruptly right at the base of the gray mountains, like they'd been plopped down by the god himself as a clear demarcation between the two nations; the dead range of Jallfoss, and the world's strongest military might of Ikrit.

Merchant villages once prospered outside the three main entrances to the mountain, but they had been abandoned a century ago after everyone inside died and rose again. The dead didn't wander from outside the mountain on their own, but the villages were long abandoned before that bit of knowledge became common. A few buildings and palisades still stood, but most had been brought down by weather or salvaged by those brave enough to get near the mountain. Now, only the bones of the outposts stood, a reminder of what resided on the other side of the mile-long tunnel to the main city of Ammerthall.

The black mouth of the tunnel faced the approaching Acolytes like the very maw of Veletos, ready to swallow a ship whole. Cirilo had approached the gateway to horror a hundred times, but the feeling of unease never lessened. The mountain itself seemed to breathe through that tunnel, pulling life in and spewing out the deadly curse. He shifted his eyes upward and steadied his nerve.

The spired towers of the Oxendine nobility and the cities of the high elves ended a few thousand feet below the highest peaks. Huge marble blocks, dug from the heart of the mountain and weighing several tons each, made up the beautiful walls and perfect structures that stretched for twenty miles in either direction. For over four thousand years, the rulers of Jallfoss constructed their palaces on the mountain tops that put to shame even the impenetrable walls of Ikrit's capital city. They would have been impervious to any modern siege weapon if they'd been on flat ground. As they stood on the sheer cliffs of Jallfoss, thousands of feet above the flat plains, no army alive could hope to even mar their perfect exteriors. Such opulence always seemed unnecessary to Cirilo, but the Oxendine sorcerers of millennia past needed something to pass the time, and architecture was the one of the least offensive hobbies he'd seen nobility undertake.

He could make the trek up the mountain side along with his other Master Acolytes, strong as they were, but it was much easier to fight undead and Sprigs than climb the shear walls that led to the Empress. No army had ever tried to conquer the mountain kingdom via siege, though a few wars of note had taken place from factions inside the mountains—dwarves against humans or something of the like. The Necromancer came from within as well, according to hearsay gathered after the catastrophe.

Cirilo would have preferred to avoid the deadly mountain all together if Lord Stavros hadn't drove the Acolytes to salvage from Jallfoss' corpse and use it as a training ground. The power and treasure they'd taken from the broken mountain had made Ikrit the most powerful nation state in the known world, but it came at the price of the lives of his Acolyte brothers and sisters—even worse, the price that thousands upon thousands of Jallfoss inhabitants paid with their endless deaths.

"That's where we're headed? Straight to the top? I've never been that far, but I always wanted to see the ruined elven castle." Eudora had noticed the Commander's stare and commented on the crumbled section of fortress amongst a handful of other castles high above them. There were several different cities built inside those towers and after a hundred years they still looked in perfect shape, except for one stretch of crumbled white marble that matched the snow-capped peaks more than its juxtaposed towers.

Eudora rode to Cirilo's left and was the most junior of the Master Acolytes on the mission by 10 Tiers and at least a decade of experience, but she'd proven herself several times over in the harsh battles against Basti's Vanguard. Cirilo hoped she would one day surpass Commander Lanthe and maybe even lead the Infantry Brigade. Her potential was there, and if she performed well on this mission Cirilo would send her to the mountain with Junior Acolytes of her own. She was a master of the partisan, a heavy-shafted halberd with unrivaled range and speed, but her Abilities to conjure weapons made her attacks equally unpredictable and deadly.

Cirilo kept his eyes on the looming towers above and noted the one knocked down castle to which Eudora referred. "The high-elven castle stood for thousands of years . . . then tumbled a week before Jallfoss' downfall. I've killed trolls by the dozens and never fought one that could cause that level of destruction. If you run into one, I recommend you turn your tail. Unless, of course, you plan to claim its Soul Essence."

The chide was in just and Eudora took her Commander's joke with a smile. Cirilo was fully confident in her capability to take on much more than a troll. He held the same confidence for the other three warriors that rode at his side. Instead of summoning an army to fight the young Acolyte's reported threat, he brought only his four most trusted Master Acolytes.

The founder of the Acolytes and former ruler of Ikrit, Lord Livadi, had created the Acolytes as his personal warriors to explore the world with him. As he grew older the Bastion turned into the source of officers for the military. Their battle prowess and might obtained from the Drift Amulets made them the ultimate fighting force with magical Abilities that turned the Ikritian army into the most feared force in the known world.

No question existed in Cirilo's mind that the four warriors he brought with him could handle any situation better than an entire battalion of un-Tiered soldiers. Besides, any larger of a group and they'd attract unnecessary attention from the horrors within, making their journey to Jallfoss's upper spires much more dangerous.

He'd carefully chosen them from the instructors at the Bastion to balance their talents against any potential threat. Cirilo himself boasted control over the forces of nature, but his greatest asset was his incredible swordsmanship which was only second to that of the deceased Master Jacoby. In a pure test of skill, Jacoby could best the Commander. However, Cirilo's overwhelming Strength, Acumen, and Merq dwarfed Jacoby's.

A shrill but stern voice responded from behind the Commander. "The high castles are a true wonder, Eudora. That is where the Empress' ghost still haunts—two peaks up from the broken elven city. All the best storytellers agree it was a troll that took out the elves' precious tower, but I have my doubts. Likely a result of a massive internal battle—fire golems, undead hordes, pure chaos trapped inside the mountain. The details are controversial, but I believe the Necromancer caused everything to turn into wharbellow dung, not a lone troll." The Acolyte looked comically small riding on the massive horse, but few would dare remark on his size. Though he was the smallest of the group, Mersin's skills were possibly the most valuable. He specialized in transmutation and was the most proficient close-range fighter Cirilo had ever seen. Once, it was rumored, Lord Stavros himself complimented the man's combat skills and had taught him physical warding magic. He carried no weapons, but his fists were faster and more deadly than any blade. He wore light leather armor, and his thick black beard poked from under a thick leather cap.

"Troll? More likely shoddy elven construction. Trolls are tough and almost impossible to kill, but there's no way a single troll could take down a castle. I've killed hundreds to trolls, and never met one that could cause such damage." Jaromak was a mountain of a man. So large, in fact, that he needed a second horse to carry his full-plate armor and his massive shield. Even then, the huge draft horse beneath him struggled to keep up with the rest under its heavy load. The Master Acolyte stood every bit of seven feet tall and could withstand an unbelievable amount of punishment in a fight, but Cirilo had hesitated to bring him along. His younger brother, Allito, had been one of the Instructor Acolytes reported dead. Cirilo had initially refused the man's request to join this mission, but Jaromak insisted so passionately that he be the one to bear witness to his brother's fate that the Commander couldn't refuse. Cirilo was more than grateful to have such a warrior at his side.

"The Scholars at the Citadel all agree it was an exceptionally large troll, and it was fighting a giant with a pet dervish." The final member of the Commander's coterie was Samos, the master alchemist and anti-mage. The man was every bit of fifty years old, but his curly golden locks and boyish face commonly left him mistaken for one of the younger Acolytes. Like Jaromak, he also had a personal investment in the mission, but of a different manner. It was well known that he was the main rival of Tekşan, the red mage of force magic. Though much older and far more powerful, Samos had routinely competed with Tekşan for the title of "Sorcerer Exalt," though the title meant little outside of the circle of mages, and the name had never officially been bestowed since the passing of the Ikritian hero known simply as Mathis. If the skeletons possessed a mage, as Koş claimed, Samos would put a stop to their magic.

With every step of his horse, Samos's heavy pack clanked with an unknown number of useful potions and components that had changed the tide of several battles in the recent war. The anti-mage's true prowess, however, lied in his skill to analyze a battlefield and initiate an Effect that would move the tide in the favor of the Ikritians.

Jaromak scoffed. "Mersin talks of wharbellow dung, but it spews from your mouth, Samos. You can't keep a dervish as a pet, they're too mean. If anything, it was a hobgoblin. At least they have magic and not just a foul temper."

"No, I heard the troll and the giant were fighting over a golden-haired princess. That makes more sense." Eudora tried to force a serious tone in her voice, but the unintentional snort betrayed her facade.

Samos, ever the scholar himself, missed her demeanor and attempted to educate the group. "To be more precise, trolls are descended from giants, as are jotuns, ettins, and various other larger races. It was not uncommon in days of old for skirmishes to erupted between rival giant clans."

"I hope the skeletons finish me before you kill us of boredom. They should call you the *bland mage*," Jaromak chided. Samos looked offended, as though the knowledge he bestowed should have been more appreciated, but the other Acolytes joined in a laugh at his expense and took turns arguing over the details of the castle's destruction.

Cirilo chuckled quietly to himself. He'd heard the same conversation dozens of times—nearly every time he approached the mountain with a group of Acolytes. Despite the limitless horrors inside the mountain that could provide an endless source of conjecture, Acolytes always preferred to speculate about the crumbled elven castle to pass the time and distract their minds as they approached Jallfoss and their possible deaths. More stories had been written about that than the actual downfall of Jallfoss, but it was mostly fiction, and the truth had been lost to the chaos created by the Necromancer's attack and Jallfoss' downfall.

Just for his own amusement, Cirilo added fuel to the fire. "I heard the Empress' sister accidently summoned an elder stone elemental after drinking too much sharinji whiskey, and it took down the castle just trying to find its way out."

Shouts of dissent against Cirilo's theory filled the still air of the abandoned village long enough for the troupe to approach an impromptu base camp and dismount. Two Acolytes met the Commander and took the horses, but they were not able to offer any information on the developments in the mountain. It would have been convenient to take the horses in the caverns, but the skeletons would attack any man or beast that happened across their path. More than once in the early days, a soldier had been thrown from a fearful mount and torn apart by attacking undead.

The group's cheerful demeaner quickly vanished along with the sun as they entered the dark tunnel and prepared themselves for the worst. At least in that expectation, they weren't disappointed.

"Commander Cirilo, I didn't expect you to make the journey yourself, but I'm glad you came. It's worse than we could have expected." Cirilo recognized the man as Acolyte Glino, a young man just into his **15th** Tier. Several destroyed skeletons littered the streets, and Cirilo was happy to see the soldiers hadn't cleared the area of the broken bone piles. For training purposes, he found value in Junior Acolytes being assaulted the moment they entered the haunted city.

Five other Acolytes stood guard in the area as Glino brought the Commander's group to the first house. "Someone was at the arena. We heard the howl from the dead animals less than a day ago. I've dispatched a team to investigate, but they haven't returned."

"Minoa's gileppo-fish perfume! I don't care about the arena. Where is Allito? Have you seen my brother?" Jaromak towered over Glino, forcing the much smaller Acolyte to cower before collecting himself.

"N . . . no, Master Jaromak. This is all we've found so far. I sent in two Acolytes as a survey team while we set up camp. One was torn apart by an attack from the undead. But the second . . ." The man trailed off as he motioned to the beheaded body.

"A sword," Eudora said as she shook her head, searching for significance in the unexpected wound. Skeletons were known to use weapons, if already equipped, but none had been seen with any level of skill and would usually resort to rending and biting.

"And what else?" Cirilo had already surveyed the carnage and come to his own conclusion, but he wanted Eudora's untainted perspective.

"I . . . I don't know what else." She gave the Commander a confused look.

"A dull blade, but a clean, single slice at the perfect angle," Samos answered for her. Sadness wavered in the mage's voice.

Cirilo tried to affirm Samos' statement, but a searing pain erupted from his chest and forced his breath to catch in his throat. Stavros's spell was starting to take its hold. Cirilo was aware of the Great Lord's Abilities, but for him to cast such a curse on the Bastion's Commander highlighted the severity of the situation. Cirilo had no choice but to trust in the Ikritian ruler. Not just his Emperor, but his longtime friend.

He tried to hide the pain from his expression, but the concerned looks on his Acolytes' faces indicated he had failed. He'd been smashed under the paw of a thunderstaunch and walked away unharmed, but Lord Stavros's spell was far more powerful than a hundred-ton jungle beast. *The old man hasn't lost his touch*, Cirilo thought.

"Commander, I warned you about eating too much bergunroot and not touching your schmeriballs?" Jaromak offered with a laugh, and Cirilo was thankful for the Acolyte's cover.

The Commander collected himself and focusing on the dead Acolyte's injuries. "It's nothing more than being disturbed at seeing two of my men dead." The other Acolytes seemed to accept his explanation and returned their attention to the bodies.

"Commander, you know as well as I what happened here. Few men in the world could wield a dull blade with such deadly precision. It wasn't a skeleton that killed this Acolyte, it was a warrior," Mersin said, careful not to say any more of his theory out loud.

"Jacoby. How would he maintain his swordsmanship after returning? And why would he run away?" Samos pointed to the boot prints that led from the carnage. The Alchemist had an astute academic mind, but he lacked the sense of tact that one would have expected of such a high-Tiered Acolyte.

Cirilo wasn't offended by Samos' accusation toward Jacoby, as the rest had likely come to the same conclusion. If Jacoby awoke, he should be a mindless undead, not a swordsman. Few undead were known to roam and none would ever flee. Jacoby searched his mind for an explanation, but none presented itself.

Eudora wasn't convinced. "I won't believe it until I see it with my own eyes, but if the returned are starting to regain their minds, surely there's some way to save our dead Acolytes."

"No Ikritian is an expert in necromancy. From everything I've seen and what the scholars will tell you, the Necromancer's spell only heals the memory of a body up to the point of the most recent death. It doesn't prevent natural decomposition, and it surely doesn't preserve the mind," Mersin countered.

If Lord Stavros said skeletons had gained sentience, then there was no question its truth. Cirilo had told his four companions what the Great Lord had given him as their mission. They were to stop the skeletons from reaching the Empress's ghost, and Stavros had also asked Cirilo to retrieve Jacoby's weapon. "What worries me even more, Master Mersin, is that the cut was made with a chipped training sword, but there is no sign of Master Jacoby's enchanted xiphos."

The Acolytes exchanged worried looks and frantically searched the surrounding area, hoping to spot Jacoby's sword. They all knew the quality and power that it held, and the fact that it was created by Lord Stavros himself spoke volumes to its value. The Great Lord had asked Cirilo to retrieve the weapon; that request alone would have been enough to send a contingent of soldiers to the haunted mountain, but given the death of fifteen Acolytes and potentially sentient skeletons, the situation was dire.

A rumble shook the ground, and a hiss filled the air, interrupting their search. Towering above the rooflines, the massive pillars that held up the cavern's ceiling trembled as one hundred years of dust accumulation billowed through the city. The sound of spraying water from broken pipes came from the surrounding houses and puddles of water started spilling from some of the doorways.

"Skeletons? Jacoby?" Eudora asked.

"No, this is from the dwarves. Glino, you and your team, come with us to the ramps," Cirilo ordered and started walking. The Master Acolytes followed in step as Glino hurriedly organized his men to accompany them.

What the hell is going on in this damned mountain, Cirilo thought as he rounded the corner of a curved street, coming into view of two skeletons. They charged, arms outstretched and mouth agape. *Jacoby, my friend, what happened to you?*

CHAPTER 24

Jacoby couldn't remember feeling so good, but then, he couldn't remember much. By the time he worked his way through the skeletal animals locked in the arena cages, he was well into Tier **5**. His muscles bulged and his metal club crushed bones like orange cramillo grapes under Fremmian toes. And that was without the use of his magic.

He combed through the icons flashing in his display.

Skeletal Animal Killed x10, Soul Essence Claimed, +3 Tiers:
STR +5, MOB +3, FOR, +3, ACU +6, PER +2, RES +3

Ability Discovered: Bolster II – Imbue a weapon with magical energy. Damage +3, ACU +2

Ability Discovered: Enhance I – Imbue armor with magical energy. Damage Resistance +1

Synergy Detected, Combining Abilities: Bolster II and Enhance I

Ability Discovered: Auric Palisade I – Imbue armor and weapons with more efficient and powerful magical energy. Damage +3, Damage Resistance +3, MOB +1, ACU +3, RES +1. Favored weapon enabled (Unchosen)

Ability Discovered: Heal I – Stitch together minor wounds

Somehow, the Amulet was channeling Soul Essence from defeated enemies, whether they be skeleton or human. What he couldn't tell was if it was bestowing Abilities upon him, or merely reporting what was happening to him as he gained Tiers.

Bolster had combined with a defensive Ability called *Enhance* to become Auric Palisade, and it now charged his weapons and armor with magical golden energy to the point that none of the skeletal animals could even touch him. He'd even learned a healing spell that had saved him from bleeding out when a skeletal cougar tore open his femoral artery.

He'd found some decent equipment in the arena's armory, but it was only slightly better than the heavy armor he'd taken from the undead soldiers. It was no wonder those young men had died as they were not properly equipped for fighting undead, not with heavy armor and chipped swords. Why then were the two men that he'd killed equipped with the much more effective clubs?

He took the time to put the skeletal animals back in their cages after he killed them. He'd already caused the death of two humans, and if these skeletons came back to life, he didn't want them attacking the men that he thought were his allies. Jacoby was starting to understand that everything in the city came back from the dead, and that was far different than actually returning to life. He pushed the thought away, telling himself that philosophy never intended to account for his current situation.

Part of him wanted to stay and explore the arena, but he only allowed himself a few minutes to check out the double doors on the arena's peripheral wall. The doors were braced with iron bands and had resisted him at first, though opened easily for him the second time he pulled on the metal rings that served as handles.

William H. Talisker, he mouthed as he read one of the brass plates in the chamber beyond. The plates were organized by year, leading Jacoby to believe the elaborate room belonged to the most recent name, but there were thousands of years of the warrior's predecessors memorialized on the wall. *I wonder about the history behind this arena. How long this city has been dead? What was it like before?*

What worried him more was the fact that someone had been in that room recently. They left behind the soldiers' armor that was missing from the dwelling from which Jacob had first awoken, and once again, the man felt he was following something. In order to solve the mystery, the only option was to make his way to the far edge of the city and search for the ghost from his vision.

His body grew sturdier with every enemy he felled, so his muscles didn't need the rest. His mind, however, had started to fatigue and he needed to sort out his thoughts. As he wandered through the streets, he followed the spiraling roads to one of the massive pillars that held up the underground city's rock ceiling and plopped down at its base, taking the opportunity to review his Auric Palisade Ability. The description indicated that he could choose a favored weapon, but it offered no indication of what came with the choice.

He unslung the metal club from his back and rotated it in his hands. Even though it had been very effective against the skeletons, he found it cumbersome and knew he preferred a sword. Jacoby unsheathed a falchion that he'd found in the coliseum's armory. He preferred a double-edged blade, but the sword was the only superior-quality weapon he'd uncovered in the mounds of rusted iron that still had a decent edge. He focused on the Ability's description, willing it to accept his decision.

Favored Weapon Selected – Sword. Auric Palisade Effects doubled when using favored weapon

As effective as the Ability had been against the animated skeletal animals, he was more excited at the prospect of doubling its strength. He didn't dwell on the choice the Ability had offered him, but one decision still plagued his mind. He hoped he was making the right choice in going up, ascending the mountain based solely on a hunch. Hope was all he had at that moment.

The stone column behind him started to rumble and hiss, jarring Jacoby from his thoughts. Water began spraying from some of the surrounding stone houses, and pools of water were streaming from their doorways. Jacoby wasn't sure what had caused the sudden flooding, but he didn't want to stick around to find out. He gathered his gear and made his way toward the massive ramps.

As he neared the far edge of the city, he saw light coming from the opening above the mile-long incline, and lighter-colored stone building at the top. He'd awoken in a city full of the undead. Whatever was above couldn't possibly be worse.

CHAPTER 25

"The worst thing about forest elves is their lack of appreciation for us. We should send a few scores of them to fight Ghara's Sprigs on their own. The sacrifice may appease her, and if not, it should keep the savages in line for a bit." Talji made no effort to hide her agitation as she stood in the Sage's hut. Being allowed in Bharat's personal dwelling was rare, even for a Sentinel, but offering her opinion to the elven leader was something only afforded to a unique few. Given her privilege, Talji's words were still uncomfortably forward, even for her.

She'd placed her Guard outside and ordered them to patrol and not let any forest elves close. She hadn't seen Jai in a few days so the beating he'd received should have been enough to keep him from sulking around, but she wanted to eliminate any chance that someone could eavesdrop.

Bharat appreciated the Sentinel's passion, but he doubted Talji would be capable of feeding elves, even forest elves, to their god, whether or not that meant there was a chance for that sacrifice to appease Ghara. She had a ferocious exterior, like a dire porcupine. Unfortunately, the elf had a kind heart that she couldn't hide from the Sage. That wasn't a bad trait, since the last truly ruthless elf he'd trusted had let him down.

"Those words could insight a rebellion. Mayur's sacrifice will be hard enough for us to manage," Bharat said. Words were everything when it came to keeping order. Far more important than actions, which could be hidden and morphed into whatever he wanted them to be. He wouldn't disclose to the warrior elf, but he had contemplated the very task that Taljipura was suggesting. He'd even sent a handful of forest elves with his Sentinels to Ghara's burrow as an offering many years ago. It did nothing to stem the tide of her monsters. He thought that if he sacrificed enough of the lower-class elves to Ghara, maybe her hunger would be satisfied and she'd stop sending her Sprigs. How wrong he was. He saw no evidence that more dead forest elves would change their god's wrath, so he'd stopped the practice.

"Did he turn before his decent?" Talji asked. She'd only seen it once, but when an elf died inside the mountain they would return, just like the skeletons, and attack every living elf they came across until slain once more. The only viable option was to dump them down one of the dead air shafts so they couldn't wreak havoc. The other choice was to turn them into a Guard, but no elf would ever admit considering such blasphemy, or so Talji thought.

"He would have . . ." Bharat rubbed his fingers along the silvery metal of his circlet. The brown flow crystal swirled like a dust storm. Talji was surprised that the Sage would allude to her that he used the spell to Hold Mayur until he could be descended, but she was, after all, his most trusted advisor. She could easily understand his actions. A preventative spell would stop the dead elf from moving. It would look much worse if a Sentinel, or even the Sage himself, had to cast the spell on one of their deceased brethren after he had awoken and killed anyone nearby. The Sage couldn't afford such bad optics when the Sentinels barely had the flood of Sprigs contained.

"The question I have for you, my child, is why you've shown so little dismay at the tragedy that has befallen your fellow Sentinel. I had hoped that you and Mayur would bond and grant us future protectors."

Talji was usually stoic, but the look on her face must have betrayed her feelings. "Mayur was far too kind to the forest elves. We were a good team when it came to fighting, but the prospect of anything more was not a possibility. His feelings for Harshmira hadn't faded in the last hundred years."

Even if it were true, to accuse a high elf, especially one who fell in combat, of relations with a forest elf was an extreme accusation. Her inability to control her tongue was only one of the reasons Bharat had not disclosed all of his secrets to Talji. Harshmira's fate, the origin of the Sentinels, even the severity of Ghara's condition, were truths that Talji was not ready to handle.

Bharat approached and put a frail hand on her forehead. "My child, the sins of the mountain have triggered the wrath of our god. Only devotion can restore our world. I understand your loss, but sadness is not the reason I've brought you here. Talji looked up at the feeble elder as he continued. "Something stirs in the mountain. I can feel it. I need you to uncover what is happening."

"Dwarves?" she asked with spite in her voice.

The Sage held her eyes until she looked away. "Maybe, but we haven't heard from them in years. If they've all died, nothing is stopping the flow of evil from below."

"There must be some way we could harness Ghara's power, even in her corrupted form," Talji suggested. "No mere sorcerer could withstand the power of a god."

"Creating life is the way of Spriggans, not bestowing power like the other gods. We know the truth . . ." Bharat said and Talji knew he was waiting for her to recite the knowledge.

"Ghara is the light that sustained the first god in his grief," she said as though she were lecturing an elfling. "Every child knows that Jallfoss sprouted from the base of the mountain and formed a tree. From that tree, the new gods grew. When they left the mountains, the tree wilted with grief. Only one god stayed to keep Jallfoss company: Ghara."

She rubbed the brown crystal embedded in the circlet on her forehead. "Flow crystals are seeds from the tree. Dwarves think they're sparks from a forge, and the Ikritians have a sad story about them being tears. Fools . . ."

"Ghara is a loving god of life, and only we can restore her." Bharat had said the words thousands of times in his sermons, but they were hollow as he spoke to his Sentinel. Talji and Bharat both knew the Sage was jealous of the celestial power bestowed to the Oxendines. Hiding his ambition to rule the mountain had never been easy for the ancient elf. Talji was even there when Bharat used a few simple words that caused the current dwarven leader to lose favor and fail his path.

Talji drifted through her ruminations until Bharat's words brought her back. "Steady your heart, young Sentinel. There is opportunity in our ill fortune, if only we can find it. Had the giant not destroyed our home, we would have been there when the Turning happened, and we'd be cursed skeletons. That would be far worse than living with savages and fighting Sprigs in this desperate forest."

She contemplated disagreeing with the Sage. The giant and his *pets* had been revered as heroes for nearly a month before the Turning. Giant was generous. He was tall and ruggedly handsome, though his undeserved confidence had driven her to despise everything he represented. Her disdain splayed across her face but before Bharat could address the hidden emotion, the ground began to rumble. Talji drew her sword and darted outside as the Sage hobbled behind her.

Geysers of hot air and water vapor blasted into the air, hundreds of feet above the tree line. Three distinct jets that Talji hadn't seen in a century sprayed their heat in the air. She knew without a doubt that the dwarves had reactivated their forges.

Bharat's voice shook in a combination of disbelief and anger. "As I feared, something *is* happening below. Go, now, and find out."

Talji bowed to the Sage, acknowledging his orders and ran off with her Guard following close behind. Hundreds of high elves poked their heads out from wooden huts, but the Sage gave them a reassuring smile. "Likely just dwarves doing dwarven things. This was common back in the day. I have dispatched my most trusted Sentinel to put the dwarves back in line." The golden-haired elves within earshot nodded, but their worried looks said that they were not convinced of the Sage's assurance.

Bharat surveyed the massive steam geysers, making sure the other elves noticed the nonchalance on his face, before slowly ducking back into his hut.

Once the elk skin flap closed behind him, however, all sense of calm vanished from the Sage, and he rushed to his personal chambers. He threw a pile of animal skins to the side and revealed a small golden chest, inlayed with precious stones and beautiful flowing elven designs. The magical wards on the chest would have stopped even the strongest weapons. Bharat channeled his Guile, and the box opened with a faint *click*. He cast a wary eye though his hut to ensure no visitors had snuck in, then he slowly opened the lid. The golden box held various flow crystals and other treasures from the high elves, but he was after something seemingly mundane.

The elf pulled out three crumpled and weathered pages and carefully held them before his eyes. The elegant penmanship and delicate strokes of the writing couldn't hide the nature of the secrets depicted by the ancient numerals; Bharat was no stranger to dark magic written in the ancient languages.

Even with a millennium of knowledge, he was only able to decipher a few spells from the text. One of those spells, *Hold Undead*, he called it, had saved the elves of upper Jallfoss, and allowed them to use the skeletons against Ghara's monsters. Though only he knew of their existence, the scraps of paper had become Bharat's reassurance that evil could beget good.

A century earlier, the city of the high elves had been ravaged by outsiders. Ironically, that ruin had saved the inhabitants from a worse fate by sending the high elves out into the forest. A month after the destruction of his home, Bharat bore witness to the events that started the Turning.

The hundred-year-old memory still sat fresh in his mind, like the event happened mere days in the past. Bharat met with other representatives of Jallfoss's inhabitants to discuss routine and trivial matters. The conversation became heated when he argued with Mathis and Skodderrfall about who would pay for the damages to the high-elven castles. Talji, then the leader of his personal security detail, and Thorodd, Skodderrfall's progeny and now Elder of the Underdeep, were there as well. What happened next changed the course of Jallfoss forever.

A gnome, one of Smyrna's famed flowsmiths, appeared before them shaking in fear and covered in blood. Conjuration is a simple enough school of magic, but to send a whole gnome to an exact location from ten miles below the mountain range was an impossible feat, especially for a dwarven engineer.

Somehow though, Smyrna had sent his distressed apprentice to them, clutching the very pages that Bharat now held. The young gnome claimed that a monster had emerged from a giant flow crystal and killed the Empress' sister, along with all his fellow flowsmiths. Tempers already strained turned to outright hostility as they discussed how to handle the critical situation.

Bharat had always felt that if it hadn't been for the discovery of flow crystals, and the dwarves' subsequent celestial lineage, they would be nothing more than lowly servants. To prove a point to the belligerent dwarven Elder, Bharat took the opportunity to educate the naive Thorodd on the finer details of his Remnant power—a secret the future dwarf king was not ready to acquire.

At the revelation, Skodderrfall had attacked Bharat. Mathis, the Empress's personal tutor and most trusted advisor, stopped the fight before blood had been shed, but the damage Bharat's words had done to Thorodd couldn't be reversed. Bharat had only spoken a truth to Thorodd. *If the dwarfling couldn't handle that truth, could he ever rule the Underdeep?* Bharat remembered thinking, justifying his actions on that faithful day.

Skodderrfall had stomped off in a rage to save his kingdom, leaving Bharat and Mathis to relay the catastrophe unfolding in the dwarven Underdeep to Empress Destria. The elven Sage had pleaded with the Empress to send her army, but she refused to take his advice, trusting that the dwarves could handle it. She had been wrong and her failure to act brought down the undead curse on the entire mountain.

If Lady Destria had dealt with the problem like Bharat advised her, he wouldn't have had to take the matter into his own hands. Unfortunately, the savage he sent to deal with the Necromancer failed, and now he was stuck in the squalor of the Amera pine valley, living side-by-side with the sordid forest elves.

Bharat hadn't disclosed to Destria that he'd taken the pages from Smyrna's messenger, and luckily, Mathis hadn't thought it of enough consequence to press the issue. From those very scraps of parchment, Bharat had derived the Hold Undead spell that had supplied his Sentinels with the resources to fend off Ghara's Sprigs.

Bharat placed the pages back into the golden chest, unsure why he'd taken them out in the first place. It may have been that he found the presence of powerful knowledge a reminder of what the elves had left behind in their castle homes, or maybe he needed the reassurance that he could control whatever changes were coming. He'd felt the rumblings from deep below the mountain, but the geysers' return could only mean one thing: the dwarves had activated their forges. The impudent dirt dwellers should have died long ago, but once again, they had somehow shaken the hive, and the bees were angry. Whatever foolishness the dwarves were up to, it could only be bad for the high elves.

CHAPTER 26

"Your father doesn't seem to be a big fan of elves," Henry said. It was the most subtle way he could think of to get Torgga to explain the dwarven aversion to elven kind. If there was the potential to encounter elves, Henry wanted to understand if they were possible allies, or more likely, a potential enemy.

Torgga scrunched her eyes as she thought, as though she'd never considered why a dwarf wouldn't get along with an elf. Henry assumed it was so ingrained in their history that it was just part of their nature at this point. "Dwarves don't typically ally themselves with elves, though we've never directly fought. At least not in Jallfoss. I do know of other dwarven and elven settlements that have warred from time to time, so the stories say. I've never heard a first-hand account. All I know is my father hates elves with a passion, but he's never said why."

"If they live on the mountain peaks, I don't imagine you come in contact with them much," Henry said.

Torgga shrugged her shoulders. "Well, they used to live on the mountain peaks, at least the high elves did. They were the nobility of the elven world, ruling over the forest elves that live in the high pine valley behind the mountain range. That was a century ago, before the high elves fled from their castles and now the remaining nobility live in the forest."

Beast had been strangely quite during the conversation, but Henry could tell she was listening. Henry wondered what type of elf Beast was, so he checked her status.

Haruspex

Under her race it still said s*keletal elf*, but nothing about *high elf* or *forest elf*. That moment didn't seem to be the time to ask, so he kept listening to Torgga explain the tense relationship between dwarves and elves. "We used to trade with them, but it got too costly to make the venture, too many deaths. We lost contact with the elves about twenty years ago. They're dealing with their own problems."

"Their own problems?" Buddy asked.

"It wasn't relevant enough for me to tell you earlier, but they worship the forest god, Ghara. When the Betrayal happened, or the *Turning* as they call it, nearly everyone in the mountain died or fled. Over the years, we taught them what we could regarding illusion and artificing, but they never returned the favor. The monsters, both above and below, have grown too strong as we've weakened, and we haven't been able to send an envoy to them in decades. Why would we bother? They never gave us much to begin with."

"You said, 'forest god.' What are we getting ourselves into?" Henry remembered Thorodd's explanation of the gods, but the dwab's account seemed more tangible than the Elder's historical narrative.

"The elves worship a giant tree, way bigger than any of our mushrooms. I don't know if it's a god for sure, but the stories say that it used to create animals and bugs and such. It would even help with the harvest and things like that, if you can believe such nonsense," the dwab explained.

"Could it be one of the Primals of which your father spoke?"

"Whatever it is, the Necromancer corrupted it, and its creations are now twisted versions of wild creatures. They're called 'Sprigs' and can be exceptionally strong and aggressive. That's one thing the Ikritian Acolytes are good for; they keep those abominations from finding their way down here."

"That's why your father is helping us so much. We're going to be fighting these monsters . . . Sprigs." At the thought of a battle, Henry instinctively reached for his sword. He felt naked when his hand grasped thin air and remembered he'd left his armor and weapons at the forge. The idea of fighting some unknown creature excited him, and he wondered how much stronger the Sprigs could be than the monsters of the Underdeep.

Torgga continued leading them through narrow passageways, gaining and losing elevation and twisting through the rocky earth. "If you avoid the elves and Sprigs and you should be fine. Just in case, my father had me bring you here—two reasons, actually. The first is to help you, the second is for you to help us. Buddy, your evocation and Henry's transmutation are more powerful than anything we dwarves can replicate. Our artificers can harness some of your magic and use it to enchant our arms and armor."

"You mean Gnaz? We know a bit more than we did, but I doubt we can help him much." Henry remembered the gnome that had worked with them to restore the magical charges in their weapons. Help wasn't exactly the best thing to call it. Gnaz nearly killed everyone when he tried to load force magic into Ox's hammer. It was Muji that had been the real star and opened the gnome's understanding enough to charge all the weapons.

Torgga smiled. "Not exactly. Gnaz is only an apprentice. I let my father know that the Master Artificer didn't show for you last time, so he was a bit more forceful in his request. Now you'll get to meet the real deal. Also, we need your help to enchant our weapons and armor."

Buddy was quiet for a few seconds before he straightened his posture and responded. "You have assisted us several times over, and we would be dead again if it wasn't for you. I can't speak for Henry, but if I can help you by aiding your artificer, then I will."

"Second that," Henry affirmed. If there was a way for him to help the dwarves and get back to killing monsters, he was happy to do whatever he could.

Torgga's eyes misted like she was going to cry before she steadied her nerves. "That's great. I promise this will be worth it. Before we go in, however, I must warn you about Skuttur, the Master Artificer. He's lost a few rocks in his quarry along the way, if you know what I mean, but he's the best artificer we have."

"If he's the Master Artificer, why did we have to teach his apprentice how to artifice?" Buddy asked.

The mage's dry sarcasm wasn't lost on the dwab. "Calling Gnaz an apprentice may be generous—glorified janitor is probably a better designation. We haven't been able to mine for decades, and Master Skuttur hasn't had much motivation to teach without the needed resources—much like Torball and his blacksmiths." Torgga's explanation seemed to satisfy Buddy, and Henry could sense the mage's expression soften.

"Enough talk, we're here." Torgga had led them through a winding series of tunnels and Henry had quickly gotten lost, but with a little bit of focus on his Perception and Acumen, he was able to mentally trace his path backward and determine where they were. It was somewhere near the edge of Hjardharfell, close to the farmlands that led to the giant mushroom trees of the Grunischwald. Torgga stopped in front of a small metal door, just a few inches shorter than Henry, and pulled on a looped handle. The door itself had three panels, all depicting geometric shapes resembling flow crystals emitting some type of radiance. The door's design made sense, based on what lay inside the chamber. It was a large room, almost forty feet across with walls of carved stone. Benches lined the round walls and held flow crystals of all shapes and sizes as though they were on display. Four stone tables sat in the middle of the room and held even more flow crystals, as well as dozens of implements and tools that Henry didn't recognize. There were wall hooks and metal stands for weapons and armor, but like the forge, the holders were all empty.

As Torgga opened the door, Henry heard a crash and saw a crystal the size of his head rolling across the floor and a gnome chasing after it. He immediately recognized the apprentice artificer.

"You're back, you dead guys with your dead eyes! How did your adventure go down below?" Gnaz's beard was still tucked into his green robes and the spiderlike apparatus on his head glinted as its crystals reflected the light of the room's sun globes."

"Successful," Torgga replied with a hurried voice, "but they don't have time for your silliness. We're here to see Skuttur."

The gnome looked flustered, but Gnaz retrieved the rolling crystal from the ground and waved them in. "Of course, or course. He should be here shortly. Master Skuttur is the greatest artificer in all Hjardharfell. He was even a student of Smyrna Skibibidi himself."

"Smyrna." Buddy said the name as if he was examining the writings in his metal tome. "He seems to be a critical player in the dwarven world."

Gnaz smiled and straightened his robe. "That he was—the most brilliant engineer of our time. Smyrna was a descendent of the greatest artificer ever, Solofur Alonofnurson,"

"Solofur . . . like the explosives?" Henry walked toward the center of the room and used his Haruspex on the implements. The Ability only returned the quality of their associated flow crystals, all of which were void of spells.

"I feel like I'm being forced to learn dwarven history against my will," Buddy said with a hint of derision and impatience in his voice.

A gruff snort came from a dark open doorway on the far side of the room. "I don't really care what you learn, but if it gets you out of my workshop, I'll do what it takes." A gnome with brilliant robes and a long white beard hobbled into the room, limping as he supported himself with a twisted wooden cane. The gnome had a bald, wrinkled head and he looked even older and worse for wear than Torbball, though his beady eyes darted across the skeletons with an unexpected keenness.

"Henry, Buddy, this is Master Artificer Skuttur. Master Skuttur, these are the dead guys who recovered the Magma Blaster." Torgga's cheerful voice seemed to wash past the grumpy looking gnome, leaving him completely unfazed.

"Returned from the dead, again. Only to send more young gnomes, dwarves, and orcs to their deaths. No one wants to go down there, but if Thorodd has ordered me to help, then I don't have a choice. Your ilk can't imagine the horrors below," Skuttur grumbled.

"My imagination is rather extensive," Buddy replied, and Henry could hear the mage's agitation.

"You were Smyrna's apprentice?" Henry asked, trying to change the subject.

"Ha!" Skuttur coughed out a laugh that sounded more like a fish gasping for water. "I'm not worthy to sweep the gem dust from Master Smyrna's work bench. But yes, I was . . ." He trailed off as the sad look on his face turned to anger. "Smyrna is the reason I'm still here. Though he was a dwarf, he was more gnome than most of us. Even his last name, Skibibidi, was gnomish."

"Henry, show him the bracers." Buddy's aggressive tone had abated, but the assertiveness was still there. Henry unslung the pack from his shoulder and fished out the crystalline armor. While Henry retrieved the Flow Bracers, Muji crawled out from Buddy's pack and perched on Buddy's shoulder, aggressively preening matted fur.

Skuttur frowned at the trogold, but when Henry presented the bracers to the old gnome, he seemed to forget about the furry creature. A combinate of fear and wonder crossed the gnome's face and his mouth shook before he could find his words. "Where did you find these?"

"We pulled them off what we believe was Smyrna's corpse. At least we think it was him. We found his bones in Lundarbrekka. We had to fight a soul-stealing golem for them and nearly died."

The old gnome's agitation had all but disappeared, and he looked with wonder at the magical items. "Thorodd said you had a surprise for me, but this steals the shroom. Do you know what you have here?"

"Flow Bracers?" Henry answered, and Buddy shot him a disappointed look for his simple answer.

"So much more than enchanted armor, they are. These are Smyrna's creation to harness the Source Crystal's power." The gnome held out his shaking hands and Henry gave him the bracers.

"You speak like you have experience with the Source Crystal," Buddy replied. The mage had never been one for small talk, but Henry agreed that Skuttur's passive mention of the Source Crystal implied he knew much more than the average resident of Hjardharfell.

"More than anyone alive," Skuttur answered, and Henry could tell by his tone the gnome's claim was true. "But that's not important. Can I keep these?"

"No." Henry shook his head. "We're on a mission to the top of the mountain. Thorodd believes these bracers can revive the ghost of Lady Destria. However, if you show us how they work, we'll try to bring them back when we're done?"

A look of confusion crossed the old dwarf's face, as though a child had just tried to explain to him that cows descended from dragons. "That's a long shot, and very speculative even for a warrior as keen as Thorodd." His brow furrowed further as he considered the theory. "However, if the Empress spent all her magic to repel the Necromancer, she would have drained most of her power. Maybe a massive burst is just what she needs to wake up."

The artificer smirked. "Fine, I can show you how they work. The genius of Smyrna was in his simplicity." Skuttur rolled back his sleeves and placed the bracers over his forearms. They were large on the gnome, but it didn't seem to bother the ancient smith. He walked over to one of the benches along the wall and placed both his hands on a spherical flow crystal that was the size of his fist. The bracers began to glow a brilliant white that drowned out the warm glow from the sun globes. A dim light swirled in the center of the flow crystal, like a goldfish being dropped in a bow, but it quickly grew in size and intensity until it filled the vessel.

Skuttur stepped back and smiled as the glow on the bracers faded. "Pure magical essence, and a thousand times more than the strongest mage's Steam could handle. And skewer my lizard if it's more than a fraction of what the Source Crystal contains. A spec of sand in a desert."

Henry stood in awe at the display. Buddy furiously scribbled in his tome and conferred with Torgga at his side.

"The humans are trying to reach the Source Crystal. Did it truly birth the Necromancer?" Henry asked.

Skuttur eyed Henry for a long moment as if he were carefully choosing his words before he simply said, "Aye, it did."

"How can you be certain? The capabilities of magic are extensive, but a flow crystal unleashing destruction on the scale of this mountain is hard to grasp. And if they're so dangerous, why do you have dozens of crystals lying about? You just filled one with magic?" Buddy asked.

"You ask many questions, but it would do you better to listen. Come here skeletons." Skuttur beckoned them closer. The artificer motioned to the various crystals displayed on the benches. Meticulously organized, each was held on a metal dais as though it were an exhibit in a museum. "Magic permeates all materials in the world, but some react more than others. Flow crystals are the perfect conduit for magic, better than any known substance. As far as I know, Jallfoss is the only place in the world you can find them."

Henry noticed that Buddy and Torgga were completely entranced by the gnome's words and even Muji seemed to be paying attention. "Flow and drift." The gnome began a lecture that sounded like Buddy's instruction on magic, though Henry didn't feel the time was appropriate to make the comparison. "Like lochs on a canal, they control the tide of magic; storing, diverting, releasing . . . transforming, but you must know what you're doing, or you'll create something very dangerous. You can use an uncut flow crystal to control magic, but if it isn't refined, there's no telling what will happen. I don't even let my apprentices try anything beyond basic cuts for the first twenty years of study." Gnaz shirked and the artificer glowered in his direction. "But it seems this one has chosen to accelerate his learning under the teachings of your trogold."

"The animal has exceeded expectation. The bracers would be lost without him. Remember that." Buddy's quick retort had him unexpectedly protecting Muji, something Henry hadn't seen until that very moment.

Skuttur only snorted in reply. "Hmpff. You're lucky he didn't bring down the whole mountain on your heads. Just keep him clear of my crystals."

"Beak," Muji squeaked in an offended tone and narrowed his eyes as he looked down on the gnome from his perch on Buddy's shoulder.

Skuttur shot the trogold an angry eye in rebuke but continued his lesson. "Now, as I was saying, unrefined flow stones can be dangerous to use. That's why we shape them to fit our needs." He held up a multifaced stone and pointed to various cuts and angles. "Quality is more important than size. A good rule of thumb is that every jump in quality has a ten-fold effect on capabilities for a constant size and shape. A Superior crystal can store ten times the magic of an Uncommon one, and Epic is ten times that, though everything is theory after Legendary quality.

"So, if a Mundane crystal was the equivalent of one point of Vitus, then a similar Transcendent crystal would be one hundred thousand?" Buddy theorized.

"I doubt you could find a Transcendent-quality flow crystal as they are almost exclusively between Superior and Legendary, but yes, that's the idea. As their quality increases, the crystals become more powerful, but exponentially more difficult to shape. The hardness increases, but the structure wanes, which means it takes an extreme amount of force applied in a precise, delicate manner. Hence the need for a Master Artificer to cut Epic quality flow crystals and beyond."

"Superior, Epic, Legendary, Transcendent," Henry said, trying to remember what he knew about the system that his Haruspex and the Drift Amulets used to organize an item's quality. "What about higher quality, beyond Transcendent?" Henry asked the gnome.

Skuttur balked at his question, but continued with his lecture, now fully enveloped in teaching. "The Source Crystal itself is the only substance I've ever seen or heard of that is of *Omega* quality. You're getting me off topic skeletons, now focus. As an artificer, I care about the shape. First you have the basic cuts. Flat edges are for storage, points for discharge. Concave radiates and convex channels. It seems simple, but with those combinations, there are millions of permutations. Your basic faceted crystal is the easiest to make and generally of a lower quality crystal used to store and release elementary spells." He held up a spherical crystal that had a divot on one side. "One like this is used for enduring enchantments. It holds a permanent spell and is powered by ambient magic. Lesser versions draw energy from the user to maintain a spell, such as the muffle rings Lady Torgga had me make for you."

Henry and Buddy both looked at Torgga, but she only blushed and turned away, pretending to look at another set of benched crystals while Skuttur continued. "This applies to simple spells: transmutation, evocation, illusion." At the mention of evocation being a simple spell type, Henry felt Buddy bristle, but the mage didn't interrupt the artificer. "Complex spells that need to anchor or identify a target require an array. Conjuration and abjuration have effects that, if put in a lesser crystal, need to be connected to one of a higher quality."

Skuttur hobbled around the room, pointing out various cuts, until he came to an egg-shaped crystal with round facets that looked very familiar to Henry.

Haruspex

Item: Golem Heart (Epic)

Description: Component, severely damaged flow crystal used to control mining golems. Hardness 30, Structure 1/10

Lore: Dwarven golems of the Underdeep, though usually inert, can be extremely dangerous and unpredictable, but their crystal hearts can be harvested as extremely rare crafting components

As Henry suspected, it was shaped like the flow crystals that powered the neglected automatons below. Skuttur continued his lecture. "Though severely damaged, this is the only golem heart we've been able to recover. It's very hard to construct spells in a flow crystal that dive into the mind, or require automation such as divination and enchantment, like the ones we once used to power our golems."

"What kind of stone would necromancy require?" Henry blurted the question without thinking. All heads turned toward him, and even Gnaz gasped.

Skuttur eyed Henry for a second, then pointed to Henry's chest. He had left his armor at the forge and now the Ikritian Drift Amulet hung exposed inside his rib cage. "You already have the answer to that question, skeleton. Drift Amulets are of Epic quality, and their main purpose is to connect souls together. Even through the barrier of death, they allow a portion of the Essence of a being to *Drift* to another."

"Could you explain how that works in more detail . . . for Henry's sake?" Buddy asked, failing to hide his own ignorance on the subject.

"Of course." The artificer hid a grin. "Necromancy is so much more than magic of the undead. It is the art of manipulating the very core of a being's soul. Death is a very emotional process, especially when it results from murder. When one kills another, or even delivers a blow that leads to death, a strong bond is formed between the souls. The Drift Amulets anchor the dying soul to that of the one that killed it, instead of letting it depart to wherever souls go. Technically, they are *anti*-drift flow stones, but no one consulted me during the naming process."

"But they also contain a divination spell that gives us information about ourselves and the world around us," Gnaz offered.

"How does the divination spell know so much?" Henry asked, not intending to pull the gnome to a further tangent.

"Fantastic question. I have no idea. Divination is the fuzziest of all schools of magic. If I were to guess, it takes knowledge from the one who cast the spell, from the user . . . you, and from the surrounding world, and spits back its best guess. Divination and Necromancy are similar in their . . ." he fumbled for the word, "*inconsistent* results."

Buddy started to ask another question, but Skuttur's tone changed to one of disgust and he cut off the mage, "Regardless of the spells in them, the cuts on the Drift Amulets are crude, as is the Ikritian understanding of the art. However, the spells themselves are of sufficient power that it manages to get the job done. I could cut a better crystal, but without the spell, it would be useless."

If Stavros is enchanting the Amulets, then he truly is the Necromancer, Henry thought, but didn't say it out loud so as not to cause more tension in the already uncomfortable room.

Buddy reached into one of the many leather pouches that hung from his body and retrieved the gem that had powered Henry's sword. "There's another crystal we're worried about. We pulled it from the hilt of an Ikritian sword." He held out his palm and unfurled his skeletal fingers, revealing the crystal and almost daring the gnome to take it. White streamers pulsed and wove their way through the green stone. Skuttur eyed Buddy suspiciously for a moment, then snatched the crystal from the mage and held it close to his eye. Buddy curled his fingers back closed and dropped his fist.

The artificer snapped his fingers toward Gnaz. "Maxilense, now," he ordered. The apprentice fumbled through his pockets and eventually produced a circle of glass and handed it to Skuttur who put it in front of his eye. "Ah, humans. They never seem to get it quite right." Henry eyed the crystal that once resided in the hilt of his melted sword.

Haruspex

Item: Drift Crystal (Legendary)

Description: Component, High quality drift crystal containing various enchantments. Hardness 50, Structure 5/5

Lore: Magical weapon created by Lord Stavros of Ikrit and given to his Acolytes

Ability: Drain Level V. Absorbs 20 Vitus/sec. RES determines transfer rate to wielder

"What do you mean, not quite right?" Torgga asked Skuttur, craning her neck to get a closer look at the crystal.

"It's a Legendary-quality flow crystal, but they've nearly

ruined it with terrible cuts. That being said, whatever spell they managed to force in it is extremely powerful." Skuttur held out the crystal with one hand then touched the pointy tip with the finger of his other hand. Henry saw a green swirl go from his finger and diffuse through the crystal, like a drop of blood in water. "It's everything I can do to resist its hunger."

"It drains Vitus, or Steam, as you dwarves so quaintly call it, and transfers it to the wielder," Buddy explained.

Skuttur continued to turn the stone and examine it. "You said it was in a sword? Shame, all the best magical items are wasted on warriors. This would be more useful for a mage. I can't imagine what a spell like this could do if the cut was right."

Buddy pulled the metal tome from his side pouch and flipped through the pages until he found the parchment from the bones of Lundarbrekka and handed it to the gnome. "Would the cut look something like this?"

Skuttur set the sword's crystal on the nearest bench, but as soon as he laid eyes on the drawing a look of fear crossed his face. He gazed at the sheet of paper, and with trembling hands he delicately lifted it from Buddy's skeletal fingers like he was plucking petals from a frail snodbell. "By Minoa's bearded mushroom, where did you get this?" The gnome's voice trembled then turned to an accusatory tone. "What did Thorodd tell you about me?"

Torgga lowered her voice, trying to calm the anxious artificer. "They knew nothing of you before I brought them to your storeroom."

Skuttur eyed her suspiciously. After a moment he seemed satisfied with the dwab's answer and spent several minutes examining the paper and muttering to himself. Henry thought the gnome had completely forgotten about them, but suddenly his voice perked up. "What we have here is a page from a spell book; one that I've seen before." He rubbed his eyes and squinted. "It comes from the tome of Lady Estreya."

"Who?" Henry asked, straining his mind to remember where he'd heard the name.

"The Empress's sister, according to the invitation to the Gladiator Supreme games that Beast found," Buddy said.

Henry recalled the event, just over a week earlier, the day after they'd found Ox. They had stumbled upon an abandoned pub in the lake cavern of Husavik called the Jolly Squid. Henry had found several bottles of whiskey, but Beast had uncovered a few scraps of paper that were invitations for the entire mountain kingdom of Jallfoss to attend the Gladiator games. It seemed like a lifetime ago, but it had been a majority of Henry's remembered life . . . afterlife.

"That's the one. She was a bit . . . odd, though no one would say she was anything less than a powerful enchantress and diviner." Skuttur pointed to the writing on the paper that Buddy had thought to be part of a spell. It was elegant, flowing, carefully scrawled. "However, if you've examined this at all, you know there are three sets of handwriting on it. I believe the first is hers."

"How do you know that it came from her spellbook?" Torgga asked.

Skuttur ignored the question and continued. "The second set, I'm certain beyond any doubt, is Smyrna's. I've read through thousands of pages of my Master's works."

"And the third?" Buddy prodded.

Skuttur shook his head. "No idea. It's rushed, almost scratched. I don't even recognize the language. Estreya's penmanship is flowery, though there's not enough to figure out the spell. Smyrna drew the sketch and wrote its specification in the dwarven style. What bothers me the most is Smyrna's drawing. Every school of magic has a unique type of cut that suits it. Based on this drawing, the crystal would house a necromantic spell."

"Why would Smyrna draw a schematic for a necromancy crystal?" Torgga asked.

"Again, no idea. Smyrna was as talented with magic as he was with engineering, but necromancy had a negative connotation, even in his day. As far as I know, he never practiced it." Skuttur traced the lines of the drawing with his finger, careful not to mar the sketch. "The drawing is detailed enough. With a high-quality flow crystal, I could probably make it myself."

Without warning, the gnomish artificer's head snapped to the sword crystal still setting on the stone bench. "No, no, no!" He picked up the crystal as his eyes bounced back and forth between the stone and the paper. "Those blasted humans. They were trying to make whatever Smyrna's drawing depicts. Luckily, the novices failed and only created a Steam-robbing sword."

"Master Skuttur, you know more than you're telling us. The Necromancer escaped and now he's ruling Ikrit. If you know something that could help, you need to tell us. The lives of everyone in Hjardharfell, even all of Jallfoss, could be at stake."

Skuttur locked eyes with Henry. The skeleton held his gaze. After a moment his stern visage relaxed, and he released a heavy sigh. "Ruling Ikrit . . . that leaves me with no choice." They waited as Skuttur resigned himself and began telling his story, "I was there, one hundred years ago . . . when Smyrna released the Necromancer."

CHAPTER 27

Tones of nostalgia and sadness filled the old gnome's voice. "There were thirteen of us, all beyond excited to be Master Smyrna's apprentices, or *flowsmiths*, as he called us. Unmatched brilliance didn't even begin to describe the artificer's knowledge and ingenuity. Any aspiring gnome or dwarf would have killed for the chance to work under him. I wasn't nearly as talented as some of the others, but I worked the hardest." Skuttur slumped on a stone chair.

The benches were small for humans or even dwarves, but Buddy, Henry, and Torgga made do as they sat and listened to the gnome's account. "The Source Crystal was the greatest discovery in the history of Jallfoss. Nothing came close in four thousand years. We almost missed it, but a tiny vein of Legendary-quality flow crystals led us to the chamber. It was at least was ten thousand paces across and filled with rivers of lava. Strangely enough, there were also trees. Hundreds of them, just like you'd see above ground. It made no sense, as there was no sunlight, but the flora helped us breathe through the lava's sulfur. We also found a ridiculous amount of golem steel and eversharp in the cavern, and it was the only place I know of where Transcendent-quality flow crystals have been found. The Source Crystal sat in the middle, bigger than anything I've seen by far. At Omega-quality, none of our tools could even scratch its surface. It took Smyrna a few weeks, but after several dozen failed prototypes, he created the Flow Bracers and an interface that could channel the structure's power."

Failed prototypes, Henry thought, then pulled out the strange cylinder with shattered flow crystals, "Interface? Any chance this is it?"

Skuttur threw his hands in the air in frustration. "You blasted skeletons are full of surprises. Minoa's lazy eye, where did you come across that, and is there anything else in your satchels I should be aware of? Yes, that is one of the prototypes—a focused crystal array that acts as a switch to activate the Source Crystal."

Henry returned the device to his pack. "We found a hidden chamber and the remains of some dwarven and gnomish miners. They caused a cave in that we think blocked the Silent. Our other skeletal friends should be helping retrieve the ore from there right now."

"So, some of my friends did survive long enough to stop the Necromancer's army from getting through the back way. Their sacrifice saved us. Good lads, all of 'em." Skuttur sniffed and rubbed his eyes, obviously hiding tears. "If only we had some whiskey to drink to their honor.

"For another time, perhaps." Skuttur dove back into his story, likely pushing the thought of his dead friends from his mind. "Through his research, Smyrna learned that the Source Crystal not only stored an unfathomable amount of magical energy, but when someone connected to the Source Crystal via the array and Flow Bracers, it amplified their spells, hundreds, even thousands of times over. He was so excited to show it off, but he didn't expect a personal visit from the Empress's sister."

The room was completely quite as the artificer told his story. "Before she came, we had conducted hundreds of experiments. We had no reason to think there was any danger. Smyrna had already extracted a huge amount of energy from the Source Crystal. The Flow Bracers worked perfectly. We didn't suspect the Necromancer was inside the crystal the whole time, probably waiting for a strong enough mage to present themselves. I was busy monitoring the equipment when it happened. The monster killed Lady Estreya first. All I heard was her scream then a terrible roar. When I looked up, a horror beyond words was slaughtering the other flowsmiths. It was horrendous. Black bone carapace and eyes deader than any skeleton. The worst part was the fear. Mentally scarring and excruciatingly painful. I still wake up screaming every night thinking of the monster."

Skuttur's hands shook as he gripped his gnarled wooden cane. "I froze. I couldn't move as the monster tore my friends apart. Estreya's spell book landed in front of me, the same one that held this very page, I believe. I reached for it but only managed to grab a few pages before Smyrna pulled me back. I don't know how he did it, but he somehow managed to use a farscroll to transport me straight up. Just imagine, transporting a whole gnome ten miles through an entire mountain range, and directly in front of the Empress's advisors.

"I appeared in Lady Destria's throne room, but she wasn't there. I remember it through the foggy lens of shock. Lord Skodderrfall, the dwarven Elder at the time, was there, along with his son, Thorodd. Bharat, the elven Sage and one of his personal guards were there as well, but I didn't know who the lady elf was at the time. There was also a human, the Empress's personal tutor and advisor, I think."

"I told them my story. Bharat and Skodderrfall nearly fought, but I was so shaken up that I don't remember what it was about. Eventually the Sage and wizard took the pages and went to tell Destria, while Skodderrfall took Thorodd and me down to Hjardharfell to prepare the troops. By the time we got back, the Underdeep had already started to fall. I've spent a century fighting with the guilt, hoping Thorodd would be able to take back our home and avenge my fallen brothers."

"It may be even worse than you think. Thorodd believes the Necromancer is actually the returned Archon King. Henry said.

"I was aware of his theory of the Archon King, and until this very moment, I never told another soul of what happened at the Source Crystal." Skuttur pressed against his cane and struggled to stand from his chair.

"So why tell your story now?" Torgga asked, assisting the frail gnome in his effort to stand.

Skuttur let out a long sigh as he steadied himself. "Because somehow, Smyrna escaped and created his golem. I never knew now he managed to survive, but if you found Smyrna's bones at Lundarbrekka, that means the story of his failure is not true. He didn't create the golem to protect our treasures from humans, he did it to stop the spread of the Necromancer's forces. I believe his golem was what held the Silent at bay all these years. It protected us for a century . . . then you destroyed it."

Henry tried to stammer a response, but nothing came to his mind. Had the golem been the force holding back the Silent, only to have Henry and his companions release the Necromancer's carnage on Hjardharfell?

Skuttur saw the worry on their faces as clear as if they still had skin. "If the golem had truly been keeping the Silent at bay, there is nothing stopping the forces of evil from streaming upward. The Silent are chasing other cave creatures toward Hjardharfell, and it will get much worse.

"Don't fret, skeletons. Hjardharfell would have been abandoned in a few years, regardless of your actions. You may have unleashed the Necromancer's forces on us, but you may also have uncovered the key to stopping him. We just need to figure out how to use the tools Smyrna left us."

Skuttur held up the parchment and Henry's hilt crystal. "This is a message from Smyrna himself, albeit unintentional. The page shows the cut, and your crystal has the spell. If you can find me a Transcendent-quality flow crystal, I can make the cut. Then, if we can figure out how to recreate the spell, we can take the Necromancer's magic and turned it against the vile creature."

"What's stopping you from transferring the spell?" Henry asked.

Skuttur pointed the pokey end of one of his instruments at the crystal. "The cut left it with too many imperfections. If we tried a transfer, it would likely unleash the spell on all of us. The process might be worth the risk at a later time, but not right now."

"If you had the right crystal and the correct spell, could you create another golem like Smyrna's, or even several?" Henry proposed.

Skuttur eyed Henry and the skeleton could see the gears in the old gnome's head turning rapidly. After a moment of heavy thinking, he nodded his head in affirmation. "Maybe. I can't do it without the spell that goes in the crystal, but if you revive Lady Destria, maybe she can offer some insight. However, if Hjardharfell is going to stand long enough for you to get to her, we've got a lot of work to do. First thing's first. If we're going to repel the Silent, we'll need magic as much as we'll need weapons and armor. These crystals . . ." Skuttur waived his hand to the daises lining the wall benches, "were created to hold powerful spells and transfer them to armaments. I hear your evocation and transmutation are slightly above acceptable, so I'll load your best spells into the storage crystals."

Before Buddy could respond to the backhanded compliment, Skuttur continued. "Second, you'll use the Flow Bracer's to wake the Empress. She was the most powerful mage of her time. She stopped the Necromancer once, hopefully she can do it again, or at least tell us how."

"Easy, what else?" Henry asked, aware that the tasks before them were far from simple.

Skuttur smiled. "The only other thing you could help with is retrieving a few Transcendent quality flow crystals for me to make Smyrna's cut. If the Empress can figure out the spell that goes in there, I just might be able to create another golem, even several, and we can fight the war on all fronts—the Silent from below, the Archon King and his Ikritians from the plains, and the Sprigs from above."

Buddy pulled the sack of flow crystals from one of his belts and placed it on the stone slab in front of Skuttur. "Like these?" the mage asked with a palpable amount of smugness.

The gnome eyed the pouch then opened it and removed a fist sized crystal. "I need you to stop holding out on me, dead mage. Or tell me what magic allows you to keep pulling surprises out of your sack."

Buddy, Henry, Skuttur, and to some extent, Gnaz, spent the next few hours loading spells into the storage crystals, much the same way they did for Ox's hammer and Beast's daggers, though the process was much more difficult. Skuttur explained that when storing a spell for further enchantments, the caster had to build the spell, not just cast it. If done correctly, the crystal would need to pull a significant amount of Vitus from them to recreate the kernel of their Abilities inside the storage crystals.

After several exhausting hours and dozens of failed attempts, Henry was able to load Blitz and Harden into two enchantment crystals. He had nearly passed out from Vitus drain, but Skuttur assured him that the gnomes could now enchant other flow crystals with the spells that would power dwarven weapons and armor, giving them a distinct advantage against the Silent. Now that the blueprint of his Ability had been captured, the dais could easily transfer that spell to another flow crystal for use in arms and armor.

The brunt of the effort didn't even come from Henry and Buddy, but from the artificers themselves. Skuttur had the expertise to guide the exercise, but not the stamina to facilitate the process. Gnaz had come a long way in just a week, but after loading Henry's Blitz into a flow crystal, he was covered in sweat and looked completely exhausted. Luckily for the gnomes, Muji had been watching, and saved the artificers from dying of Vitus drain. At first, Skuttur was against the trogold's help, but when Muji and Buddy loaded his frost spell in just half an hour, the ancient artificer acquiesced to his assistance. After seeing what a Tier-15 trogold could do, Skuttur even praised the furry creature, and the gnome and Buddy began to get along.

Henry could tell that Buddy was completely in his element. The academic research was right up his alley, and the mage even had a cheerful tone in his voice. He was so engrossed with his work that he didn't even notice Torgga's departure. The dwab had watched the spectacle intently, pride and other emotions gleaming in her eyes, but she let Henry know that she had to check on the front lines and would return in the morning.

While they worked, Henry and Buddy tried to pry more

information about Smyrna and the Necromancer from the Master Artificer, but Skuttur was done talking on the subject. Instead, he pressed Buddy to fill more crystals with offensive magic. The mage complied, and he and Muji charged more dais-held storage crystals with evocation.

He started with fire, force, water, and frost, but when he got to lightning, Henry took a nervous step back.

"You don't strike me as the wary type. Afraid of a little spark?" Skuttur commented.

Henry shook his head. "No, I'm actually resistant to lightning and weak to fire, but every time I get hit with lightning, I have strange visions."

"Visions?" the gnome asked, raising a curious eyebrow.

"Just a continued vision I guess, of a desert and a storm, but I get weaker every time I have one. Strangely, the last one gave me an Ability," Henry explained.

"I doubt lightning could cause weakening visions, and it definitely won't give you Abilities. However, this is worth investigating and likely something you need to fix. We could always try to induce another . . . vision. Better here than on the battlefield, wouldn't you say?" Skuttur suggested.

"Master Skuttur does have a point. In a controlled environment we may have a chance to gain some understanding of your plight," Buddy offered.

Henry agreed that he needed to learn what was causing the strange reveries, but he preferred to avoid the experience all together.

Buddy put a hand on Henry's shoulder. "Henry, if we're going to undertake this mission, we need to be able to rely on you. I don't question your determination, and our last battle against the Silent proved your capabilities, but if something is inhibiting your ability to fight. We need to understand it. Otherwise, you not only put yourself and us in danger, but the potential salvation of the entire mountain."

Henry acquiesced. "I guess I have a duty to see this though."

"That you do. We've come too far to let our limitations hold us back," Buddy said.

Buddy was right, Henry admitted to himself. The others were relying on him to lead them to the Empress and save the mountain. "Fine, but how do we do this?" He asked.

"Not in my workshop. This way," Skuttur said and led them through the door. They followed the artificer through a series of tunnels that lead to an open pavilion with mushroom-filled planters, a sun globe-filled chandelier, and a balcony that overlooked the mushroom fields. High above the ground level, Henry could see the grid-like layout of mushroom farms and various cages that looked like they held livestock, but he was still too far away to make out what they contained. Far in the distance, he could see the green iridescence of the tall mushroom tress that made up the vast underground forest of the Grunischwald. Just above, the lumimoss dotted a rock dome that was so high and sparkly that it resembled the night sky. The inhabitants below rushed as they prepared for the imminent danger. Henry could see wagons pulled by dwarves coming and going into the forest, likely taking arms to the front lines and bringing back ore for the forges.

"This is safer. Stand here," Skuttur ordered, directing Henry to a spot in the middle of the tiled courtyard. Stone benches and potted mushrooms made the pavilion look like a relaxing spot.

Henry complied and took his place where he was instructed. Buddy and Skuttur stood near the entrance, opposite the balcony and talked about the best way to conduct their experiment. When Henry was in position, Buddy asked if he was ready. Henry, still unsure, nodded and widened his stance.

Buddy lifted his palm and a white ball of lightning the size of an acorn formed in his hand, cracking with arcs of electricity. Buddy aimed the spell, and it flashed toward Henry, hitting him square in the chest. His body tensed and he felt a burning sensation, but it wasn't significant. The spell's effects quickly faded. He acknowledged a flashing icon and looked at his Health.

Lightning resistance applied: 8/8 damage negated
Health: 115/115

"Anything?" Skuttur asked.

"No. My lightning resistance stopped everything. I think the spell was too weak—" Henry realized the folly of his words too late to mitigate the impact as a blast of lightning twice the size of his head hit him with the force of Ox's hammer. His entire body seized. A new notification appeared in his view.

Lightning Resistance applied: 10/43 damage negated
Health: 82/115

CHAPTER 28

Howling wind and rumbling thunder rocked Henry's senses. Heavy raindrops pelted his face and blurred his vision, making it even harder to adjust his eyes to the near pitch black around him. The cold rain chilled his skin, and the hard stone pressed against his back, sure signs that his skeletal body had been replaced with flesh. A brilliant flash lit up the sky, silhouetting jagged stones all around him.

It had worked. Buddy's last lightning bolt had sent him back to the desert and the ominous howl in the storm indicated he wasn't alone.

Henry sat up, frantically searching the sky for the dragon, but the dark clouds, driving rain, and black of night obscured any sign of a threat.

"Warrior. To me." Henry turned toward the sound of the prisoner's voice—aged and strained, yet still forceful. He could barely make out the man's face behind the stone spikes of his cage, but a distant flash of lightning revealed his pale visage spiderwebbed with black veins. "Hurry, the Primal returns. Free me, and together we will kill it."

Henry brought himself to unsteady feet, though his body

now strengthened with muscle and tendons righted itself much easier than bones by themselves. He felt strong, though cold. "I'm coming," Henry assured the man, making his way over to the cage while continuing to search the sky for the winged monster. *He just called it a Primal. Could it be a real dragon?*

Haruspex

Like before, the divination didn't work in this place. Without magic, he would have to rely on his flesh instead of his Vitus-fueled Abilities. Strangely, he felt much more in tune with his extended Attributes. He pulled in a deep breath, spreading his awareness as far as it would reach and felt his Harmony connect to the environment. He could sense the rain, wind, and rocks and their linkage leading back to him like he was a spider in the middle of a huge web.

With his Affinity, he pulled on the connection, hauling that energy toward him and feeling it flow through his channels. Then he pushed that energy out, flexing his Might as his skin warmed and shoved away to cold feeling. He felt like his first six Attributes, Strength through Resolve, governed the capabilities of his mind and body, but the newest three, Might, Affinity, and Harmony, had more to do with his connection to the outside world.

A rasping voice interrupted his introspection. "Your skills won't work here, warrior. Now hurry. You need to find a way to get me out." The man insisted as his mouth stretched into a strange combination of smile and snarl, though the panic in his eyes never wavered.

Henry reached the jagged stone spikes that confined the emaciated man and pressed hard to test their resilience. The yellow glass gave no indication of budging. "How can I get you out? I'm strong, but I can't break the stone. How did you get in here, and who are you?"

The man clung to the yellow glass pillars that held him. "You must find a way, for both our sake. My name is Raynott."

"Raynott Degonhart? The one that imprisoned the Necromancer?" Henry asked. The man gave him a confused look, so Henry pressed again. "The Archon King? You fought him, right?"

The slightest hint of recognition crossed the man's frantic eyes, and the corners of his mouth twitched. "Yes, we must stop the Archon King and the Necromancer. Once we defeat the dragon, your enemies will fall to our regency. Free me, warrior, and I shall join your charge."

Henry paused as he tried to work through Raynott's response. Before he could reply, the earth shook, and a jolt of pressure sent him flying backward. The surge was stronger than the force from Buddy's evocation, it felt like a powerful will was bearing down on him. Shock hit him harder than the pressure when he realized the sensation was exactly like the presence of the Silent, only the dragon's was a hundred-fold more powerful. It wasn't an aura, more of an intrinsic part of its being.

His mind resisted the onslaught . . . barely, but his body couldn't withstand the intensity, and the cyclone launched him away. As he tumbled, he saw the form of a huge, winged monster perched atop the spire that rose above the prisoner's cage. He couldn't see much detail, but he could make out jutting horns, bat-like wings, and powerful legs. It was large enough to dwarf the bearded salamander. The monster crouched and launched itself into the sky, vanishing into the swirling tempest above.

Henry came to a halt with his face down in a puddle. He lifted himself up and wiped the water from his eyes. Lightning flashed above him and reflected off the water. The ripples obscured the reflection, but he saw a face that he both did and didn't recognize. He had a strong jaw covered in a bit of stubble. Shaggy brown hair partially covered sapphire blue eyes, and a stream of blood trickled down from a wound on his cheek. He paused for a moment, transfixed by his own image, but another flash of lightning revealed an open maw descending from the clouds above him and growing larger at an alarming rate.

Henry rolled as a jaw large enough to swallow a team of horses and their cart smashed into the rock where he had been just a second prior. Shale exploded beneath the force of the monster. Dark blue scales the size of Henry's hand covered its face, but its horns and spikes were the same yellow glass that made up the stone he'd found in the desert as well as the cage that held Raynott.

The behemoth afforded Henry precious few seconds to analyze its features. The dragon's throat rumbled with a growl that shook the very stones beneath Henry's feet, then it snapped at him with another chop that seemed much too fast for a creature so massive.

Henry dodged close to the dragon's body, forcing it to maneuver itself off balance just to reach him. Henry knew that if he got any further away from the dragon that it would have no trouble crushing him. Powerful hind legs tipped with claws longer than Henry was tall churned through the stone like freshly tilled earth. Thick, leathery skin stretched from its body to its long, winged fore legs, then on to a further spine that gave the colossal lizard a wingspan easily over a hundred feet.

The scales on its body were much larger and more rugged than those on its face. Henry grabbed one and tried to lift himself onto the dragon's back, but the monster whipped around at an incredible speed and kicked him with a flash of a back leg. The impact sent him rocketing through the air. He felt like he was soaring fast enough to keep going back to where he had started in the desert, had a jagged stone pillar not stopped his flight. He caught the pillar on the flat edge, square on his back. Ribs broke, and air and blood spurted from his mouth. Henry righted himself as he dropped and somehow landed on his feet, though still riddled with pain and gasping for breath. The dragon didn't give him time to recover.

The monstrous blue lizard faced Henry just over a hundred paces away, and a deep guttural growl formed in its throat. Its yellow horns flashed as sparks of lightning danced across the dark scales and reflected off yellow, cat-like eyes.

Those eyes. They were filled with pure animalistic rage, like the entire storm above had been compressed into those two marvelous, dangerous orbs. His awe only lasted a breath before he felt his skin tingle. The air around him charged with static, but he was already jumping out of the way. The dragon opened its mouth, and an arc of blue and white lightning blasted forth, shattering the stone pillar and melting whatever hadn't been blown away.

Henry didn't take the time to gawk at the pulsing ball of destruction with coronas of electricity spiraling from its center. The shards of exploded and melted rock that tore at his skin were enough incentive to keep him moving. Though his Affinity screamed a warning at him, it wasn't necessary for him to understand that suffering a direct blast from the monster would spell his end, even if his lightning resistance still worked in the desert.

Henry ran, and the dragon gave chase. Sharp stones tore at his bare feet but he paid them little notice as he jumped, spun, and skidded around jagged spikes and pillars. The dragon gained on him. It wasn't as fast as Henry on the ground, but it could topple the stones impedances instead of going around them, allowing it to quickly gain on its prey.

He couldn't use magic, though his heightened Attributes were still available. With none of the restrictions of his *Skeletal Body* or *Path of the Desert* Status Effects, he felt faster and more formidable than ever. However, Strength and Mobility weren't the Attributes he needed most. Henry polled his Perception and Acumen, willing his mind to map the layout of the stone oasis. There was a straight path, maybe fifty yards long that led to the prisoner's cage, and he was running perpendicular and just few paces away from the loose stones at its start.

Henry crossed the rubble and feigned a trip, exaggerating a stumble as he sped forward. He felt wet heat from the dragon's breath and smelled something he could only describe as burnt rot. The dragon made a rumbling guttural sound of excitement, likely envisioning chomping on the fleeing man.

It took the bait.

The dragon lunged as Henry planted his foot on a firm rock just past the loose stones. He launched his body to the side as a deafening snap of dragon's teeth filled the space he had just left. He heard the monster's claws skid as it tried and failed to overpower its own momentum. Rock exploded and lightning arced. The dragon tumbled. Henry didn't look back until he reached Raynott's cage.

Shock mixed with a small bit of impressed approval—that was the emotion on the prisoner's face as Henry spun and put his back to the yellow glass prison. The dragon had already righted itself, and the low angry growl it released as it looked at the Henry and Raynott was far more terrifying than all the dread monsters he'd faced combined.

"Fool warrior, what are you doing?" Raynott spat, more

forceful than Henry thought the emaciated prisoner should be capable.

"Taking a page from Lord Oxendine's book." Henry curled his lips into a smile, preparing himself to face the dragon head-on.

"Osyrian was no fool . . ." Raynott's shocked voice fell on deaf ears as Henry's complete focus spread though his awareness. The dragon narrowed its eyes and snarled as dirt and broken rock cascaded off its thick hide.

It was time for Henry to put his newest Attributes to the test. The connection he felt with the dragon was still there, the same one he felt with the Silent, but much stronger. It wasn't like a connection to its mind, but more like if the monster was a candle in a dark room. His entire being felt like a moth drawn to the flicker.

That feeling must be Harmony, Henry thought, flexing the Attribute until he felt the connection anchor itself, *but I need it to be more*. He pressed his will against the connection, forcing it to bend and mold from a thread into a channel. It was like building a sandcastle under the water, across an ocean. The more he pressed, the more it wanted to fall apart, but with a final flex of his Affinity, the connection solidified. It wasn't the flood of emotions that the Drift Amulet imparted on him, but rather a small trickle of the most prevalent workings in the dragon's intent; hunger, the excitement of a chase, and no small amount of embarrassment from having been tricked by its prey.

The dragon must have sensed Henry forming the channel because it halted and eyed him. He felt the slightest bit of curiosity boil to the surface of the monster's mind.

It's working, Henry thought. *Now to send it one of my emotions.* He burst through the fog of his own mind and reached into his core. The swirling tempest had nearly turned black as it violently churned and flung relentless bolts of lightning. Henry pulled as much power as he could from the storm and used it to bolster his Might. He forced a single but powerful thought through the channel—a challenge.

Unexpectedly, the dragon winced as though Ox had caught it in the face with his maul. The monster's curiosity turned to confusion then to disbelief in a heartbeat. Its mouth opened into a vicious snarl, revealing a forest of sword-sized teeth. A wave of rage washed the lesser emotions away like a wooden raft beneath the force of a tidal wave. Its prey had just rebuked its authority, as though it were an equal.

The dragon stretched its behemoth maw and released a roar that shook the entire oasis. Jagged pillars crumbled and Henry couldn't tell if it was from the dragon's bellow or the rumble of the behemoth's footfalls as it charged.

"So, you choose to die as a brave fool? Very well, warrior." Raynott's words faded under the roar of the storm and the quake of the enraged colossus. Henry pushed off the stone cage and launched himself forward. In the space of a breath, he neared within a few paces of the dragon and forced all the mental energy he could from his core and into his challenge, further driving the monster into its blind rage.

The dragon opened its mouth to swallow Henry, and he felt its heavy breath blow back his hair. He dropped his body and let momentum carry him sliding on the wet rocks. Jagged, curved teeth longer than his arm filled Henry's vision as the shale tore into his back.

The dragon closed its mouth around empty air, inches above the evading warrior. The snap of its jaw was louder than any lightning strike; almost as loud as the crash of monster and rock as the mountain-sized lizard plowed into Raynott's cage. Henry turned just in time to see Raynott's head duck before the dragon smashed into his prison. The entire structure exploded under the shear mass of the monster, sending yellow rock flying like shrapnel that impacted and destroyed any nearby jagged stone structures.

Henry scrambled to his feet and ran toward the tumbling dragon. Through the channel between them, Henry felt the dragon's rage soar to a frenzied mania. He cut off the connection, not needing his Affinity to perceive the creature's wrath. Lightning erupted across the churning mass of scales, wings, and claws, illuminating the stone oasis and destroying any remaining pillars in the vicinity.

With the Mobility of a cat, the dragon righted itself and spun in place. Its spiked tail scattered any rubble within a hundred feet as wild eyes searched for the eluding warrior. Raynott was gone, as was his prison, and in its place was a dark, gaping hole in the earth. It was just a few feet wide, but the bottom disappeared into darkness. Exposed and vulnerable, Henry had no other options. He ran.

He was just a few steps from the black hole when he locked eyes with the dragon. The lightning arcing across its scales erupted. The monster stretched its jaw fully open and released a roar that drowned out the thunder in the storm above. A blazing orb of blinding white energy formed in the opening between its teeth. The rain around its maw instantly turned to steam.

The beam that spewed from dragon was a thousand times the power of any of Buddy's lightning bolts. Henry dove into the hole as the rush of light and heat blew past the opening. Waves and waves of electricity surged through his body, wracking him with convulsions. He bounced off the rocky walls of the hole and tumbled into darkness. Stone fell all around him, and he plummeted into the abyss.

—

Status Effect: Fourth Path of the Desert. STR -12, MOB -12, FOR -4, ACU -4 Health -20, Fire Resistance -20, Lightning resistance +20

Ability Discovered: Primal Urge I. Only a—

"Henry! Henry!" Buddy shouted. The mage forced a healing crystal into Henry's palm as the warrior flailed and tried to gather his senses. "My apologies, Henry. With your lightning Resistance that high, my magic shouldn't have damaged you that much, but your bones nearly crumbled under the bolt."

Henry could make out his Health bar at the top of his vision—well below **25%**. It took a few minutes to calm himself and the healing crystal brought his Health above **50%**. "It wasn't your bolt. Whatever I endure in the Path affects me here as well. I nearly died this time."

"We only saw you flying backward and your bones crisping. What happened in your vision?" Buddy asked.

"I fought a dragon . . . ran away from a dragon, really. But I also figured out who the man in my visions is. He's Raynott Degonhart. He told me we have to stop the Archon King *and* the Necromancer.

Buddy cocked his head and looked at Henry. "Are you sure he said *and?*"

"Without a doubt," Henry affirmed.

"That implies the two are not the same . . . and that both exist . . . There is more at play here than we realize. I recommend that until we learn more, you remain wary of the revelations in your visions."

Henry flexed and rotated his bones, still unsure that they would hold together after the punishment he took. "Our mission still stands: we must hurry to Destria."

Henry's body and mind had taken a beating. He attempted to review his Status updates and dive into his core, but he drifted off to sleep before he could accomplish either.

While Henry recovered in the deserted dwarven plaza, Skuttur brought Buddy and Muji back to the flow crystal room. Gnaz retrieved several hundred superior quality flow crystals, and the four spent the rest of the night transferring various spells into the smaller shard and delivering the enchanted devices to the forge to be combined with weapons and armor.

CHAPTER 29

The woman's cry pierced his mind like Beast's arrow through a salamander's head. *"Henry!"*

He jolted awake, reaching for his sword and preparing for battle. He found neither a weapon nor an adversary in the empty pavilion. Even his time unconscious didn't allow him a moment of peace.

He had slept on one of several stone benches that lined the outside of the dwarven parlor, having drifted off shortly after returning from his desert vision. Had he really fought a dragon? His head sure felt like it. Though his body couldn't experience actual pain, the exhaustion present in both his mind and bones confirmed that his Desert Path was much more than a dream.

With shaking skeletal fingers, he rubbed the sleep from his eyes—an action that did nothing to sooth his non-existent flesh, though the familiar motion calmed him, nonetheless. He looked around and noticed some of the potted mushrooms on the far side of the plaza had been smashed and scattered, leaving clods of dirt on the wall.

No, he thought, those were scorch marks from Buddy's lightning blast. The mage hadn't held back when he unleashed the second bolt, and the damage to the plaza—and Henry's bones—proved it.

He groaned, bringing himself to his feet and looking out over the balcony. Most of Hjardharfell was a series of caves and tunnels carved into the mountain, but the city extended into a monstrous, open cavern a thousand feet high, and several miles long called the Grunischwald. Far below, mushroom-construction homes extended to a defensive wall, then the landscape turned into farms with lines of oddly shaped fungus and cages for various animals. The farmlands were busy with movement, like someone had disturbed an ant colony. A constant stream of carts made their way from Hjardharfell to the base of the thousand-foot mushroom trees that made up the underground forest. The dwarves and carts below were far away, but at **40**, Henry's Perception was his highest Attribute, and it was easily up to the task. He focused and saw the carts were filled with various weapons and armor.

Good. The dwarves must have been busy all night at the forges. Hopefully Beast, Ox, and Buddy were able to assist the smiths and artificers.

The sun globes around him had begun to brighten, indicating that it was morning. He had no idea how long he'd slept, but he felt it was the most restful slumber he'd gotten since he'd woken as undead. Though he was weak from the Desert Path Status Effect, the damage from Buddy's spell, and days of fighting, he felt he was as close to refreshed as a skeleton could get. He acknowledged the glyphs flashing in his vision and reviewed his full Status.

Haruspex

Name: Henry

Race: Human Skeleton

Tier: 12

Health: 105/105

Vitus: 109/113

Attributes:

STR: 19

MOB: 32

FOR: 30

ACU: 23

PER: 40

RES: 36

MIG: 5

AFI: 8

HAR: 4

Resistances: Physical, Environmental, Lightning, Poison (Immune)

Weakness: Fire

Thresholds:

MOB +10%. -10% Vitus requirement for all transmutation Abilities

FOR +10%. Health +1 per point of FOR, +1 Health regeneration per hour

PER +10%. Transmutation Abilities extend to Equipment. Divinity Abilities expanded

RES +10%. Mental Damage Resistance +1, +1 Vitus regeneration per hour

Status Effects:

Soul Anchor: Slowly regenerate all damage, even beyond death. Degradation of the mind can vary and is much more pronounced in sentient beings. This Effect does not stop natural decay. +2 Health/Hour

Skeletal Body: Without flesh and blood, your STR and FOR are

> greatly reduced. However, your body no longer suffers from many ailments common to living forms. STR -20%, FOR -20%, Damage Resistance: Physical -1 (Bludgeoning -2), Environmental +1, Poison: Immune

Fourth Path of the Desert. STR -12, MOB -12, FOR -4, ACU -4 Health -20, Fire Resistance -20, Lightning resistance +20

Abilities:

> Spark I (Evocation)
>
> Sacrifice II (Transmutation)
>
> Blitz III (Transmutation)
>
> Harden II (Transmutation)
>
> Haruspex IV (Divinity)
>
> Consume II (Necromancy, Passive)
>
> Taunt I (Enchantment)
>
> Primal Urge I (Enchantment)

The last two Abilities caught his attention. He'd been too tired the night before and didn't take time to examine them. He let their descriptions expand.

Taunt I (Enchantment). Pit your Resolve against a target's and goad them to attack you

Primal Urge I (Enchantment). Only a fool would challenge a dragon. Now that you've confronted a Primal, there is no going back

Henry remembered the powerful emotions running through the dragon's mind and how he had forged a connection between him and the monster. Somehow, he had used his new Attributes—Might, Affinity, and Harmony—to create and affect that connection, but the specifics on how the process worked still eluded him. If Strength, Mobility, and Fortitude were characteristics of his body, and Acumen, Perception, and Resolve corresponded to his mind, then what aspect of him did the newest Attributes reflect? The Soul Anchor Status Effect that kept him alive, as well as the Soul Essence he harvested from fallen enemies, suggested that souls were a real thing . . . and that he had one. To say that his Remnant Attributes were facets of his soul felt incomplete, and didn't explain the way those aspects allowed him to interact with the dragon. The strange Abilities that his Desert Path had given him only added to the mystery.

Taunt seemed straight forward enough—it was enchantment magic, which Buddy had explained was magic of the mind. His Resolve must have been enough to allow him to goad the dragon while they were fighting. *Fighting* was a stretch. He mostly ran and evaded, but it worked nonetheless, allowing him to use the monster's anger against it.

The second line of expanded text was ominous and more of a warning than an Ability. Primal Urge must have originated from his use of Harmony to form a connection with the dragon, Affinity to strengthen that connection, and Might to force his challenge into the monster's psyche. Thorodd and Ox were both Remnants, apparently, but their explanations were vague at best, and didn't help clarify either his visions, or the strange happenings with his Status. At a loss for a better alternative, he decided to test the Ability.

Primal Urge

Primal Urge Failed: No valid target available

No valid target? Henry wondered with a stifled laugh, *I guess I need to track down a Primal.* After a few more failed attempts, he gave up trying to activate the Ability and turned his attention to his Attributes—namely the Threshold section.

The Desert Path Status Effect had dropped his Strength down to **19**. He was even further away from the Strength Threshold than he had been, but he still had four Attributes above **25**. The Effects of the Mobility, Fortitude, and Resolve Thresholds were simple to comprehend—they affected Vitus usage and Health recovery. The Perception Threshold, however, was less quantifiable. It allowed him to extend transmutation Abilities to his equipment, and it also expanded his divination magic.

He thought back to his fight with the dread mantids, where he used the Perception Threshold buff to transfer his Harden Ability directly into his shield. That made sense, as it was a transmutation Ability, but what about the claim of expanding his divination? Before Henry could explore the thought, his Perception alerted him to a presence in the small courtyard. Henry dismissed his Status, then turned to see who had joined him.

"I'm glad to see you're well after yesterday's battles," the gnome said.

"Olafur! Great to see you're safe. How fare the front lines?" Henry lifted a hand to wave. The bone fingers sticking from his leather bracers caught his attention, reminding him of the undead curse—a stark contrast to the flesh he possessed in his Desert Path.

"Each cluster had a few run-ins with the Silent. We took some losses, but now that arms and armor have started to arrive we're faring much better. I was sent back to help enchant healing crystals now that my magic is less needed in the tunnels. Thorodd asked me to retrieve you. He and your fellow skeletons are waiting for you in the main hall."

"Lead the way." Henry gathered his pack and followed the gnome. The tunnel portion of the city of Hjardharfell was confusing, and many of the paths doubled back on themselves or led to dead ends, but Henry's Perception and Acumen were growing enough that he had no trouble understanding the layout. After a few minutes following Olafur, they came to the open cave of Hjardharfell proper. It was a mile-wide carved-out sphere filled with crossing ramps, platforms, dwellings, and various shops. Supported in the middle of the city, like the yolk of a giant smeendavear egg, sat an enormous stone structure with windows and balconies that served as Hjardharfell's capital building.

Word of the skeletons' achievements must have spread, because the reception he received from the city's inhabitants was completely different than his first arrival. The city was a bustling hive of activity with gnomes, dwarves, orcs, and even a few humans, running about. Every one of them wanted to stop and talk to him. They all greeted Henry and thanked him for saving their city, offering him various baubles, mushrooms, and grilled meats.

Henry politely refused as Olafur pushed through the gathering crowd of citizens. "Move along, move along. Stop holding him up. He's on his way to see Lord Thorodd. Get out of the way, you jabbering chonkeros!"

Henry followed Olafur away from the crowd and into the central structure. In the dwarven world, wood was a sign of opulence. Doors, chairs, and tables made of the scarce material were carved with precise geometric shapes. Valuable looking gems were fixed in chandeliers, diffusing the light from sun globes that reflected off perfectly polished marble floors. They went up several flights of a winding staircase and through the open gear-mounted doors of Thorodd's chamber.

White stone pillars lined the expansive, domed room, and a singular sun globe hung from the ceiling directly over top a huge stone table. Three dwarves, Thorodd, Torgga, and Skuttur, stood next to Buddy, Beast, and Ox around the table. Each turned to Henry and Olafur as the two walked across the onyx floor.

Ox immediately caught Henry's attention. He sported armor that made him look like a dread ram was standing upright. Various dread bones were fastened together with metal links, golem steel plates, and leather straps. The dread-ram skull Ox had taken as a trophy had been fashioned into helmet, and Ox peered through its open maw.

"Ghakk," Gator squawked from Ox's left shoulder plate. The amalgamator wore a dread mantid skull as a helmet and looked content with his perch on the massive skeleton's new armor. Several heads taller than Henry and as wide as an actual bull, Ox was an intimidating sight for sure, and Henry was glad to have to the huge skeleton on his side. He assessed the armor as he approached.

Haruspex

Item: Molten Dreadmail (Epic)

Description: Armor. Heavy platemail assembled from the husks of fallen dread monsters and forged together with golem steal. Physical Damage Resistance 20 (Slashing +8, Bludgeoning +5, Piercing +8). Fire resistance +15, Heat Resistance +15, Magic Resistance +5. MOB -10. Hardness 30, Structure 200/200

Ability: Adapt II. Silent components hunger for the living. Ensure a perfect fit by sacrificing Health to affect the armor's size and shape

"I thought there was a dread ram in here, and I almost attacked," Henry jested. "You look good, Lord Oxendine."

"Oh, stop. You're making me blush." Ox laughed and puffed out his chest.

"Nice of you to join us, sleepy bones," Torgga chirped with her signature giggle.

"Yeah, I may have overdone it a bit yesterday, but I'm ready to head out," Henry returned. "Lord Thorodd, were the forges successful?"

"Very, and as promised, we've set you up for your journey." Thorodd motioned to a pile of weapons and armor setting on the table.

Henry approached and nearly gasped when he saw the equipment. "The dwarves made all this in a single night?"

"That and much more. Let none say that Hjardharfell left you wanting." Thorodd grumbled, unable to hide the pride in his voice over the exceptional job his smiths had done. The dwarven king smiled and downed a heavy swig from his stein.

"I will. I can't believe you took bones, ore, and broken armor, and turned it into this!" Henry said, barely containing his excitement as he identified and donned the kit.

Haruspex

Item: Gladiator's Dreadmail (Epic)

Description: Armor. Light scalemail assembled from the husks of fallen dread monsters. Physical Damage Resistance 12 (Slashing +5, Bludgeoning +2, Piercing +5). MOB -4. Hardness 30, Structure 100/100

Ability: Adapt

Item: Dread Claw Javelin (Epic)

Description: Ranged weapon. Due to master craftsmanship, the range and accuracy of this weapon is greatly increased. Piercing damage +3. Accuracy +3. Hardness 30, Structure 100/100

Ability: Adapt

Item: Dread Mantid Shield (Epic)
Description: Kite Shield. Crafted from a dread mantid chest plate, this weapon can grow from the size of a buckler to that of a tower shield. Hardness 30, Structure 100/100
Ability: Adapt

The dwarves had taken the high-quality leather from his Gladiator Supreme armor and used it to fashion together various dread bones. They had even forged an open-faced helmet from spiked plates of golem steel. The set was a bit loose on him until he used Sacrifice to activate the armor's Adapt Ability. His Vitus dropped a few points, and the armor contracted to a perfect fit. It would marginally restrict his Mobility, but with **32** points in the Attribute, the protection it offered easily offset the restriction of movement.

The shield was the size of a dinner plate, but when he secured it to his forearm and pushed Vitus into it, the dread bone expanded to the size of a kite shield. It was light, but harder than steel. Few weapons would be able to overcome a Hardness of **30** before chipping away at all **100** points of its structure.

The dwarves had also modified five dread claw spikes into perfectly balanced javelins. He reduced them all to the size of daggers, refilling his Vitus, and secured them to his hip with a provided leather carrier.

"This is amazing!" Henry shouted when he was finished securing the gear. "I still can't believe the Mastersmith made this in a single day!"

Buddy handed him a sheathed blade, hilt first. "One more thing. This should hold up a bit better than your last sword."

Henry took the weapon and pulled it from the holster. The

prismatic metal, eversharp, composed the double-edged blade and glistened under the light of the sun globe. It looked like it had been grown from a single piece of metallic crystal instead of forged by dwarven lava. It was the most beautiful weapon he'd ever seen.

Haruspex

Item: Slyngur (Legendary)

Description: Weapon (Enchanted). Contains Drift Crystal (Legendary). Forged entirely of eversharp alloy, this double-edged xiphos is both perpetually sharp and extremely resilient. Slashing damage +7, Piercing damage +5. Hardness 50, Structure 150/150

Abilities:

Drain V. Absorb magical energy from an enemy. Absorbs 20 Vitus per second. Resolve determines transfer rate to wielder

Restore. If damaged, this weapon can use the bearer's Steam to return to its original shape

"*Slyngur,*" Henry read aloud.

"Dwarven for *lucky skeleton,*" Skuttur quipped and snorted at his own joke.

"Now you can quit complaining about not having a decent sword," Beast added.

Henry noticed Beast had some new equipment as well.

Haruspex

Item: Farscroll Quiver (Superior)

Description: This modified farscroll can retrieve any item placed in its paired vessel. Hardness 15, Structure 40/40

Ability: Retrieve. This item is paired with a weapon container in the Hjardharfell forges

Item: Veiled Brigade Daggers (Epic)

Description: Weapon (Enchanted), Contains flow crystals (Superior).
  Veiled Brigade Daggers plated with eversharp. Slashing damage +7, Piercing damage +5. Hardness 20, Structure 50/50

Ability: Frozen Strike. 22/22 charges. +10% ice damage. High chance to inflict Slow on a damaged enemy

Henry nodded in approval. "You've got some upgraded equipment as well."

Beast pulled an arrow from her quiver and twirled it in her hand. "I got tired of running out of these. It took a few tries, but Skuttur helped me modify a Farscroll. We paired it with a barrel in the armory filled with arrows. The dwarves promised to keep it full for me. They also gave me some fresh Solofurnos." Beast patted a metal case secured at her hip.

"You mean the unstable explosives that caused the cave in?" Henry asked, not hiding the concern in his voice.

"Not to worry," Buddy said. "We tested a few out. They're reliable and pack more of a punch than one of my basic fireballs."

Henry noticed that Buddy had also allowed the dwarves to upgrade his equipment. The mage's blue mantle had been modified into battle robes. The cloth still hung tightly to his body and was secured with several leather straps including his bandolier. Dread bone made up the shoulder plates and bracers, and he also sported a new set of boots.

Haruspex

Item: Dread Battle Robes (Epic)

Description: Armor (Enchanted). Mage's battle robe reinforced with the husks of fallen dread monsters and thin sheets of golem

steel. Physical Damage Resistance 5 (Slashing +2, Bludgeoning +1, Piercing +2). RES +5, Fire Resistance +5, Heat Resistance +5, Magic Resistance +5. MOB -10. Hardness 30, Structure 100/100

Ability: Adapt.

Buddy motioned with his thumb to his leather rucksack. "Muji is sleeping in my pack, but they even made a salamander leather harness for him to keep his Drift Amulet secure."

Thorodd cleared his throat. "If we're done with the fashion show, we need to get down to business. I'll be heading to the front lines, but I can at least show you where you'll be going. I'm one of the few that has been there."

The skeletons turned their attention to the mosaic of precious gems that made up the stone tabletop. Hundreds of tunnels and caverns wove together like the intricate designs of a fine silk carpet. Some of the sections between the city of Ammerthall, where the skeletons awoke, and the stronghold of Lundarbrekka, where they fought Smyrna's golem, were starting to look familiar to Henry.

Thorodd pointed to the opposite section of the table from the dwarven Underdeep. "The high cities of Jallfoss; they get smaller but more elaborate as you go up. Follow this path to the Oxendine palaces. About twenty miles of castles line the front range. You'll want to make your way to the highest peak. It contains a chamber that was mostly used for formal meetings and ceremonies. That's where Destria fought the Necromancer, and where her ghost still haunts.

"Make sure you stay away for the back side of the mountain—this section here, labeled Amera." Thorodd pointed to the mosaic's peripheral where a flow of emeralds and topaz depicted parallel mountain ridges lining a long and narrow forest. "That's where the Sprigs are concentrated. Also, the traitorous elves are worse than Minoa's thorny rose."

Henry made a mental note of the path that Thorodd pointed out, and Buddy scribbled as much as he could in his metal tome. He looked back at the path to Lundarbrekka. "That's where we fought Smyrna's Golem. All the roads lead to and from Lundarbrekka, but none around it. Skuttur, I know there are thousands of miles of uncharted tunnels in Jallfoss, but I don't see any other connecting Hjardharfell to the rest of the Underdeep."

"The choke points were meant as a defensive measure if we were attacked from above. We could retreat to Lundarbrekka and not get surrounded. Ironically, that layout and Smyrna's Golem kept us safe from the horrors below for a century. There is another way to the lower Underdeep. It was lost during the Betrayal. We used it for fast access to the Source Crystal. I thought it was lost, but the treasure room you found is likely the entrance to the only way around. We'll keep it sealed until we've reclaimed the Underdeep. Afterward, we'll pay tribute to my fellow flowsmiths that sacrificed themselves to seal the tunnel and keep us safe," the artificer croaked.

"Your friends were true warriors. We'll drink to their memory when this is over," Ox promised.

"Agreed . . . when this is over . . ." Henry said. "Lord Thorodd, thank you for the gear and the information. We can't delay any longer, but once we revive the Empress and break the curse, we'll return to help you retake the Underdeep. However, before we go, I have one more question for you."

Thorodd raised an eyebrow, and Henry continued. "I had another vision last night. I spoke to Raynott. He's being held prisoner. I also fought a dragon."

A grave countenance took hold of Thorodd's features. "Aye, that's what Buddy told me. Raynott died four thousand years ago. After the battle with Malek, Raynott and Osyrian founded our mountain nation. Osyrian took the mantle of emperor, and Raynott left to explore the world. Eventually, he returned to establish his bloodline as some of the deadliest warriors the world has ever seen. I can't tell you if the man you saw is truly Raynott, or just a creation of your mind. I can only say that your journey is of grave importance. Not only to you, but because of the circumstances, all of Jallfoss as well."

"You told me not to fail this Path, and nothing more. You know more than you're letting on, and I think you know who we are," Henry accused.

Thorodd gave Henry a sad look. "I have an idea who you were . . ."

"But you're not going to tell us," Buddy finished the Elders trailing thought.

Thorodd let out a long sigh and took another drink from his stein. He looked around the room at the skeletons, then shook his head. "You can see in my Status that I'm *Thorodd the Broken*. A long time ago, someone gave me information that I wasn't ready for. I can't blame the bastard for my failure, but I won't do the same thing to you. You four walk an uncertain path—you most of all, Henry. I believe you have all you need to save Jallfoss. Don't fail."

Silence hung in the room for a moment before Ox bellowed, "You heard the dwarf. We have what we need. Now, off to more battles."

Thorodd lifted his stein. "My daughter will take you as far as she can. Good luck."

Being dismissed without having all his questions answered left Henry frustrated, even though he knew pressing the Elder further wouldn't bear the fruit his blank mind and curiosity desired. He and the other skeletons filed out of the Elder's chamber behind Torgga and Olafur.

Giant gears rotated on well-oiled bearings and closed the heavy doors behind the undead. The loudest sound the portal made was a hiss of pressure when the doors formed a near air-tight seal, testifying to the precision of dwarven engineering. Thorodd continued to eat, shoveling lizard meat and mushroom gravy into his mouth and washing it down with the bitter sharinji beer.

The skeletons had provided Hjardharfell with the means to finally create the delicious brew he hadn't tasted in decades. However, until he defeated whatever evil was boiling up from the lower Underdeep, he couldn't justify diverting resources from the war effort to make ale, no matter how delectable. For several minutes, he distracted himself with memories of the savory liquid, until Skuttur cleared his throat.

"You have something to say?" Thorodd grumbled between bites.

"Your daughter seems quite fond of the skeletons, especially the mage."

Thorodd emptied his stein and set it down hard on the stone table. "What's your point, old dwarf?"

"I'm not questioning your judgement, but I am questioning Torgga's. Can we trust the undead? More importantly, can we trust her to lead Hjardharfell when she surpasses you?"

"She's already surpassed me. She did so yesterday when she defeated the Bearded Salamander. She will succeed where I failed and return Hjardharfell to all its glory. I choose to trust the skeletons because I trust my daughter."

"A full-blown Remnant and one halfway through his Path just walked out of your chamber. I would hope they don't turn against us. That would be catastrophic, considering who they were in life. I'm too old to disagree with you, my friend. I just hope you're right."

CHAPTER 30

Jacoby laid on his back and stared at the ceiling fifty feet above. Chandeliers filled with ornate sun globes hung from each of the five open chambers, slowly increasing in brightness to indicate the morning's arrival. Jacoby had found what he assumed was a cathedral the night before and tucked himself into a hidden nook that gave him decent cover and a good view of the entrances. Judging by the ornate but faded paintings, the place of worship was dedicated to some god he didn't recognize with white, feathered wings.

It was by far the most lavish place he'd found in two days traveling through the cities, and it likely took hundreds of years to construct. The huge building was filled with extravagant decorations, golden tapestries, and ornate rugs and curtains. Several had been charred or burned completely, but since the place was made entirely of stone the fire hadn't spread and destroyed the structure.

Standing around like they were waiting for a ceremony to start. Dozens of skeletons also occupied the building. Not just in this building and the several hundred others in the underground maze, but the undead were scattered throughout every cave-city and tunnel he passed. The skeletons were everywhere, though Jacoby felt they had been concentrated in certain areas, and he could tell that someone had deliberately moved them out of sight of the main roads—most likely to make traveling the cites faster and less dangerous. However, there were still thousands of the undead and he was glad he didn't have to fight his way through them.

Jacoby had torn down one of the smaller tapestries and rolled it up to use as a pillow. The hum of wind and water rushing through the various utilities was great background noise and lulled him right to sleep. It also served to cover any sounds he made. For that, he was grateful, as he knew stealth was key to his survival in the dangerous locales.

In addition to skeletons, he'd passed dozens of putrid, disfigured creatures in the two days he'd been traveling through the upper cities—insects the size of eagles, a giant cougar with three heads, and a caterpillar that shot spikes from its body, just to name a few. They were all extremely hostile. He'd picked off a few of the weaker ones, gaining another **2** Tiers and passing three Attribute Thresholds, giving him a significant bump to Strength, Acumen, and Resolve. However, he'd avoided several monsters that were obviously beyond his capabilities. The noise of wind and water from the various utilities helped him stalk his prey undetected, but also hid the sounds of larger monsters.

He had entered the current city when the sun globes were dimming, but now they were starting to brighten, giving the impression of dawn. He gathered his gear, drew his mace, and quietly made his way toward the cathedral's exit.

Huge wooden doors carved with beautiful designs hung open on large metal hinges. Jacoby peered over the city from the top of tiered steps. The city was half a mile across and in the shape of a spumera bean, with a bulge in one of the walls. The cities had grown more immaculate as he made his way up. The dwellings got larger, and the stone used to construct them got lighter, but every city he'd come across had dozens of paths leading in and out. He felt lost, though he knew that if he kept going up, he would eventually break through the ground, get outside, and be able to orient himself. As he gazed out and looked for his next direction of travel, he saw sunlight coming from one of the largest tunnels.

Finally, a way out, he thought. He started toward it, but within a few steps he heard a clicking sound from above him.

More reaction than intention, Jacoby sprung forward and tumbled down the stairs. Though the stone steps hurt as he rolled to the bottom, the alternative would have been much worse. Where he had stood just a second earlier, a huge creature smashed into the stone platform, sending stone chunks flying. It was the size of a bull and a hideous combination of centipede and wolf, with six legs on one side and five on the other. It had clawed talons at the end of each foot and spiked hair like a porcupine. Black skin covered its body, and its jaw curved into more of a jagged beak than teeth. It eyed him with malicious intent and clicked with its mouth in anticipation of a kill as it took a step toward the still tumbling warrior.

Jacoby righted himself before he reached the bottom. He dropped the mace and drew his falchion in one fluid motion. The blunt weapon was less effective against living creatures, and he preferred the sword. Defending from a lower position and fighting a much larger opponent, he needed every advantage he could muster.

Auric Palisade

A golden sheen surrounded his blade, casting shadows across the cathedral's stonework and causing the stalking monster to hesitate its advance. He took advantage of the short pause to view the creature's Status.

Assess

Type: Sprig, Tainted Jackal

Health: Full

Vitus: Full

Attributes:

    STR: 18

    MOB: 28

    FOR: 15

    ACU: 12

    PER: 11

    RES: 8

Damage Resistance: Physical

Weakness: Magic

Lore: Tainted Sprigs are the creations of the corrupted forest god, Ghara. They can be extremely dangerous and should only be fought with groups

He'd seen the name "Sprig" on these corrupted creatures and was thankful for the information the Amulet provided. The only clue the item gave him on how to kill it was its weakness to magic.

"Magic it is," he said to the monster. It stalked toward him and lowered its body, preparing for another pounce.

Jacoby needed better ground to fight the jackal. Behind him was an open plaza with buildings on the other side roughly fifty feet away. It seemed like a more advantageous spot for him to fight and he knew how he wanted to get the Sprig over there.

He loaded magic into his left hand, focusing the golden warmth of his core into a swirling mass, and released it as a spray of brilliant light. He knew it wouldn't be enough to even hurt the monster, but he didn't need to damage it yet.

Dazzle

The monster couldn't dodge the wide arc of magic blasting its face. The attack forced the creature back in a daze. By the time it cleared the fuzz from its head, Jacoby was already halfway across the plaza and running toward one of the open doorways. The Sprig screeched in anger and took off after the man. Its eleven legs tore up cobblestones as it powered its way toward the running human.

Jacoby dodged several standing skeletons as he heard the monster's heavy body slam into the ground and spring after him. The Sprig was faster than he expected, but he didn't waste time looking back. The monster had nearly reached him by the time he got to the doorway.

Jacoby ducked to his left inside the building and spun, forcing all the Vitus he could manage into the magic around his blade.

Auric Palisade

When the monster's head came through the doorway, Jacoby chopped down as hard as he could. Leathery skin and thick neck muscles tried to resist the heavy slice, but the increased damage from his Ability allowed him to force the blade most of the way through. The monster's head fell to the floor, but its body was still moving so fast that it crashed through the stone entrance and took Jacoby with it. The Sprig momentum and huge body destroyed half of the front of the building along with chairs, tables, and several innocent skeletons standing in the dwelling.

By the time everything stopped moving, Jacoby was on his back, staring up at the ceiling for the second time that morning. This time, he was covered in Sprig blood. Like a mixture of rotting meat and wet dog, the smell was terrible. He pulled himself free of the rubble and retrieved his sword, then acknowledged the glyphs flashing in his vision.

Sprig Killed, Soul Essence Claimed

Ability Discovered: Dazzle I. Discharge a cone of magical energy with a chance to . . .

Jacoby cut off the view as several skeletons rushed through the open hole where the doorway once stood. They had armor and brandished weapons—some of them very high quality—but Jacoby didn't have time to admire their equipment. Though they looked like the normal skeletons that didn't react to him, these were very much animated and were obviously attacking him.

Dazzle

The golden cone sprayed from his hand and blasted into the charging skeletons, but it had no effect.

Idiot, Jacoby thought. He should have known his new Ability wouldn't work on skeletons, and now he was even lower on Vitus. Even worse, his mace was at the base of the cathedral stairs. He'd have to make do with his sword.

Auric Palisade

He powered the protective sheen around his armor and lifted his sword. The skeletons swung at him with wild chops, but Jacoby danced and spun between their attacks. His strikes were drawn to the weak spots in their armor, and he crushed bone like a child stepping on guilian fruit at a harvest festival. His attacks were clean, direct, and most of all, devastating. On top of that, the skeletons were poor swordsmen, and he cleaved through them with little effort.

He sliced through the last skeleton, stopping just outside the damaged building. Movement to his left made him turn, as red auras seared into his vision and engulfed his psyche.

Status Effect: Enraged (Severe)

A heavily armored skeleton stood just a few paces from him, but he barely saw the undead due to the three crimson auras behind it. Two of the elves stood inside raging blazes like funeral pyres consuming an honored dead. The middle aura, however, was a series of thick vines wrapping around an elf wearing animals furs and white armor.

Overcome with killing intent, Jacoby sprang forward. He saw shock in the faces of the elves on the left and right, but the middle one looked calm. "Kill the human!" she shouted.

The skeleton attacked. It was much larger than the others and sported elaborate armor and a shining steel blade. It raised its weapon, but Jacoby's sword removed its head before it could finish the strike. Jacoby barely noted the felled enemy under the influence of the red auras as he continued his charge.

One elf fired an arrow and the other shot a bolt of green magic. Both projectiles impacted his Auric Palisade shielding and bounced off. The only impact they had on his magic was a slight dimming as the damage pulled Vitus from his mind.

Just a few feet away from the center elf, Jacoby cocked his sword and prepared for a deadly thrust.

The elf lifted her palm toward him. "Hold!"

Status Effect: Hold Undead. No actions may be taken without the direction of the caster. Command Link Established 46/2300

Jacoby's magic cut off. Every muscle in his body locked, and he smashed his head into the ground, skidding to a stop at the elf's feet.

Status Effect: Concussion (Mild): MOB -5%, ACU -5%, PER -5%, RES -5%

He tried to speak, or even move, but he was unable. His muscles refused to respond to his demands.

"Stand, Human," the elf ordered. To Jacoby's surprise, his body reacted and righted itself, refusing his violent urges. His Resolve floundered against the Hold Undead Effect, and the rage continued. Though now that his body was unable to move, the Attribute found purchase against the aura's influence and allowed him to regain some semblance of control.

Status Effect: Enraged (Moderate)

With the Effect slightly reduced, Jacoby could think at last. The elf before him wore fur-covered white armor and held an elegant-looking blade. However, what struck Jacoby was her beauty. Though Jacoby only had the memory span of a few days, he felt the woman before him would be gorgeous by any standard. He tried to talk, but his jaw held firm.

"How did you hold an Acolyte, Talji?" one of the other elves asked—a female, judging from the sound of her voice.

The center elf, Talji, apparently, turned and responded. "He *used* to be an Acolyte. Say what you want about the Ikritian soldiers, they keep their heads in a fight. Not this one. I recognized his actions as that of an undead, though he's clearly alive. What do you think, Lata?"

"How can he be aware if he's undead, and why isn't he decomposing?" the second elf, Lata, asked.

Talji walked toward him and put a hand on Jacoby's face, pinching his chin between her thumb and index finger. She stood on her toes to match his height and looked deep into his eyes. Hers were green with sparkles of gold and brown. Soft pale skin, and cheeks flushed with a bit of red highlighted her delicate features. Her eyebrows furrowed in a serious expression as she studied him. If it weren't for the red aura urging him to rip into her apart, he would have found the experience pleasant.

She let go of his face, then smacked him hard enough to make his ears ring.

Status Effect: Enraged (Minor)
RES +1

The blow shook his senses and allowed him to stave off most of the aura's Effect, but he still couldn't move. He felt the control the elf had over him weaking ever so slightly, but compared to the total power she wielded over him, the gain was insubstantial. Talji stared into his eyes with a combination of anger and curiosity.

"You're alive, and an Ikritian Acolyte. You're also undead, otherwise the Hold Undead spell wouldn't have worked," the elf mused. "You're very strong, human. You may be what we need to turn the tide on Ghara's Sprigs."

Jacoby struggled again to speak, but no amount of Resolve allowed him to overcome the spell.

"Are you the one that's been giving the dwarves trouble?" Talji's voice softened as she asked the question, more to herself than Jacoby.

"What do we do with him?" the third elf asked.

Talji's eyes narrowed in anger. Jacoby sensed the elf didn't appreciate her thoughts being interrupted. Nevertheless, she replied. "It's very strange, Surat. His Resolve ticked up, likely from fighting off the violent urges. When that happened, my internment weakened. Even so, he's only taking **46** points, and it's nothing at all to control him."

"He just went through our guard like they were children, and he has **7** Tiers. Bharat will want to meet him." Surat said.

Talji's lips turned up in a dangerous smile, revealing perfect teeth and a pink tongue that danced just behind them. "I agree. And on the way, this dead Acolyte will tell me everything he knows."

CHAPTER 31

With one quick stroke, Cirilo removed Sigurjon's head from his undead shoulders. Though the Acolyte had been resurrected as one of the mindless creatures of Jallfoss's curse, it still pained Cirilo to strike down one of his own men.

Sigurjon was one of the best instructors that had come out of the Bastion in decades, on par with Jacoby; his students always excelled. Sadly, Cirilo had no choice but to kill the Master-Acolyte-turned-undead to keep him from attacking. The headless body dropped to its knees and Cirilo booted it in the chest, sending it smashing into a rubble pile thirty feet away. There was no room for a light hand when dealing with the undead. Cirilo had seen too many soldiers sympathize with the fallen Acolytes. Most ended up torn apart by their former allies.

Beside him, Jaromak smashed the two Junior Acolytes that were Sigurjon's students into a rotting puree without showing the slightest bit of remorse. Jaromak was nearly as enraged as the undead that attacked them. The huge soldier shook as he stared at the bodies. Congealed blood oozed from their destroyed corpses, and piles of innards spilled onto the sand.

"Burnt like a pig on a spicket and robbed of our family maul and crest. Whatever skeleton killed by brother will pay. It even had the gall to loot his corpse," Jaromak spat. He knelt beside the parts of the former Junior Acolytes. "These boys didn't deserve to die any more than Alito did."

Cirilo knew the dead Acolytes would rise again in a few days, completely repaired of any amount of damage he could deal to them. The worse part was the pain it inflicted on the minds of the living. Fighting undead did something to a soldier's head, especially when the undead they found were former allies, or even worse, family, in Jaromak's case.

"I understand your anger, Master Jaromak. Your brother was a model of grit for all Acolytes. However, you will maintain control as you promised," Cirilo said with a calm but stern voice.

Jaromak outwardly agreed, but anger still held firm in his voice. "Aye, Commander."

"I'm sorry for your loss, Master Jaromak," Eudora offered, watching from a few feet away.

Jaromak wiped globs of blood from his massive tower shield. "I don't want your feelings, Eudora. I want to crush the bones of the ones who killed our Acolytes."

The five Master Acolytes and five younger Acolytes had quickly fought through the city and come to the base of the ramps at the far cavern wall of Ammerthall. Cirilo surveyed the open area. Homes had been smashed there a hundred years ago, but there were also fresh signs of battle—boot prints, scorch marks in the sand, broken arrows scattered about. The Commander approached the stone monolith at the center of the plaza and read the inscription as he had every time he came to the ramps.

These roads of stone that lead to the worlds above and below
Are dedicated to the Great Emperor Ortegus Oxendine
Father of the lasting peace between Humans and Dwarves
May the nations of Stone and Sky, Fire and Water
Forever prosper under the watchful eye of our Guardian
3012-3098

"The lasting peace . . ." Cirilo mouthed the words as he ran his fingers over the inscription of the monument. He had always preferred the life of a philosopher, but the moment called for a warrior.

He stood tall and spoke as only a Commander could. "Several things worry me. First, the utilities that have come back on. Something is amiss below, and I have a feeling the skeletons Lord Stavros sent us to stop have something to do with it. Jaromak, Samos, you stay here with the other Acolytes. This is the only ramp to get from the Underdeep, so I'm counting on you to stop anything that would try to rise from below. Eudora, Mersin, and I will proceed to the Oxendine summit."

"Yes, Commander. No enemy will get past us." Samos replied.

Cirilo regarded the vanquished undead. "Everything that Koş told us is true, including where his troupe died, and the description of the skeletons that attacked him. The three unique skeletons in Ammerthall are missing: the mage, the rogue, and the giant. They match Koş's description of his assailants . . . and according to the boy, there was one more, another warrior type."

"If they have a mage in their group, I'm prepared." Samos ran his fingers along a black metal broach secured around his neck.

"That's why you're here." Cirilo smiled, acknowledging the Master Acolyte.

Jaromak tightened his grip on the leather straps securing his huge tower shield. "I don't care what they are. Any undead that comes up that ramp will face my wrath."

"I'm counting on that." Cirilo patted the huge Acolyte on the back then motioned with his head to the others. "Eudora and Mersin will come with me. We're the fastest and can make our way to the Empress in the least amount of time."

Jaromak turned to the other Acolytes and barked his orders. "You heard the Commander. Prepare for battle."

CHAPTER 32

Ox trudged along at the back of the skeletal convoy. His massive dread armor fit perfectly, and his extreme Strength allowed him to move with almost no hindrance, but no amount of brawn could help him find the motivation to keep moving his feet. The monsters he'd fought since leaving Hjardharfell no longer posed a threat to him and did little to distract his mind.

He'd chosen to follow Henry and the other three simply because it seemed like fun. He didn't really mind being a skeleton, and without a memory to distract him—or a body to enjoy women and booze—there was nothing he would rather do than battle the monsters of Jallfoss. That all changed when he started fighting the Silent. He didn't know if it was just because he was getting stronger, or if there was something significant about the dread monsters, but his display had started giving him a message that caused him no small amount of anguish. Henry and Buddy seemed concerned about Primals and Remnants; something Ox cared little about when a single word kept rolling through his mind: Failure.

The four skeletons were halfway through the mining city of

Hershwald with its metal beams and beetle-like contraptions that were used to transport and organize various stones and ores.

Ox looked ahead to the three skeletons in front of him. They were moving with a purpose. Ox's eyes fixed on exposed bone and noted how his companion's bodies had grown more robust, and how their minds had sharpened like the keen edge of a blade. Buddy and Beast had uncovered hidden potential that made them powerful allies, and though Henry was obviously degraded by the visions he had been experiencing, the warrior was determined to fight to his last breath if it meant saving the undead in this mountain. That determination impressed Ox, and because of that, he didn't mind letting Henry lead. That responsibility was too much work to shoulder with the additional duty of being the mountain's emperor. Ox almost laughed thinking about how much his regal claims annoyed Beast.

Henry had been pushing them hard to make up for lost time, and Ox had protested when the warrior said they couldn't stop at the Jolly Squid in Husavik. "When we get our bodies back, I'll buy you all the whiskey you can drink." Henry had promised. Ox reluctantly conceded, agreeing not to waste the precious liquid until he had a tongue to enjoy it. A lack of tastebuds, however, wasn't the true reason that he allowed the group to bypass the pub. Something was bothering him, and Ox felt that only a decent fight could quiet the uncertainty that plagued his thoughts.

Like Henry, Ox had several unexplained and concerning occurrences in his Status. He had the same Attributes and Abilities as Henry, and according to Thorodd, he was something called a Remnant. Ox had little idea what that meant besides granting him certain powers similar to those of the Drift Amulets. The dwarven Elder was unwilling to offer further explanation.

Lost in thought, Ox followed the other three to the bottom of the curved ramp that made up the exit from the industrial cavern of Hershwald. Like the other ramps and tunnels throughout the main passageways in Jallfoss, the ramp's center chain had begun moving. The chain clanked and groaned as it shed a century of rust and dirt, but it was still much quieter than would have been expected from thousands of pounds of metal links and gears. Buddy still scoffed at the dwarven machinery, while the others appreciated the resilient engineering.

Ahead of Ox, Buddy had his head down and was reading from a tome that Torgga gave him as they parted ways. A question had been burning in Ox's mind and he wanted to ask the mage, but he knew Buddy wasn't one for small talk. Ox decided to try anyway. With a few large steps he caught up to the mage. "Barney, what are you reading?"

Buddy didn't lift his head from the book to reply. "Lady Torgga gifted me with this tome. It is a collection of all evocation references she recovered from the dwarven archives. Though limited in scope, its relevance to the elements makes it quite valuable to me. In exchange, I gave her the golem heart that the trogold found."

Ox recalled the parting but had been distracted with his thoughts at the time. "So, the dwarf gave you a book, and you gave her a rock? Not the way I would court a lady, but she seemed excited. You were right—dwarven women love rocks."

Buddy sighed and closed the tome. "I am not courting Lady Torgga, and as I said, it wasn't a rock; it was a golem heart. A mage of her caliber should be able to put it to use. Also, she gave me much more than a book. This is a collection of all dwarven knowledge related to evocation. Their society revolves around mining and subterranean farming, so most of this information involves earth magic, though there is a bit on acid and poison. They even found a way to combine wind magic with the miasma vector to keep noxious gas for harming the miners."

"*Vector?*" Ox asked.

Buddy stowed the tome in a leather pouch and raised his hands to lecture. "Yes, that's how most evokers organize their magic. We chose a type, such as fire or lightning, then a vector, such as bolt or shield, which you've seen me use most often. Interestingly, this collection has taught me four new elemental types—earth, acid, poison, and wind—and three new vectors—*miasma*, as I said, and also *detonate*. I was reading a section on *nullify* when you interrupted me."

"What do those do?" Ox asked.

"Miasma is a cloud of concentrated elements. Detonate is a remotely-activated discharge. Nullify cancels out an equivalent form of magic. The dwarves only used nullify with the earth and poison elements to reduce the danger associated with cave-ins and trapped poisonous gasses, but I believe I can expand it to other uses and forms of magic. The most interesting spell I've found is one call *Enduring Sphere*. Where most evocation . . ."

Ox had lost interest in Buddy's explanation and tried to change the conversation. "You may not realize this Barney, but I am an accomplished mage myself. Though I only need a single spell to smite my enemies. Cast Iron . . . get it? *Cast* iron?" Ox swung his hammer in a massive arc over Buddy's head and waited for the mage's response.

Buddy only cocked his head and looked at Ox. "That is not a spell, it's merely you hitting things with your maul . . ."

Ox lowered his hammer and shrugged his shoulders. "Anyway . . . I need to ask you a magic question, but you can't tell the grumpy minion."

Buddy continued to give Ox a curious look. "Very well. What?"

"Promise you won't tell her?"

"I have no interest in discussion your lack of knowledge with the elf."

Good enough, Ox thought. "Have you ever heard of an Astral Covenant?"

Buddy quickly pulled out the red mage's metal tome and thumbed through it until he found the passage he was searching for. "A Covenant is a rare and dangerous magical technique that involves sharing power between mages. There are many types, but this account doesn't describe them in detail."

"Like a thrall?" Ox asked.

"No," Buddy replied bluntly. "A thrall is subservient to its mage. A Covenant is a more . . . intimate, yet unpredictable connection. A consensual exchange between equals. Why do you ask, Lord Oxendine?"

Ox hesitated, but he had no reason to believe the mage was anything less than worthy of his secrets. "I . . . have one, but it's broken." Ox brought up the Status Effect in his display.

Haruspex

Astral Covenant: Disabled
>   **Bond 1 of 3 broken: Resistance, All -5**
>   **Bond 2 of 3 broken: MOB -30%**
>   **Bond 3 of 3 broken: ACU -30%**

Ox read the Status Effect out loud. Buddy listened intently to Ox's description and scribbled furiously in the margins of the metal tome. "Interesting. I didn't think a Covenant could exist between more than two individuals. It appears that who-ever you shared it with is dead, understandably so. If you died, then so did whoever you were connected to. It appears the consequences of a broken Covenant are quite severe—even more so between multiple mages. You are degraded like Henry, though from a source of your own making in a past life."

Ox's shoulders slumped with the revelation. He wanted to argue with the Buddy's assessment, but deep down he knew it was true. "So, what do I do?"

Buddy gave Ox as sympathetic of a look as a skeleton was capable and patted him on the shoulder. "Exactly what we're doing. Henry seems confident the Empress can fix this curse and bring all the skeletons back. I trust the warrior with my life, but there are forces at play we don't understand. Our current plan is the best we have, until we figure out some of the mysteries of this mountain."

"What mysteries are *you* trying to figure out?" Ox asked glumly.

Now a few hundred feet from the top of the ramp, Buddy looked up to the opening to Ammerthall. "For starters, the magic in this area is . . . off. As we get closer to the top of this ramp, I'm sensing interference in the flow of magic. I suspected yet dismissed the sensation earlier. Now that my Magic Sense Ability has evolved into Mystic Revelation, it's clear that something strange is here. Maybe the pillar in the plaza is enchanted with some type of warding ma—"

"Everyone, stop! Something is wrong. Defend!" Henry's shout interrupted Buddy's musings.

CHAPTER 33

Ox looked up just in time to witness a fiery blast erupt in front of Henry. Buddy lifted his hands and formed a force wall around the four skeletons, diverting the emulsion around them. The concussive force rattled the ramp's chain and sent loose dirt cascading down the steep walls.

Billowing dust spread like smoke from a wildfire. Through the particles, Ox saw a massive, armor-clad warrior standing at the top of the stone incline—stoic and patient, like he'd been waiting for them. Then man carried a huge, elaborate tower shield, and wore a full set of shiny steel platemail and the red tunic of the human Acolytes. Ox paid little credence to the soldier's gear as rings of crimson flared from a central, brilliant red aura, urging Ox to violently extinguish it.

Status Effect: Enraged (Minor)

"Acolytes!" Henry shouted as more red-cloaked soldiers appeared around the first. The men fired arrows and launched brilliantly-colored bolts of magic.

The volley deflected harmlessly off Buddy's shield, and

Henry laid out their plan. "Multiple ranged attacks coming from above. We have to get to their level, but there are probably more traps blocking the way. Buddy, get you, me, and Ox up there. Beast, find some high ground and take out any humans you can."

Henry had barely finished talking when the mage's force magic launched the three skeletons in the air and over the attacking soldiers like they'd been flung from a trebuchet. Ox saw seven Acolytes total: five armed with bows and magic, the big one at the top, and a robed man further back. All seven craned their necks to watch three skeletons soaring over their heads. Each human's blazing red aura drove a spike of mania into Ox's psyche that he found nearly impossible to overcome while careening through the air.

Status Effect: Enraged (Moderate)

Buddy slowed their descent with more force magic, but he hadn't mastered the art of a gentle landing. They hit the sandy plaza and rolled to a stop. Luckily, their new armor and Tier-**11** Attributes kept their bones from shattering on impact. More importantly, they were no longer on the lower ramp and at the mercy of enemies with the high ground.

Henry shouted something, but the Enraged Effect overpowered Ox's Resolve. The collection of red auras beckoned him forward as he raised his hammer and charged the large soldier. His heavy boots thundered across the sand as arrows and magic struck him. His new armor allowed him to shrug off most of the damage and heal the rest with minimal Vitus.

At the edges of his vision, he saw Buddy's blue fire bolts careening toward a grouping of Acolytes, so he focused completely on the huge man. Ox was a head and shoulders taller, but the man was still much larger than a normal soldier. He sported a six-foot tower shield with intricate designs that matched his heavy platemail. Ox noticed, but didn't bother to care, that the man carried no weapon—only the huge, curved plate of steel.

The man's helmet had an open face and as Ox drew near, he could see the man's snarl change to a smile. The soldier mouthed the words, "Found you."

A wave of pressure from behind took Ox's feet out from under him, and he tumbled to the ground. The blast jolted his head enough for his Resolve overcome the aura's influence.

Status Effect: Enraged (Minor)

Thinking a little more clearly, Ox saw that the large man had lifted his shield and slowly prowled forward. Ox looked down to pick up his hammer and noticed that the intricate carvings on his maul matched the man's armor and shield.

"So much for your mage," the man said as his smile grew even more menacing. Only then did Ox notice that Buddy's fireballs had not impacted. He looked back to where Buddy had once stood only to see a black, shimmering dome had covered the skeleton.

Henry had already stood and began running toward the grouping of soldiers. He shouted to Ox, "The mage did something to Buddy. Take the big guy. Beast and I will get the rest."

"My pleasure." Ox lifted himself to his full height and brandished his maul.

Now within twenty paces, the Acolyte picked up his speed. "You'll pay for what you did to my brother! You killed a great man, and now you wield a weapon you don't deserve! I will tear you apart!"

"I was born with this hammer. At least in this life. You'll

have to kill me again and pull it from my dead fingers." Ox didn't specifically remember killing any brothers, but the possibility was definitely there. Regardless, he was eager to fight.

Ox loaded his hammer with force magic and swung. He expected to smash through the steel armor and pulverize the soldier into bloody bits, but the Acolyte tipped his shield just enough to send the maul and its force magic glancing off harmlessly. A wave of force erupted from the point of impact and sent sand blasting away from them. The man stepped inside Ox's range and lunged with his elbow. He caught Ox directly in the center of the dread bone breastplate with enough force to knock Ox back several steps.

The attack didn't inflict any physical damage, but it was the first time a smaller opponent had managed to stagger him. Ox opened his jaw to speak but the edge of the man's shield caught him in the face. He didn't see the blow coming . . . or the dozen that followed. The man's Strength was lower than Ox's, but not by much. However, the Acolyte was much, much faster. Blow after blow landed, directly targeting the few vulnerable spots in the dread armor.

Heal

Ox's bones cracked under the assault, though he repaired them instantly and with minimal effort. Healing himself was easy, crushing the man was going to be difficult. The Acolyte easily dodged every one of Ox's heavy swings and retaliated with lightning-fast attacks of his own. Ox knew Henry and Beast were faster than this enemy, but they didn't have a quarter of his devastating Strength to back it up. Ox tried to use Haruspex to divine any information he could. The constant barrage of shield bashes, powerful kicks, and devastating punches stopped the Ability from working. Ox tried to pull Torgga's ring from his finger and release his Temperance Aura, but he lacked the dexterity to pluck the jewelry from his digit under the heavy onslaught from the Acolyte.

For the first time, Ox realized just how much of a detriment his Astral Covenant Effects truly were. With all his Strength, Ox's mind and body were too slow to hit the soldier. What's more, the blows were getting stronger. Though his armor was resisting just fine, his bones weren't, and the man was finding and exploiting every weak spot in the dreadmail.

"How could my brother lose to such a weak opponent?" The man taunted in between strikes. "You don't deserve that armor and maul. I will take them away and grind your bones to dust. Curse or no, I will make sure you never return."

"Ghakk!" Gator chomped from Ox's shoulder. A two-headed skeletal giant sporting dread-skull helmets should have struck fear into the heart of any man, but this Acolyte seemed unfazed.

"Gator fears no human," Ox roared.

The soldier shouted back between continued attacks, "I am no simple human. I am Jaromak, brother of Allito, progeny of the strongest warrior house in all Ikrit. You are a monster and should not exist. I will correct that mistake."

Jaromak grabbed one of the curved horns of Ox's dread ram helmet and smashed his own steel-covered dome directly into Ox's face. Ocular bones cracked, and Ox stumbled backward. The blows were starting to add up, and Ox's Vitus was below half. He was running low on options and saw that Henry and Beast were busy with the other Acolytes. They wouldn't be coming to his aid anytime soon. He had to squash this bug himself.

Ox raised his hammer and loaded several force charges into it, then brought it straight down with all his Strength. Even if he missed, the blast would catch the man and give Ox enough time to follow up.

Instead of dodging, the soldier jammed the bottom of his shield into the ground and tilted it back, leaning the giant chunk of metal at an angle away from Ox. The maul impacted the shield and released a magical attack strong enough to shatter granite. Just before the weapon landed, a layer of scale-like rock formed over the human's shield. Ox's hammer impacted a palisade as sturdy as Smyrna's Golem. The earth magic from the Acolyte's spell reflected the discharge from Ox's hammer, blasting the skeleton with his own magic and sending him tumbling backward.

Status Effect: Enraged Dismissed

Status Effect: Stunned (Moderate): MOB -10%, ACU -10%, RES -5%

Ox skidded to a stop in the sand. The blast had cleared the rage from his head but replaced it with a foggy concussion. He tried and failed to stand as the flow of rock from the Acolyte's shield splashed to the ground and rushed toward him like a mudslide covering an unsuspecting village. It washed over him, filling the empty cavity between his bones and armor and forcing him back to the ground. The instant he was covered, the liquid rock solidified, trapping him in darkness and crushing him under its pressure.

Status Effect: Entombed (Severe): MOB -100%

—

Beast Blinked to one of the rooftops and watched as the idiot men flew over the battlefield. They were slow to recover and take up the fight, but at least they were no longer on the vulnerable ramp.

Her Resolve had grown enough that only a minor Rage Effect plagued her, giving her ample room to target the enemies. Beast fired arrow after arrow at the Acolytes. Her Farquiver worked amazingly well, supplying her with an endless source of projectiles, though they did little good. As her arrows and Buddy's flames approached the men, the red-robed mage pulled something from the vast assortment of items that hung from his clothing. A pressure wave rolled across the plaza, knocking her arrows from the sky and extinguished Buddy's blue fire. It also sent Henry and Ox sprawling. Beast lifted an arm to shield herself from an intense wind blast. When she looked up, a black dome had been erected over Buddy.

"The idiots are about to get themselves killed," she cursed.

"The mage did something to Buddy. Ox, take the big guy. Beast and I will get the rest." She heard Henry yell. She knew the warrior wasn't equipped to fight the mage, so, as usual, it was up to her to save to male skeletons.

Blink

It should have been simple to sneak behind the mage and slip a dagger into his back, but as she appeared, her conjuration magic rebounded off the man and sent her tumbling back.

Status Effect: Stunned (Minor): MOB -5%, ACU -5%

Beast rolled to her feet and shook the Effect from her head. The man whirled around and narrowed his eyes. Golden-brown curls hung from his head and his eyes held an intense focus. Had it not been for the lines around his eyes and mouth, Beast would have thought him a youth. However, the confidence the man displayed said he was very much experienced in battle.

He wore red robes with the white Acolyte crest, but he had so much equipment strapped to him that he looked like a comical version of Buddy. All sorts of crystals and magical devices hung from leather straps and stuck out of satchels. A huge metal container hung on one hip, and a spell book sat holstered in the other.

The man's lips parted as he looked Beast up and down. "Very sneaky, arena guardian, but your magic won't work near me. Without your mage, this battle will be over quickly."

"I don't need magic to flay skin," Beast snarled and sprang forward. The last thing she wanted was condescension from a man, so she gave into the Enraged Effect's violent suggestion.

From her first attack, she had gathered that Blink wouldn't work to get her close enough to strike, but she was faster than any mage. As she charged, the man didn't move, he just watched her. His confidence should have given her pause, but her unhindered rage pushed her to attack and extinguish his offensive aura.

She activated frost charges into her daggers and launched herself forward. Unfortunately, her speed did her little good. Within a few feet she lunged with her dagger, but her movement slowed to a near standstill. She felt like her body had completely sunk in quicksand or been plunged into water—there was so much resistance in the air that she could barely move.

The man stepped to the side, pulled a mace from a holster, and cracked her across the skull. The tumble backwards wasn't slowed like her approach had been, and she slammed into the sandy plaza.

The man twirled the mace and taunted, "Speed and magic don't work on me, skeleton. I am Samos, the Anti-Mage. Now, tell me before I kill you and the other abominations, how did you come back to life?"

"What did you do to Buddy?" Beast hissed.

"The skeletal mage? A stasis field given to me by the great Lord Stavros himself." Samos held up a black Flow Crystal embedded in a pendant and hung around his neck. "The ruler of Ikrit and most powerful sorcerer in the known world sent us to handle his dirty work."

Status Effect: Enraged (Moderate)

Siren

Beast unleashed her ear-splitting shriek and launched herself forward again. The man's words had allowed the aura's Effect to take full hold of her, and she attacked without regard, overcome by rage.

Unaffected by her aural attack, the man smiled the way one would look at a child throwing a temper tantrum and dodged her slowed thrust. "I see the undead madness still afflicts you. Your death will relieve you of that curse."

CHAPTER 34

Fighting five Acolytes was more of a challenge than Henry had anticipated. He realized he hadn't directly fought one of the human warriors since Ox had awoken a week earlier. In the very same location in which they now found themselves, the skeletons had ambushed a single experienced soldier and three novice Acolytes and had barely claimed victory. The current fight saw them with neither the advantage of numbers nor initiative.

Even so, Henry's improved Attributes, his new Abilities, and his new weapons and armor proved a match for the soldiers. Though he loved slaying monsters, clashing swords with another warrior fit perfectly with his combat style.

Henry could tell the humans had trained together. Their attacks were synchronized, and they seamlessly supported each other. Three of the Acolytes had dropped their bows and drew black maces. Between the mace-wielding fighters and the two mages firing bolts of magic at Henry, the skeleton had his hands full, though he found himself enjoying the exchange on the razor's edge of a second death far more than he should. Every dodge and parry, every thrust and block, filled him with a deep satisfaction—an abiding clam, foreign to the heat of battle.

A quick Haruspex told Henry that the five Acolytes before him were between Tier **15** and **20**, and their Abilities were on par with that level. The three melee soldiers rushed him and pummeled him with heavy attacks from the maces that Henry assumed were designed to crush the undead. His Skeletal Body Effect and subsequent weakness to bludgeoning damage made him vulnerable to those weapons, but that only made the fight that much more exciting.

Blitz

A black mace came straight for his head and Henry had to activate his magic to avoid the attack. He thrust with Slyngur, aiming at the vulnerable spots between the man's platemail. The Acolyte, however, had a set of skills of his own. Henry's sword bounced off a sheen that covered the man's armor.

Vitus +2

His sword was living up to its make and it pulled from the ward enough magic to keep him fueled. Henry doubled back, dodging another mace and two more magical bolts.

One, two, three . . . Henry counted in his head before another volley of magical attacks zinged toward him. He narrowly dodged the bolts, only to find himself directly in the path of a third mace. Henry raised his left arm and activated his dread shield.

Sacrifice

Adapt

Vitus pumped into his armor and expanded the buckler at his wrist to the size of a kite shield. The mace smashed into his defense and rebounded, leaving Henry completely unscathed. He would have these men defeated in short order.

Thanks dwarves, even after a hundred years you've still got smithing skills, Henry thought with a smile. He began pumping Vitus into his attack, but a loud *crack* brought his attention to the surrounding battlefield. While Henry had been enjoying the exchange, he had lost track of the trouble the other three skeletons were having. Beast had just been smacked to the ground, Ox was covered in rock, and Buddy was still trapped inside a black dome.

Henry cursed to any nameless deity willing to listen. He was supposed to be leading them in battle, and instead, he had let them get separated and overwhelmed. He needed to—

The ground below Henry shook and churned. Five whirlpools of liquid rock swirled, the fluid stone rising and solidifying into rocky homunculi.

Haruspex

Earth Elemental (Lesser)
Type: Construct
Health: 153/153
Vitus: 0/0
Attributes:
    STR: 45
    MOB: 8
    FOR: 38
    ACU: 0
    PER: 15
    RES: 0
Damage Resistance: Physical, Environmental
Lore: Lesser elementals, especially those of earth, are only dangerous when not left alone. When harnessed by a mage and sent into the fray, they become deadly adversaries

Just like Buddy's elementals. Before he could react, all five earthen constructs rushed him. He sliced and his sword bounced off their hard bodies.

Blitz

Henry raised his shield and propelled himself forward. He impacted an elemental and sent it flying backward. It cracked and pieces crumbled off, but it reformed and resumed its charge. Now with ten enemies, Henry had no reprieve from the onslaught. Every time he tried to attack one, another hit him.

Harden

Magic flowed into his legs and reinforced their structure. He kicked one of the elementals as hard as he could, hoping his bones would hold up. They did, and the construct blasted in half.

A magic bolt flew toward him, and Henry blocked with his shield just in time. He'd been watching and he knew it would take the mage a moment to recharge, *3* . . . Henry locked onto the Acolyte, counting down the seconds in his head, *2* . . .

Blitz

He dodged and ducked under a series of stone and mace attacks, *1* . . . Magic formed in the mage's hand. The charge fizzled as Henry's shield impacted his chest. The man tumbled backward, but before Henry could slay the Acolyte, the rest came to his rescue.

A yell rang though the battlefield, and Ox erupted from the stone that had covered him. The second Acolyte mage turned his attention to the giant skeleton and sent a volley of bolts into Ox. Amidst the fray, Henry saw Ox cock back a massive skeletal arm and throw something with such force and speed that its impact took the offending mage off his feet. That's when things got weird.

—

Ox was trapped. The liquid stone had solidified around his bones and held him in a crushing earthen tomb. Even with the Strength of a dozen men he could do little to escape Jaromak's spell.

Solid rock usually gave him little resistance, but the magic-reinforced earth left him struggling to break free. The damage he had taken from the human's attacks had weakened his bones enough to prevent his escape. Ox cursed his frailty. His minions were relying on him. Henry, Beast, and Buddy were out there fighting for not only their lives, but his entire mountain, and what was he doing? Getting pummeled by a single human and lying on his back? *Pitiful*, he thought. How can I call myself Emperor Ortegus Oxendine if I can't even save myself? Wallowing in self-pity, he focused on the glyphs in his view.

Status

Astral Covenant: Disabled

    Bond 1 of 3 broken: Resistance, All -5

    Bond 2 of 3 broken: MOB -30%

    Bond 3 of 3 broken: ACU -30%

Ox knew Buddy was right, he had let someone down in the past—three someone's apparently. He despised his own weakness. The entire mountain was counting on him, and he was failing. Had his failure allowed the Necromancer to curse the mountain in the first place? He had no way of knowing, but anger quickly replaced his shame and boiled away his doubts. No rock could hold back his Strength. A yell reverberated from his skull as he dove into his mind—past the fog of his memories and into his core space.

Brilliant white nearly blinded him as he broke through the dark murk and emerged into a blizzard. Blowing snow gathered over a massive sheet of ice. The glacier in his mind was so colossal that its size couldn't be determined by sight alone. It was long and wound its way up and around mountains until it disappeared into the low cloud tops. In the middle, it was a deep, brilliant blue. The sides of the glacier were nearly black with dirt that had been ground from the surrounding mountains over thousands of years. The bottom of the ice ended at the edge of a turquoise bay. Several bergs and smaller chunks of ice floated peacefully just off the glacier's edge.

A piece of the glacier broke off and crashed into the water below, sending a spray high into the air. The huge chunk of ice broke as it impacted the surface and bobbed in the water until it began to float out toward the other pieces of ice.

His own Strength radiated from the chunk of ice, almost pulsing with a heartbeat of its own. With every bit of Acumen he had, Ox pulled on the Vitus within the ice. The blizzard swirled around him. He grabbed it and forced its magic into his bones.

Ability Discovered: Heart of the Jotun I. Increase STR by 20% for a single attack.

Stone crumbled and ground to dust as Ox released the pent-up energy. He roared, and the tomb around him cracked open like fault lines from an earthquake. He tore from the stone and brought himself to his full height, shaking the remaining rocks from under his armor.

Jaromak stood before Ox with a strange combination of excitement and anger betraying the calm visage of a seasoned warrior. "Good, I was hoping you had more for me," he growled.

Ox pumped another force charge into his hammer. "Much more." Jaromak lifted his shield and Ox stepped forward to engage the Acolyte. Before they could begin, a yellow and green bolt of magic crashed into the giant skeleton.

Ox halted his advance and turned his attention to where Henry was fighting the other Acolytes and five . . . mud men? One of the Acolytes had broken away and launched a magical bolt at Ox. The dread armor stopped any damage, but the jolt forced Ox to survey the battlefield and what he saw worried him. Henry and Beast were struggling, and Buddy was still under the black dome. They needed help, and Ox only had one option to provide them reinforcement.

He reached up to his shoulder and wrapped a massive hand around Gator and the amalgamator's dread mantid helmet. With a snap, Ox tore the animated skull from his shoulder plate, pumped Vitus into his bones, and launched Gator at the offending mage.

Heart of the Jotun

"Gator, attack!" Ox ordered, flinging his monstrous companion.

"GHAAAKKK!" Gator shouted as Ox's immense Strength, bolstered by his new Ability, sent the amalgamator careening through the air faster than any normal being's Perception could follow.

"Humpff!" the Acolyte grunted as Gator hit him square in the chest. The force of the impact lifted the soldier off his feet and sent him tumbling backward.

Everyone on the battlefield froze in their tracks and careened their heads to the sound of cracking bones, bending metal, and screams of agony. The Acolyte writhed on the ground, thrashing his arms and legs in the sand. His limbs contorted and bent as bones broke through skin, and blood spurted in the air. Chest up, the man's arms and legs lifted him from the ground like a grotesque spider. Gator had melded with the man's amor—and likely his flesh—and was now sitting on top of his torso like the amalgamator was riding a horse.

"Ghakk!" Gator turned toward the nearest soldier and used his Acolyte mount to charge. The still living man shrieked in pain as Gator forced his limbs to claw forward.

Seeing the horror of their inverted compatriot screaming and scrabbling toward them, two of the Acolytes fighting Henry tuned and ran with Gator in hot pursuit.

Ox had given Henry an ally and the warrior skeleton didn't waste the opportunity. Ox watched as Henry's body blurred under the speed of his Blitz Ability. Arcs of red blood and explosions of dirt filled the air as Henry slayed an Acolyte and bashed through two rocky earth men.

Like a piranha sensing blood in the water, Gator suspended his chase of the fleeing Acolytes and pounced on the body of the fallen man. Armor, weapons, and body parts rolled together as the Amalgamator absorbed the second Acolyte. Now the size of a small horse, the abomination resumed his charge, leaving Henry fighting a single mage and the last three earth elementals.

"Monsters," Jaromak said with a combination of disbelief and horror in his voice.

His face flushed with red, and he shouted, "Samos, we've played enough! I need this turtle out of his shell!"

"Understood!" Samos replied and immediately opened the large container on his hip. The mage seemed very unbothered by Beast's proximity to him, and Ox wondered why the elf hadn't killed him yet. The distance dulled his Perception, but Beast seemed like she was barely moving. The mage procured something from his pack and threw it at Jaromak. The massive

Acolyte caught the glass bauble and immediately launched a fresh assault on Ox.

Heart of the Jotun

Ox pumped more Strength into his bones, but the increase did little to stop the Acolyte. Jaromak deftly avoided another heavy swing and smashed the glass container into Ox's chest plate. Ox tried to attack again, but the man ducked under his maul and circled to his back. Jaromak jammed the edge of his shield into the back of Ox's legs, forcing the massive skeleton to his knees. Ox tried to spin and catch the man with a backhand, but Jaromak put a knee in his back and grabbed both of his biceps, stretching Ox out and holding him still. Ox struggled to free himself from the awkward grip, when a burning sensation quickly formed on his chest and spread through his body.

Status Effect: Scalding Embrace (Minor): 2 Heat damage per second

The heat quickly spread over his dreadmail, and within seconds the armor turned into a furnace that rivaled the forges of Hjardharfell. Ox's Health started ticking down, and with his Vitus almost gone, there was little he could do stop the burning.

Status Effect: Scalding Embrace (Severe): 10 Heat damage per second

His Health plummeted, and Ox had no choice but to abandon the dwarven armor.

Adapt

He felt his bones weaken as he pumped the little Health he had left into the dread bones. The armor expanded, giving him enough room to wriggle free of the mail and escape Jaromak's grasp. Ox tumbled forward and struggled to stand with his damaged bones.

Status Effect: Scalding Embrace Dismissed
Status Effect: Health Drought (Severe): STR -10%, MOB -10%

"Ah, much better. Now I can breathe," Ox said with a chuckle, even though his vision was blurry and his movement was sluggish.

"Every faux breath you take is an insult to my family. Die, skeleton." Jaromak tossed the dread armor aside and lunged forward.

Ox prepared himself for an inevitable pummeling. Now that his armor was gone, and his Health was dangerously low, he knew there was little he could do to stop the attacks. He may die, but hopefully he'd given the others enough room to claim victory.

Apparently, he had. Just as he braced for the Acolytes attack, Gator plowed into Jaromak's shield. Now the size of a bull after absorbing the bodies of all five lesser Acolytes, the amalgamator sent the Acolyte reeling.

Jaromak recovered quickly and used Gator's momentum to send the mass of flesh and metal tumbling through the destroyed plaza.

"Enough!" Jaromak's frustration laced through his shout as dark brown magic swirled around his hands. He pressed his palms into the sand and a wave of earth burst forward. It swept away the amalgamator. Gator, still squawking from inside his dread-mantid helmet, tumbled through the churning earth as it solidified around him.

Ox rushed, hoping the catch the man off guard, but Jaromak caught his forearm. The Acolyte slowly turned his head. The rage in the man's eyes would have given any normal being pause, but it only fueled Ox's determination to finish him.

Both warriors moved to strike.

An explosion ripped through the battlefield, interrupting their fight with a blast of fire, sand, and rock.

CHAPTER 35

Beast's Perception and Acumen was high enough that she'd kept track of everything on the battlefield. Gator had helped, but now that he was trapped and Ox was without his armor, the large Acolyte would have him beaten shortly. Henry was down to two opponents, but there was little the fighter could do against either of the Master Acolytes. Worst of all, Buddy was still inside the dome. Things were looking bad, and Beast knew she needed to even up the odds. She had a plan. It was dangerous, but she had no choice.

Samos, the Anti-Mage, as the prat called himself, was full of surprises. Every time she attacked, the man let her get close enough to see every line on his smug visage before smashing her with his mace. Arrows, daggers, magic . . . nothing worked. She had been punished severely for every failed attack. She'd gone through both of her healing crystals, and her Health was now dangerously low.

"You're not learning," Samos taunted after another thwarted attack.

Beast disagreed; she had learned two critical pieces of information. One—when inside his slow dome, she could move back with only minor hinderances, and two—the Anti-Mage severely underestimated her. That information would have to be enough to bring the sorcerer down.

Beast ran forward again, both daggers shining with frost magic. Her body slowed as she watched Samos lift his mace. She stopped her charge and pulled back as the weapon whizzed in front of her face. She pivoted and lunged again, immediately slowing under Samos's magic. She eyed the glowing jewel on the man's chest that ran the slow field.

"I know what you're after," Samos laughed, noticing her skeletal gaze. "This is what is causing your trouble, but you'll never get it." He swung the mace again.

Beast ducked back just a bit too slowly. The weapon glanced off her skull, but she pivoted again and stepped forward, thrusting her daggers straight out.

"You keep doing the same thing and expecting to even-tually get through. I'll help you focus." Samos stepped back and smashed her hands, sending her daggers into the sand. Beast knew he expected her to dodge back, but instead she kept coming forward, forcing her Strength and Mobility to the Attributes' limits. The movement caught the mage off guard and Beast plowed into him. Her hand crept up to the jewel on his neck and the tip of her boney finger touched the crystal.

"Too slow again," Samos responded, but a twinge of frus-tration ran through his voice. He swatted her hand aside and stepped back while procuring a jeweled wand from his robes. He activated the device, and a magical blast of light and heat sent her tumbling backward.

"I tire of these games. It's time to end you all." He reached to open the oversized alchemical pack on his hip. Confusion ran across his face when he touched a metal box instead of his leather alchemy satchel. Puzzlement turned to shock as he watched a lit fuse burn and disappear inside the container. His eyes widened, and he clawed at the metal. The anti-mage looked up at Beast.

"I was tired of your rambling before we started." She held up his alchemical bag. "Do you know how hard it is to covertly light a fuse while fighting in your slow field? Very." Then she disappeared, satisfied that the smug look on his face would never return.

Samos tried and failed to pull the solofurno box free. The explosion of dwarven engineering incinerated his body and tore apart the surrounding plaza.

—

Ox halted his attack to brace against the concussive force. The explosion had caught him by surprise, but his massive frame and heft kept him from getting knocked over. A quick glance at the origin of the fireball revealed that Henry was nearby and hadn't fared as well.

The detonation blasted through the open plaza, crumbling Jaromak's earth elementals and ripping apart the two remaining Acolytes. Henry barely had time to expand his dread shield, but the blast still sent him skull over femur. The warrior skeleton lay in the sand, unmoving. Ox reached with his Affinity, letting it flow along hidden currents until it touched Henry. The warrior was alive but hurt. Though Ox couldn't reach out to Buddy and Beast in the same way, he trusted they could take care of themselves.

Jaromak lifted his massive tower shield and deflected the incoming debris like a boulder holding firm in heavy rapids. Though he was a hundred yards from the explosion, rocks still pelted the metal slab with the force of a cannon. "No!"

Jaromak screamed as the ball of fire dissipated, revealing a crater where Samos had once stood.

Ox heard the dismay in the Acolyte leader's voice. The battle had nearly been won, and in an instant all the Acolyte forces, save for the massive warrior himself, had been annihilated.

Jaromak rocketed forward, propelled by earth magic and leaving a wake of jagged stone behind him. Ox barely had time to brace before the man bashed into him, lifting him off the ground then slamming him back down. Ox felt ribs crack under the force of the takedown. Jaromak stood above Ox with a boot on his chest. The man lifted his shield and brought the edge down hard on Ox's upper arm bones, first one then the other. Ox's bone couldn't resist the force of the heavy steel, and both of his arms shattered.

"No final words for you." Jaromak raised his shield once more, just above Ox's face and brought it down with all the Strength he possessed. "I will have my justice. Die, Necromancer spawn!"

Heal

Ox's arm shot back into place and the bone melded together. He'd used the last of his Vitus to re-attach the limb. He was out of magic, but not out of Strength. The massive shield descended toward his throat, and Ox caught its edge. His bones creaked and threatened to shatter again but held firm.

"I'm not dead again yet!" Ox cried and forced the Acolyte back.

Jaromak lifted a steel-covered boot. "Justice for Ikrit!" he shouted, slamming his foot down to crush Ox's skull.

A blue fireball smashed into Jaromak's shield. The heat from the flame melted the slab of metal and the force sent the Acolyte staggering back.

Jaromak cast the warped and steaming tower shield aside.

The hair on his head and beard had been singed and he wore the scowl of a wolf who had been denied its prey.

Buddy's hoarse voice echoed through the landscape. "Your justice is misguided, Acolyte. He didn't kill your brother."

Jaromak's gaze locked on the skeletal mage, a hundred paces away on the other side of the ravaged plaza. "He wields my brother's maul. That is all the evidence I need. Don't worry mage, your second death is shortly behind his."

Buddy reached under his robes and pulled out the pendant he had retrieved from Allito's body. He held the necklace high and spat, "The giant didn't kill your brother, *I* did. I burned the flesh from his bones. His screams are my earliest memory."

True rage filled Jaromak's eyes. The human brute took a slow step toward Buddy, then another, having completely forgotten about Ox.

Beast appeared at Buddy's left and brandished her daggers. Henry had pulled himself from the sand and stood at Buddy's right. The blast had taken its toll on Henry, but he was alive. "Ox is out, but it's still three on one, we can take him." Henry said.

"No." Buddy's stern voice made Henry pause. "This fight will be a duel between me and the human. You will not interfere."

Without averting his gaze from Acolyte, Buddy handed the skeletal elf his leather pack. Muji poked his head out from under the top flap and beaked softly.

"Beast, hold my trogold."

CHAPTER 36

The tone in Buddy's gruff voice left no room for protest. Beast took the pack from the mage as Muji crawled out and climbed up to a perch on her shoulders. The trogold growled and bared his teeth as the Acolyte approached with thundering footsteps. Beast nodded and retreated, as did Henry.

Whatever magic Samos had used to trap Buddy, it was powerful. The spell had covered him with a conjured dome that looked like a thick oil sheen on the surface of a smooth lake. The shell rendered him completely immobile and quickly drained most of his Vitus.

Though Beast had killed the mage and freed Buddy of the spell's hold, the dome's Effects left him frazzled and his vision blurry. He'd also spent most of his remaining magic shielding himself from the blast. Using the entire case of solofurnos to slay her opponent was overkill, even for Beast. The excess annoyed Buddy, though he was still thankful to be free.

The huge Acolyte was fifty paces away and closing the distance quickly. Buddy focused his dazed vision and the two imposing shapes coming toward him joined into one massive, angry soldier. Though Buddy's Resolve easily overcame the rage Effect of the soldier's red aura, he couldn't help but want to give into the anger—to burn the flesh from the man's bones and rejoice in the shrieks of his death throughs. Though staggered, Buddy refused to give into the rage. Instead, he used the last few seconds before the man reached him to check his Status and shore up his plan.

Status

Health: 78/94
Vitus: 47/426

Status Effect: Aberrant Torrent (Severe): Max Vitus -50, ACU -12, 10% chance of spell failure

Anti-mage was an accurate description of Samos's Abilities. A few more moments in the spell's grip would have seen Buddy drained completely. The black dome had been agony, eroding his Acumen point by point. Without any Vitus crystals there was no way to restore his magic, and Buddy mentally kicked himself for not persuading Olafur to give him even a single enchanted shard.

The explosion had only taken Buddy's Health down a bit, and he felt—hoped—he had enough to win. He had seen everything from within the dome as it withered him down. That was the weakness of the spell that had trapped him. He had remained conscious and aware of the events transpiring around him. With nothing to do but wait, Buddy spent that time reviewing and categorizing the full extent of his magical prowess. He had ample time to create a strategy.

The Acolyte approached within twenty paces and picked up speed. Buddy saw the determination in his eyes and knew the man wouldn't hesitate to extract revenge.

Buddy clearly recalled his first memory, waking shortly after killing Jaromak's brother. The first thing he could remember seeing was the man's body crisping under the intense heat of blue flames. Buddy could still see the man's shocked expression, especially the tremor in his eyes before they popped from the heat as his flesh melted. Those same eyes now rushed toward him, ready for combat.

Buddy couldn't blame the man for his vindictive intent, though that wasn't why he had demanded a duel. After watching everything transpire, Buddy knew he was the only one that could defeat Jaromak. He couldn't risk any of the other three skeletons dying again. Keeping them out of the battle was the only way Buddy could ensure their safety.

The anti-magic dome left him with little magical reserves. However, the few minutes it afforded him to ruminate were more than sufficient. First, he would test the man's response to magic.

Buddy dove into the fog of his mind. The past week had afforded him little time to examine the blank space where his memories should have been. The infrequent moments he had been able to devote to meditation gave him no indication that he would ever recall his past under his own power. At that moment, though, Buddy wasn't searching for memories.

With the hardened Resolve of a practiced sorcerer, the skeletal mage forced his awareness deep into his core, and the clear image of a volcano appeared before his mind's eye. Jagged crags of black stone stretched toward the heavens like the ground itself lusted for the sky's embrace. Fissures spewed noxious vapors as dark blue lava gushed from multiple cavities and ran down the landscape in scorching rivers and cataracts.

Deep within the volcano, magma of a brilliant azure churned and boiled, though its power was muted. Buddy pulled from its depths and watched the molten rock recede as he channeled the magic into his bones.

Evoke

Type: Flame, Lightning, Ice
Vector: Bolt
Modifier: 6X

Bolts of evocation magic conjured around Buddy—two each of the elements he'd selected. Whoever he'd been in his past life, his mastery over magic had surely carried over into this existence. He'd quickly moved past specific named Abilities for each of the hundreds of iterations of spells he could cast. Instead, he shaped the magic of the natural world as he saw fit. This instance was in the form of six bolts of magic, each powerful enough to strip the armor and flesh from any normal opponent.

Buddy knew, however, that Jaromak wasn't a normal opponent. As the magical attacks approached the running Acolyte, the man thrust his arm upward in a scooping motion. In response, the earth in front of him shot forward in the form of three-foot spikes that impacted Buddy's bolts. Four elements mixed in an explosion of blue flame, clear ice, white lightning, and red earth. Jaromak burst through the occlusion, unharmed and now within ten paces of Buddy.

As expected, Buddy thought, thankful his face couldn't betray him with the tell of a smile.

Evoke

Type: Flame, Force
Vector: Elemental
Modifier: X5

Buddy loaded Vitus into his hands and pressed his palms into the ground, sending the magic forward and swirling up from the ground in the form of five fire elementals. Buddy's contingent of flame soldiers, reinforced with force magic, rushed to engage the Acolyte in melee and afforded Buddy the chance to circle away, creating more distance, and thus time, between him and Jaromak. The Acolyte responded with five earth elementals of his own.

The man dropped to his knees and skidded to a stop, then slammed his fists into the ground. Brown and red magic spun through the sand and five more earth elementals sprang forward, engaging the soldiers of blue fire. The troops met in the middle with an explosion of blue and brown. Normal earth elementals would have gone right through the fire types, but Buddy had reinforced his summons with force magic—at least enough to pose a physical threat.

Fire and rock blasted in all directions as the magical automatons struck each other with heavy blows. Buddy cared little for the outcome of the tangential battle. He only needed Jaromak to activate as much earth magic as possible while reserving the maximum amount of his own magic.

Mystic Revelation

Multicolored lines of energy lit up the battlefield before Buddy. Blue and pearl for his evocation, and dark brown for that of the Acolyte. There was also a haze in this area that Buddy hadn't noticed in any other part of Jallfoss. It slightly obscured his Mystic Revelation. He'd first become aware of the occlusion a few minutes early, just before the battle had started. At that moment, he didn't have the spare faculties to determine its source. Instead, he reached with his mind and grabbed ahold of Jaromak's earth magic.

Nullify

Ability Discovered: Nullify I – Cancel out the effect of one single element of magic. Amount of cancellation depends on the ratio of Acumen between both casters

He'd learned and successfully replicated the Ability that Torgga had put in the dwarven tome, but dissolving the man's magic wouldn't be enough with Buddy's low Vitus. He reached further through the flow of Jaromak's earth magic and into the warrior himself.

Ability Altered: Nullify I has become Sovereign Convergence I

Ability Discovered: Sovereign Convergence . . .

Buddy cut off the display. He knew how to execute the Ability he'd just created without the Drift Amulet describing his own spell. He wasn't Henry—he didn't need the item's divination to tell him what he already knew. Instead, he watched the earth elementals crumble to dust.

"Don't waste your time, mage. Samos may be dead, but his dome left you with little Merq to spare. Even if your magic is stronger than mine, you don't have enough left to counter my spells for long." Jaromak lifted his hands toward the five fire elementals converging on him. A wall of liquid earth rose from the sand and smashed into the conjured flames, snuffing out Buddy's coterie and burying them below the cascade.

Sovereign Convergence
Evoke

Type: Force
Vector: Wave

Buddy's Convergence Ability wove itself through the earth magic, weakening its structure like termites devouring a wooden truss. His own force wave shot forward and collided into the wall of terrain roaring toward him. The two magical tsunamis met and erupted into a geyser a hundred feet high that sent a shower of rocks through the plaza.

Jaromak didn't wait for the spells to settle. He charged right though the falling debris and emerged on the other side, ready to pound the mage into bone dust. Buddy anticipated the charge and retreated the moment he released his own wave. As Jaromak emerged from the fountain of earth and force magic, Buddy unleashed all his remaining Vitus. Then he reached further, pulling from his mind a store of magic beyond the capabilities of normal mage.

Evoke

Type: Fire, Ice, Lightning, Force, Acid, Wind
Vector: Bolt
Modifier: X24

Status Effect: Vitus Drought (Minor): Your Vitus had dropped 5% below zero.

Jaromak deftly dodged the first few bolts, then formed earthen spears to counter the others.

Sovereign Convergence

Buddy latched onto the Acolyte's magic and tore it apart at its most basic level. Jaromak's bolts dissolved, forcing the Acolyte to block Buddy's attack with another summoned rock wall. The barrier crumbled under the barrage, and Jaromak roared in anger as the various elements ripped into him.

Buddy knew the attacks would do little to damage the

human. Their value was in the split-second of time they provided to mage to surveille the battlefield. Beast had retreated with Buddy's pack to a nearby rooftop, and Henry had dragged Ox off the plaza to the safety of an alley. *Hopefully they're far enough away,* Buddy thought as he tried to ignore the strain of the Vitus Drought.

"Beak!" Muji's angry trill echoed across the rubble-strewn court. The trogold struggled in Beast's arms, fighting in vain against the clutches of the skeletal elf to join Buddy.

"A trogold? How pitiful. Is that your thrall, mage?" Jaromak sneered as brown spirals of magic coalesced around his clenched fists. The skin on his face was scorched, frozen, and bleeding, but the scorn for the undead hadn't left his eyes.

"His name is Muji. Your fight is with me . . . *human.*"

Evoke

Type: Flame, Force
Vector: Elemental
Modifier: Empower

Buddy compelled his magic into the ground and dipped further past the limits of his empty core. A spot of churning blue flame appeared just in front of the mage and began to swirl. The magic turned white under its own intense heat and quickly expanded to a circle fifteen feet wide. A flaming hand emerged and grabbed the edge of the circle, pulling its owner from the depths of Buddy's powerful evocation.

Status Effect: Vitus Drought (Moderate): Your Vitus had dropped 15% below zero.

The greater fire elemental stood to its full height of nearly twenty feet, towering over the surrounding plaza. Searing heat turned the surrounding rubble into a melted pool of stone. The blue fire giant charged.

Jaromak recovered what remained of his tower shield and shrouded it with a layer of rock just in time to deflect a heavy strike. The skin on his face blistered under the ambient heat. The Acolyte growled in anger as he dodged and blocked.

The man rolled to the side to avoid another fiery blow, then cast his shield to the ground and gave Buddy's elemental a look of angry defiance. The fire giant responded with another heavy slam. As the attack drew near, Jaromak lifted his palm and discharged a spell in a burst of brown earth magic.

A hand, nearly the size of the Acolyte himself shot from the ground and caught the fire elemental's attack. The sand churned like a raging sea, and a greater earth elemental that rivaled the size of its fire-based twin rose from the ground. Dirt and rock cascaded down the rising monster like an avalanche tumbling from a living mountain. For just a moment, the two forces of nature stared at each other with an almost human-like reverie, somewhere between deep respect and fierce hatred.

The giants of earth and fire pummeled each other with heavy fists—neither relenting, neither giving an inch. Bouts of solid fire and chunks of animated earth were flung across the battlefield as the two enormous monsters tore into each other.

Sovereign Convergence

Buddy didn't wait for the victor to be decided. He sent his magic through Jaromak's elemental and ripped apart the bonds that held its form in place. The earthen monster exploded in a shower of dirt as Buddy's creation burst through it and charged at Jaromak.

The Acolyte was ready. Lifting his arms like he was

excavating the very bowels of the Underdeep miles below, he summoned a huge spike of stone that thrust upward and impaled the fire giant. The elemental died under the force of the massive earthen lance, but not before a wave of liquid flame washed over the Acolyte. Another wall of stone to block the deluge, and the fire crashed against the bulwark.

Both the spike and the wall crumbled under Buddy's Sovereign Convergence, leaving the skeletal mage and massive Acolyte staring at each other across a suddenly quiet battlefield.

"If you weren't out of magic, you may be able to win," Jaromak shouted as though the duel was already over. "With your Merq empty, you can do little more than Nullify my attacks. It's time I end this."

"Now you want to talk, human. How fortunate am I to hear your derision? The only sounds I witnessed from your brother were gargled screams as his throat turned to ash," Buddy spewed words of venom in the guise of a taunt. The insult worked.

Jaromak sprang forward, covering himself in living stone and growing to the size of Smyrna's Golem. "You will die! I'll crush you, then I'll rip apart the other three and stuff that trogold!"

"I already told you, his name is Muji, and you'll be dead before you can touch him."

Sovereign Convergence

Buddy reached deep into the volcano of his core and pulled until the blue lava disappeared. He took all that he could, trusting . . . hoping it wouldn't kill him before he could release the spell. He knew he had only seconds before the Drought's Effect incapacitated him. He gathered all the magic he stole from himself and forced it into his Ability.

Status Effect: Vitus Drought (Severe): Your Vitus had dropped 25% below zero.

The particles of earth magic that had formed around the Acolyte appeared to Buddy as trillions of individual grains, each connected to the others through Jaromak's mastery over the element. Buddy took that connection and sundered it.

The thundering golem before him crumbled and Jaromak crashed into the ground just in front of Buddy. The mage dropped to his knees, fighting for consciousness.

The Acolyte lifted himself to his feet and sneered. "All you did was waste my time. Prepare for Justice."

Buddy didn't hear the man's words as he struggled to keep from blacking out. Darkness clawed at his psyche. It took every point of Resolve Buddy had to maintain his awareness. He could only focus on the glyphs in his display.

Sovereign Convergence: Capacity reached. Opponent's spent and remaining Vitus available for 5 seconds . . . 4 seconds . . .

The volcano that made up Buddy's core rumbled and quaked. The cragged ridges that formed the mountain's peak toppled outward as fissures of black smoke burst forth and filled the atmosphere. With a force of a million solofurnos, a geyser of sapphire magma erupted into the sky. Buddy harnessed every last drop of the magic in his core and forced it into his spell. Jaromak's eyes widened as Vitus drained from his mind.

Evoke . . .

Buddy didn't have the mental endurance remaining to pick the specifics for his spell. Instead, he forced all the magic he could at an infinitely small point in the center of the Acolyte's chest.

"Justice . . ." Buddy whispered. He compelled the Vitus to erupt. The Acolyte's face contorted, and his skin stretched. Blue fire burst from his eyes and mouth. A swirling ball of pure emulsion ripped through the man's flesh and armor. The magic grew in intensity and exploded outward, sending Buddy flying.

In his last moment of consciousness, calm and relief filled the mage's mind. His sacrifice would save the others, hopefully giving them the chance they needed to break the Necromancer's spell and save Jallfoss.

—

Blitz

Henry caught the falling mage and turned his back to shield himself from the growing ball of fire. Searing blue and white spun faster and faster, tearing apart and swallowing up the earth below it. The golem steel in Henry's dread armor did little to protect him from the intense heat, and the damage compounded with his negative fire Resistance.

Buddy's duel with the formidable Acolyte had given Henry time to stabilize Ox and free Gator. "Ox, Beast, we have to go! Up the ramp, now!" Henry shouted and started sprinting for his life.

"Agreed, Harry. No time to stay for the after show." Ox had managed to heal himself enough to run alongside Henry.

"Ghakk!" Gator squawked from Ox's shoulder.

"Move your asses, boys! The spell is getting bigger!" Beast yelled from a hundred paces up the ramp. Muji squirmed in her arms, still struggling to get close to Buddy.

The roaring inferno grasped for the fleeing skeletons as they ascended the ramps of Ammerthall. Their journey to the highest spires of Jallfoss had just begun.

EPILOGUE

Stavros's weary mount clopped through the cobble-stone streets and into the poor slum district. The Great Lord could have pressed through the night and made it all the way to Ikrit's capital city and the familiar fires of the Citadel, but he didn't have the motivation to keep going. Maybe he dreaded what he would be forced to do when he got there.

Within a dozen miles of the Ikritian capital, the merchant city of Çaraki was kept clean and orderly for the most part, but every city had its less-reputable districts. Stavros and his horse slowly made their way through the narrow winding streets of the least respectable part of the town. Sporadic lanterns cast shadows, and equally shady figures ducked into those shades, keeping a watchful eye on the unexpected traveler.

Stavros was familiar with this area, he just hadn't been through in a very, very long time. His horse slowly clopped down the winding streets until he heard boisterous music and loud cheers that came from the only brightly lit building he'd seen in several blocks. It was of wooden construction that had once been extravagant, but years of neglect left it in moderate disrepair. Painted words in faded red and white lettering above the doorway hung a sign that read: "Dirty Merv's Pub and Inn. Come for the beer, stay for the cheer." Stavros laughed. It had only gotten dirtier over the years.

A stable boy dozed near the patio. Stavros cleared his throat, and the lad lifted his head, revealing a tired and annoyed expression.

"I'll only be an hour. Have her groomed and fed." Stavros dismounted and handed the reins to the boy who still rubbed sleep from his eyes. Stavros placed a silver in youth's outstretched palm.

The boy looked at the coin and rubbed it with his fingers. "Do you know how late it is, old man? I know you fancy folk are used to making demands, but I've been working all day."

"Three silvers then? And another two when you have her ready for me." Stavros handed the boy two more coins. The lad nodded in approval, taking the reins and leading the horse toward the stable. The mare was worth more than every building in the slum combined, but Stavros hoped the boy was too tired to notice the quality of his mount at the late hour.

Stavros watched the boy and his horse disappear around a dark corner, then the Great Lord pushed his way through a door that looked like it was hanging on the frame by more hope than hardware. The portal creaked on its hinges, but none could have heard the sound over the ruckus coming from inside. He left up his hood, though the chance of the patrons recognizing him as their Emperor was very low.

Drown me in liquor
And wash off my strife
Hold me tonight
But don't tell my wife

Three bards—harp, drum, and singer—entertained the rowdy crowd of tipsy patrons sloshing beer back and forth as they swayed in time to the rousing tune.

Don't tell my wife
Why should she know
Just pour me a beer
And give me a show

The drunken mob shouted the refrain. Stavros barely stopped himself from mouthing the words of the familiar song. He caught a few glances as he made his way into the parlor. His Perception was far higher than anyone's Attributes in the room, and he was aware they were discussing his fine adornment that was uncommon in such a place, especially this late.

Stavros dodged drunken bodies and made his way to a seat at a long bar. The wooden top had divots worn from years of elbows resting on its edges. He sat on one of the few empty barstools. A blonde woman, a bit past her prime, offered him a coaster and a smile that still had most of her teeth. Her low-cut dress left little to the imagination and had likely earned her a hundredfold in tips beyond what she had paid for it. "What'll it be, fancy pants?"

"Pint of ale," he said with a soft smile as he looked around the parlor. A few younger waitresses ran through the crowd, serving food to various tables. An older man stood behind the bar on the opposite side from where Stavros had taken his seat. The barkeep had a huge pot belly and a long handlebar mustache. He was contently polishing a mug and watching the patrons. Though he was well beyond fifty years old, his bare arms were bigger around than most men's legs.

"Can do, sugar. Any food? Fresh stew . . . just a few days old," the woman offered.

Stavros shook his head, then asked, "It's a busy night. Celebration?"

"I'm surprised you haven't heard. We defeated the Varanasi. Sent Basti and his cowards back behind their walls. Commander Alicos gave the order to bring everyone home except a single peacekeeping Brigade. Our boys have come back, and they're drinking like they haven't tasted the stuff in years. Some of 'em haven't. If you ask me, Lord Stavros should have pressed until Basti's head rested on the tip of a pike, but I hear the Great Lord has always been a bit too far on the merciful side."

A drunken boy, just a few years into manhood bumped into Stavros and leaned on the bar's edge. "Bar wench, four pints and a smile."

The woman grabbed the drunk by his ear and nearly pulled him across the bar top. "You're lucky you're cute and a good tipper, or I wouldn't be so gentle."

"Ow, Rosie! You know I'm just jokin'. Let go, will ya?" The boy squawked and the three other men at the table he had come from burst into laughter, some almost crying.

"That's better, sweetie." The bartender, Rosie apparently, let go and gave the man a wink. She turned around and started to fill a beer until the tap ran dry. Dumping out the foam, she shouted to the portly man, "Merv, this one's out. Fetch the lad four draughts and I'll roll in another keg."

"My pleasure, Rosie." The man looked up from the mug he was cleaning, but when his glance crossed Stavros, his eyes narrowed. It would have been imperceptible to most, but Stavros's Perception saw it clearly.

The man grabbed a mug and started pouring as the young man beside Stavros sat on the stool and started jabbering. "Rosie is meaner than a rattlesnake, but I sure did miss her."

"Have you been gone a while?" Stavros asked.

"Nearly two years on the front lines, but we finally sent the Varanasi running."

"You're one of the brave men protecting us from the foreign aggressors. For keeping me safe, you have my gratitude. This round is on me." Stavros reached into his pocket and procured a few coins, which he placed on the bar.

"I won't turn down free beer, old man, but I didn't do much until the end. I was working supply the whole time. It was the Acolytes who did the heavy lifting. They led the infantry, the calvary, and the artillery like the young gods themselves had returned. They even captured Basti's Vanguard. Just think . . . twenty of the most dangerous assassins in the world, shackled like common criminals. That's where I came in. Worked the convoy that brought 'em back in chains. That evil contingent now rots in the dungeon below the Citadel."

The barkeep plopped four pints in front of the young soldier. "Don't forget, Yilmaz, your stories have to be at least ten percent true."

"I swear on Minoa's soggy tulips, the black-hearted Vanguard are now safe in the Citadel's dungeons."

Then the young soldier leaned toward Stavros. "You're not from around here, old man, but if you think Rosie is mean, don't mess with Merv. He used to be an Acolyte, and even fought beside Lord Stavros in the battle of Krislokan. Rumor has it he killed a demonthorn mandrake with nothing more than broken cossamor tusk."

"Mix a story like that with sweet bread, and all you'll have is a vegetarian sausage roll. Now get back to your friends and stop bothering the old-timer." Merv shooed the lad away.

The boy did as he was told and brought the beer back to another round of jaunts from his friends.

"Killed a demonthorn mandrake with a cossamor tusk . . .

not bad for an old barkeep," Stavros said, barely concealing a smile.

"That was a lifetime ago. I've told the stories so many times that I forget what is truth and what is artistic interpretation. What intrigues me, however, is that a ghost from that former life has shown up. It's good to see you, old friend." Merv sat a foaming pint of ale in front of Stavros.

"I'm sorry it took me so long to make my way back. You retired from the Acolytes twenty years ago and I came for your pub's grand opening. I'm glad to see it's doing so well." Stavros took a long swig from the mug. It had a fantastic aroma of candied sugars, roasted nuts, and a mildly perky spiciness that augmented all the other smells. Deep caramel and nougat notes were accented with honey, brown sugar, and just a bit of boozy undertone. There was no real bitterness per se, but more of a phenol bite.

"Much better, now that my customers are back from the war. I'm glad you decided to keep them alive instead of throwing them into the meat grinder that a siege would have been." Merv grinned as he watched Stavros fail to hide his enjoyment of the draughts exquisite flavor.

"We could break them, but the sacrifice it would take is more than I'm willing to pay." Stavros wiped a drop of ale from his chin, sad to have wasted even the smallest amount.

"That's good to hear, but I doubt you came this far just to talk war strategy."

"I'm on my way back from the Bastion. There was an . . . incident . . . at Jallfoss I had to attend to."

Merv studied him for a long moment. "You have a look about you that I've seen in this place thousands of times. Normally it belongs to a man that isn't ready to go home to a nagging wife. I doubt a woman is keeping you from your lofty towers in the Citadel. What type of incident at Jallfoss would require the personal attention of the Great Lord himself?"

Stavros wasn't trying to hide his identity, but he also wasn't keen on making it known to everyone in the bar. Thankfully, the band and patrons were loud enough to overpower the conversation between him and the barkeep. Stavros smiled and nodded. "Am I still that easy to read?"

Merv returned the smirk. "Whatever is bothering you, this should help." The barkeep touched a panel of wood on the far wall. It spread into an opening that revealed a secret compartment. Merv reached into the dark hole and retrieved a clear glass bottle filled with a dark liquid. It was a soft golden caramel, and the bottle had a faded, hand-written label.

"After all these years, you haven't finished it." Stavros could barely contain the excitement in his voice.

"Haven't had a patron worthy of drinking it in twenty years," Merv said as he pulled the cork free from the bottle with a satisfying *thunk*.

"I hope I'm worthy," Stavros said, a sullen tone encroaching on his voice.

Merv pulled out two tumblers from below the bar and poured a dram in both, then replaced the cap. He set the bottle on the bar. "I was just a boy when Livadi departed on his last mission. Fifty years ago, your uncle set out with his Acolytes. He died on that quest, along with every Acolyte that went along, except one. That expedition managed to prevent an army of ethereal defilers from descending upon the planes of Ikrit. Only one Acolyte came back with Livadi's last decree, that you would be his successor. The greatest Emperor this country has ever seen found you the most deserving to rule this nation. So, if you're not worthy, what does that make me?"

"The best damn Acolyte and barkeep this side of Shargala," Stavros replied with a smile and lifted his glass.

Merv roared out a laugh loud enough to grab the attention of a few nearby patrons. He picked up his tumbler and held it toward Stavros. "Have it your way. To liars and old friends."

"To old friends." Stavros returned the toast and took a swig. The memories came flooding back to him of the first time he'd tasted Lunga whiskey. "I remember when you got this bottle. Stole it from the nightstand of the ugliest Yalifafu woman any of us had ever seen. It's still some of the best whiskey I've ever had, and I've had a lot."

"She may not have been a looker, but she quenched my thirst in more ways than one."

It was Stavros's turn to laugh. "That's why you named your bar *Dirty Merv's*."

"One of many reasons." Merv smirked, but then he picked up the bottle and his expression turned somber. "You're about to do something drastic, aren't you?"

"Too many Acolytes have died in that mountain. Jallfoss has stolen so much from me. It's time to take it back."

"What are the chances you return to finish this bottle with me?" Merv asked.

Stavros lifted his glass and stared at the brown essence. He swirled the liquid and watched legs of perfectly aged whiskey slowly run down the side of his tumbler. Looking straight into Merv's eyes, Stavros told him the truth. "I fear this is the last drink we'll share."

"A dram quenched in solitude is a dram wasted," Merv said, then split the rest of the bottle between the two tumblers. "If this is the last drink between us, we'll have to make it a good one."

Merv lifted his glass and shouted, "To Ikrit!"

"To Ikrit!" Every patron within earshot returned. Neither Stavros nor Merv shot the whiskey. They each took a small sip, savoring the taste as much as the memories they'd shared. For a long while, the two old men recounted stories of their adventures, each more exciting than the last.

Eventually, Merv sat his tumbler down. "Why do you think I saved this bottle all these years. Do you think I like remembering the garlic in that woman's breath?"

"Maybe," Stavros said with a grin.

"Fine. Maybe a bit, but that's not the point. I can drink garbage sharinji by myself, but a good whiskey is meant to be drunk with friends. I'd rather pour this out than drink it with anyone other than you."

Stavros took another sip, slowly letting the caramel and smoke, the citrus and the lavender, flow over his tongue. "I've done terrible things, Merv. You are a true friend to still share such treasure with me."

"I didn't follow you to the ends of the world because you were perfect. I followed you because you did what you had to for the good of Ikrit. You could have sent me to prison for not following orders a dozen times over, but you only threated that once or twice."

"Prison is for criminals. This . . ." Stavros motioned to the entirety of the pub. "This is for heroes."

The juvenile soldier from before bumped into Stavros's shoulder. Having finished several rounds of beer, the man had returned for another. Much less sober than earlier, the man reached for Stavros's whiskey. "That's not how you shoot liquor, old man. Let me show you how a soldier in the Ikritian army does it."

Merv slapped the soldier's hand away before he could touch the Emperor's glass. "This isn't shooting whiskey, son. Take your ale, and get back to your girlfriends." The soldier gladly accepted another round and stumbled back to his table.

Merv shook his head as he watched the lad spill more beer than he delivered to his companions. "They're excited to be home, and we're happy to have them back. The war's been hard on us all. I can only hope this is a lasting peace."

Sadness crept into the Great Lord's voice. "It will take years for Basti to recover from his defeat, if he can even survive the wrath of the Varanasi nobles. I'm only concerned with Jallfoss. The evil in that mountain is begging to be stopped. Livadi threw entire legions at the graveyard nation, and nothing changed—a century of young lives wasted."

"That mountain has taken something from all of us. Whatever it stole from you, I hope you get it back," Merv offered.

Stavros nodded. "This nation needs more men like you and less like me."

"We've disagreed on much, and continue to do so," Merv said before raising his glass and downing the last of his whiskey.

Stavros followed suit, then lifted his old bones from the bar stool. "It was good to see you, old friend. Until the next sun."

I hope you enjoyed reading Book 2 of the Dead Again series as much as I did writing it. New authors like me thrive on your feedback, so please go to Amazon, Goodreads, or wherever you prefer, and leave a review. You can also reach me directly at brucejamisonbooks@gmail.com.

If you enjoyed this book, please leave a review at your favorite online retailer's website!

Enthusiastic reviews from readers like you
are incredibly helpful.

Thank you!

NEF HOUSE PUBLISHING

Discover more awesome fantasy and LitRPG at
www.nefhousepublishing.com

www.ingramcontent.com/pod-product-compliance
Lightning Source LLC
Chambersburg PA
CBHW021846010726
47493CB00005B/1569